Legacy of the Vampire

Nael Roberts

Copyright 1988 (2013) by Nael Roberts

CW01498540

DEDICATION

To Pat, Paddy, Tracy, Graham and Moo.

All digital artwork by Trevor Storey, concept by Nael Roberts. (2013)

www.naelroberts.com

CONTENTS

Introduction

LIFE IS A GAME OF MANIPULATION,

A CONFRONTATION OF WILLS.

WHERE THE VICTOR CAN

SOMETIMES BE THE VANQUISHED

AND THE AGGRESSOR, THE PROTAGONIST.

MEMORIES CAN LIVE FOREVER IN TIME,

AND THEIR CONSEQUENCES CAN BE

FELT BY THE GENERATIONS YET TO FOLLOW.

LIFE, IS A GAME.

Prologue

Consciousness ravaged his cadaverous mind as atavistic emotions rushed like intervallic lightning throughout his malodorous and corroded carcass. The dark sensuality of the harsh coldness of the clay that surrounded him enhanced the dankness of his earthly prison; exacerbated his new-born lust for life. His body began to contort and convulse as provenance regained tenure of this once abandoned and fragile earthly coil, sending great spasms of preternatural life pulsating throughout this diabolical festering frame.

Putrefied fingers moved for the first time in centuries, gripping handfuls of heavy incarcerating dank clay. This most obtuse, yet altruistic of sensations excavated emotions that danced with pure pleasure at these insignificant emanations that ravenously stimulated his immortal touch; he was alive.

No! He was more than alive, he was un-dead.

He could feel an incalculable anguish as his ancient muscles ached to move; they had once been strong and able to carry his muscular frame across mountains and into conflict, but now they were old and ravaged by the demonic spectral bane of time. They tensed at his upward push as he endeavoured to drag his semi-decayed remains towards the surface. Warm air greeted his hand as it broke through the earth's surface, intensifying his tenuous, juvenile emotions. Within moments his second hand was free and both searched for something to abet them back into this repugnant world of mortality. They found the gnarled root of an ancient tree, which enabled him to drag his rotting corpse from its abominable resting place. Soil fell from his eyes and he, a new born aberration to a callous modern world, glimpsed the moon as if for the first time.

Lifting himself from this grave he stood proud, allowing his decayed eyes to grow accustomed to the cold winter's night.

He had made it.

He was reborn.

His preternatural eyes surveyed this new world with intense hunger.

Drawing back his lips he released a primordial scream that was filled the night with the eternal rage of a recalcitrant soul.

****

Part One

FROM THE CRADLE TO THE GRAVE...AND BEYOND.

One

She knew she was in the depths of a baleful dream, but somehow the complexities of its fabric wove an interlaced chronicle that somehow reached far into the essence of her own truth. The light from the candles made everything shine with an almost fairy-tale incandescence as the revellers danced in dresses of gold and silver that shone like stars on a deep crimson sky. Wigs were powdered and built high, faces were painted with heavy fard, as those assembled glided as if on air, totally unaware of each other, or even their own presence or surroundings.

They began to dance unnaturally faster, accompanied by the music, their actions becoming wild and outrageously exaggerated. The very essence of the room began to spin and she realised that something was wrong. Voices from beyond her perception, began to rise. She endeavoured to understand their cries but the language was foreign to her, yet somehow familiar. She turned to her fellow revellers to find that they had ceased their merriment and were now focusing their collective attention solely upon her.

From the centre of the crowd stepped a stranger; his movements were slow, feline and calculated as he glided towards her with his arms outstretched. He smiled, and then looked as if to turn away. With the speed of an animal he sprang at her, his mouth open wide, savage teeth grinning, framed by decayed lips. He hit her with the full force of his body, sending her screaming backwards, her hands clawing at his cold clammy flesh. As she fell to the floor panic ravaged her emotions. She opened her mouth to cry out for help but the only sound that came was a long, soulful scream.

She sat up in bed as sweat ran down her forehead and onto her cheeks. For a moment, she could not understand her situation.

Where was she?

What was happening?

Then reality hit her with the full force of its might and she realised that she was alone, at home, in her own bed. Lying back against her pillows, she breathed a deep sigh of relief. In the back of her mind a sound registered over and over again. The dark clouds of sleep still hung heavy in her thoughts, masking the melodies of this modern life. She concentrated harder upon the noise, trying to comprehend its meaning; its constant rhythmic ringing. Then a brief flash of realisation assaulted her as her senses burst into life.

'The telephone!' she thought to herself, as she fought her way through her cluttered mind.

The ringing was now becoming more distinct as its harsh peel began to pull and tear at the air, desperate for attention. She rolled over in bed and reached out her hand across the bedside table, knocking to the floor an empty wine bottle, a casualty from the previous night. Lifting the receiver from the telephone to her ear, she muttered almost incoherently into its mouthpiece.

"Hello!" Her voice was dry and broken, a legacy from the night before. "Hello, this is Ann-Marie Harrington."

An urgent voice called from the other side.

"Ann-Marie! Are you going to come into work today or not?" At once she recognised the fierce tones of her editor's voice. "I know that it was your birthday yesterday, and I made allowances so that you could leave early and meet all of your friends for a night out together but if you don't mind, that was yesterday and today I would like you to justify the reason why I haven't fired you yet."

"Oh Harry, calm down," she replied, in an almost lucid tone. "I think that you've been drinking too much coffee. It's bad for you this early in the morning."

"What do you mean, this early? It's almost lunch-time," he harshly replied.

Ann-Marie sat bolt up-right in surprise, her eyes attempting to focus upon the clock on her bedside cabinet.

"Shit! Sorry Harry. I guess I got a little merry last night," she said.

"I know what you northern girls are like," his tone softened. "Well, you're only forty once in your lifetime."

"Once again, thanks for reminding me," she said. "I seem to be spending most of my adult life lying about my age or blinding myself to the advancing years by looking to the bottom of a bottle for comfort."

"Well, if you look as bad as you sound, then I don't want you coming into the office and putting me off my lunch. Get your act together and interview someone for me. It's an assignment that's nice and arty, something that you would really appreciate. Talk to some spoilt brat about her strange abstract art, just the thing to clear a hang-over."

"Thanks a lot, Harry," she exclaimed.

"Don't mention it," he said, in a sarcastic tone. "Here's the info, her name is Susan Ward, she's eighteen years old and she's supposed to be the best in her league. I've arranged for you to meet her at about three p.m. so that gives you plenty of time to get yourself together and sober up. I expect a nice, balanced article from you; after all, you are older and wiser than when we last met."

"Thank you for reminding me," Ann-Marie said, trying once again to focus her attentions upon the bedside clock. It's digital red numbers screaming at her through her post drunken haze. 'Twelve-fifteen p.m.'

"It's at the Dane's Art Gallery, just off Oxford Street. Can I make a suggestion?" he enquired. "Walk there and get some fresh air; you never know you might even like it, get a differing sense of sobriety."

"Thanks Harry. You're all that I need to help me forget my troubles. Tell me, do you work at being miserable or does it just come naturally? Like breathing and being demanding?" she wryly enquired.

"I never knew that you cared so much Ann-Marie," he said, laughing.

"I don't!" she quickly replied before slamming the telephone handset down.

Lying back onto the bed, she stretched herself out and relished the warmth of her own body heat. Closing her eyes she could almost feel the minutes as they ticked by, bringing the memories of her birthday celebration rolling back and filling her with inner warmth; a warmth that was closely followed by the chilling wind of uncertainty.

The images of the masked ball haunted the darker recesses of her consciousness. Sitting up in bed, she endeavoured to focus her thoughts upon these pictures, but only the cold embers of lost memories returned to her mind.

After showering, dressing and respectively pampering herself, Ann-Marie was ready to face the day, although most of it had already passed. Picking her car keys from the key rack next to the front door she remembered Harry's words and smiled to herself, before rejecting them and stepping out into the cold winter's day. Behind her, her home fell into an almost reverent silence as a sense of anticipation filled her world. It had been a long time since she had walked about this city, a city that had been her home for almost ten years since her relocation from her rural idyllic life in the tumultuous, weather savaged wilds of the outskirts of Durham City, to the collective calamity that was London.

Reaching the gallery her greatest horror was recognised, for there on an advertising poster staring back at her was a picture of the artist with whom she would undertake an interview in less than ten minutes.

'My, you're ugly,' Ann-Marie thought to her-self as she passed the picture and made her way through the main doors and into the entrance hall.

The main gallery was big, bright and exuded a smell of cleaning fluid and aerosol spray; it reminded Ann-Marie of an operating theatre, all clinical and clean. 'No cynical, impure thoughts could invade.' she thought as she moved into the gallery and towards the first picture that drew her attention, its vivid colours and bright shapes reminded her of a painting achieved by an infant child, its structure was a barrage of grotesque colours, criss-crossing and assaulting the canvas. She turned and looked about at the other individuals in the gallery and laughed a little to herself as she muttered under her breath.

"A fool and their money are soon parted."

A noise alerted her to the advancing intensions of another and to her left a private door opened and a frail looking teenage girl entered the room, her emaciated features and the savage pallor of her skin initiated a gasp from Ann-Marie, who immediately recognised her from the image on the poster. She moved to meet her, hand outstretched, speaking as she walked.

"Hello I'm Ann-Marie Harrington, journalist; I work for the..." before she could finish her rehearsed introductory sentence the young girl anticipated her words and smiled.

"Yes, I know, I've been expecting you."

The warmth of her voice caused a smile to break across Ann-Marie's lips.

"I was just admiring your work" she said, turning and pointing to the painting that she had recently insulted.

"Thank you. Where would you like to do the interview?" The artist enquired.

Ann-Marie shrugged her shoulders and thought for a moment.

"Why don't you show me your paintings and I can interview you as we go?"

The young girl smiled at the proposition and motioned for Ann-Marie to follow.

"How long have you been actively painting?" Ann-Marie enquired.

"As far back I can remember, I have always been able to discern and mix colours. I've always had a natural flair for painting, it's a bit like second nature," Susan paused. "No! It's more like I've always have been and will be, an artist of some sort."

Ann-Marie smirked.

"I guess you're one of those hardnosed journalists who only believe in what they can see?" Susan said; gesturing to one of the paintings upon the gallery wall. "Are you trying to tell me that this is made up purely of paint and perspiration? What about the imagination? The inspiration? Where does that come from? Is it merely the passing of electric impulses in our brains granting us thoughts or is there something deeper?"

"Are you trying to say that your artwork is inspired by something greater?" Ann-Marie, enquired inquisitively.

"Yes and no," Susan replied.

Ann-Marie placed her hand thoughtfully upon her own chin.

"Then what does that make us? Puppets for the Gods?" Creatures to be manipulated? Pets for a greater force? I don't think so. Humankind has advanced so much over the centuries by use of its own brainpower," she half-heartedly smiled at the artist. "If there was a greater force then why not give us all the answers? Instead of giving us trivia, dark shadows in corners or stigmata, why not a cure for cancer..?"

Susan smiled and thought purposefully before interjecting. "They do, but indirectly; they gave us Marie Curie, Einstein, prominent doctors, outstanding teachers, or some spoilt kid who thinks that she can paint a picture or two?" Susan continued but corrected her analogy. "Not that I would ever dream of putting myself into the same league as any of those people who I have fore-mentioned."

Ann-Marie smiled. "Now if I were a 'hardnosed journalist.' I would first ask myself. 'Why has this girl put herself or her talents in the same category as holy divinity?' But I'm not, and I can plainly see that your paintings, even though very delightful, are nothing special," Ann-Marie said, pointing to one of the portraits on the far wall. The picture was slightly cumbersome but well structured.

Susan smiled. "I agree, but I did paint that one when I was only five."

Susan turned slightly and walked further into the exhibition, leaving Ann-Marie to fall deeper into her own ignorance.

As the interview progressed Ann-Marie's perception of this fragile soul dispelled and she realised that below the surface of the interviewee's delicate frame rested the heart and a determination of one who could have been further advanced in her earthly years. It was when they came to the more recent portraits that Ann-Marie understood the complexities of their construction and began to realise the rare talent which presented itself to her. She allowed her imagination to delve into the deliberate yet soft brush strokes that appeared to build the artistic dichotomy before her. She marvelled at the piercing eyes of the male subject; his image demanded recognition, demanded tenure. Her mind ransacked her memories, creating chaos in her thoughts. Only after she had studied the images for several moments did a distant wisp of recognition which partially elude her thoughts, alert her to the recognition of the artists subject but also her own undesired attention, and it was at this point that she realised that she was now the centre of that attention and not the canvas. She turned to the artist and smiled.

"What's wrong Miss Ward? Is there cause for amusement?"

Susan smiled. "Please, call me Susan, Miss Ward adds years on me. Makes me sound like my mother."

Ann-Marie returned her smile.

"The subject in that picture came to me in a dream, I've no idea why or who he was." Susan's mood lighted. "Tell me, have you ever thought of posing for a portrait?"

Ann-Marie returned a rather nervous look.

"Me!" she cried, her startled emotions echoing around the gallery.

"No, think about it," Susan interjected. "You have the perfect face for it; features any artist would sell their soul to paint. Just think of it; your face captured upon canvas for an eternity. In centuries to follow, people would marvel at your beauty and confidence. You would, in some way, be immortalised. A minute essence of yourself would be locked within the painting, surviving the cruel passage of time. All of this will be gone soon," Susan said, waving her hand close to Ann-Marie's face. "Just think of it, your face, captured forever," Susan's excitement began to grow. "Can I be permitted to take a few photographs of you? I just want to see if I can do it. Please, you must allow me. If it turns out the way I hope it will, I'll give you the painting; a form of payment for being my model, so to speak," Before Ann-Marie had time to answer Susan rushed off and returned a moment later with a small, handheld digital camera.

"Try to look natural," Susan said, as the camera clicked over and over again, as she instructing her startled subject in the ways of an artist's muse.

"That's it, hold your head back a little and open your eyes wider."

Ann-Marie smiled the best she could, but embarrassment quickly took hold of her. Seeing this, Susan took a final photograph and thanked her subject profusely. Ann-Marie couldn't help but feel that the interview tables had been well and truly turned. She laughed, easing the uncomfortable atmosphere.

Susan smiled again, "You really can have the painting if you want it. I'm not just saying it to get you to write nice things about me. Write what you like, I don't care."

"Thank you. I really am flattered by your proposition. After all, who wouldn't want a portrait of themselves hung on their living-room wall? Especially one done by such a prominent artist?" Ann-Marie said in genuine delight.

"When will your article be in the paper?" Susan enquired.

Ann-Marie thought for a moment. "Well, if I start it straight way then it should hit the press in about two days." Delving into her pocket she produced a business card and presented it to the Susan.

"If you need anything give me a call, you never know I might do a follow up story," Susan smiled, and offered Ann-Marie her own business card in polite response.

The interview had taken the remainder of the afternoon and by the time Ann-Marie left the gallery the skies were already turning a dull, dirty grey. A thin film of ice covered the steps which led down from the front of the gallery and she wished that she had worn a more sensible shoe, as heels were too cumbersome for the ravages of winter. It was just as this thought danced through her mind that she noticed the delicate drift of Christmas snow as it fell softly from the heavens.

"Blast!" she said out-loud, as a cold winter wind blew down the street and around her naked ankles. She moved about, endeavouring to generate a little warmth as she waited for a taxi to come into view. Almost ten minutes had passed before one turned the corner and stopped outside the gallery. The passengers alighted and made their way to the galleries entrance. Ann-Marie, not waiting to see if the driver had another fare, stepped into the back of the vehicle and closed the door behind her. She muttered her address and without giving the driver a second glance she began to work feverously upon her story.

The traffic was heavy and laboured, almost coming to a standstill at one point as the clouds overhead relinquished their festive cargo, covering the city with a soft blanket of wistful snow. In stark contrast, dark, heavy sleet issued across the roads and onto the human traffic laden pavements, bringing a sinister foreboding to this joyous festive season. The taxi gathered speed as the main throng of traffic passed one of the major intersections of the road, but the increasing noise of the vehicles did little to distract Ann-Marie from her work.

The taxi driver began to chatter about the decline in the weather and oncoming festivities, and Ann-Marie gave the occasional acknowledgment as a response in the hope of appeasing the drivers increasing conversation. His chattering voice became a mere distant distraction as she wrote frantically onto her note pad. Sentence after sentence flowed from her pen as outside of the window the throng of traffic gathered in ferocity. Cars sped by, manoeuvring through the evening rush, demonstrating the anger of the traffic's flow. It appeared urgent and demanding as its main body began to swell as the hunger of the swarm began to display its true nature as sinister emotion enveloped all without.

A large red London bus hurried from a side-street eager to reach its destination only to find that its anticipated pathway was marred with thick black ice and cumbersome slush. It advanced forward at an almost calculated pace, its tyres weak with their uneasy lumber. The driver gripped the steering wheel in anticipation of perceived dangers and manoeuvred the vehicle slowly into the raging thoroughfare of the evening rush-hour. He tentatively placed his foot upon the accelerator, drawing the monstrous steel colossus forward into the icy evening air. All about, the demonic vehicles hissed and scorned his harsh advancements and snarled with their displeasure as the red leviathan advanced.

Less than a street away a motorcycle messenger impishly darted in and out of the ravenous traffic, weaving his deadly path through the small gaps, which appeared almost inhumanly possible to transcend, but did little to deter his Machiavellian pace. This insignificant purveyor of tragedy was unaware of his cataclysmic role in the passion-play which unfurled before him. Leaning more exaggeratedly from side to side he brought his vehicle through the angry torrent of London's vehicular commuter's until it appeared that his destiny became increasingly apparent. He moved into the centre of the raging inundation, and as he advanced feverishly down Oxford Street he swerved uncontrollably upon the ice and clipped the side of the heavy London bus, cars swerved to miss this oncoming catastrophe but mirrored the messenger's calamity. The side of the bus buckled from the vehicle's impact, sending it spinning erratically upon the ice. Undulating slowly sideways it sent plumes of snow and slush in sinister, festive waves ahead of the cumbersome vehicle, creating a malevolent wake that seemed to exacerbate the eerie silence that captured this brief moment in time. The air was filled with silence, as all earthly motion appeared to slow as a preternatural realisation alerted the taxi's passenger to the forthcoming disaster. Ann-Marie urgently looked up from her work.

Hitting the taxi with the full force of its rage, the side of the bus crushed the back section of the vehicle, sending fragments of glass and metal into the air. Inside, the passenger's world fell into silence as a universe of darkness enveloped her.

Two

The light that shone all about was bright but not blinding, and it seemed to soothe - almost comfort - Ann-Marie as she stood alone in the perpetuity of her mind, an existence no longer complicated by the rigours of mortal life. It was as if her thoughts were her own and the indulgence and misgivings of others were washed away by the resonance of this gentle ethereal glow. Then life hit her with the full force of its reality and she felt herself being drawn downwards at a great speed, hurtling blindly into an unearthly void, the ground rushing up to meet her and she abruptly opened her eyes.

The lights were gone, taking with them the feelings of gentle tranquillity, and in front of her stood a solitary hospital bed upon which lay a young woman. At first Ann-Marie felt as though she were intruding upon a strangers rest until reality hit her with the full force of its truth. With a horror greater than anything she could envisage, her mind assaulted her with the stark reality that the stranger that lay in front of her was none other than Ann-Marie Harrington herself, the physical was now being observed by the spiritual.

Escape, was the only emotion she could sense, and it gripped her at an exponential rage, sending her fleeing from the hospital room where her mortal remains lay, standing motionless in the corridor, her very existence a paradoxical anathema to science but little solace to herself. She stood motionless for what seemed an eternity before she turned and looked through the unkempt windows of the hospital ward and out into the winter world beyond, and fell deeper into her own despair as she observed mortal life returning to its self-regulating normality and she grew envious of it all as it perpetually continued in its day-to-day mundane existence. How she longed for the sensuality of human kindness as the winter sun reached tentatively across the evening almond-grey sky.

A gentle voice that spoke from behind Ann-Marie, snatching her from the very brink of despair.

"Young lady, aren't you going to come in?" he enquired. "I've been waiting for you for a number of days."

She turned around over and over again to find the source of the conversation; it was only when the voice called again did she find its origin. Just off to her left lay a set of private rooms, above which read the sign 'Long Stay Ward.' Venturing along this short corridor she came to a door that was left ajar. Ann-Marie stepped tentatively inside the room and was surprised to find an elderly gentleman seated on the bed; he appeared to be waiting for her.

"Yes my dear, I'm talking to you," he said with a smile.

Ann-Marie looked at him in surprise.

"You can hear me?" she said.

The elderly gentleman smiled and nodded his head.

"Yes my dear I can hear and see you."

"But how?" Ann-Marie enquired with surprise.

"Please sit and I'll tell you the reason why we are both here, he said. "You may think that all of the events which have befallen you are all by chance, or accident, but I'm afraid that nothing could be further from the truth."

Ann-Marie tentatively sat next to her elderly companion and listened to his words. "I have been sent here by the spirit world, by a people known as the Qareen. They have asked me to meet with you and teach and guide you through the conflict that you are about to enter and could consume your very existence. From this point on, time will never seem the same to you. Your world will change in such an immeasurable way that even you will doubt the dramatic transformation that your life will take. You will need to forget all of your yesterdays. Discount and abandon all of the theories and scientific boundaries which have been placed upon you since childhood, and forge forward with new eyes and a fresh grasp upon perception. Observe the world anew with more than just your five basic senses."

The old man smiled to offer Ann-Marie reassurance.

"I have offered my services to those of a higher order so that I can fulfil my own destiny and transcend this pitiful realm of existence. Those services to which I refer are those of a medium. You see, I have been a medium for nearly thirty years, and now, after assisting those from one side of life to contact those on the other, I have been asked by those on the spirit side to do a great and just task." He paused and thought deeply before continuing. "You see, all of the events which have taken place over these past few hours, if not over the entire period of your life, have been nothing if not fixed. You have been guided, coaxed by a greater force; a force so dynamic and powerful that it is far greater than anything you could ever imagine. You are one in a million, and the only reason why things have now come to fruition is because there is a danger; a danger so strong and powerful, that, with time, it could bring down the heavens themselves. You see, you are responsible for an act that took place several centuries ago; an act that has filled a creature of destruction with vengeance so powerful that even now he is hunting you and will stop at nothing until you are destroyed. His presence and potential could have a considerably detrimental effect upon the very future of humankind itself."

Ann-Marie held up her hand in amazement.

"Hold on! I think that things are going a little too fast here. One minute I'm interviewing an artist in one of London's finest art galleries and the next..."

The other interjected, "..Susan Ward?"

Ann-Marie slowed her words, puzzled.

"Yes. And then I'm in an accident and I find myself in this situation, out of my body, confronted by a whole plethora of horrors that could have easily come from a Victorian gothic horror. I don't understand, please tell me what's going on."

Her teacher offered her another comforting, reassuring smile.

"I cannot say that I have all of the answers but I can try to alleviate some of your fears and justify your emotions. Let's start from the beginning, as I know it. I can only repeat what I have been given by the spirit world, and that information is very limited. First of all; I can show my manners and introduce myself. I am James Jackson, Medium to the stars and heads of governments."

"Really?" whispered, Ann-Marie, in surprise.

"No, but it sounds good, doesn't it?"

They both smiled. "There's no need for you to introduce yourself Ann-Marie, as I already feel as though I have known you for a lifetime," he paused.

"Let us begin. Question one, and I feel the most urgent of your questions; the reason why you and I are here at this moment in time. Firstly, to get you back into your body, a task that will take a lot of effort on your part, my dear, and secondly and most importantly, I must tell you of a power at your disposal and the acts that you are about to perpetrate and those that you have already executed. I will begin with the latter as this is, for me the easiest hill to climb. You my dear are very special, a child born one in a generation. You have a power that others could only dream of possessing. You are what we call a 'Communicator', a bridge between this world and the next, a bond between the living and the dead. However, do not deceive yourself; you are not a medium or a clairvoyant. You have nothing in common with these charlatans who would swindle the desperate and the lonely, but you are a genuine 'Communicator.' You may ask yourself what is the difference? Are they not one and the same? But the answer that you must give yourself is a fervent no. For there is a universe of distinct subtle differences."

James paused once again. "How best can I explain?" he said.

"You see in every one of us there is a tiny fragment of our former self, that person who we were in our previous existence. Something of that former self stays with us even when the physical form is consumed by time. The spirit is somehow perpetual, immortal, transcending the barriers of death. We are born, procreate and then die. There are a few other insignificant events which occur somewhere in the middle, this is the basic pattern for life. Don't you agree?" he said looking to Ann-Marie. But before she could answer he continued. "No! This is not how it should be; it is only this way because human kind has made it thus; our thirst for knowledge has been washed away by a sea of indifference; we no longer care for, or understand this world in which we live. Life ceases to exist outside the confines of man's superficial mind. Minds filled with the mundane, the obscene. The lust for life has gone, replaced with the trappings of a disintegrating, disingenuous civilisation. A civilisation hypnotised by the context of their words, guided, as if blind, by political fools and vagabonds. Hypocrisy reigns supreme. The society of the world as a whole is based upon the oppression and denial of others, by a people who will not accept the findings of their own senses. They are propelled by a science, which is less than a few centuries old and yet allow it to set itself against the laws of nature and other sciences older than history itself. To man, if something exists which he has not yet named, or he has not yet discovered, he assumes with his arrogance that it cannot and does not exist, there is no margin for possibility, no shades of grey in his black and white world. It is all perception; he cannot understand that the universe is far greater than imagination could ever comprehend and the souls of his fellow kin are as diverse as the seasons, and for what may be heaven to one could be hell to another. You must learn to grasp the improbable as well as the impossible for they may be closer to your own ideologies than initially perceived. Was it not apparent, that only a few years ago space flight was considered something of fantasy? Yet now it is a mundane reality. Readily accepted by all who are confronted by its overwhelming evidence. And yet, even though there is insurmountable truth which stares science in the face, it still refuses to acknowledge that it may be wrong or that the boundaries which it has set itself, may in some way require revising."

James looked at Ann-Marie.

"You must believe what I am saying; otherwise you could never accept that I am sitting here before you. A remembered mortal, long since deceased, yet an immortal never forgotten."

Ann-Marie smiled her acceptance of his preposition.

"Are we all the same?" she enquired. "And what makes me different from these other spiritual people?"

James smiled "What sets you apart from the others? Well, one major thing is your talent. Please try to understand you are not restrained by the boundaries that restrict other mortals, you can follow your soul's desire and savour the delights and experiences long forgotten to this world. You can visit places and people who have long since entered the realms of fantasy and folklore. Civilisations forever forgotten, lost in the annals of a darker time. You see, you are a traveller. An observer, recorder of the ancients, an alchemist of time."

Realising that he may have been confusing his student, James began to explain in a finer detail. "Locked within us all are those experiences and emotions that make up each individual. When death claims the mortal form, the splinters of their experience bind themselves to the immortal self and journey with it through the constant cycle of birth and rebirth, fading at the passing of each generation but existing there perpetually. They are waiting to be touched, to allow their memories to once again flow free in the vast seas of recollection. It is this, 'something' which you have, this ability to activate and manipulate these memories. You can use the hidden fragments of D.N.A. locked within your inner-self and travel into the past, using the previous incarnation of your former selves as a staging post and then move freely about time and space at will. Humankind has always known of the existence of your brethren but because of prejudice and ignorance, you have been kept a protected secret by the likes of my kind."

He briefly paused.

"I am sorry if I seem to be hurrying but time is neither on your side nor mine. Where was I?" he said correcting himself. "Travel: Yes, when you travel onto the pathways of D.N.A. you must remember - when you do this you send out a signal to anyone who is sensitive enough to pick it up. Unfortunately your greatest enemy is sensitive to your thoughts and for that reason and that reason alone I must plead with you to use your powers sparingly and only when it is necessary."

"Enemy? I don't have any enemies," she looked deep into his eyes. "Who would want to harm me?" Ann-Marie demanded.

James smiled and continued.

"I know that this all sounds very much like a fantasy but I must assure you it is not and everything that I am telling you is the truth. I felt that I had to tell you of the travel and your dark talents, for this next piece of information will go far beyond these realms of this reality and your own juvenile preconceptions. Please forget all of the images of these creatures that you have seen in the Hollywood pictures or read in books and magazines and acknowledged them for the abominations, which they truly are. They have existed since the dawn of time and some would say before. Yet many centuries ago, using the powers that I have described, you sent one of these demons into the bowels of the earth, but now he has risen in order to claim just retribution against those who set out to destroy him and his kind; he seeks his revenge."

Ann-Marie suppressed a tiny laugh as James became more dramatic at the passing of each sentence. She apologised, "I'm sorry, but no creature known to man can live in the ground for several hundred years. Now this spiritual travelling I can slightly take on board but a creature that is immortal, what is he, a God?"

James smiled once again. "He would have you believe this, but no, Christian is no god. He is the scorn of anything that is good in this world and if this world is to have a future then you must do what you have already done and fulfil what is in your destiny to achieve. Christian and his kind are nothing but a disease that infects this world of man and it is your duty to destroy him and other of his dark brethren, those born from the pages of the Necronomicon, those born of the dark mother."

Ann-Marie stood in silence, contemplating his words.

"A Necro ... what? This is too much; I can't take in all of this information."

James lowered his head and contemplated his answer.

"In simple terms, its basic translation means 'The Book of the Dead.' Written many thousands of years ago by a wandering soul of a lost, and some say original civilisation, long before the Egyptians and it contains the dark incantations and spells lost to history and its like has not been seen for several millennia. The book was torn asunder and an integral part was thought destroyed, burnt in the destruction of the library at Alexandria in Egypt in 48 BC, but its name and whereabouts have presented itself to history on a number of occasions, which causes great concern and embarrassment to the Catholic Church."

"Why?" Ann-Marie enquired.

"The surviving elements of this book were entrusted to the Catholic Church, and their dark antecedence has been eternally apparent throughout the barbaric history of man's fight against the dark unholy elements of this world, and even now, the church are mustering a holy expedition to destroy those devilish creatures who would seek to harm you."

He took a deep breath.

"There has been a supervisory regime called the Illuminati, established by the Catholic Church since its own inception, following the crucifixion of Christ. They later became a military order known as the Hospitallers of St John or the Knights Templar, formed around the twelfth century, but prior to this, in 600 A.D. Pope Gregory commissioned the Ravannate Abbot Probus to build a hospital in Jerusalem to treat and care for Christian pilgrims to the Holy Land. Through-out the ages of Man, this order has splintered and fragmented. Initially, they cared and nursed the weak and later became military figures that became known as The Protectorate and they followed a more sinister doctrine. It was to these chosen men that all things spiritual and holy were entrusted," James Paused. "It was from this Order that elements of the book was entrusted and by one whom they wished to destroy."

Ann-Marie urged him to continue.

"The book contains knowledge far beyond the imagination of modern man and its whereabouts is unknown. The creature who wrote its contents remains lost in the mists of time and with her those sacrosanct pages written in the blood of infidels. For within this sacred lost volume there is a dark and powerful inscription that holds the true and sacred name of the Lord. And he who knows the names of God holds absolute power."

Ann-Marie allowed the magnitude of this information to envelop her before enquiring. "So it can be used for evil as well as good?" she asked in a slow deliberate way.

James smiled and nodded.

"And the only weapon we have to fight with is faith," Ann-Marie whispered.

"In this modern world faith appears to be lost in the priorities of acquisition, maybe man should not look too see if he has lost faith in God but whether God has lost his faith in man," James stated.

Ann-Marie contemplated his words.

"This, however, is not your most demanding of predicaments," he continued.

"Christian!" she said. "What is he?"

"First of all, he is as you are, a Communicator: One born of a twin, both born of extraordinary power, both given over to the father of darkness, disciples of the dark gift."

James sighed as a flood of incomprehensible thoughts filled his mind. "Man is such a weak creature but for all of his failings we are what we are. I suppose where there is light there must be darkness, and in the depths of human sorrow, there must be a little joy. But those who hunt you realise that to feel perfection and serenity one must first taste temptation - a temptation that has damned them for an eternity. For the one who hunts you is a creature that can never be trusted, a drinker of souls, a destroyer and a vagabond. This abomination is a true emissary from the devil himself. He is a vampire!"

For some reason unknown to Ann-Marie she understood that James was telling the truth and a dark cloud of justifiable terror passed over her soul.

"A vampire!" she could hear her own words ringing in the air about her, echoing with their discordant, nonsensical chime.

"Do you believe me?" James enquired.

Ann-Marie remained silent.

"It would seem that you have very little choice," James said, offering a reassuring smile. "These creatures have hunted on this and other realms of existence since time immemorial. They were here long before Jesus brought Lazarus back from the dead and Judas hanged himself after betraying his master in the garden of Gethsemane. For if we look into the creature's own origins we may find the pathway that will lead to its own demise and it was felt that Judas may have been the father to the third and most recent branch of this abominable race. To understand the connection we must look deeper into the tales original intention. In endeavouring to unwrap the cultural words of the Bible you are required to steer away from the old western inclination in which it is so blatantly fermented. In our western eyes it is perceived that Judas hanged himself, but to Middle-Eastern doctrine this is far from the tale's true account and in some perverse way offers you an insight in the creature's greatest weakness. Judas, in fact, leapt onto a large military spear which left his body hanging in the air and according to the writings of Luke, his entrails poured out onto the field, which was later purchased by his own bloodied thirty pieces of silver and used as a burial site for foreign pilgrims to the blessed lands."

"This is why Matthew then states that Judas hanged himself when in fact these actions are one and the same thing. This action and this action alone brought about the inception of the vampires greatest weakness; a stake driven with faith through their black heart is the Christian and only true way to destroy a vampire and release their immortal soul into the Lord's compassionate care."

James looked sensitively at Ann-Marie and continued.

"Two other primary factors are highlighted by this tale, Judas and Lazarus did not and cannot die in a mortal sense, and all that these aforementioned actions accomplished was to create a different cultural line of the same abomination, for they themselves became the servants of a darker force, the children of a lesser God. There were also many innocents who were also drawn into this scarlet passion play, for the field that was purchased from the polluted silver acquired by Judas were damned for an eternity. All those hapless souls buried in virtue, rose from the earth after their death to join their dark creator. His blood permeated the earth with its satanic toxic virus and this group of un-dead brethren who would later be known as the Poor Fellow Soldiers of Christ were created. Please look for evidence of their existence when your body and soul are reunited, for knowledge is always power."

He thought deeply before continuing.

"In European literature it is evident that these creatures were first recorded in England as far back as the eleventh century in holy documentation entitled 'Creatures of the Night', and later dark arts such as Nigromancy and the existence of the aforementioned Necronomicon was pondered in the manuscript, 'The Clavicle of Solomon', from which the holy name is given as documented in its originality by King Ptolomeus the Grecian."

James leaned back and exhaled strongly.

"I cannot emphasis enough that when your unification is complete you must seek out this knowledge in order for you to fully understand your enemy, for knowledge is power and power in your case is the salvation of life itself. History is pitted with dark tales of the origins of these festering abominations, some as far back as recorded history itself. Even in pre-dynastic Egypt there were tales, even some linked to the gods and associated with these creature's dark origins. For you to understand these abominations to a greater degree, I feel I must delve into the far-reaches of their own history and in some perverse way this may give you insight into ending their wicked lives."

James continued in a slow and deliberate manor.

"Now to the second strand of this dark heritage. It was told that in ancient Egypt the God Set was jealous of his brother Osiris and plotted his downfall and so threw a magnificent banquet in his honour. At the banquet there was a beautiful gold sarcophagus inlaid with diamonds and precious stones and Set announced that whoever lay within its exact confines may keep the box and the riches it held. Each of the party guests endeavoured to lay within its boundaries, but to no avail and it was only when Osiris positioned himself in the box did he match perfectly. It was unknown to him that his sinister brother had the box created to his perfect dimensions. It was then locked and Set ordered his brother to be cut into fourteen pieces and those pieces were to be scattered into the Nile."

"Following this dark deed his beloved sister Isis, discovering the abomination which has befallen her true love, scoured the Nile endeavouring to find all of the pieces of her adored Osiris. Unable to bring him back to life using the Necronomicon she begged the sun god Ra to intercede. Ra agreed to her demands but instigated a severe warning with damnable conditions. These conditions were dark and foreboding. Primarily, they stipulated that Osiris must sleep within the confines of an illustrious sarcophagus during the daylight hours, as he was damned never to walk in the blessing of Ra's sunlight; to do so would curse his immortal soul to everlasting torment. The second and most heinous of these stipulations was that he must drink the blood of the living to sustain his dark damnation, and only after agreeing to these conditions did Ra fulfil his obligation and Osiris was then brought, deceased, into the land of the living to be forever known as the un-living one, king of the afterlife, father of the blessed un-dead."

"You can see how modern perceptions of these creatures and their habits have been absorbed into folk-lore and become the very fabric of some civilisation's foundation. A simple stake through the heart, the purifying touch of the morning sunlight, these actions can free their tormented souls. If you look about this contemporary realm, ancient evidence of their existence haunts this modern world."

He looked about the room for an example before his eyes were fixed upon the moon outside of the hospital window. "It is surmised that there are fourteen phases to a single moon's cycle, one sliver cut off each night for 14 days, then reassembled over the next fourteen days, as were the pieces of Osiris," James smiled, "It could have been fifteen but for the oxyrhynchus fish, but that is another tale," he smirked lightly to himself before continuing. He then stopped his merriment and looked purposefully into Ann-Marie's eyes. "Remember, there are other dark creatures who you must be aware of, who are locked within the cycle of the moon and their origins sit closer to your own home than you realise."

An unwelcome shudder ran down Ann-Marie's spine.

"Now, we must hurry and I will endeavour to teach you the skills you require to return to your earthly body as we have very little time left as I know that there are much darker forces plotting and conspiring and it is apparent that Christian is about to form a diabolic coalition with a creature of pure evil."

Ann-Marie moved her hand slowly to her mouth "What kind of creature can be worse than Christian?" she said, her eyes filled with both terror and horror.

James let out an abject sigh and waited a moment before answering.

"I have held this information till last as I knew it would overshadow all that I have already said... I know little of him apart from his name, Caliban - Devourer of Souls. Even his name elicits fear from his own debauched offspring. He was also known as the devourer of flesh, even his name is a loose anagram of the word cannibal. His presence within dark history reaches as far back as the ancient Romans and beyond, for they understood the most malevolent of his baleful attributes and called him, 'The Dark One' - 'Kaliban.' Roughly translated from ancient texts as meaning 'with blackness.' He is the third master of this Vampire race, or Tribe. He is what you would call a Demon, an insignificant creature of the lower denominations, but a demon, none-the-same. He and his kind have sought entrance into this earthly realm for centuries and would forge a coalition with anyone willing to fulfil his dark desire," James looked at Ann-Marie in despair. "Now child, we must hurry."

Three

Susan stepped back from the painting as the dying light from the sun shone in through the attic window giving the whole room an incandescent warmth, alighting upon the features of the subject immortalised upon the canvas. She smiled to herself and placed the paint brush into the murky jar of turpentine.

From behind, she heard a noise, turning she saw her mother standing in the doorway to her workroom. Her mother was young looking for her age; she had passed the dreaded forty with ease and sailed into middle age as though it were designed totally for her. Susan studied her mother's features, wondering if time would be as kind to her as it had been to her mother. Her strong feature almost moulded from marble, her precise dark copper hair cut into a perfectly cut bob, just touching her shoulders, her delicate frame, strong yet yielding, and those eyes, green and piercing. They almost looked into Susan's very soul as if searching for the secrets locked within. She could have watched her all night, this vision that was her mother but words broke the spell of concentration that she had cast over herself. Her mother spoke in soft deliberate tones.

"Is that the reporter that you met the other day?" she said, nodding towards the painting.

"Yes I'm going to give it to her, a sort of present for being kind. Most journalists don't give a damn about what they say or how they treat their subjects but she was different; she had compassion, something that costs nothing but meant so much."

Susan's eyes moved from those of her mother and back onto the painting; it seemed to mesmerise her, draw her into it. A recollection that refused to be viewed. "I feel as though I've met her before."

"That's possible," her mother said. "You've talked to so many journalists, I can't see how this one's any different," she then changed the track of conversation. "I was going to make some tea, would you like some?" Susan nodded, not taking her eyes away from the painting, her mind captured by the presence of Ann-Marie. 'I have met you before Ann-Marie Harrington, that much I know," she said quietly to herself.

Four

Ann-Marie sat on the hospital bed her mind raging with a multitude of questions. Besides her stood the delicate frame of James, his smiling eyes comforting his pupil as he proceeded with the lesson. As he spoke, his voice was warm and compelling almost urging Ann-Marie to remember his every word.

"You must try and clear your mind; it is important to concentrate on everything that I say, for if you do not follow my exact words then you will never achieve the reunification of your body and soul," James took a deep breath in readiness for the first and only lesson.

"Walking, breathing, laughing, crying, remember these emotions, remember how it felt to be in pain, the warmth of the summer sun upon your face, the sensation of winter's rain on your skin. Anything! Just try to recall how it feels to be alive. When you have this mixture of emotions pulling at you, you are then required to concentrate them, focus them into a beam of pure light and direct it just above where your mortal body lies. For what you are trying to do is to make your spirit form act the way in which it was intended. We want you to float; only a few inches off the bed at first, but with time this will become to you as natural as walking. For it is with this power that you will reunify your own body and soul and in time return to Christian's century and correct the sands of time, so that your destiny can be fulfilled."

"Why must I return to his century, can't I confront him here?" she enquired.

James smiled.

"From the past, he searches for you, as you are the key to his own future. However, you are also his nemesis. For you are the one who wronged him, caused him great pain both physical and emotional. His driving force is hatred and the focal point is you, which is why you must prepare yourself for the task ahead, for if he finds weakness or insecurity then we are all damned. For Christian is about to forge a dark alliance with a force so powerful that it very essence could tear your soul asunder, and his dark alley has never been known for his compassion. Never underestimate your enemies, for they will never underestimate you; understand them and then you will truly understand yourself. As I have said, you must return to the past for it has already been written and therefore history must be fulfilled. Confront him upon his own ground."

James smiled to offer reassurance.

 "Now, we must get over our main predicament. The reunification of your body to soul; first of all you will feel the sensation of your spirit trying to travel, this is totally natural; it is your spirit searching, trying to move into the realm of another dimension, a simple action that man neglected to remember when he transcended into this modern, less spiritual form of being."

"You have been away from your physical form for some time now. We can only pray that the lower elementals have not taken hold and forced their dark bidding upon it, for they frequently venture into the realm of man in the hope of discovering or possessing a vacant shell. Be it through illness, torment or basic sleep as with all of these, the soul may be inclined to leave the physical form and venture into the unknown. It may be for the briefest of moments, but that is all that it takes. This is one reason why there are so many risks and responsibilities, not just for yourself but for those whom you decide to carry with you."

Ann-Marie gasped, "What are you trying to say?"

"I'm not trying to say anything; I'm telling you that you can move into another living soul's domain. You can travel and manipulate another individual's dreams and therefore alter the outcome of decisions that they may make in the future. That is one primary reason why your kind has been kept so much a secret. Can you imagine what would happen if your powers were to fall in the hands of a less than honest government? Presidents could be manipulated, politicians moulded. The ramifications go far beyond man's futile imagination. It is a great burden to bear, but you are responsible not only for yourself and this power that is at your touch, you are also responsible for denying that I or any of my kind has ever existed. You must build a defence against the inquisitive thoughts of others, for each government, employs the likes of yourself, albeit very much weaker, but if they were to sense a fraction of your powers then they could locate you and use these great gifts for negative purposes. Never tell anyone, no matter how much you trust them, for there is no such thing as a kept secret. You are responsible, that is why you were born in times past as you were born now, a Communicator."

"You do not have a choice about your future, it has been preordained, written in the stars. Nothing that you say or do in connection with the gift can be altered; it is yours and always has been. Accept it and your life will be fulfilled; yes it has its dangers, but so does living. Life in the modern jungle of man is a torture in itself; use your gift for the furtherment of good. Reject it and I cannot say the tortuous outcome that may prevail, but be reassured you cannot lose it. It is yours and always has been. Now, shall we continue with your lesson?"

Ann-Marie lay back upon the bed and concentrated, using the full force of the turmoil that raged within her, focusing upon the space above her head. She could feel her spirit form moving but only slowly at first, urgency gripped her as tension filled her mind.

"Why can't I do it?" she exclaimed, pushing her thoughts forward. James' voice seemed to add to her dilemma.

"Don't force it, nature will proceed at its own pace; you will progress to the next level only when this one has been truly understood. Use that power that you know is deep within you and try to guide it slowly to the surface."

"Tease it, manipulate it, encourage it; dissipate your negative energies and use your positive. If you always remember this you can achieve anything, now concentrate."

Ann-Marie focused her mind and allowed herself to fall into the darkness that was her uncharted soul. The domain of the forgotten world that was unconscious, where the darkest desires of an individual would wait and fester, putrefying in their impotency. She could feel the strength of her inner-self drawing her desires to their conclusion, infinitesimal in their presence, yet gathering in their force. The space above Ann-Marie began to shimmer and buckle and to her surprise, all at once, she could feel herself rising from the bed. It was only when she stopped concentration and just thought that she could feel the true magnitude of this power surge through her.

"That's it! That's it!" James exclaimed in excitement, "You've done it."

To Ann-Marie's amazement she found that her actions were presenting at her will, and she moved forward and upwards until she stood vertical looking in James' direction.

The light from the window behind her tutor shone through, casting shadows of light across the whole room, a kaleidoscope of soft broken images. She hovered for a moment, drinking the images of delight; falling backwards into her fertile imagination she noticed the changes which had taken place. James looked somehow different, somehow vulnerable.

"Never underestimate yourself or others. You see mortality and immortality will always follow the same dark theories and distinct parallels. For those who are perceived as painfully vulnerable, are fundamentally those who are the most aggressive. Paradoxically, those who seek to control their environment, and the individuals inhabiting their chaotic realm, can only reach their true potential by first plunging themselves into the turbulent depths of submission. Only then, can they savour a true deprivation of the soul, and thus comprehend their own sanctity and taste the essence of an individual's pure worth."

"You see my dear," he continued. "All you needed was the key and now that I have given this to you, my job is over. Fulfil your destiny. Love and hate are powerful emotions and the trauma they procure will haunt us through the centuries, but in your case it is evident that some wounds get deeper with time."

James smiled and stepped away, observing Ann-Marie as he moved, however it was only when he reached the far wall that it happened; slowly at first, then gathering in intensity, a great light filled the room, sending Ann-Marie's spirit self-backwards. Her emotions were captured by its brilliance as the radiance which issued offered solace and comfort and it was only when this light faded did her senses bring her thoughts back into order she found herself alone.

The room behind her began to darken as the malevolent forces gathered in readiness to claim her mortal form. She moved closer to the bed, unaware of the shadows that crept and slithered across the walls and ceiling, festering above her mortal remains. She took a deep breath and layback in the air, as if in sleep. Hovering for a moment she allowed the sensation of weightlessness to wash over her, she felt that at that moment her soul had found true peace. Opening her eyes, she was amazed to find that night had already descended but when reality alerted her senses, fear gripped her thoughts.

'What was going on?'

Then, her mind cast itself back to the conversation with James and the sinister tale of dark elementals. With an inner rage she targeted the centre of her mortal body with her thoughts and directed the beam of her mind directly into her physical self. A great wind gathered her up, taking with it every sensation that she had ever experienced in her life and maximising them until she felt as though she were about to implode. Pressure filled her very essence and it was as if the world were bearing down upon her. The dark elementals grasped and reached forward to capture her soul as she opened her mouth and shrieked a terrorised mortal scream.

Reality sent her senses into turmoil, for the scream that issued from her mouth was not that of a spiritual being, but that of flesh and blood. Nursing staff came rushing from all directions as Ann-Marie thrashed and twisted upon the hospital bed. Life had returned as the two halves of this being were now re-united in a dark coalition.

Five

Susan Ward lay in her bed contemplating the events that had taken place over the past few days, a great sense of bewilderment hung over her thoughts. Why hadn't Ann-Marie contacted her as promised, and why hadn't her story appeared in any of the newspapers?

She moved further down the bed between the sheets, as the warmth generated by her body began to rise around her, soothing her, bringing upon her the tales of night. Sleep slowly filled her mind, bringing the images of the day's events across the screen of her thoughts. The painting of Ann-Marie seemed to be the foremost of these images, almost burning itself upon her memory, as if urging her to recall a past-perceived encounter.

Her dream world came and went; images dancing and spinning, playing over and over again the life that she longed to live and yearned for. The night had passed uneventfully and the first chorus of dawn began to awaken the new day. It was from this angelic melody that a noise issued from beyond her dream, yet was somehow part of it. A distant rhythmic pulse that moved and played at regular intervals, manoeuvring itself in and out of her imagination.

It was soon to be followed by a calling, beginning almost silently at first then gathering in volume. It was only after she concentrated, did Susan realise that these events were taking place beyond her thoughts. They were events in the real world. Opening her eyes she looked about the room that lay in total darkness except for the gentle slivers of blue silver moonlight that crept in through the curtained window. The sound came once again followed by the calling; Susan recognised it at once as her mother's voice, but it somehow seemed different, changed. She was calling to her but her voice contained an urgent tone.

"Susan, can I come in? There's someone here to see you."

Immediately Susan's mind rushed to thoughts of Ann-Marie.

"Come in mother," she called.

The door to the room opened slowly allowing the light from the landing to bathe the bedroom in a soft, pale light. Jennifer stepped into the room and almost immediately Susan realised that something was wrong.

Her mother moved towards the bed, a fixed smile upon her face. It was only when she was almost level with Susan did Jennifer speak.

"Look who's here to see you," her voice was shrill and painful.

From outside the door a great shadow filled the room, sending a deep shudder across Susan's soul. Terror gripped her as this aberration entered her restful domain, its great bulk emanating dark vibrations and she knew that this creature was not of earthly origins. It held human form but Susan knew that this was not a manifestation of man. It moved forward, head bowed as if in prayer. A white ruff hung from its neck, extending two short tails down onto his chest. The remainder of his garments were black, except for the bright silver buckle that sat in the middle of his cap. As he moved, his cape billowed out behind him like a ship's sail lost in a winter's storm.

27

His head snapped sharply up and he stared into Susan's fearful eyes; a wry smile broke across his lips. Time seemed to stand still as the stranger dominated the situation. Then, as if following a silent command he lunged forward and fell upon Susan; his dark words filled the air as he descended.

"Follow me child, for ye be a sinner," his voice was abrupt and abrasive.

His long, bony fingers reached out and gripped Susan's wrist, sending a cold sinister spasm of revulsion through her whole body. She tried to pull away, but as their bodies touched the whole scene before her changed. The wallpaper blistered and melted, contorting into a myriad of shapes until it resembled something that looked like wood. To her left, the walls that were once deep pink and soft became harsh and whitewashed.

Beneath her the bed began to change; no longer was it the soft, comforting mattress full of memories of contented slumber, but now it was a hard wooden board, which irritated and hurt her body. The vision that returned to her eyes was that of a room barren of comfort and lacking of hope. She sat motionless as the silence began to build, fear had passed its saturation point and a strange calm had fallen over her. Everything that she saw was unfamiliar, but in some strange way she recognised everything. Confusion became her enemy. After a moment she realised that she was alone and rose from the bed and moved tentatively over to the small picturesque window on the far wall.

Outside, the world had taken on a dramatic change; gone were the streets and houses that she knew so well and in their place stood an old English village, the type that Susan recognised as being mid seventeenth century. In front of her stretched a village square, in which stood several inhabitants who moved about their daily business as though this was the natural order of the day. With the realisation, that what she saw could be real, a deep sense of fear began to build within her.

Her eyes moved from the square and out past the village boundaries and onto the fields that stretched out as far as the eye could see. There she saw children playing next to the stream, and heard the birds singing. It seemed as if life continued unaware of this stranger that had fallen into this eccentric and forgotten world.

It was at this point that Susan realised that those villagers who stood in the square were staring at her and a deep sense of embarrassment began to envelop her. For their looks were not those of inquisitive strangers but those of hatred, deep, pure and vicious. She moved back from the window just enough to conceal herself from their view.

Watching the life below filled her head with questions, the primary being, 'Where am I?'

This was answered in a way that she would never forget. From inside of what she assumed was the church hall, came a great pouring of people, all of whom were screaming and shouting. It was only when they advanced did she realise the reason for their outburst and at whom it was directed.

They gathered in the village-square and marched, as if an army towards the house in which she stood. As they reached the front door the rabble stopped and looked directly at the window from which Susan was watching. The villagers began to chant in unison, gathering in volume as they progressed. A single word fell upon Susan's ears, filling her will horror; as that word that rang out over and over again was…

"…WITCH!"

A loud shattering sent Susan rushing over to the bed, as the villagers sent rocks hurtling through the small glass window. Susan began to cry as fear of the unknown haunted her, she prayed that this ordeal would not gather in magnitude, but as her prayer slipped from her lips it was joined by another sound. The bolt from the other side of her bedroom door was being drawn back, ready for a stranger to enter. Susan fell backwards onto the bed, sure that death would claim her. The door opened, a little at first then it swung to its full extent, crashing off the wall, sending it shuddering back and forth on its metal hinges. Susan waited for the hoard to enter but to her surprise, a young woman stepped into the room carrying a basket laden with clothes.

 Her manner was harsh and this was matched by her features and the expression held upon her face.

Throwing the basket upon the floor the young woman hissed a command for Susan to dress and abruptly left the room, closing and locking the door as she exited. After several minutes she returned, giving Susan just enough time to dress in this medieval garb. The woman stood for a moment watching her captive, her eyes almost boring into Susan's mind. Then she spoke again but this time in a gentle, almost pitiful tone.

"The fathers wish to see thee in the congregation hall, by half past noon. That time is almost upon us and if thee doesn't hurry then it will be a further black mark against thee." The young woman ushered Susan out of the bedroom and into the hallway of the building.

"Follow me," she said, not looking back at her ward.

She walked down a large, wooden stairway that echoed to the sound of her heavy leather boots. Descending, they passed stern looking paintings and small stained glass windows. Susan was amazed by the sheer size of the house and realised that it was broken into two levels, a prison on the upper and a courtroom on the lower. As she looked about she could feel the eternal coldness of this building. Stopping at the mid-point of the stairs, she looked out of the polished window that faced the village-square. Horror gripped her; for it was not the pyre and stake that sat in the centre of the square that terrified her, but the reflection in the eyes that looked back at her. For they were not her own. They belonged to a woman whose age, she surmised as being in her late twenties with a soft almost sensitive complexion. Susan muttered under her breath.

"What's going on?"

The companion turned and spoke. "What did you say, Witch?"

Susan swallowed hard as she mouthed the word. "Witch?"

When they reached the bottom of the staircase she found herself in a large courtroom filled to capacity with the rebellious villagers that she had seen only a moment before from her window. Their expressions were less than compassionate. Several of them spat at her as she passed. She was immediately directed to the defendant's stand; there she stood in silence awaiting the court to begin.

From the windows, black curtains hung, restricting the bright summer light from entering the courtroom; it seemed to match the heart of those gathered for this trial. A single man moved forward to the chair that sat directly in front of Susan, she recognised him at once as the stranger that had entered her bedroom almost a lifetime ago. He stood for a moment, turning his head slowly from side to side as a mark of pure arrogant, reaffirming his powerful social and legal position to those who sat before him. A subdued chatter began to rise from the back of the courtroom. This was extinguished by a single well-place command.

"Silence!" he commanded.

Silence reigned supreme. The Judge leaned closer towards Susan. Observing her every feature, he smiled a dark wry smile.

"Listen to me Rebecca Cane," he began, "Ye have been summoned to this courtroom to give an account of your actions, and to cast light upon the dark events which took place on these nights hence past: When a number of these gentle village folk did see thee committing thy dark deeds. They have made claims and accusations against thee about assignations with the Devil and passion with his minions. Look deep into your black heart for the strong reverence which you will need if you are to survive these rigours which are about to befall thee."

The Judge cleared his throat before speaking.

"Who is the first witness in this case against this Witch, Rebecca Cane?"

"It is I, Joshua," said a young man who rose from the crowd and slowly walked to the vacant witness stand.

"Michael Smith, ye are known to us all as a strong, upstanding, honest member of this community, and I am convinced that the evidence that ye shall give within this courtroom shall be that of a truthful and unbiased viewpoint. But I will say to ye all here and now that this is a court of the law and therefore your opinions are not what we are asking for, we are asking for your evidence. Please try to keep your personal view of this creature to one side. We want the facts that is all." Joshua motioned for him to continue.

"It was on the night of the fourteenth that I did see Rebecca Cain with several other girls walk in the moonlight in the meadows over yonder. The clock had not yet struck the tenth hour and night was not yet truly upon us. Her companions did leave her alone and return to their respective homes, as they were girls of virtue and honour. It was as time progressed that I did then observe Miss Cain masquerade with evil and it was an abomination such as I have ever had the misfortune to behold. For she did dance as naked as the day of her birth, casting spells and singing in the hope of calling the dark forces of the Devil for solicitous deeds."

The courtroom erupted.

Silence was called.

"Continue," the Judge instructed.

"I was so horrified by that which I witnessed that I returned home and took straight to my bed; my own wife fell into deep concern over my actions, for I was very much a changed man after this incident."

"Did ye see any sign of the Devil?" Joshua enquired.

Michael thought for a moment before answering.

"No! But I did hear his hoofs pounding upon the ground behind me as I ran in fear of my own life. It was as if the night were filled by sound of his advancing armies," he bowed his head. "I feared for all our souls that night."

Several of the women held their hands to their mouths in horror, feigning their revulsion; deeply damning Rebecca with their contrived actions.

"Thank you," Joshua said, dismissing his first witness, whose eyes were wandering about the courtroom helplessly. Never once making contact with those of the defendant.

He then turned his attentions directly to the presence of an elderly woman who sat next to the witness stand.

"I call ye as the second witness," he cried. "Tell me and those assembled your name and what ye witnessed on the night last," he demanded.

From within the Council gathered an elderly lady stood, walked to the vacant witness stand and cleared her throat before beginning to speak; pointing an accusing finger at Susan, she began.

"I did see this daughter of Satan ride upon her broom over to the graveyard, out yonder," she said, pointing to the east. "And, summon up my dead son upon whom she had cast a spell before his death, to entice him from beyond the grave to be her dark companion. I was horrified as I watched this creature create passionate carnal lust with him. I do claim before this court that she is responsible for the accident that did kill him. It has been witnessed by several of our villagers that this imp of the devil has been casting her seductive spells over the minds of our weak men folk. She has been seen cavorting in gay abandon in the meadows on moon lit nights, dancing, in the hope of conjuring her master. It was there that she took my son, and after less than a day had passed he was taken from us by a violent fever, a fever, which this she-devil had brewed. Mark my words; she has several other innocent young men under her spell. Will you wait until the same fate that has befallen your own flesh and blood takes your own? I implore that this court gives out the sentence that her black crimes demand."

With this final accusation the courtroom erupted only to be quelled by the Judge's calls for silence, then after several minutes of contemplation he addressed the waiting court.

"The allegations brought against this woman are of the gravest magnitude, we must have evidence that brings no doubt or inflection into my mind of this woman's guilt or innocence. With the testimonies of this villager, and those who have spoken over the last few days, I cannot help but pass the sentence that is demanded by law and mankind. Otherwise, this evil that she represents will spread across this God-fearing country and the name of Pendle will be damned forever in the annals of history."

The Judge turned from those gathered in the courtroom, and looked directly into Rebecca's eyes, his features and expression almost enveloped by the darkness that surrounded him.

"Rebecca Cain: As it is stated in the good book, 'Thou shalt not suffer a witch to live.' It is the finding of this court that you should be taken from this place immediately, and your soul be cleansed by the only means known by man to rid the earth of the evil that you represent. These crimes that have been brought before us are of the gravest magnitude and therefore demand the severest of punishments. We generally hang our witches to allow the evil spirit buried deep within to escape in the last vestiges of earthly breath, but for ye, dark daughter of Satan, this demise is too lenient."

He paused and took a deep breath, as tears filled his eyes.

"Burn her!" he whispered, as moral pain wracked his body.

The courtroom erupted as cries of "Heresy!" and "Satanist!" were hurled at the accused. She was taken from behind and bound. The rope bit deep into her wrist, causing her great pain. Her cries of innocence were ignored as she was lifted from the witness stand and carried out into the village square and into the pale afternoon sunlight.

Inside the abandoned courtroom, Joshua Cane fell to his knees as tears ran down his cheeks. His bloodshot eyes looked to the heavens as his heart sank into despair.

"Help her Lord! Be gentle with her soul."

He covered his face with his hands as he began to cry uncontrollably.

"Forgive me daughter, for I have damned you."

The door closed in front of him, sending the room once again into darkness and he fell back against his chair. His soul began to fill with a deep regret, which he knew would haunt him into the next world as the echoes of his daughter's voice pleading for fatherly salvation rung savagely in the air.

Rebecca screamed as she was tied to the pyre; flaming torches were flaunted before her as if to entice her demise. She screamed of her innocence, pleaded for compassion; but the savage beasts who were once her brethren were now her executioners.

"I am not who you think I am. I am not Rebecca Cain. This is a mistake, someone help me, oh God, please 'HELP ME!'"

Her eyes widened with fear as a blazing torch was brought closer, its flames sending dark, choking smoke into her face causing her to gasp for breath. The villagers took great delight in bringing down this daughter of evil, the destroyer of crops, turner of cream and caster of spells. To the women she was beautiful and a threat, to the men she was a temptation; something to have, or to destroy. One of the villagers moved forward and placed a blazing torch deep into the base of the pyre, sending great curls of red flames licking up towards Rebecca's legs. She began to scream, struggling to free herself; she could feel the ropes as they bit deeper into the flesh of her wrists sending a river of blood hissing into the flames.

Her thoughts began to spin; images began to blend into one mass of confusion. The orange glow of the sun merged with the flicker of the rising flames, sending a mellow haze into the air. She closed her eyes and prayed to the heavens for deliverance.

Opening her eyes Susan realised that the world had changed and she once again bathed in its serenity of her own home. She closed her eyes and lay back in bed as the images of her dream rushed once again to the front of her mind. A dream, and that was all.

A nervous laugh broke from her lips as she rose from the bed and moved to the window. Morning had come, and with it the refreshing sunlight of a new day. Stepping from her bed, Susan reached up and gripped the curtains, pulling them apart she allowed herself to be bathed in the glory of the morning. She opened her eyes and witnessed the world as if anew, smiling at the familiar landmarks that greeted her.

Susan raised her hand to cover her eyes from the strong greeting of the morning light she stood for a moment relishing its magnificence. Her eyes marvelled at the gentle rays of sunshine as they danced between her fingertips. 'It was winter,' she thought to herself, but the sun's presence was strong yet welcoming. As her eyes became accustomed to its purity they followed the soft undulations of her own youthful skin and her slender delicate fingers. She turned and walked into the subdued light of her bedroom, rubbing her wrists in acknowledgment of an irritation which she began to experience. Sitting at the dressing table she endeavoured to look closer at her wrists. Almost immediately she recognised that something was not right. Purposefully her hand reached to the small table lamp and she tentatively pressed the on switch. The room about her was illuminated by its harsh, unnatural glair and Susan recoiled in horror at the image that befell her eyes, for there, deeply engraved into the flesh of her wrists were the rope burns worn by the witch Rebecca Cane.

Six

Initially, the sensation of movement was very foreign to her; it was as if she had the weight of the world pressing down upon her mortal frame. It felt as though her limbs were made from lead, a stark contrast to the weightless freedom she had experienced while in spiritual form. To the doctors, it was the side effect of the coma; to Ann-Marie it was something more preternatural. She had recalled the events that had taken place while her physical form remained within the confines of this hospital room and her spiritual-self had partaken of an adventure that would have chilled the soul of the most intrepid of explorers.

'Could she really travel in time?' she thought.

Had this been a dream induced by the coma and the multitude of medicines which ravaged her body? Was there really a vampire called Christian, searching the world, ready to kill her?

Ann-Marie was informed that there was no lasting physical damage and she could feel her physical strength returning; she had never liked hospitals and was so pleased to returning to the comfort of her own home a few days later.

****

It had been almost a week before Ann-Marie had returned home and never once had she tried to use her powers, for the words spoken by James rang as a death knell in her mind every time she contemplated this act. (The signal that she sent out would attract the attention of anyone sensitive enough to feel its presence.) These words hung heavy over her. She tried to clear her mind of any thoughts except for those needed for her day-to-day existence, yet the more she endeavoured to sweep the idea of testing her skills to the back of her mind the further to the front of her thoughts they seemed to progress. A tension began to build deep within her and she felt powerless against the danger that could confront her at any moment. She required information, a source of knowledge that she could draw upon if she were to destroy this abhorrent creature that hunted her.

As she sat in her favourite chair, allowing her eyes to wander her living room, she realised how little all of this superficial physical accumulation of chattels really meant; how transitory her life had become. She understood more than most that death was not the end of our existence, but the thought of loving another living soul and watching them grow old and depart this mortal life brought a shudder to her very soul. She thought of the void between worlds and the existence lived by those who could somehow cheat death. She could feel the embers of her gift beginning to stir as a great well of power erupted within, filling her whole being with a warm, radiant light that surpassed the brightest Sun, bathing her in its gentle glow. The experience culminated in a white river, which cascaded in her mind, taking her to the highest peak of spiritual pleasure. To the onlooker she was only day-dreaming but to Ann-Marie it was as if life itself were dancing through her whole form, forcing her to move to its melody and for the first time to feel truly alive.

When she opened her eyes a strange calm befell her and it was as if the weight of this existence had been lifted from her shoulders and she were about to start life anew. She sat for a while watching the world outside follow its pattern of life as the dark clouds of the evening drifting across the darkening sky. The sun, moving as if to rest, relinquishing its hold upon the Earth and giving over its sovereignty to the queen of the night. The street lights radiating their warm, yellow glow, offering artificial illumination to this dark modern world.

Seven

The black heavens greeted Christian as he entered London; change had swept across the capital with a mighty hand, taking with it many of the landmarks that he could associate with his own time and replaced them with great steel structures that reached into the sky almost raping the stars with their harsh unemotional touch. Their great expanses of glass reflected the moonlight and sent a blue sheen across the city below. Christian wandered hungrily through the streets as a greater urge pursued him - that of knowledge. This modern world had advanced far beyond his imagination; it was truly hell on earth. Beggars wandered the streets, calling to passers-by for assistance as the pain of hunger ate into their very souls. Christian observed life in this time of space travel and exploration. How much man had advanced, he thought, but how little he had really changed. As a creature, he remained that; a creature. Nothing more. Nothing less. Still following his baser instincts. Still striving for self-perpetuation. The vampire smiled and spoke almost silently to himself.

"This will be easier than I first anticipated, for man and myself are closer than either of us had realised. How pitiful!"

He moved on, leaving the rundown parts of this metropolis behind and entered into the grander, more affluent part of this city. Great buildings reached skywards but this time they had a more majestic manner, complimenting their surroundings and adding to the harmony of view. He felt at home with this grand facade of life. This financially-controlled existence, this was the true essence of man and it captivated him, drew him like a spider into a monitory web, a web of deceit and mistrust, of lust and hunger, a true reflection of himself he thought; a true bridge between man and superman.

Using his preternatural powers, Christian allowed his thoughts to wander aimlessly through the minds of those who inhabited the rich buildings that surrounded him. A yearning to accumulate wealth and possessions returned; a black longing for a prize almost as dark as the gift that he himself possessed, both aspired to for the same reason. Money, as with the dark gift meant power, sovereignty over those weaker or less financially powerful than oneself. A standpoint, from which to dictate to others your values, your ideologies. He smiled to himself as he thought how little everything had changed. London was at bursting point with potential victims, beggars and whores, rich and poor, saints and sinners; all were the same in Christian's eyes. All second best to the delights that he aspired to. These pathetic inconsequential's meant nothing to him, for he could feel her presence grow closer, as if her very soul emitted a signal to his own, calling for them to be one again, reunited. He could recall the past as if it were yesterday, drawing upon the delights and the disappointments alike, using them as a catalyst to move himself forward, fuelling his rage against time.

Christian stood for a moment upon a street corner, an intersection between roads. Without warning, his senses once again burst into life. His eyes searched the night, scanning buildings and roadways, all around life pulled at his senses, sending them spiralling into misdirection. Then, as if a great beacon called, his eyes fell upon a dark building that rested at the far end of the street in which he stood. Moving forward he gathered pace and soon found himself standing at the steps of a vast stone building; his heart began to race as his imagination began to play tricks upon his mind. A young woman came into view, her long dark hair bringing back a recollection that had remained buried for over two centuries. Without realising his actions, Christian let out a heavy breath and air gagged in his throat; his eyes began to water as recollection assaulted his emotions, calling him hypocrite and liar. Denying himself any human frailty, he watched the figure as she moved along the hallway and through a vast set of wooden doors.

A single name broke from his lips as he moved away from the steps and observed the human traffic from the security of a dark alleyway opposite. Closing his eyes, he allowed a human tide of pain to wash over him, as he muttered her name.

"Marie-Anne!"

Eight

The gentle light from the ceiling chandelier softened the atmosphere of the library's entrance, giving the lobby's dark wooden walls and marble floor an almost sensual appearance. It was at the far end of the entrance lobby where Ann-Marie stood, searching through her pockets for the scrap of paper given to her by Susan Ward which contained her telephone number. Finding it, she held it to her lips, thinking for a moment the words spoken to her by James and the ramification of involving another in this foreboding tale, and the darkness that would ensue. She recalled how he knew Susan's name and occupation and how he stated that fate had a stronger pull on man's destiny that he realised or desired. She plunged her hand once again into her pocket and produced several coins of varying denominations. Placing one onto the telephone slot she lifted the receiver and held it to her ear; the sound of the dialling tone was almost deafening in the pure silence of the lobby.

She closed her eyes, ignoring her inner voices and pushed the coin into the slot. Taking a deep breath she looked at the paper and followed the number with her thoughts, recalling it over and over again, giving herself time in which to think. Her fingers pushed the first number on the telephone's pad then followed by a second and a third until the sound of ringing could be heard from the handset.

A voice almost exploded into Ann-Marie's ear as the recipient answered.

"Hello, Ward's residence."

Silence returned the acknowledgement of her call; Ann-Marie stood frozen, lost for words.

"Hello! Who's calling?"

The voice seemed a little less accommodating and warm, this second time; it held a timbre of authority.

Ann-Marie breathed heavily, gathering her senses.

"I'm sorry, could I speak to Susan Ward please?"

There was a short silence, and then the voice returned to its original soft tone.

"Yes of course, can I ask who's calling please?"

Ann-Marie stuttered, "Yes, it's Ann-Marie Harrington, I'm the journalist who interviewed Susan a week or so ago, I just need to talk to her about a few things."

The voice hesitated on the other side, a pause that seemed to build as the seconds passed. Then she spoke.

"I'll just get her."

Ann-Marie stood for a moment as if in a trance, her eyes searching the surroundings, alone, the dark wood on the walls, deeply engraved and polished to a sheen that almost reflected the light from her eyes. She looked past the reception and out through the vast glass door and into the world outside. The traffic moved at an almost redundant pace, crawling along the road outside of the library. The snows had begun to fall again and the warmth of her surroundings seemed to offer a warm and reassuring comfort on this harsh winter's night. An inquisitive look swept across her face as she peered questioningly into the darkness of the shadowy alleyway opposite. She could have sworn that she had witnessed the image of a stranger dressed in darkness, looking directly back at her. The voice from the telephone brought her senses back to reality, making her jump a little with shock and forget her reason for calling.

"Hello, Hello, Susan? This is Ann-Marie Harrington, we met a while ago at the Dane's Art Gallery, you took a few photographs of me for a portrait, do you remember me?" Her voice was shallow and bothered.

This was not matched by the bright youthful chorus that greeted her with a sharp joy of recollection.

"Why yes, of course I remember you, I've finished the painting it's almost dry, you can come and see it if you want."

Her hurried words washed over Ann-Marie filling her with confusion. Stemming Susan's enthusiasm, she broke in to her one way conversation.

"Yes, I'm happy you remembered me. I was wondering if you could meet me tonight?"

The voice at the other end suddenly became reserved and withdrawn.

"Yes but why? It's dark, can't this wait until morning?" Susan enquired.

Ann-Marie pondered for a moment as Susan's words were cast adrift upon the stormy seas of her own self-doubt.

"I, I would be grateful if you could, I'm at the main library, the one next to the University of London, behind the British Museum, off Bloomsbury street."

"Is this to do with the article that you're writing about my work?" Susan asked, as a note of caution entered her voice.

Ann-Marie though for a brief moment, turmoil pulling at her every thought.

"Yes... No." Confusion built up deep within her. "You could say, I just need to tell you a few things and sort out a few facts, that's all."

Susan paused, thinking to herself.

"I'll be about twenty minutes. If I get a taxi now I should miss the main part of the traffic jam."

Ann-Marie replaced the telephone handset without saying goodbye; her mind was full of questions yet screaming for answers. Walking back along the entrance lobby she stopped at the main desk and enquired whether they had a section on mythology and the occult. The receptionist pointed her in the direction of a set of lesser grand doors that stood to the right of the entrance. Ann-Marie thanked him and made her way through the doors and into a great, heavy dark room, filled with silence and shadows. All about her literary volumes reaches skyward, towering high above, undisturbed by the inquisitive yearnings of man. In the middle of these literary towers stood a small desk at which sat an elderly gentleman who pondered over a heavy volume that almost covered the entire surface of the desk's top. Moving over to him, Ann-Marie allowed her eyes to marvel at the vast panorama of volumes that inhabited the cases, meandering like written streets of knowledge awaiting a stranger to lose themselves in their imagined alleyways and scribed avenues.

As she reached the desk the old man looked up and offered her a warm and welcoming smile, his features bathed in the soft, artificial light from above.

"Can I help you my dear?" his voice was soft and comforting.

Ann-Marie swallowed as a deep sense of embarrassment came over her, washing her in a pool of self-consciousness.

"I'm looking for a book," she said, smiling.

"Well, we do have the odd one or two," he said, casting his eyes about the room. "Can you be a little more specific?"

Embarrassment filled her as her features became flushed.

"Anything on Vampires?" she muttered.

"Why, yes" he said, rising from his chair. "Whole sections. Follow me."

He moved from behind his desk and walked away into the darkness; Ann-Marie followed intently, listening to his words as he spoke.

"Well, we have a vast section on vampires, those of old legends, from the movies, modern writings, take your pick," he paused by a column of old volumes and looked at the bewilderment upon Ann-Marie's face.

"May I make a suggestion?" Ann-Marie nodded her approval. Reaching up he took hold of a great leather -bound volume and dusted off its cover. "Now this is the one that I like; 'Vampires, Myth and Legend.' It's got them all in here, from the earliest stories of Darius I, Pharaoh of Egypt, to the modern images that we see on the cinema screen today. I think that this is the one that you're looking for," he said handing the book to her. "If you need any more assistance I'll be at my desk, you've got plenty of time to read through it, we don't close for a few more hours."

Ann-Marie smiled with gratitude and moved to a table in the corner of the room; there she sat allowing her fingers to move slowly over the worn leather of the book's heavy cover, her mind eager to savour the information within.

As she lifted the main binding of the book, the pages fell open at the ancient portrait of the Egyptian Pharaoh Darius I. The splendour of his features captivated Ann-Marie. She had not witnessed anything such as this in her lifetime; the soft curves and strong line of his face drew her into him, yet, it was the sheer blue of his eyes that pulled her closer to the image. They brought back a recollection, a strange and distant recollection of something long forgotten. Brushing her feelings aside she continued with her search. As the pages turned she beheld images and tales both ancient and modern, stories of creatures that could exist beyond the realms of man and time. They captivated and enthralled her imagination.

It was as she turned the worn pages, in an almost haze like trance, when she came across a painting, which appeared delicate yet foreboding. The scene depicted was that of six people around a fire, drinking from great golden goblets the blood of an innocent child that lay slaughtered at their feet. A seventh individual stood away from the others, as if in distaste against her comrade's actions. Ann-Marie felt drawn to this woman, the only female in the group, and she surmised that this individual held a tender human soul. She studied her features, her long curled hair that almost touched her waist, her bright skin almost marble in texture. Yet, once again it was the eyes that drew her attention. Bright, alive and very blue.

She then looked at the others, six men, five holding goblets brimming with blood and a sixth in the centre, a teller of tales, communicating with his comrades, deep in conversation with the night. The others seemed too preoccupied with their unearthly drinking to listen to him, but he continued unperturbed, relaying the tales for himself, to keep them fresh in his own mind rather than in those of others.

As she followed the line of drinkers her eyes fell upon the face of one who sat next to the story teller. His face was half in shadow, but it brought something of a remembrance back to Ann-Marie's mind. A recollection. She looked at the bottom of the painting and read the title.

'THE TRIBE.'

Nine

Christian slowly climbed the steps of the library, ignoring the sounds of the city and the inquisitive stares of those people who passed, witnessing this creation of evil. Entering the lobby, he followed the signal left by Ann-Marie. As he touched the doors that led into the reference library where she sat, a great feeling of energy surged into his system, pushing him back. With a feeling of determination Christian pushed the doors once again and watched as they silently opened, admitting him access to his quarry. As if a silent phantom, he manoeuvred his way through the aisles of books that towered to the ceiling, passed the attendant and glided closer to his nemesis. Pausing in the shadows he observed her for a moment, recalling his image of her. He moved closer marvelling at the features of this mortal incarnation of his love that betrayed and damned him for an eternity. As he reached her desk the great tide of his accomplishment receded, leaving him feeling incomplete. This confrontation which he had prayed for, for over two centuries, was now at hand and yet it was somehow barren; he had prayed to the dark god of vengeance for this moment and now that it had arrived he felt impotent. He thought for a moment, casting his inhibitions into the dark seas of self-doubt. If he were to destroy her now then what would fuel him for the future? For over two hundred years he had languished in the pits of the earth dreaming of this bitter moment, and now that it was here, doubt crept into his heart. He moved closer, realising that he must conclude his act and perpetuate his destiny, for everything had its path and he must follow his own.

A dark shadow fell across Ann-Marie as she sat pondering over her book, savouring the information within. Her long hair had fallen over her eyes as she continued reading, she pushed it to one side and allowed the distant defused light to dance across the page in front of her. It was into this light that a stranger stepped, blocking the soft caress of its touch.

Ann-Marie looked up to the stranger and smiled.

"You've come?"

"Yes, how could I not?" Susan said, her words soft and comforting. She sat in the chair opposite, unbuttoned her heavy winter coat and unwrapped the scarf that hung about her neck. Placing it on the table in front of her she looked to Ann-Marie and spoke. "So, are you going to tell me what was so urgent? My mother's not too pleased that you've dragged me out across London at this hour, it took me all of my time to persuade her that I could go alone."

Ann-Marie lowered her eyes and focused them upon the book in front of her, she thought for a moment.

"It's too quiet in here, let's go somewhere else. There's something that I think you should know."

Susan gave Ann-Marie an inquisitive look as she watched her close the book and rise from her chair. Slowly, she walked over to the assistant and several words of gratitude were passed before Ann-Marie looked over to Susan and motioned for her to follow. Susan lifted her scarf from the table and walked from the shadows into the light of the main part of the room, it was as she passed the stranger that her senses danced, bringing her to an abrupt halt. The stranger observed her actions from his vantage-point in the shadows of one of the literary alleyways. Susan peered at him and Christian smiled, offering her a gentle, deep bow. A strange sense of bewilderment came over her.

"How strange!" she muttered under her breath.

"What's strange?" Ann-Marie's abrupt words made her jump.

"That man down there," Susan said, pointing at the cold emptiness that was once occupied by the stranger.

Ann-Marie looked into the shadows and shrugged her shoulders.

"Well, whoever he was he's made a sharp exit just as we should, it's getting late."

As they left the library Susan continued to think of the stranger; her mind was a rage with questions searching for answers. They stopped at the bottom of the library steps; not noticing the ancient visitor, who watched from the darkness of the alleyway, opposite.

"Well, where do you suggest we go?" Susan enquired.

Ann-Marie thought for a moment.

"I know, there's an all-night cafe just down the road, we'll go there."

Christian watched as the women walked away, his passions burning deep within, mixing with his animal yearning for blood, sending his emotions pulsating to bursting point. Keeping a safe distance from his prey, he slipped from the safety of the shadows and followed his intended victim into the torrent of human traffic, which was London.

By the time they had reached the small cafe the snow was falling in a gentle torrent, spiralling in the air above their heads then landing all around, covering the world in a soft white carpet. The gentle yellow glow of the cafe's lights seemed to invite them to enter, promising warmth on this cold and inhospitable night. Ann-Marie ushered Susan onto a seat as she purchased a two large mugs of strong hot coffee, which she placed on the table between them. Sitting with her hands around the cup she savoured the warmth that seemed to bring a contentment to her very soul. Closing her eyes she realised that the noise of the traffic outside seemed to be silenced into a distant melody by the contentment that washed over her, bringing an inner calm to her thoughts. It was Susan's words that broke the spell that she was weaving over herself. Bringing her abruptly back to reality.

"So, why did you ask me to meet you?"

Ann-Marie opened her eyes and smiled and then she set her mind into action.

'What could she say? How could she explain?'

She leaned forward on her chair and took a deep breath and after exhaling she drank from her cup, savouring the coffee's bitter taste.

"I don't know how to begin; you're going to think that I've gone mad or something."

She began. "You see, after I met you I had an experience." This was the best way in which she felt that she could describe her adventure, as not to bring scorn or ridicule. "Just after I left the gallery there was an..." she paused, as a deep sense of shame came over her as she thought about the next sentence that entered into her mind. She thought over and over again of the ramifications of her words if she were to tell anyone of the events that had taken place over the last few days. Could she trust Susan enough to give her the power to bring down her career? Even though she was as much involved as Ann-Marie.

"There have been several strange events that have occurred in my life," she began. "You see just after I left the gallery a strange thing happened. I had taken a taxi and was on my way home when there was an accident."

Susan's eyes opened wide with shock.

Ann-Marie lifted her hand to reassure her that everything was all right.

"It's all right, I'm fine. You see, it was when I was in hospital when something happened, something that is almost beyond explanation. Even I sometimes find it hard to comprehend what my mind is trying to tell me actually occurred. I must stress to you that these events were not a dream or the ramblings of a panic-stricken mind. They happened and you must believe me for you are the first living soul that I am telling, and the only reason that I am doing this is because..."

Ann-Marie paused and took a deep breath. ."..because, the events affect you as much as they affect me."

Susan's look turned to that of deep bemusement, which grew darker at the passing of each moment.

Ann-Marie put her coffee mug onto the table and took hold of Susan's hand.

"Please try and keep an open mind and remember that these events really did happen. No matter how abstract or bizarre they may sound, all of which I am about to tell you is true; I must emphasise that you need keep an open mind. Wipe away all of your preconceived ideas about the powers of darkness as I have been forced to do by the sheer strength of evidence that has assaulted me. Forget the tales of bedtime and the boogieman. Forget the stories of demons and Shakespeare, the sprites of 'A Midsummer Night's Dream' or the ghost in 'Hamlet.' This is as real as this table in front of us," she said moving her hand across the table's polished surface. "Or that window that looks out onto the street..," she said pointing in the direction of the glass. She turned her attentions to follow the direction of her instruction and brought her senses to a cold and abrupt halt. Even though the streets were a throng with pedestrians and the night was thick with its inhabitants, her eyes fell upon the stranger who stood below the street lamp, almost inviting her to notice his presence. She turned to whisper to Susan but in that instant he was gone, no more than a memory, a grain in the passing of time. She swallowed hard and sat back in her chair, doubting her senses.

"What's wrong?" Susan said, rising from her chair and peering out of the dirt stained window. "Someone you know?"

Ann-Marie smiled and composed herself. 'I'm becoming scared of shadows,' she thought as her senses calmed, bringing a warm red glow to her cheeks. "Oh God! I feel so stupid. When I think about it to myself it sounds great but when I try to put everything into words it just comes out as nonsense, complete folly."

Susan took a deep breath.

"Maybe I can beat you at the nonsense stakes. The events that have taken over my life in the past few days are nothing if not strange. So believe me, anything that you have to say would not amaze me."

Ann-Marie knitted her eyebrows as her journalistic instincts began to stir, pulling at her curiosity, begging for her to learn more.

"What do you mean?"

Susan blushed in her embarrassment; her fingers rubbed the deep wound on her wrist drawing Ann-Marie's attention in its direction.

"What's wrong?"

Susan pulled the woollen glove from her hand and held up her wrist for Ann-Marie to see. A gasp issued from her friends lips.

"Who did this? Was it your parents?" Ann-Marie enquired with deep concern.

"No!" Susan exclaimed. "It was..."

The back of her throat began to dry as the words jostled and fought for their freedom, emerging from her mouth as a mixture of half sentences peppered with a bountiful serving of frustration. Her mind began to cloud as the thoughts that had once inhabited the mind of her alter ego danced their way into her consciousness, bringing with them the dark rains of self-doubt. She stood and put her hand to her lips.

"This is going to sound crazy, I can't tell you here, isn't there anywhere else with a bit more privacy?"

Ann-Marie stood and put her arm around Susan.

"You can come to my place; I only live about ten minutes away. Wait here, I'll ring a taxi."

Susan stood for a moment, allowing her thoughts to accumulate, filling her with a deep sense of dread.

'How could something in fantasy, something in the world of dreams, find its way into this reality? Leaving a physical mark, proclaiming a bridging point between worlds?' Pulling the glove into place she smiled as the light from the taxi alerted her of its presence.

The journey to Ann-Marie's home was extremely uneventful, as little communication had passed between the two women and even when they entered the house an uncomfortable silence hung over the situation, forcing a mental wedge between the natural flow conversation. Ann-Marie had left Susan in the living room as she went into the kitchen to make refreshments. She returned moments later with a tray laden with assorted confectionery and a pot of hot coffee, which sent steam billowing into the air from its spout.

Placing the tray on the table she sat heavily onto an armchair, allowing the soft cushions to envelop her, bringing a comfort to the physical pains that she had endured that day. It was the sound of Susan pouring the coffee which drew Ann-Marie's attention.

"It's strange, all of our lives we keep asking the question. What is this all for? If you really get down to it, I mean right down to the questions of life and what this whole existence is for, you always seem to come up with the same answers. The priests and religious folk will tell you that this is penance and we must all suffer. Others will tell you that we should all have fun now, for this is it. All the world's a stage and there's only the one act, so get it right," she stopped and leaned forward taking her cup from the table. "But what if I were to tell you that there was more, more to this?" she raised her hand as if acknowledging the room. "What if I were to tell you that there was more to everything?"

Susan placed her cup onto the table and thought about Ann-Marie's words, but the answer that she eventually gave was not that which her companion was expected.

"I know."

These simple words brought Ann-Marie down from her tower of self-importance and crashing painfully back into reality.

"You see. Something has happened to me and I feel that if I don't tell anyone about it soon then I'll go mad. I don't care if after what I've told you, you think that I'm crazy, you think that I should be carted off to some form of institute for the mentally infirm. I have to tell someone; it's the feeling of confiding in another living soul that I want. It's having that certain someone say, to have dreams such as those are 'normal' or 'I've heard of this before.' I just need some reinforcement for my ideas, someone to say, 'you're not mad'."

Susan lifted her wrist.

"It's this. You see, I dreamt that I was in another time and I was burned as a witch and these are the marks made by the rope that bound me to the pyre," her words issued at an ever increasing rate until her manner was almost frantic." All I want is the answer to my questions"

A cold shudder raced down Ann-Marie's spine when Susan mentioned time, it was as if a bolt from the heavens had struck her, transfixing her to the spot. Just as Susan finished her speech she realised that her words were falling upon deaf ears.

"Ann-Marie, What's wrong?"

She jumped with fright, sending her cup onto the floor, spilling its dark contents onto the carpet. Slowly she rose from the chair and walked across the room.

"I think that what I have to say will be understood to a greater degree than I initially thought. There is something of a parallel going on here; we have both been subjected to similar encounters. It's as if someone or something is controlling us, or this situation."

Susan stood. "I know what you mean."

After a brief pause Ann-Marie began her own tale, recalling her meeting with James, of the story that he told and how their two lives were intertwined. Of Christian and his sister and a darker force that controlled the pathways of man's destiny and the power that was at her call, the power of the Communicator. It was only when she had finished that both women realised how the events of the past few weeks had ruled their lives, drawing them closer for a purpose that was not yet truly apparent.

"We're both sane, that's for sure" Susan said. "I just wish that I had an answer to my question. I wish I knew who Rebecca Cane was and why she was burned as a witch. In the brief time I inhabited her life the only emotion that I experienced, apart from fear, was pure loneliness."

Ann-Marie thought deeply to herself before speaking, realising the magnitude of her next comment.

"There is a way that you can find out."

Susan looked at Ann-Marie as puzzlement swept across her face.

"How?"

Embarrassment washed over her.

"It seems that I can travel into another person's dreams. James told me, there are a lot of people who can do it, but the governments of their countries take them into what they would call 'custody' and use them for their own dark deeds. Just think of it, an assassin that could kill an important politician, without leaving the comfort of his or her own bed. No weapon, no evidence. A perfect crime."

"A power that could be used for good or abused by man, manipulated for evil. People such as I could be used to help children plagued by nightmares. To help the Doctors in their fight against mental illness. Anything! But no, what my kind is being trained for is to be pawns in the struggle of the cold war of the nineteen sixties and seventies. Or now, in the present day, to be used for industrial espionage, stealing secrets from the minds of scientists."

"I know that my powers are in their embryonic stages of development. But if what James has told me is true, then I am about to become one of the most powerful Communicators in the history of mankind and if I were to make a mistake at this early stage of my education then I could experience the fate which befell my predecessors. That is why I think that I have found a solution that could help us both. If James's preposition is correct and I can in fact travel into another person's dream to help them, then let me travel into yours to find some answers to your questions and reasons for the events that seem to be haunting both of us."

****

Christian watched as the light burst into life in the bedroom of Ann-Marie's home. He was amazed by the inventions of man and how he had advanced in a physical sense, but he also derived a great amount of amusement from the reality of this world in which he found himself. As he stood below the window he could sense a change in the balance between spirit and physical; a fluctuation in the equilibrium between worlds and he knew at once that his love was weaving her magic.

Ten

Susan could feel the room begin to spin as sleep began to weave its own images into those of the real world, constantly turning and rearranging the pictures of her thoughts until her mind became a blank canvas, leaving the screen of her inner-self pure, a recipient for the images sent from another place of existence. Deep sleep seemed to gather her up in its dark arms and carry her along with its gentle reassuring touch. Within, her senses still registered the movements from without. They still recognised the human noises made by her companion. The darkness that filled her began to grow in intensity as she fell deeper and deeper into her own mind. An inner yearning longed for this journey to come to an end, but a hidden terror urged for it to continue for infinity. To carry her forever on its wave of pleasure and serenity, where pain and suffering were mere words and hunger could only be appeased by knowledge.

Just as her emotions were becoming accustomed to this dark haven, the sensation of floating was surpassed by another less gentle feeling. It was as if she were falling further and further down into the bowels of the earth and no matter how much she struggled she could not release the scream that was building within.

Wind rushed passed her face bringing with it the cold sensation of the environment into which she was unceremoniously plunging. Then, all at once everything came to an abrupt and startling halt and she realised that she had arrived. Her hands touched the ground below her and to her amazement a sensation that she recognised was returned. Her fingers traced the soft surface of the polished wooden floorboards and she knew in an instant where she was.

A small table lamp sent out its soft light to fill the corner of the room, bathing Susan's face in a soft warm light. Ann-Marie sat in the chair next to the bed observing her companion's features as they contorted with an inquisitive torment that brought the reality to Ann-Marie that Susan had arrived at her destination. Sitting back in her chair she concentrated, focusing her mind onto one point, just as James had taught her in the hospital. In an instant she could feel the warm, astral wind rushing past her as her spirit moved forward in readiness to join with the mind of Susan Ward.

Then there was nothing. No space. No time. Just consciousness. Pure and unadulterated. The bright light seemed to engulf her, lifting her higher. As she looked up she realised that she was being carried towards a rainbow of light that seemed to reach across the whole horizon before her. This image invaded the feeling of emptiness that surrounded her, but this invasion was as welcome as dawn was to night. She reached forward as she came close to the brilliant colours, hoping in some way to capture their brilliance for a brief inspiring moment, but as her fingers penetrated the soft flesh of the colours a scream filled the air, sending Ann-Marie spiralling backwards and downwards away from the rainbow. As her world tumbled she looked back at the arch that had brought her so much joy but the image that met her gaze was not that which she had expected, for there in the place of her colourful cavalcade was a great figure, grinning with pleasure. Its red skin that seemed to claw its way across his naked chest, and black horns that protruded, sent a chill to her very core. Ann-Marie realised at that point; that she had met the one that she had been warned against, the ally to her own enemy. A single word broke from her lips: "Caliban."

Ann-Marie opened her eyes but this did little to alleviate the terror that was building up within her, for all around darkness had fallen covering all object that could bring a hope of recognition. Then, without prompting, a hand reached from the shadows and offered her assistance. Ann-Marie reached forward and gripped hold; realisation hit her.

"Susan, is that you?"

"Yes, be quiet. I don't think that were alone."

"Where are we?" Ann-Marie asked.

"You know that church that I told you about, the one in the dream, with the witches?"

Ann-Marie nodded.

"I'm here, in your dream. Our minds have merged together. He was right, James was right."

Susan put her hand over her mouth to stop the laugh that was building within.

"That's right. You are. I just thought that this was part of my dream, but it can't be; it feels too real."

They hugged as a feeling of accomplishment filled them. A feeling that was short lived.

It was Susan who heard it first. That deep, deliberate breathing that filled the hall.

"There's someone in here with us," she whispered.

Ann-Marie nodded her acknowledgement and allowed her hands to fall from Susan's shoulders.

"I know I can hear them," she quietly replied.

At the far end of the room a candle exploded into life, sending its soft light into the harsh inky blackness that enveloped the courtroom.

"So you've come, daughters of darkness, to help your sister in sin."

Susan at once recognised the voice.

"It's him; it's Joshua Cane, from my dream," she said, as fear rose within.

The candle moved closer, bringing with it the softness of its light that reached into the shadows, banishing them for a briefest of moments.

Joshua placed the candle on the table in front of the women and allowed the light to dance over his features. Immediately, Ann-Marie notice the long sword, which he held in his left hand.

"You have come to save your sister? I would hurry, for they be tying her to the pyre as we speak. Hurry, then we shall have three Sisters of Satan to burn. Three vessels of evil to release."

"How could you? She was your daughter," Susan's screamed, her words burrowing into his heart.

His face changed from that of an arrogant man and contorted and twisting with the pain that boiled deep within.

"She is a witch; I am the law and must be followed. Do not pity her, for you will gladly change places with another as you join her as her soul is released by the cleansing flames of the Lord."

"I don't think so," she said, hitting him with her open hand. Ann-Marie's reaction caught him off guard, sending his emotions repelling backwards.

Joshua righted himself; gathering his senses he raised his arm and brought the sword crashing down in Ann-Marie's direction.

Ann-Marie gasped as the blade stopped just above her head, she could feel the wind produced by the sword descent pass her. Stepping backwards she saw the instrument that brought the weapon's journey to an abrupt halt. For a moment she thought that it was a statue as its flesh was as hard and as white as marble. But this statue moved, its presence became all the more apparent as it stepped from the safety of the shadows, his features almost blessed by the soft light that fell all about.

"We meet again" he said to Ann-Marie; a deep sense of confusion filled her.

"Oh my love, would you forget me so soon?" Sarcasm filled his words. Christian smiled revealing his identity.

"Christian," the word escaped viciously from Ann-Marie's lips.

"Have you missed me, beloved?" His words dripped with dark condemnation.

"But how?" she mumbled. "In this dream."

Christian laughed. "It is not only you who are a Communicator, my dear. The world is full of them. I just happen to be doubly blessed," he lifted the sword and smiled.

"A child's toy." With that, he broke the weapon with the slightest of effort and sent it crashing to the floor. "How the years have been kind to you, this incarnation of your essence is as beautiful as your last; I will savour each moment as I devour your soul."

Joshua pulled a crucifix from his pocket and held it in front of Christian in a vain attempt to repel the danger that confronted him.

Sending his hand out before him, Christian hit the object, dispatching it spinning into the darkness.

"You dare!" He hissed and gripped the sides of Joshua's coat and lifted him from the ground as his legs kicked in the air below him. As their faces drew level, Christian smiled. "What should we do with you little man? You pathetic creature that places himself above all others, spouting your sanctimonious rubbish. Proclaiming everything in the name of your God, yet neglecting your fellow man's suffering."

Joshua pulled away in repulsion.

"You hate me, don't you little man?" Christian continued. "I am the personification of evil. I am everything that your darkest of nightmares could portray - the Devil incarnate."

Joshua began to tremble.

"They say that the punishment should fit the crime, and as I am Judge, Jury and Prosecutor I have the perfect punishment," Christian said offering Joshua a sardonic smile. "So that you may feel the sweet suffering that haunts my every moment, I shall make you that which you most despise. I shall make you...Me!"

Christian laughed as Joshua struggled, slowly he pulled him closer, almost sensually he placed his lips upon those of his captive, savouring each moment of his impotency, then as quick as lightning he buried his teeth into his victim's neck, drinking the liquid deep into himself he allowed his soul to ride high upon its dark crimson tide.

Ann-Marie motioned for Susan to step back into the comfort of the shadows.

"We must get back, otherwise we will suffer the same fate as your friend."

"How?" she whispered.

"The same way we got here, I assume. If we managed to travel into this world then we must be able to get out. Take hold my hand and let's see what happens," Ann-Marie concentrated, forcing her mind into action, pulling at the power deep within her core. After several moments she opened her eyes and to her dismay she was still in the court-room and there was a greater horror about to assault her. For Christian has finished his task and she knew that they were next to appease his disgusting palette.

"Leaving so soon my dear?" Christian said, slowly moving towards her. This simple action brought the pictures of her own nocturnal travel flooding back to the forefront of her mind; she recalled her own dreams, dreams of the past, dreams of the masquerade ball and France. It was as if her nightmare had revisited her and she was reliving it anew.

She gasped as Christian reached for her. She could almost feel his dank breath upon her skin, her senses screamed in anticipation of his touch as darkness engulfed her. Falling backwards she awaited the harsh reality of the wall behind her but that reality never came, she was once again floating in the sky of her mind. Drifting through the clouds of her thoughts, she once again felt safe, as the sanctity of her own inner self became apparent to her fragile anxieties. She floated happily through the lost haven of her thoughts until suddenly she could feel the calling, a pulling from another dimension and all at once, with a little sadness, she could feel her physical self, enveloping her.

"Wake up! Wake up!" Susan demanded, pulling at her arm.

"If he can get into my dreams then he could get into yours and kill us both at any time."

Ann-Marie looked about the room, her mind still a cavalcade of distant images, one fading into another.

"No! He must be close to do that," she said in her sleepy haze, "but I agree we must get away and put as much distance between the two of us; we have to leave now. What time is it?"

Susan looked at her watch. "My God! It's six a.m. It's almost morning."

Ann-Marie moved to the window and pulled open the blinds to witness a sky streaked with red and black, a sky that announced a new day.

"Quick, ring a taxi. I'll pack a few things; we must get out of here, otherwise next time we won't be so lucky."

"Where will you go?" Susan Said.

"I don't care" Ann-Marie replied, pushing several articles of clothing into a bag. "I'll get a hotel room. I'll even sleep on the streets to get away from him. I'll be all right. I did this story on a woman's refuge that's in town. I'll call them; they'll let me stay. I'll pretend that I'm doing a follow up story and I'm doing it from the viewpoint of a woman on the run, first hand and all that. They'll swallow it; they received a lot of good publicity from the last feature."

"You can't do that," Susan said.

Ann-Marie stopped her frantic packing and looked at Susan. "What do you mean? I don't think that you understand, our lives are in danger."

"I know, what I mean is that you can stay with me, if we're together he may find it difficult to track us down. After all, two heads are better than one and there's always safety in numbers. Stay with me, please."

"What will you say to your mother?" Ann-Marie enquired.

"We'll cross that bridge when we get to it," Susan replied.

Ann-Marie thought for a moment. "Well, it's the best offer that I've had in these past few days. Your place it is and let's hope that we can put enough distance and time between ourselves and our troubles so that we can figure some way of confronting them head on and as equals."

Ann-Marie finished her packing and made her way to the kitchen at the back of the house. There she stood for a brief moment, turning the dark thoughts over and over again in her troubled mind. She turned and looked at Susan's sympathetic face as she stood silently beside her.

"What have I got you into, child?" she whispered.

Susan smiled and lifted one of Ann-Marie's cases from the floor and stepped out through the back door into the morning.

As they left the Harrington home through the rear garden neither women noticed the disturbed soil next to the back gate, for beneath slept an enemy that would stop at nothing to reclaim his prize.

Eleven

There it hung, a silent witness to the abortions of man, drifting through time and space, turned by clouds of purple light. The silent, majestic moon that shone through the large windows of the Cardinal's private quarters, sending rivers of gentle silver light across his room and onto the desk; a desk that was laden with ancient hand-written papers that should have long since perished with the devouring hunger of time. He stood with his back to the calling moon, the only light allowed in his dark chamber on this thoughtful night. He moved to the table and studied the assorted time-worn pages, lifting a document to his eyes and reading the passages over and over again.

To my beloved sister Mica.

Christian Pontmercy.

(Paris 1788.)

His eyes searched further up the page, re-reading the lines of hand written messages that had plagued him for almost half a century. His mind tearing itself asunder with unanswered questions. His lips moving silently, mouthing the words as he followed the lines on the dark worn, time ravaged page.

20th December 1788

My dear Mica,

It was with a sad heart that I left you behind with the tribe, for you are as alive and bright as I. Now that I am in Paris it is as if the heavens themselves have opened for me. Granted this may be due to the dark gift which we creatures of the night possess, but that aside, civilisation has many pleasures to offer those such as ourselves. Please, reconsider your actions. Join me. With your beauty, you would set this fragile world of mortal man alight. We could conquer the world and become immortal King and Queen of the night, sovereign above all others, as it was meant to be. Do not remain with those creatures that abuse the gift that was granted to us all by the Gods themselves.

How I hated my pathetic past life within the confines of the mountains. Living in our underground chambers, away from man is no way to exist for magnificent creatures such as ourselves. We are the hunters and man the hunted. It is natural selection and we should never have fought our true nature. Our natural instinct is to kill and it would be a joyous time for us all, if Callum and those of the Council Elders would accept their chosen path and face their own destiny.

Excitement is all around Paris as the smell of revolution hangs in the air and with it the strong hand of change. I am only saddened that this hand cannot reach those whom I love, for I know that you feel as I do that your immortal life is wasted and freedom for your soul will only come when you are released from the shackles of your subservient living.

I will today and forever love you; your beloved brother.

Christian

X

He slowly placed the letter onto the desk before lifting his eyes skyward in disbelief.

"A tribe of vampires living beneath the Pyrenees Mountains?" he whispered. Once again torturing himself with fantasies of such creatures, a persecution which he had endured for almost half a century, tormenting his mind with unanswerable thoughts, too impossible to believe but too fantastic to ignore. Many times he has asked the Holy Father and the Illuminati for funding to hunt out and destroy these abominations, but each time his request was denied. For forty years his earthly prayers were unanswered and now, at the culmination of his earthly life, he felt that his final appeal which would be once again rejected. In despair he allowed his hand to fall to his sides; closing his eyes he expelled a laboured and painful breath. He turned and looked at his reflection in the large mirror that hung over the fireplace; defeat had painted its victory across his features many times and the deep lines of frustration had criss-crossed his face with an almost vicious vigour. The long - case clock chimed the witching hour as the Cardinal's face sank into his chest in despair.

As the chimes reached their conclusion there was a gentle knock on the outer wooden door to his chambers, which caused his pulse to quicken. The Cardinal's throat was dry and unyielding.

"Enter!" he proclaimed, in an almost anxious voice.

After a brief moment a frail elderly gentleman entered the room and offered the Cardinal a deep respectful bow. He spoke briefly but his words conveyed so much, filling the dark chamber with light.

"His Holiness has granted your request."

The words raced through his mind, dancing across his thoughts, bringing light into the darkness where self-doubt and uncertainty lingered. Lifting his hand to his chest he began to breathe as if he were infused with invigorating energy. "Gather the team together, we must work quickly" he said.

The Cardinal moved to the desk and gently lifted the letter, held it in the subtle light of the moon. A deep anger slowly crossed his features as he crushed the decaying pages within his grip.

"I will, have my answers," he whispered.

Part Two

CREATURES OF THE NIGHT

One

It was the enticing sound of the birds calling that drew Jess closer to the entrance of the cave. Outside, the winter sun rained down with a brilliance, more enticing than gold, which flooded the valley with a shower of diamond light. His skin began to tingle in anticipation of the joy he had perceived would follow, but he never fully understood the severe warnings which his mother had given him and how the sun could do him harm. Yes, he understood that they were the people of the caves, the creatures of perpetual night, but this attainment of a gift was a prize far greater than anything his imagination could covet. He could bring his mother a souvenir, something from the upper world, something caressed by the sensual rays of the winter sun.

There had been a calling, and all were summoned to the great hall, for the dream-seer Callum had grave news. All were required to be present as this portentous omen would affect each and every one of them. All were present; all except Jess. His mother had not noticed that he wasn't by her side and when this realisation did occur, it would be too late.

Jess could feel the sun's strong presence even as he stood in the deep, dark shadows of the cave; its anticipated touch danced upon the hairs of his skin, bringing a multitude of sensual delights to his senses. As he stepped closer to his quest, the warmth of the waking world gathered up his thoughts and carried them upon a wave of sensual empty promises. He drew closer to the cave's entrance as the scent of nature's bouquet drifted gently past, enticing him to follow.

He could feel his heart beat with a tentative urgency as he caught a glimpse of the lush, green grass of the valley's floor as it stretched out before him. He closed his eyes as the sensation of nature's breath danced upon the naked flesh of his arms. Turning his head he marvelled at the corporeal impression of the wind as its essence raged at great speed along the sides of the valley walls, conveying a mournful orchestral sound of a sympathy that rang aloud like an anthem to nature's savage beauty.

His pale blue eyes searched the horizon as they marvelled at the clouds that cast gentle shadows across the valley's floor as they passed tentatively by, enticing the harsh rays of the winter sun and defusing their glare with their alluring presence. This was a world of which he had momentary, mortal recollection but had always longed to experience; it was a world of colour and light, a place of honest, extreme sensation. He could feel his excitement as he reservedly stepped into the embittered sunlight that bathed the surface world as a ravenous, devouring sensation which muted and raged across his senses, whispering malicious lies, which momentarily made him feel truly alive. He began to drown in his own wonder, asphyxiate in his own hedonistic pleasures, as he stood motionless on the floor of the valley, out in the open, drinking in the pure epicurean delights. He slowly walked with an anticipatory excitement into the centre of the valley's floor, the innocent sensuality of nature tormenting his soul and enticing him to fall into her awaiting deceitful, pestiferous arms, a place where the sun's rays touched the ground at their strongest; naive delight had captured his soul with a dark satisfaction that would be his downfall.

He held his hand out in front of himself and watched the soft pattern made by the gentle sunlight as it danced sensually across his skin. He marvelled at the warmth that this indulgence brought him both physically and emotionally, and with an exhilaration that pure emotion could not surpass he danced blindly in the harsh, fresh light of the soft afternoon sun, blindly oblivious to the suffering which was about to befall him. He stopped and looked to the valley floor as a broad smile broke across his face; leaning forward he reached down to the delicate mountain flowers which grew in great swaths beneath his feet. Lowering himself closer, he was intoxicated by their subtle perfume, which was momentarily exaggerated as he pulled handfuls of these exquisite mountain beauties from their natural habitat and gathered them into a deathly bouquet. Minutes began to exaggerate themselves into hours as the very essence of this new world invigorated him with a new and purposeful life-force. Jess had never felt so alive. Exhaling, he smiled a wide purposeful smile and allowed his head to fall back and drink in the full sanctity of the afternoon sunlight. It was only when he looked at his bare upper arms that he noticed that his skin was subtly changing colour; only gently at first but exacerbating as the seconds passed. Looking closer upon the soft skin of his forearm he could see the delicate transformation that was beginning to ensue. The entire surface area began to darken and change its subtle complexity as the light from above began to consume his immortal flesh; his skin began to slowly blister as a gentle issue of blood rose to the surface through the pores of his preternatural tissue. He could feel the inexorable pain of his own bodily fluids as they raged to preserve their living presence from the decaying vigour of the harsh winter sun. Dismay gripped his emotions and he dropped the noxious bouquet, his eyes searching for the cave's entrance and the sanctity of its merciful shadows. Fixing his sight aggressively at the cavern's gaping mouth, he began to move with mortal speed towards the enveloping inviolability of its beckoning salvation as fear began to rise savagely throughout his whole form. He could feel the strange sensation of warmth as its presence began to build from deep within his immortal frame as all about the gentle issue of heat began to rise from his panic ravaged body, signalling the impending vicious demise of this once-innocent soul. He could feel his potency wane as the ark of the sun's zenith continued its ravenous journey devouring his inner strength with each phase of its enchanted cycle.

Stumbling forward he fell aggressively to his knees; the shimmering aura of the world around assaulted his senses as preternatural fear filled his heart. He raised his hands to block the light of the sun in a vain attempt to shields his dying eyes from the devastating warmth of the comforting mortal glare. Blood-red tears ran down his cheeks as his flesh began to violently burn and blister; momentarily flames leapt across the surface of his forearms as his muscles fell in charred pieces upon the soft surface of the Valley's floor. A single soul-wrenching word raged from his dying throat as he collapsed almost lifeless upon the ground, its echo resonated angrily around the valley's walls.

"MOTHERRR!!!"

He struggled as the final embers of his life pulled his decaying shell towards the dark safety of the cave, but as life departed this charred form an ominous, dark shadow filled the valley, bringing sadness to this world for the suffering of this bastard child of Icarus.

Callum, the dream-seer, stood motionless in the doorway of the great meeting hall, his huge frame blotting out the subtle light from the corridor beyond. He watched as Mica darted around chairs and behind pillars in her fruitless search for her lost vagabond child. Even in such a traumatic emotion her beauty captivated him, her long black hair falling in strong curls past her shoulder and down her back, framing her almost perfect features sculptured across her ivory skin. She stopped her frantic endeavours and turned sharply in Callum's direction.

"Jess! Have you seen Jess?" her voice was soft and pleading.

Callum moved from the safety of the Machiavellian shadows and stepped resolutely towards Mica. Turning his head purposefully to one side he offered her a tainted, reassuring smile.

"No, sorry, the last time I saw him was just before the gathering."

His apologies bit deep into his soul. She slowly moved towards him, her feline movements capturing his primordial, carnal emotions.

Callum shook his head once again in denial - or knowledge of Jess's locality.

"He was with me a moment ago; I swear he was by my side," she pleaded, as tears began to fill her eyes.

Callum opened his arms to offer comfort but Mica raised her hands, rebuking his consoling advance.

"No!" she insisted. "We must find him."

He moved to one side and offered her a slow purposeful bow as she passed him and exited the room; his eyes captivated by her every movement.

Mica moved hurriedly along the dark corridor, sparsely illuminated by tar torches, which hung high above, offering a sporadic, cumbersome light. Her eyes darted back and forth, unhindered by the dark apparel as their vision was accustomed to this domain. Her mind was a rage as dark thoughts ravaged and tore at her consciousness, whispering their baleful woes. They surmised and stipulated, goaded and provoked, tearing at her mother's doubt in an attempt to turn her mind. Placing one hand upon the cold cave wall she raised the other and placed her palm harshly upon her forehead in a vain attempt to alleviate the inexorable pain, exorcising the demonic rage building within. Breathing deeply she closed her eyes to gather her thoughts in a vain attempt to calm her darkening emotions. Allowing time to wash over her she opened her eyes and looked purposefully along the corridor. Silence filled the air and at that very point in her life she felt truly abandoned. She turned to look from whence she came and an abundant silence greeted her, as the corridor stretched blindly into the distance.

She knew of the gathering, the calling of the Tribe to the chamber, but even the usual debating outcries which were regularly, feverishly apparent were silent and forlorn and the whole world appeared reverent and subdued. This heightened her fear as the silence became almost unbearable, rising like an impending storm that was bereft of witness. She then heard her name, quietly at first, but the urgency of its calling alerted her to the exigency of its importance. She moved at preternatural speed, enhanced by the overwhelming fears of a mother who knew she was eternally damned. She passed friends and foe alike, all bowed with their head in a subdued respectful manner, it wasn't until she came to the entrance of the cave that she truly appreciated the sanctity of their respect.

She observed, as one of the great female elders stepped back into the comfort of the cave's shadows from the searing light of the mortal world. Her skin had long since lost its favour for the light of man and the damage which it had experienced was negligible.

She moved with an unearthly grace towards Mica and held out her quivering, ivory hands. Mica rushed forward, her eyes transfixed upon the delicate leather belt held in sorrowful concession; her hands trembled as they took it from another, only too willing to part with their sorrowful gift. In a brief moment in time she had moved from parent to mourner, a transition that she had neither wished for nor desired. Silently she sank to her knees, holding the object tenderly to her lips. She looked mournfully to the elders and whispered.

"I'd like to be alone."

One of the elder vampire smiled and raised her arms, palms open and outwards, and ushered all gathered to leave.

Mica sat harshly against the cave's wall and slowly gathered her feet beneath her, allowing her mind to stir, bringing forward the soft images of her lost brother, which mingled and danced with those of her fallen child. She recalled the features of her beloved with a soft delight, a brother who perished at the time of the revolution in France in 1789, and their carefree childhood in England, a time of everlasting life and happiness. Then, a harshness filled her very core with the recent image of Jess; young, alone and dead. Twisting in an agonising torment which haunted her very thoughts and chilled her long dead soul, she stood as if in deep pain, gripping the cave's walls for solace and comfort. Standing, she held her hands to her eyes and wept deeply and uncontrollably.

Turning, she walked with a soulful decorum back into the lair, with a stoical dignity she passed her companions, deaf to their sympathies she moved to the only place of comfort that she knew, the Library. She could now hear the usual clutter of noise, which regularly accompanied everyday life within the caves as social normality urgently regained domain over the preternatural order of life.

In the great hall the elders tried to calm those who were gathered for the meeting, but the touch of death had unsettled several of the more volatile members of the Tribe. She could hear Cantor as he took command of the situation, bringing peace and silence in a moment, by use of his powerful voice.

"Brethren, please listen. I speak for us all when I say that we feel the suffering of our beloved Mica and I do not mean to trivialise her pain, but we must stress that what Callum has to say is of utmost importance."

"I know you understand, but you are not a woman and you cannot comprehend the death of a beloved child. Mere men cannot even comprehend the significance that such a loss would have upon the very core of a mother, be she mortal or immortal." a female vampire shouted in ridicule.

Callum moved forward into view, taking the collective gaze from Cantor.

"I, above all others share the suffering that is felt by Mica, for was it not I who taught the children of this tribe the ways of our kind? I was witness to their transformation from mortal to immortal. Just because we are the elders of this tribe, older than most and unfortunately primarily men, that does not mean that we do not have emotions. All humans have emotions and no matter how far we progress along the road of immortality we can never escape our corporeal roots. Yes, we are vampires, but before we were granted the dark gift we were human, and for that reason and that reason

60

alone we turned from the act of taking another life, for our kind can feel ambient emotion on a higher level than any mortals. So do not tell me that I am unable to feel the loss of little Jess. I am a vampire but I am also human and feel his loss as much as I would feel the loss of any of our kind. For, was it not I who taught him the ways of our world, the peaceful coexistence with nature which we have procured and nurtured for centuries? Was it not I who supported him at the most crucial time in his existence, his rebirth? Is it not I who has offered each and every one of you gathered here this early evening this guiding governance at your most vulnerable and crucial of times?

His anger was growing more apparent.

"Have I ever turned my back upon my responsibilities to each and every individual here? Then do not offer me the demeaning provenance of your half-hearted and bitter-sweet mellifluous words."

 Callum allowed his words to echo reverently about the great chamber and be absorbed by his companions. He took an almost human breath before he allowed himself to continue. "There is a danger far greater than anything which we have encountered in our time upon this realm of existence and this danger is almost upon us. I cannot emphasise the urgency of my words."

Then, an interruption came from a male vampire who stood and screamed a question at the seer.

."..but what could be worse than the death of one of our children?"

Callum turned to the purveyor of the question, his stare almost melting the aggressor's heart. He spoke in an almost inaudible whisper

"The death of us all."

A hush fell over the hall.

"I take that by your silence you wish for me to continue? he enquired, with a sense of menace.

"With the passing of the next cycle of the moon, many of you here shall be vanquished." Sounds of surprise and horror filled the air, but Callum raised his hand to stem any questions and continued. "Since the great battle which divided our kind all those centuries ago, our tribe has taken to living in our subterranean world, sustained by the blood of cattle, leaving mortals to exist in peace. So that in time we became creatures of folklore and legend and after the revelation that I am about to reveal to you, some may consider returning to the old ways. This, however, is very much out of the question, for man is no longer the fool that he used to be. He now has a great many technological wonders at his command. It is ourselves who have become the prodigal lost sheep in need of comfort and guidance. The world which we all knew is long since dead and fear for our kind has passed taking with it any reverence or respect which we once knew. Man has created wonders which are incomprehensible to our immortal, antediluvian minds. He has great metal machines that can fly through the air, steel ships that tear through the very waters of the world's oceans and vast machines that ravage and devour the land. His cities have spread throughout the skin of the earth like a great plague, covering and destroying anything natural. These times which man has created are strong and vicious; there is no mercy, there is no natural place for our kind to linger. I am not exaggerating when I tell you that man will show you no compassion; he is cold and brutal, far beyond any loathing which could be conjured by the dark tales of our kind. Tales of our gothic portrayal and sinister presence which kept the lonely wanderer company on a dark and malevolent night are now fodder for their children who demonstrate a vicious and callous greed that would far eclipse any malicious wrongdoing ever imagined by any one of you. Mankind now has a nature that is rancorous, resentful and unforgiving. His malicious hunger for the servitude of every creature that exists on this planet is unbound. His acerbic touch fetters and destroys hope with a vindictive bitterness that would surmount even the darkest of immortal hearts. Deeds are portrayed and solutions are sought in the name of a greater glory. Empires are built and destroyed but their true cost is never calculated. The innocent which we knew in our mortal lives has long since been surpassed by a dual horned demon that has censured man into abeyance and commanded him to undertake his dark malevolent bidding."

Callum paused for thought, allowing himself to choose his words very carefully.

"Unfortunately the technical transition of man into this barbaric abomination is not our only concern," Callum smiled briefly to himself. "If only it were... then some of our kind may truly adapt and survive, integrate as other renegade vampires have achieved in the past. But no! Our problem comes from a stronger source than man. Our nemesis since the origins of our species and other factions thereafter; our true antagonist and the second horn to this un-majestic king without a crown, is religion. However, this creature which we once understood and respected, has undertaken a dark metamorphosis and the intertwined transactions of commerce and faith have become interwoven bedfellows. The destructive advancements of science, enlightening precarious pathways with its theories and proclamations, destroying the theologies and appeasing them with the comforting solace of remuneration. One symbiotic creature offering succour to another; a truly unholy alliance."

Callum brought his hand to his mouth and with his thumb pushed his lips together as he briefly closed his eyes. As he opened his eyes an almost mortal vulnerability enveloped him and he spoke in a slow deliberate tone.

"And so, it is with grave apprehension I must inform you that it has come to my attention that secret letters written many centuries ago, telling of the exact location of this Tribe, have fallen, or been given into, the hands of those who would see the demise and destruction of our kind. Whether this was accidental or deliberate we do not know and it is unrewarding to point the finger of blame in the direction of one who may have perished centuries ago. We are in the 'here and now' and this is the predicament which we must face together, we must be vigilant but even as we speak those who would see our downfall are mustering their resources and will be upon us within less than 48 hours."

One of the younger vampires, respectful of Callum's status, stood and asked a poignant question.

"I don't understand; how can man destroy us all? We number in the hundreds. Could we not fight, or are we to accept our destiny and await the slaughter that is imminent?"

"I understand," Callum said. "We are powerful beings, creatures that can live for a perceived eternity, surviving not for the moment as mortal man but for the challenge and the knowledge. Many of you here have lived several human spans of existence, but by the laws of nature, something I agree that we do not truly adhere to, everything must come to and does have a natural end. I am not saying lie down and allow this abomination to consume us; that is the furthermost desire that I have. The reason why I may sound defeated, as though the battle was already over, is the future which has let itself be known to me. You all know that I am the oldest of the known Communicators and for that reason my powers are stronger than most. For several weeks now I have been privy to dreams and witnessed visions of destruction, the habitual genocide of our race. You may feel that my words are empty, barren of substance. If so, please take your chances and flee the confines of the subterranean world when nightfall comes. Any hope of life, even in this cold, modern world, is more precious than gold itself but you cannot outrun what fate has decreed. I feel that it is only my compelling duty to inform you that man is no longer scared of the dark and that which he does not know; he rushes blindly forward, consuming with a vicious hunger, destroying everything in his path."

The young vampire sat slowly back into his chair. "But what does man have that we should all be so afraid of, that we should lay down our lives for?"

Callum took a deep breath and closed his eyes; allowing his head to fall back a little as he drowned in the silence of the hall. After a brief moment to compose himself, he looked the questioner directly in the eyes and spoke a single word.

"Science!"

The young vampire stood and shouted belligerently in Callum's direction; "Tell me story teller, how do we know that you are telling the truth? Your visions have been wrong before. If you're so sure that this is the end for us all why don't we just go out now into the evening light and allow the sun to do its work?"

"I will tell you why. We are vampires, and for that reason we are a proud race. We do not accept fate, we dictate it."

A cheer issued from his companions as Callum moved closer to answer his questioner. When their faces were almost touching, he spoke in a low deliberate tone.

"I will take into consideration the things that you have spoken of, but do not let your own self-importance protect you, for it will not. Man will no longer hang garlic behind his door to ward off evil spirits or demons. He no longer believes in ghosts or witches; this time in history has passed. The time into which you wish to condemn us all is an empty one. There is no compassion just servitude, even for creatures such as ourselves. Yes! You may live but it will be a damned existence; we will be shadows of our former selves."

Callum returned to the centre of the hall, speaking as he walked, his back to his audience.

"Man is the master of his own destiny; he has created weapons of destruction that could destroy this planet several times over," he turned and stared at those gathered. "These weapons of mass destruction are far beyond anything that you could ever imagine in your wildest of nightmares. Do you think that because we have cultivated our old ways that man has chosen to do this also? If you think this, then you are sadly disillusioned. We have lived our peaceful existence while man has fought many great wars, killing millions of his own kind. He had expanded his mind and developed his technology, a technology that has outreached the bounds of all our insignificant imaginations.

He is no longer content with bringing Mother Nature to her knees, he has raped and ravaged this planet of all that is good and now his conquest is reaching for a greater goal. Man has touched the stars. He has built great metal machines that can carry people to the heavens and touch the moon. There are objects, which float around this planet, the flotsam and jetsam of man's scientific mistakes. Machines send images in seconds across the world. There are moving pictures that captivate and entice, and this may sound intriguing - almost alluring - but a world of science has no place for our kind. We will be a curiosity. Something to be studied and dissected. Then cast aside when we are no longer of use. We are all of the Old World, a time before this great hunger for knowledge."

He paused.

"Our perpetuity and immortality could be used to procreate their wars. In this modern world we too could become a weapon of destruction, an army of diabolical darkness," he looked deep into the young vampire's eyes, allowing time for his harsh words to permeate his thoughts.

"Don't you see? How many of you here could live with the dark knowledge that you were responsible for the perpetual life of a great dictator? Caesar, Genghis Khan, Stalin, Hitler. Would that make you proud? His words dripped with sarcasm.

Can you recall the last great human uprising? The war they said would end all wars? Could you imagine if their leaders were given the dark gift? Yes, my friends, a war that would never end. Armies of darkness. Immortals perpetuating a suffering for an eternity. Such a proud inheritance."

His words softened. "We can never allow this."

"Science has advanced to such a degree that it would be easy for man to take a sample of blood from any one of you, analyse it, then find the component that makes you what you are and duplicate it. Synthesise it, this essence of your immortal soul."

Callum moved over to the large chairs of office that stood in a semi- circle at the far reaches of the chamber. He sat in his own elders' chair; a chair given to those granted office in this parliament of the underworld. A parliament that he himself had formed many millennia before many of those gathered were born into their own mortal bindings.

"Death would be the end for us all, as we are not truly immortal; insanity or weakness eventually consumes our immortal soul and are we only delaying our inevitable demise. I cannot and will not bind you to my words for you are all free spirits and you must make your own choice or mistake. But, I must beg you to consider all that you have heard this day and make your choice in all urgency."

****

The great meeting continued as possibilities were exchanged and ideologies explored. The world outside pursued its natural course as the days fell by, allowing the soft colours of night to enter into this forgotten valley. A soft mist seemed to rise from the valley's floor as a gentle fall of rain cleansed and purified the horizon, bringing the tears of heaven to wash away the pain from the sole stranger who stood at the entrance of the cave. When darkness had claimed its hold upon the night Mica left the safety of her world to gather the ashes of her fallen son. Wrapping them in an animal skin she placed them in a pouch about her neck, so that he would be once again close to her heart.

As she walked across the valley floor, not caring where her wandering took her, she thought of happier times, when her brother would play with Jess, making him laugh. The tricks that they would play upon her and the mischief into which they would fall! Now both were gone and this hung heavy upon her heart. Together in life, separated in death. She turned and looked to the entrance to the cave; this sight felt as alien to her as much as this feeling of being alone. There was nothing to keep her here, no child to care for, no love to hold.

Her mind once again turned to thoughts of her twin, buried alone in a grave. Unknown and forgotten. Her hand reached for the pouch about her neck and she knew then what she must do. She would find her brother's final resting-place and there he would lay with her son. Without a backward glance, Mica left the valley and made her way to the village at the base of the mountain, there she hoped to mingle with mortals and learn their ways.

****

As she stood at the base of the mountain, watching the lights of the village flicker in the night's sky, she wondered how much of this world had changed since she had last ventured into the realm of mortal man. With a great deal of trepidation she moved to the outskirts of the village. All about her the ski chalets stood in their picturesque setting topped by a thick blanket of snow. The buildings increased as she moved closer to the centre of the resort. The night was silent and bereft of another living creature; that was until she turned a corner and found herself on the main thoroughfare of the village. Noise screamed all about as the shops sound systems pumped loud rock music from their speaker out into the streets to entice the customer to buy their wares. Neon lights flashed. Cars swerved and sounded their horns. The red glow of the street lamps warmed the crushed snow that was piled up along the roadside. Following the direction in which the crowd pushed, Mica allowed herself to be carried along on their stream, offering little resistance to their urgency, anathema to this modern world. She passed shops laden with a thousand delights, displayed to those rich enough to be able to afford their exclusive wares. A café filled with the living, deep in their conversations, relating over and over again the traumas of their insignificant existence, never realising their own mortality until it was too late. Students filling their heads with politics and the ideologies of philosophers who had long since perished at the hands of time; their words a gentle guidance to support man in his troubled history which was now exalted and proclaimed with a vengeance as the right and true word, used to assault his fellow brethren to subjugate and subdue his own ideologies with the preference of another.

Mica continued with her journey of exploration into this world of the unknown, along streets and down alleyways. Turning another corner she found herself standing in a quiet square, which was surrounded by small picturesque buildings that seemed to huddle together for warmth against the cold of that winter's night. Peace reigned supreme. The noise and turmoil that assaulted her moments before were now lost in a memory, replaced by a heavenly silence that calmed and comforted. Standing alone, she purposefully allowed the benevolent melancholy of this night to envelop her and soothe her embattled soul. She smiled as silence swathed her with its sensual caress and brought her hope.

It was then that she heard a call, a cry in the night. It rang like a child's symphony upon the wind, its melody assaulting her maternal senses. Her hands rushed to her ears, as if to block out the sound of this forgotten chorus, but to no avail. For the music of suffering that was carried upon the wind was not that of memory, but that of reality. Slowly stepping from the roadside she ventured deeper into the centre of the square, her preternatural vision searching the dark shadows and recesses of the buildings.

All about her the night hung heavy and it did not wish to reveal any of its secrets, even to one so manipulative of its emotions. She turned and turned again, lost in the insecurity of her own failings.

Then she noticed it, a great building that sat at the far corner of the square, reverent in its own disposition and she marvelled at this construction to an empty and jealous god. Walking slowly towards the main bulk of the building, the wind caught her imperial coat, sending it out behind her like the wings of a great bat.

As she reached the stone steps, crowned by a set of great wooden doors, locked against the cold of this winter's night, she sensed the faint pulse of a human life. Climbing upward she could feel the spirit of the other intensifying, as she grew closer. Reaching the plateau of her quest the heavens opened, letting down their gentle kisses of winter. Looking up, Mica watched as the light flakes of snow drifted slowly to the ground, concealing her movements.

A humble moan issued from the shadows of the church doorway, bringing Mica's senses sharply back to her. "Jess?" she whispered, knowing full-well that her kin was dead, but a mother's hope still burned deep within her heart.

The child that her senses discovered was starved and alone and even to her harsh vampire touch, she could feel the cold that had already penetrated the very core of this young mortal's flesh. Lowering herself to her knees, she moved closer to the child. Displaying her most human smile Mica spoke gently.

"Are you alone? Where are your parents?"

The sight of this child burned a rage deep in Mica's heart. Here she was, a childless mother, staring at a motherless child, abandoned. The child spoke; uttered words foreign to Mica's ears. She felt helpless, as all she could do was pay witness as the chill of winter drew the life-giving warmth from this little innocent's mortal body. Tentatively standing, the child moved forward and placed its arms about Mica's neck, a single word fell from her lips, a word that tore at Mica's soul.

"Mama."

Mica tried to pull away, but she knew that if she did then her heart may well break with the immeasurable pain. The sensation of motherhood washed over her, bringing a brief moment of joy. She pressed her lips gently against the child's soft neck, hoping to reproduce the tenderness shown to this orphan of the night by its own true mother. Mica could feel the warm blood that flowed just below the surface of the child's skin and a hunger began to build deep within her. Not a hunger eager to appease the appetite for one such as her own, but a hunger for her sex, the hunger of motherhood. She knew that this child could never replace Jess, but its very existence, as an immortal in need of guidance would fill the void within. Her tongue began to move across the delicate skin of the child's neck, passing back and forth over the point of entry, anaesthetising and comforting. Looking at the church, her thoughts were full of questions. She had not feasted on human blood for almost two centuries, so why now, tonight, in front of the house of God?

'Why not?' she thought.

Yes, I would take pleasure in this one, simple act for one reason and one reason alone; here is a child outside the house of the Lord. Who chose to ignore her cries, thus sending her into the arm of this so-called daughter of darkness? Who was to blame for the demise of this child? The vampire that followed its own true basic instinct, an instinct that it has suppressed for centuries? Or could it be the church that turned a deaf ear to this sole child that cried in the dark on this bitter winter's night?

Closing her eyes, Mica bit deep.

The taste of human blood pushed her senses spiralling skyward, sending her into a spasm of ecstasy. The warm salt of the fluid burned as it danced across her tongue and down her throat. It ravaged her system, filling it with a power that surpassed her deepest nightmare. It plunged into the pit of her stomach then subsequently rushed about her body, drawn to all parts with vampiric speed to rejuvenate and quench her yearning. The sound of the child's heart beat like the rhythm of a great drum, pounding in her ears. Pulling the infant closer she drank deeper, for the most basic of instincts captured her; she was the true predator of mankind.

It was all over in a brief moment, but to Mica it could have lasted an eternity; it was the culmination of a two hundred-year hunger that lay dormant, fighting against her true emotions. The infant's head fell against her shoulder as life departed its hollow shell. Pulling away, she realised to her horror the full extent of her actions and dropped the child's lifeless body irreverently to the ground.

"Am I to be cursed, to be childless? Why won't this God tell me?" she screamed, her eyes never leaving the innocent that lay at her feet. Tears filled her eyes; not the tears of pain or suffering but the tears of rage and bitterness. She screamed again and again into the empty night, calling to the shadows for an answer. She could feel her emotions heighten and soar with the rejuvenating mortal life force, its energy invigorating her very soul. She turned again and again upon the spot, desperate for an answer. Stopping, she wept and whispered "Why?"

A mournful compassion compelled her and she moved closer to the lifeless corpse. She raised her head and looked blindly upon the motionless body, staring without vision at its silent form.

She looked helplessly into the dark that surrounded her as her preternatural senses became aware of a subtle shimmer in the atmosphere and then she noticed the change that had taken place with the night. The dark shadows seemed somehow lighter, more vibrant; an anticipatory sensuality gripped her senses and looking at her feet she realised that the radiance was issuing from the child, a strong spiritual glow emanated all around and Mica watched as the spirit of the infant's true form rose from its mortal bonds and drifted into the air above her. A soft radiance touched the air all about, sending gentle glimmers of gold and light dancing into the sky, an ethereal amnesty lighted her presence as Mica advanced towards the spirit. Even though she hastened this child's demise by only moments, its passing would haunt her soul for an eternity. She watched enviously as the spirit gently graduated towards the heavens, its very presence an epiphany for this sole observer.

It was as this pure brilliance began to capture her imagination that a soulless noise began to assault her senses as the grand doors of the church began to move, it was as if the wind was gently pulling at their great metal locks, wishing to gain entrance against this cold abandoned night. They moved slowly at first then gathering in strength until they crashed back and forth, restrained only by the bolts that held them closed from within. Mica backed away, for her senses screamed danger and her body began to shake as fear rose in her very soul.

All around the sound of the assault rang in the air like thunder, crashing back and forth, filling the world with an unholy discord. Then, as quickly as it began, they ceased their movement and returned to their resting position, but Mica retained her distance. Anticipation filled the night, anticipation that was soon rewarded. A gentle aura issued from the centre of the doors, gathering strength and colour as time proceeded. Mica anticipated that this was the tunnel of light recorded by man in so many near-death recollections, documented throughout history. She waited with baited breath as the colours merged and danced and after a moment it was as if the very fabric of the wood were ablaze as the colours rages all about. Then, just as fear had reached the zenith of her emotions, it stopped and there in the middle of the church doors hovered a vast circle of pure unadulterated light.

Mica smiled as she watched the child's spirit rise majestically and move closer to her heavily rest.

Then, without mercy, a great fiery muscle-bound arm punched its way outward, not through the wood but through its essence, creating a portal from another, darker world. Mica recoiled in horror as terror gripped her very essence. That arm was followed by another, its skin red and pulsating, covering muscles that winced against the cold of the winter air. Its fingers were tipped with great razor-sharp claws that pulled at the very fabric of the night, as if to perpetuate its entrance into this dimension. A black, cloven hoof forced it way through the portal and stamped itself with a strong irreverence onto the snow-covered ground outside if the church. This was followed by another, topped by a great muscle bound torso.

Watching in revulsion, Mica merged into the shadows, for she knew the name of this creature of damnation. It was when the abomination stood to its full potential that she realised the quest of the atrocity that was before her. Her eyes stared, transfixed at his features, following the contours of his face, down from the great horns that protruded from his head and onto the yellow eyes that flicked back and forth. A single name issued from her lips as she closed her own eyes and prayed for deliverance from the God of mortals, for there before her was her own true God whose name was forgotten by the centuries and damned by her kind. For there stood Caliban, creator and master of all things immortal that follow the path of darkness.

His attentions, however, were not for those of his fledgling kin, but for the innocent that drifted above him. He smiled a sardonic smile as he reached tenderly upwards, brushing the child's ankle with his finger. Mica wanted to scream, but a deeper emotion prevented her outburst. Not an emotion of human proportion but an emotion that bonded her to her kind. For if Caliban was to find her, then he would surely find the

Tribe. Those gentle humans who, centuries before, he himself had damned into immortality and perpetual night and abandoning them to discover the abominations that he had inflicted upon their now immortal souls.

She watched in horror as his grip tightened about the child's ankle, causing immeasurable distress and discomfort. The infant screamed and pulled away, but this enticed him all the more as his black emotions thrilled at her discomfort. This feast of souls was long overdue and eagerly anticipated, for Caliban, the creator of the European Tribe, could only feast on the souls of those hunted by his kin. Pulling her close to his face, he blew her a demonic kiss and allowed his black tongue to issue from his tormented mouth and drag its atrocious, cancerous self across her soft, soulful flesh. His free hand gripped her from behind and pulled her tight to himself. She kicked as a fear unknown to mortals filled her, tearing at her emotions and damning her for an eternity. Pulling her close to his chest he looked at the night sky with a dark irreverence and stepped backward into the portal. His body disappearing into the bright light that issued from within, the air was almost electric with his presence. Then as quickly as he had entered into this dimension he was gone and the night was once again ruler of its own domain as darkness hung malevolently all around. Moving over to the discarded child that lay on the snow covered steps, Mica stared at the abandoned shell that was once host to a living soul, a soul that she had cast into the very clutches of damnation.

****

It had taken Mica almost an hour to gather her broken thoughts; the splinters of her once powerful mind were now cast upon the seas of her fractured consciousness, a lost ship aimlessly drifting through the bloodied oceans of her wayward thoughts. Wandering the streets in an almost distant haze she neglected to realise that the morning was approaching and the horizon was dancing with rays of golden sunlight. As she wandered through the approaching morning, blind to the world about her, she found herself standing before the impressive gates of an old unloved cemetery. Gently pushing the gates, she found them responsive to her touch, they swung silently open, gathering the snow as they followed their path, piling it up against the rusted bars.

Her feet were the first to invade this sacrosanct ground; she was not the first human to walk this burial place of God's creatures, but she was the first of her kind to venture into this place of death. To man, death was the end, the final curtain to a hollow life and when the culmination of his existence was upon him they would wait patiently for his inevitable demise, but the phantom that would cast their downfall meant nothing to her kin. This ghost which they had banished from their own horizons at their point of turning would now be a welcoming comfort to this gentle creature of the night.

Silently she moved, as if a spectre through the soft folds of winter, leaving no evidence of her journey, no path to follow. All about her reached great monoliths to the departed, tributes to the achievements of the dead, long since forgotten. Her fingers traced their way across the cold, harsh stone, sending the snow that had piled up in the gaps, drifting off into the air to dance on the bitter winter winds that blew like the breath of fallen angels.

Mica stopped at the greatest of these monuments, the centrepiece of this mausoleum of death. How they reminded her of the living, huddling together as they did in life. The rich: never wishing to distribute their wealth and scared that others may take it from them. Now, in death, they banded together like wolves, eager to tear and bite at those who would venture too close to their sacred hoard, these final displays to their wanton lust. A house; to hide the decaying remains of a once self-important fool who lived and died in splendour while those around existed in squalor and deprivation, with disease and pollution issuing through the very fabric of their homes. A dwelling for the living that could never match the grandeur of a structure whose sole aim was to house the remains of one who could no longer suffer the indignities and horrors of this world.

Mica moved to the back of the building and there she studied its form and construction. Her eyes following the lines and patterns of the brick work, searching for a weakness, a vantage point. Her vampiric eyes found their quest and gently she prized and teased at the cement, easing it free from its rest until the brick that it surrounded was loose to her touch and she could pull it from its resting-place. After one was freed, then came another and another until she had created an entrance large enough to grant her admission into this dark chamber. Inside, the shadows that clung to the walls comforted her, bringing a soothing gentle calm to her fevered mind. She could sense the impending morning and her preternatural inner self called to her to rest as it relinquished its command over the dark forces that gathered within her.

Lying in the safe darkness of the chamber, how she wished that he had followed. How she now hungered for the comfort of his touch. In a way she was pleased that they had never grown too close, for she knew that the pain that she felt now would be intensified beyond endurance and the thought of leaving him behind would torture her for an eternity. Concentrating her mind she reached out to touch another, briefly she felt his presence but then he was gone.

"Be safe, my Callum," she whispered, as immortal sleep captured her thoughts and gathered them up in its arms so that she could dream beyond this world of shadows and into the reality beyond.

Outside, the colours of night were receding from the skies as morning reached across the horizon, comforting all that it touched with its soft, sensual glow.

****

Callum watched as life around him fell apart, the very fabric of his dreams was breaking asunder and drifting out of reach, carried upon the sad winds of destiny. Time had never been their enemy but their companion, and now all of that had changed for the dark avenger who stood sharpening his scythe and pointing it in the direction of the unfortunate ones was poised, ready to strike and bring down the race of supermen who were already old when the earth was still young. Callum closed his eyes as a single tear of sadness tore its way down the hardened flesh of his face. After a brief moment he composed himself and watched the chaos that had captured the minds of his people. Several of the younger tribal members had brought the cattle from the deep bowels of the caves, setting them free to wander out into the bright world above and mingle with those domesticated creatures of man. Cattle that had sustained life and brought anonymity to all that sheltered beneath the black cloak of the Tribe. A deeper sadness consumed Callum. A sadness called loneliness.

He had day-dreamed for the briefest of moments before he realised that he was being observed. An innocent girl stood before him peering into his sad, ancient eyes, searching for an answer. She stood momentarily then broke the spell that she was weaving over him.

"They are all waiting for you in the great hall," she whispered.

Callum smiled his acknowledgement and moved to leave, but she stood before him denying his exit.

"Is there something that I can do for you?" he enquired.

Once again the girl looked pitifully into his eyes.

"I know this great talent that you've been gifted with for eternity is powerful and portentous, and that you are rarely incorrect with your predictions, but may I reiterate, have all these ominous destructions which you claim to be witness to, are they about to expire and bring about our noble tribe's passing? Are we all about to suffer this great indignity at the hands of mere mortals?"

Callum smiled and lowered his great stance so that he was level with the girl's eye-line.

"What is your name?" he enquired.

"Elizabetha," she replied.

"Tell me beautiful one, how long have you lived with us here in this dark, cold world?"

His words sent a shudder down Elizabetha's spine, but she concealed her fear and answered him in a strong, controlled voice.

"I have been immortal for sixty years now," she said.

"Do you fear your destiny?" he enquired.

Elizabetha smiled and nodded her head.

"Then you are braver than most, for many of our kind have lived with the preconceived idea that we are invincible; demigods above man. Little do they realise that many of our kind destroy themselves before they reach the infancy of five hundred years. Madness consumes them, either that or loneliness."

Callum looked deep into her eyes, eyes that reflected a pure, precious soul. It was then that he committed a crime against himself and offered this innocent a glimpse of her own destiny.

"Give me your hand," he whispered.

Elizabetha did so without question. No sooner had he taken it up, he let it go, dropping it roughly onto her lap. He turned his head away, thinking for a moment. When he looked back at her the vision of pain that was etched upon his face filled Elizabetha with fear.

"What is it, have you seen my destiny?"

Callum smiled a wry smile and looked to the ground in shame.

"Yes."

Elizabetha took his hand and held it in her own.

"I know that I have no right to understand what the heavens have in store for me, and if you feel that the information which you possess it too great for me to comprehend then I will understand if you refuse to tell me if my fate lies with that of my kind."

Callum breathed a laboured sigh, allowing the air to slowly escape from his lungs as he looked painfully at Elizabetha.

"I will break the bonds of my own council and tell you what you are eager to hear. Yes, the Reaper will cull many of our kind before this day is over; however, after the counting of vanquished immortal souls is finished I can tell you that your name will not be with those presented to the Almighty to account for their time upon this transient world."

Callum smiled and embraced her hands in his own as he rose to his full height.

"Come we must go to the meeting in the great hall, for many must make peace with themselves before they can make peace with their maker."

****

An uproar issued from those gathered as Callum entered the great hall. He moved silently to the centre of the meeting place and stood with his head bowed, allowing their urgent questions to wash over him. After a moment he slowly lifted his head and looked directly at those gathered; this action alone was enough to quell the anger of those searching for a deliverer in this their hour of need.

"Little has changed since we last met; several members of the tribe have taken it upon themselves to leave and not face the destiny that has been written for them, for those who come to destroy us are but a few hours away," he said.

A young vampire stood and directed a question to Callum.

"I know the reasons that you have given us are for the best intent, but why must we lay down our lives for these mortals? Why can't we fight?"

"We have never needed to involve ourselves in the external politics of mortals, for they are willingly throwing themselves deeper into the abyss that is knowledge and perpetual destruction which they choose to call their advancements in science. They build their hopes upon these wanton desires without turning their search for knowledge inwardly too save their own damned souls from destruction and damnation."

He paused before continuing.

"I must reiterate that at no point in the whole of these proceedings have I ever asked any of our kind to offer themselves as a sacrifice to those who come to destroy us. What I have said is that many of you will die. Now that may come as an act of violence in the struggle for life as the conflict between mortal and immortal occurs. I do not want you to lie at man's feet and allow him to walk all over you. No! That is the last thing that I would wish. There are a number of reasons why I informed you of the events that are about to occur and the ramifications that they will bring to us. There are those that I have already mentioned, so that you may turn to your brother, your sister, your lover, husband or wife and tell them from the depth of your vampire heart how much you love and respect them. I am not trying to scaremonger or exacerbate the situation but the death knell is ringing and if you are too ignorant to understand this or too deaf to hear it, then I pity you. For, mark my words, there is no turning back. This is our day of judgement."

"Will any of our kind survive?" the young man said in a lower, more respectful tone.

Callum looked to Elizabetha and offered her a half-sympathetic smile.

"I would be lying if I said no. Who they are and how the destructive hand of man will spare them, I do not know. If you are among those left alive after the dark angel has taken your brothers and sisters into the realm beyond, then please try to integrate yourself into the pattern of existence dictated by modern man and give him no cause to suspect that you are more than that which you first appear. Life in the world outside may be a greater torture than that of death. In this immortal life within the Tribe you have comfort, but in the perpetual world of winter, that is man, you will feel nothing but the bitter kiss of his touch. He will spurn you, reject you and even try to destroy you for you are neither human nor animal. You are beyond that realm. There is one blessing. An animal will only kill for food and man will always kill for faith, but as we are a faithless race and as long as man and animals inhabit this world we shall never go hungry."

Callum stopped and moved over to the great council chairs that stood in reverence at the back of the chamber, pausing for a moment to admire the dark, polished sheen of their wooden surface, he sat down in the chair reserved for one elected to grand council elder, and not appertaining to his position. A great whisper danced about the air as those who witnessed this blasphemy protested in shallow tones. After a minute had passed, an eternity for those gathered, Callum raised his hand and enquired the reason for their unrest.

The vampire who had questioned him minutes before stood and looked at him with a defiant glare.

"You have sat in Cantor's chair, which is sacred as are the others appertaining those members of the Upper Great Council. Is this your way of electing yourself our leader? A grand dictator of the un-dead?

Callum stood at a speed greater than that which any of those gathered could comprehend, sending the questioner backwards with his presence.

"Can you not see what is before you? Do not look with your eyes for only fools look with their eyes. Eyes can be deceived, misguided. Look closer; look with your heart. Can't you see...?" Callum sat back down on the chair as he spoke. "... this, this is nothing?" He raised his hand and brought it crashing down upon the arm of the chair. "They are chairs, symbols of command and power. An image to show balance within our society's structure, something to aspire to. That is all; this is why I am showing them so much disrespect. They are only chairs! With the passing of time we have given them a name - a respect - and they have become great icons. They have become the symbol of power within our world. As have other lost and forgotten artefacts. The great chalice of Raphael. The sacred book of the Necronomicon. The holy stone of the Lukal. They are all mere objects. That is what I am trying to tell you. We no longer respect the individuals who hold the office of council for their integrity or compassion. We respect them for the objects which they worship, or we respect them because they sit upon these hallowed chairs, and there is no other reason."

He slowly stood allowing all present to bathe in his words, then, with the speed of the ancients he turned and gripped the chair in which he previously sat and lifted its great bulk above his head. Pausing for a moment to allow his lesson to hit home he then sent the wooden icon crashing into a thousand shards into the stone floor of the chamber.

"Take a look at these shattered pieces that lie on this cold stone, for they will be your lives and our kind when less than a few hours have passed. So before you scream sacrilege, remember that it was only a chair, but this..." - he curled his fingers into a fist and sent it crashing into his chest – "...this is a life and should be cherished to the bitter end. Why do you look to me for an answer? It is always Callum that you run to, and when I tell you of the fate that is about to befall you all, you mistrust my words and question me. Have I ever, in all the time that you have known me, given false counsel or advice? He paused for an answer. "Never!" he screamed. "And for that reason I shall leave you all to decide your own destiny. I wash my hands of my elected position and leave you all with a clear heart and conscience. I fear that you are all damned."

Kicking his way through the debris he left the great hall, closely followed by Elizabetha who called for him to listen to her. Only when they reached the door to his private apartment did he stop and confront her words.

"Callum, please do not allow their words to hurt you; they are like children, scared of what they do not know or cannot understand. I know that you are angry with them as a father is with their child endeavouring to hide the pain that he feels deep within. If any of our kind is to survive then it should be you, for you are the most human of us all; your gentle ways and understanding set you high above any other who could call themselves friend."

Callum allowed the anger to fall from his face and smiled at Elizabetha.

"My child, you are wiser that you comprehend and for that, I love you," he leaned forward and held her face in his great hands, holding it for a moment he then kissed her gently upon the forehead. "I have no reason to perpetuate this existence. No, I will join my friends in their destiny; life for me now has little meaning," he then moved into his chambers and closed the door, destroying the bridge between himself and the world he once knew. Looking about the room at the objects that he had amassed over the centuries he realised how foreign this all seemed to him. The sailing charts from China, silks and spices from India and scientific instruments from across the globe. All acquired before man's curiosity had put an end to his earthly travels.

For a moment, he allowed Elizabetha's words to sink into his thoughts, turning them over and over in his mind. Never once since the beginning of this whole episode has he ever thought of his own destiny. For the whole of his time living in this dark, forgotten world he had always put others before himself, refusing to acknowledge his own desires and yearnings for the sake of preaching sound advice to those who required his understanding. Yet never in all of that time had he thought of his own needs. Reflecting upon the past few days a deep sense of want and bitterness came over him, for he had allowed that which he loved above life itself to leave and enter into the dark world of mortals.

He moved to a dusty shelf chiselled from the grey rock. There, searching until he found the object of his quest, he lifted the small leather bound object to his chest, waiting several moments before unwrapping its contents. He gently pulled at the

74

leather-bound straps until they relinquished the portrait within, a picture that brought so much comfort to his heart. He sat for a moment, tracing her delicate features with his eyes and at that moment he knew that his destiny would not follow the disparaging path of others. He loved her and for centuries he had denied that fact but now he would find her and confess his undying love.

Callum moved about the room, gathering possessions ready for the journey ahead. Outside, the turmoil that consumed his fellow immortals spilled into the corridors close to his chambers. He could hear his fellow kin's cries, desperate for guidance but their demands fell upon deaf ears. For Callum, the councillor was no more. Gone was the storyteller, the guide, a shadow in the dark, a philosopher following the exploits of mortal man, the constant in this vampire universe.

In increasing urgency he searched, turning over tables and objects, blind to the damage that he was inflicting upon the shelter that he had called home for many centuries. A deep anger possessed him as his search continued with a fruitless endeavour. Then, just as his anger was about to consume his rational thoughts he observed the object of his quest and slowly moved to the corner of the dark room. He lifted the small box from its hiding place and dropped it onto the floor in the centre of the chamber. Falling to his knees beside it he allowed his emotions to recede and drift upon the calming seas of a now rational mind.

His fingers began to pull at the ancient lock that secured the wooden box closed. This offered little resistance and shattered at his strong touch, sending a thin powder of rust into the air. Lifting the lid, Callum smiled to see that its contents were still intact. Reaching in, he lifted the time worn papers up and out into the soft light of his room. The once white sheet was now brown and brittle with time, ever decaying as the seconds passed. He opened the object to its full extent and placed it upon the floor. His eyes searching across the lines and passageways drawn onto the map before him. A map that he himself had crafted centuries before, telling of the secrets of this dark underground world. He allowed his fingers to follow the lines of the chart, searching for an escape route or some assistance to his own self-perpetuation. Finding such a route he allowed the image to burn itself into his thoughts before gathering up the map and placing it along with the other objects that he wished to save from the abomination that was about to consume his kind, and placing them in his leather satchel.

Leaving his room, he searched for a suitable pathway to follow. Instead of moving towards the entrance of this underground world he ventured deeper into the caverns behind. Passing the library and the great hall, he refused to offer a backward glance to a world that he now rejected for the ignorance that it had perpetuated through its own self-gratification and denial. Moving down past the stables the stench of life assaulted his senses. These simple aromas, basic and primitive, brought back emotions long since forgotten, yet associated with his mortal years. He realised he had for too long sat upon the plateau of authority, forgetting the innocence of life. Binding himself to his own penance and self-importance. He turned over in his mind the questions put to him throughout the centuries and the answers that he had given. He wondered how could he, this tiny cog that moved through the machine of life, make a difference and change the destiny of his fellow immortal man when others, greater in mind and stature, could surpass his wisdom?

It was as he slowly stepped into the darker regions of his world that he realised how unjust his proclamation and counsel could have been for some would follow his words blindly, holding his ideologies higher than their own. They held an almost religious reverence for him, a reverence granted by the sheer fact that he was one of the founders of this dark dynasty. He knew in his soul that his counsel was a sound one, but the dark shadows of doubt still drifted across his heart.

All about him the shadows of the underworld gathered, concealing his pathway, restricting his escape. He had no light to guide him, only his preternatural senses. His eyes searched the path in front of him, urgently seeking a sign that would give him hope. Returning empty, he travelled deeper into this dark world, moving further down into the blackness that engulfed him, devouring his very presence.

 It was as he came to an intersection of corridors that doubt entered his thoughts and he once again took reference from the map; holding it close to his face he could see from the detailed drawing that he had found his destination. Placing the parchment back into his pack he turned and viewed the vast, dark avenues that stretched out before him, as if veins bringing life-blood to this cold and forgotten place. Vigilantly, he moved slowly forward, deeper into the bowels of this dark world.

Eventually he could go no further and found his path was blocked by a great stone wall. Once again pulling the papers from his pack he studied their writings, analysing their long forgotten meaning. He thought for a moment as recollection assaulted him, before stepping forward and reaching high into the stone of the wall, searching its contours with his eyes he allowed his fingers to find their quest. For there, just above his head, sat a thin ledge of granite. His fingers moved slowly along its surface, disturbing the dust and sending it drifting into the air above. Gently touching the smooth surface he allowed his senses to guide his way. Then, he found it. Just left of centre was his goal; a small, rounded button carved from the same stone as its host. For a moment he stood motionless, recalling his own words and his caution about the world of man. Then, almost involuntarily his finger exerted pressure upon the small, stone button, forcing it down until it became level with the ledge. For a few moments silence filled the chamber, then air, vacant and hollow began to escape from behind the wall, as ancient mechanisms made to move. This was soon to be joined by the low, gentle beating of an expectant heart. His mouth became dry as the deep sense of expectation filled him. From beyond the wall there came a hollow turning sound, which was accompanied by the grinding of other, lesser tuneful cries of ancient machinery. Callum's eyes searched his surrounding for the slightest recognition of change. Then, all at once the wall before him began to move, drawing itself away from him. The wall receded for a few inches then slid sideways along tracks, allowing Callum to step into this hidden realm of darkness, seeking governance from this ancient Massimo. Turning briefly, as if to bid farewell to his old life, he gave a sorrowful glance to that which he once knew and was about to leave behind. No sooner had he entered the chamber than the mechanisms controlling the wall moved eagerly into life and with a gracious ease returned it to its original stoical position, refusing him exit. He now knew that he must follow his emotions and cast aside his own council. Human emotions began to fill him with both dread and trepidation.

The darkness of the chamber intrigued him, for he knew this place. These were the halls of banishment, for it was here where those who had perpetrated crimes against the Tribe, or were no longer desired by the Tribe were sent, before they would make their way into the outside world and eventual ostracism from all immortal life.

It had fallen into decay centuries before and was now forgotten by even those upon the Grand Council. All save one. For Callum would wander these dark corridors without, deep in contemplation, alone, but content. Settling hypothetical arguments with his own thoughts with a deeper desire to understand himself and to respond and reduce the feeling, which burned within his ancient heart. Feeling for one so gentle, so pure. His love for Mica was fathomless, infinite. Beyond the boundaries of man. He could not bear to pass her without drinking in the sweet scent of her perfume and doing so, he would hide deep within his own lost world, for the fear of rejection tore at his heart; a rejection which he would need to confront if his desires became apparent. He would sit for hours, lost in the pleasures of his imagination, pleasures that would in time turn to torment and send him dangerously close to the edge of despair. His denial over the centuries had been controlled by inner yearning for knowledge and understanding of all that surrounded him, but these shackles of the soul were broken that night when his preternatural eyes fell upon the beauty that would become his secret beloved, forever locked within the passions of his soul. And now, centuries later that secret still remained buried even deeper in his fragile heart.

From above there came a gentle rush of winter wind that danced delicately upon his skin; with a deep sense of sorrow he realised then that he had achieved his quest. He could feel his heart pounding in his chest, sending great rhythms through his whole body. Calling for him to rest, for he was tired both mentally and physically. A dream world began to capture his thoughts, sending images of genocide and destruction across his mind.

"How could I allow them to die?" he thought. "They are my people, they trusted me."

No sooner had he pondered the question did the answer avail its self to him and he knew that this sacrifice to man's curiosity had to be offered. It was almost incomprehensible for most vampires to accept and understand death, for it was something foreign to them, something alien. A dark beast that would rise and feast upon mortality. It was the harbinger of mortals, a slayer of man. But he also knew that man needed to be appeased, his desire for understanding and his deep yearning to understand why. A sense of calm filled him as sleep captured his soul and comforting thoughts entered his mind, for surely if he were to survive, then so could other members of the tribe.

Two

The meeting had been called at an urgent pace and the group gathered consisted of three, all of whom sat in stony silence. Observers and those being observed. Eyes passed comments that lips needed not to utter and shadows hovered offering deep suspicion and mistrust. The sound of the wood burning in the open fire punctuated the time that built uncomfortably in the mounting silence. They had all received the phone call that contained a garbled urgent message, commanding their presence in Pyrenees, and now that they were there, a thousand questions demanded answers, yet, none were forthcoming.

A noise from behind closed doors drew their attention and they stood collectively in anticipation. A deep Italian voice mumbled from without just before the handle was turned and the door opened slightly. They all peered into the blackness of the hallway, but the darkness would not give up its secrets easily. The stranger stepped into the room and walked immediately over to the fireside, thus gaining a position of dominance over his fellow group members. He stood motionless for a moment observing their expressions, his own blank and unyielding.

"Thank you for being so vigilant and coming at such short notice, I myself would have liked to have given you more time to gather yourselves and to give you more information as to why you were all summoned with very little briefing or insight into the dilemma that has arisen. Now, you have all been chosen because you are experts in your field of work. First of all I will, by means of an introduction and beginning with myself, introduce everyone in this little group to each other and give a basic outline of their field of expertise and the input that they can and hopefully will contribute to this group. Please keep any questions that you feel you need to ask until the end, for time is not on our side and we must get underway as soon as possible.

"First of all, myself. My name is Antonio Johnson. As you will have guessed, I am part Italian, part English. My field of expertise is field combat and self-defence. I am what you could say, in a loose way, the leader or navigator of this group. It was I who, upon the instructions of a higher person, contacted you all individually. You will remember that you all put your names forward to become a member of this conservation, exploration group. I know that this may have been several years ago, but we do vet our candidates extremely well. Now, please sit and we will continue," he instructed.

Turning to the first member of this gathered group he smiled and offered an open hand as an expression of welcome. This is Dr Janet Childs, who, at present, is situated in London's Natural History Museum. Her field of work mainly consists of anthropology, archaeology and ethnology. She studied at the University of Newcastle and passed with a first in her degree. She has been working in London as a freelancer for several years before landing the position as head of archaeology at the Natural History Museum."

"Next!" he said, looking to the middle-aged gentleman that sat next to Janet, "This is Gustave Holt; he is a military man who retired several years ago because of an injury. But, I am assured that all is well now," Gustave offered him a reassuring smile. "Gustave was born in Germany some forty five years ago and joined the army when he was eighteen. There, he had an illustrious career and became honourably decorated with several prominent medals. He was injured while serving on border patrol in Bosnia in the early 1990's and so was pensioned out of the forces. His capacity within the group is to act as my second in command and to keep us all out of trouble," he smiled at Gustave in an attempt to lighten the darkening mood.

"Finally, there is Leon. Leon Jazdzewsiki who is, or was, a journalist before he became an anthropologist and an expert on ancient tribal ways and the structure of the world's earliest known civilisations. Leon originates from Poland and worked for a prestigious New York magazine for five years before continuing his studies and becoming a lecturer in ancient cultures."

Antonio took a deep breath before continuing.

"I have made this very simple, leaving out basic information. If you wish to discover more about each other, then feel free to pass on that information after this meeting. The information which you gave to the Bureau is confidential and shall go no further, even to those involved, unless they have specific clearance."

"The main question that burns in your mind is... Why? Why was I called away from what I was doing to race across the world to a meeting in a desolate hotel on the edge of an ice field, high in the Pyrenees Mountains? Well there is a reason and a very good one. I must say this to you now and give you the opportunity to leave without any incrimination, for there could be some considerable risk to your own safety. This is one of the primary reasons why we picked each one of you, for you do not have any dependants, no ties to a social or structured society. You are all rebels, individuals who would not be missed. So if any of you would like to leave then please do so now with the knowledge that your actions will be honoured and no retribution undertaken."

Observing the group, he found little intention of movement. Taking this as conformation of their willingness to stay and partake in this mission, he continued.

"Over a hundred years ago a series of letters were unearthed in differing localities all over France; letters that could bring down the ideologies of modern civilisation as we know it. It would bring a new view on the structure of the world and the chain of events that govern it. For man would no longer be that which he aspired to become. He would no longer be at the head of the food chain, no longer the master of his own destiny. Everything that was rejected by science centuries before would come tumbling forward into this and the next century bringing with it nothing but turmoil and destruction; the desolation of man's endeavours over this past millennium.

Since the beginning of recorded time man has crowned himself king of all that he surveys. Now, it would appear that in all this time man has been nothing but a puppet king, a false sovereign of his own destiny. It would seem that there is a creature that is stronger, deadlier and immeasurably superior to us, his weaker brethren. This creature is..." - he stopped to correct himself – "...this creature was man. When the earth was young they were already old; they were the elders of a waning civilisation, their time of prosperity had long since passed, but their existence still resounds within society's thorough-out this modern world. We know very little about them, except from the letter which came into our possession. They are dated around the spring to the summer of 1789 and all signed by the same person and all sent to the same recipient. The perpetrator, one Christian Pontmercy and the recipient, Mica Pontmercy. We understand that she is his younger, twin sister. You may ask what have the uttering and whims of a series of letters that are centuries old got to do with this modern time and why should they bring concern to us in this technological age? After all, their writer would have long since perished and his thoughts with him, and if they had not been so diligently preserved by the authorities, would their meaning hold any rational now, in this modern world?"

Pausing, Antonio took a deep breath realising the absurdity of his words. "What if I were to tell you that this is not so? What if I were to tell you that either the writer or its intended recipient may be alive today? The documentation highlights the existence of a tribe; a breed of supermen who still roam this fragile earth, never falling prey to disease or illness, never crippled by the ravages of time or their families torn asunder by the presence of death."

A sarcastic smile broke across Janet's lips. "What are they? Gods? Little green men? How can an individual survive hundreds of years without death? It's impossible. The longest living thing that has been recorded is a tree, and there have been seeds that are thousands of years old discovered in the tombs in Egypt that have been germinated and flourished, providing a basic crop in laboratory conditions. All of this is hard evidence, not fiction."

Antonio smiled and leaned against the fire surround, his arms folded.

"Scientists! You can never observe with your eyes, only your brains. You must have an explanation for everything, and if it cannot be explained then in your view it does not exist. Don't you comprehend what I am trying to explain? If these creatures have been around since time immemorial then how much control have they had in the development of mankind? How much have they manipulated us, moulded us into the creations that we had now become? This paranoid, self-opinionated, arrogant race that pollutes and devastates all that it comes into contact with! I know what I am saying may sound a little far-fetched but understand I have had several years to become accustomed to the evidence that has been set before me and I must ask you all to do the same, but in a brief period of time, we do not have the leisure of procrastination."

"Please let me explain. The letters and maps which we have at our disposal give a great insight into the workings and whereabouts of a race of people simply known as 'The Tribe'. They have lived something of a forgotten existence and have fallen into the realms of folklore and fantasy. They have perpetuated these delusions and in so doing have remained unobserved and distant from mortal history, but now their actions have called us all together. It was decided to send a reconnaissance agent to gather information and confirm if such a place exists. For several days the contact between the agent and the Bureau was regular and uneventful. All of these contacts were recorded, as a matter of protocol. The final recording I would like you to listen to; it will in some way give you an insight into the magnitude of the events into which you may find yourself placed."

Antonio turned to the table next to the fire; upon which sat a small recording device. He pushed the play button and immediately the air was filled with the sound of static.

"Lynn calling home, are you receiving over? There's something going on in the valley below, there are signs of movement ... I don't know how long I can stay in contact with you, over. The valley walls will block the signal soon ...set up satellite link ...will try to video over... It's mid-afternoon... I didn't think that they could come out in the sunlight...it looks like a child over..."

Then static.

"The signal became too weak to pick up at this point, but luckily one of our spy satellites was overhead and managed to pick up the signal from Lynn's video transmitter. I must warn you that the images that came back are not pleasant."

Antonio picked up the television remote control from the mantle shelf and pointed it to the machine in the corner of the room. Immediately it burst into life, revealing images of the valley vibrant colours across its screen. Those gathered in the room squinted and peered closer in the hope of gaining a better vantage point. The commentary continued, but this time it was accompanied by the images of the events which have transpired.

"I can see someone in the darkness of the cave. I'm using the zoom to see if it can make out any features." The camera lens zoomed in and out in a rather unprofessional manor. The images were somewhat disorientated, yet understandable. They could see the distant shape of a child stumbling closer to the entrance of the cave, its demeanour resembled something human, yet somehow different. "I don't know if you're getting this, but it's a child; I can see a child. It looks to be only early teens, about twelve. I don't know..."

The images moved in and out of focus.

"I can't get any closer or they might see me." The vision became a little darker. "I'm in a little cavern just at the base of the valley floor, directly opposite of the cave's entrance. We should be able to see what's going on... I can see the child clearer now he's moving to the cave entrance. He's moving into the sunlight. I can see him really clearly..."

The images began to change as the child began to contort and twist as pain ravaged its body and blistered its flesh. Flames burst from within, devouring his innocent immortal frame.

."..My God! Oh...shit..." The camera movements began to shudder and shake as they turned away from the valley and into the small cave in which Lynn hid.

"I'm sorry.... I can't film anymore." The camera was then lifted and focused upon a dark figure at the back of the cave.

"Shit, there's something in here with me and it's big..."

The shadows on the screen moved closer until they engulfed everything within the view of the camera's lens. A high shrill scream pierced the air as the shadows fell upon their victim. Antonio froze the picture as a hideous vampiric face passed across the screen.

"This, ladies and gentlemen is your superman, the race of super-humans that has lived since time has begun."

Leon sat back in his chair: "What the hell is it?"

Silence filled the room, as the group could not take their attentions from the face of terror that looked back at them from the screen.

"In ancient times they were called the enlightened ones, the Wamphyri. Later they were known as the Nosferatu, Chupacabras or Vrukalakos, and now they are called the un-dead. Vampires. Before you laugh or ridicule all that I have said, look at the evidence that your scientific mind had demanded. Use all of your senses, you have all witnessed the images that had moved across this screen. Read the letters sent by a tormented immortal to his sister," he lifted a folder from the table and cast onto the floor in full view of the group. "There! If you can find a better explanation then I will be glad to listen."

****

Almost an hour had passed since Antonio had given his ultimatum. The dossiers had been read and re-read over and over again to see if their contents could offer another, less sensational explanation to the events which had transpired over the days since the disappearance of the Bureau's top field agent. The video had given little or no information other than that which could be perceived by human eye, it held no secrets, no hidden messages or agenda. It simply contained the deaths of two innocent individuals, both in search of that something which would fulfil their lives.

Leon placed the folder on the floor in front of him and sat back in his seat. "Alright! Just say we believe this story, what happens next?" he enquired of Antonio.

"Well, whatever happens next will happen with or without your participation. A truck will be leaving from outside this hotel at 8:30am. That's just over an hour from now. It will be taking me and whoever else cares to join me, as far into the Pyrenees Mountains as possible. From there we will continue the rest of the journey upon foot until we reach the valley which is described in those letters and Lynn's report. We are there only as observers, that is all. To accumulate and co-ordinate as much information as is possible. So! If you're all in, then great; if not, then I am sorry, but you must stay here until this mission is over. We cannot have any of these facts falling into the wrong hands."

Gustave quickly stood up.

"Great! We either do as you say or we are prisoners."

"No you are not prisoners; you are employees of the Bureau, and while you are here you are under both their and my jurisdiction."

Gustave slowly sat back onto the seat.

Janet closed her folder and took off her reading glasses.

"Well, I'm in. I'd rather chase phantoms across the hills that be cooped up in this hellhole. After all, it's a chance to see the scenery."

Antonio smiled and looked for compliance from the others.

Leon pulled his camera from his pocket.

"I'm in if I can take the holiday photos."

Antonio laughed.

"Now that I'm counting on," he allowed a few seconds of silence to pass "I will take this as confirmation that you are all in."

Everyone nodded in unison.

"Let's get going."

Gustave and Leon stood and quickly made their way out of the room leaving Antonio and Janet alone.

Janet sat further back into the chair, lowering her eyes as she stared into the fire.

"Why didn't you call me? Just because our relationship was over didn't mean that our friendship had to be. I valued you. I loved you once; couldn't live with you, but I loved you."

"Loved me!" he said, in surprise.

"You still love me then," she said, "Does the Bureau know?"

"Yes, I informed them but I told them that it had been over for years. I had to tell them something; after all it was I who asked for you specifically for this assignment. You're the best in your field and someone that I can trust. And were going to need trust if this thing turns out to as big as the Bureau imagines."

Janet looked at Antonio with concern.

"Thank you for asking me personally but what do you mean, 'trust'?"

"Everything will become apparent in time," Antonio said.

"And is everything between us over?"

"As far as the Bureau is concerned, yes."

"And as far as Antonio is concerned?" she seductively enquired.

"As far as Antonio is concerned...We have a truck to catch."

He held out his hand to offer Janet assistance to her feet. Taking his hand gingerly, she stood. Their eyes searched one another for signs of passion. Antonio moved closer, his lips brushing her face gently. Janet stepped back.

"What will the Bureau say?" she said, sarcastically before leaving the room.

Three

As the truck struggled its uneasy way along the steep mountain paths, ominous rocks reached forward in a sinister, malevolent manor. The driver, who was supplied by the Bureau but was not one of the team, seemed familiar with the twisting, undulating pathways. Their journey was long and arduous, taking them deep into the uninhabited regions of the mountains. As they travelled a thin mist descended, bringing an almost romantic presence to that winter's day. The sun gave deceiving warmth to the surroundings. Its bright winter shine illuminated the mountains all about, washing them in a golden glow.

Antonio looked at his watch. 12:30pm. He was about to ask the driver when they would reach their destination when the truck came to an abrupt halt.

"I can't take you any further," the driver instructed. "This path turns at the top of this hill and continues, but eventually returns us to the base of the mountain. I'm afraid you'll have to continue the rest of your journey on foot."

"Can you return for us before nightfall?" Antonio enquired of the driver. "I don't want to be stuck on this mountain in the dark."

The driver nodded.

"Alright, everyone out," Antonio called as he alighted from the truck.

Leon began to take the boxes from the back of the vehicle, stacking them on the ground.

Gustave slowly walked to Antonio.

"Why can't the driver stay?"

"The Bureau wants as few people to know about this expedition as possible. The driver thinks that we are collecting soil samples. He's a local, employed by the Bureau, but a local nonetheless. If he goes down the mountain screaming 'vampires' we'll have a thousand villagers following us with burning torches and handfuls of garlic. Not a pleasant sight. It looked preposterous in the old movies, just think how ridiculous it would look in real life?"

Gustave smiled. "I don't know what looks more ridiculous; the image that you've just conjured in my mind or the thought of four people, all probably with an I.Q. over 160 each, running about on the side of a mountain hunting vampires."

Antonio smiled and nodded his head slowly in agreement.

They watched as the truck pulled away and disappeared into the light mist.

"Great way to spend your winter holidays," Janet said, pulling the zipper up tightly on her ski jacket, her breath escaping in clouds of moisture that danced in the chilly afternoon air. Picking up one of the boxes she asked, "What's in these things anyway?"

"All will be revealed in time my dear," Antonio said in a mocking sinister voice.

"I suppose it is beautiful," she said, looking at the great mountains that were bathed in the soft light of the afternoon sun. This idyllic scene offered a false serenity and a gentle haven for the naive soul.

"Very romantic. Come on; let's set the pace. Just like the old days," Antonio said with something of a sexual connotation to his voice. Pulling a laminated map from his pocket he pointed in the direction they should follow. Without hesitation or care for his fellow travellers he walked off the trail and up onto the forgotten pathways that criss-crossed the mountains.

Following the guidance of the ancient map he quickly manoeuvred his way through the dangerously loose scree and higher onto the more stable part of the pathways. Passing trees and waterways he couldn't help but feel that he was one of the first living souls to witness this beauty for centuries. The sheer size of this forgotten terrain filled him with an awe that brought home the reality that he was truly emotionally alone and only a minimal part of this complex existence that was the universe. He thought of those creatures, which he hunted, perpetual and immortal. How would it feel to never have an end to your existence? A life that could transcend those fears that haunts the mortal soul? He deliberately moved further from the main body of the group to allow his thoughts to capture his deep imagination. To the others it looked as if he were making sure that their pathway was safe but this was more of a selfish action. He wanted to be alone in this wilderness and savour its unhindered passions.

It was only when he reached the first ridge did the spell that he was casting over his imagination break and he was once again forced to focus upon reality. He had not realised the distance which he had travelled until he looked back at his companions. Lowering the box he was carrying to the ground he gathered his thoughts and looked once again at the map. From the directions written he could see that their quest was less than thirty minutes away. How close, yet how distant he felt; it was as if the culmination and preparation of many years work were about to come into fruition and the slightest mistake could counterbalance the odds against their favour. His heart hung heavy, for he knew the full extent of his actions and the outcome which they would perpetuate.

He could hear the noise of the group as it drew nearer, their distant voices shattering the natural silence of the mountains. Taking a deep breath he turned and offered them a smile for their endeavours in keeping up with his hurried pace. He couldn't help but feel that they were somehow lost in the turmoil of their actions, set adrift upon the sea of their desires. The inner burning to succeed and to achieve recognition for that success, blinding them all against the true reality into which they would soon find themselves cast. He tried to shake these dark thoughts but he realised that a price would be set upon each of them, a price that may be too much for each individual to pay.

"The valley is only about thirty minutes away. If we follow this ridge it will take us around the side of the mountain and hopefully to the pathway, which will lead to our quest. Does anyone need to rest?" He enquired, not caring for the answer. There was no reply so he lifted his box and continued along the ridge, moving slowly away from his companions in the hope of recapturing the soulful memories that had visited him for the briefest of moments.

The afternoon was quickly falling by and the sun gathering speed, reaching high into the sky, its gentle rays warming the traveller's skin, making their troubled journey a little more pleasant. Janet moved past the group and to Antonio's side.

"Penny for them," she said, knowing that he was deep in contemplation.

"You could always read me," he replied.

"Like a book, my friend."

"What am I thinking now?" he said, staring at her with a playful look in his eye.

She thought for a moment before commenting.

"That we should all piss off and leave you alone on your mountain to follow your desires and to be at one with everything that surrounds you. Am I close?"

Antonio smiled.

"No you're not close...That's exactly what I was thinking. How perfect everything is, how balanced. Are we doing the right thing coming here?"

"Indecision, coming from you of all people. I've told you before, I know you better than I know myself. Why, what's wrong? What haven't you told us?" She returned his smile. A smile that lasted briefly. "Will you answer me honestly if I ask you a salient question?"

He nodded.

"Since I agreed to come onto this expedition I will follow it through, against my better judgement. But there is something that I must know. If we do find that this forgotten race of immortals exists here in this beautiful God-forsaken place, then what do we do with them? Are we only here to observe, take notes, and make contact? What?" Her eyes narrowed. "Or is there something a little more sinister about to happen to our new-found kin, something that you haven't yet informed us about? Something that you are little ashamed of maybe?"

Antonio stopped and bit his bottom lip. He tried to look her directly in the eyes, but a dark cloud of deception came over him.

Janet's expression turned to that of shock and dismay.

"Genocide! You're going to kill them, aren't you? Because you don't understand them, because there different from us? You feel the need to destroy them. Believe me I am in no way condoning their existence but this is information that I think we should have all been privy prior to us making our initial decision to undertake this quest. Why didn't you tell us? Was it because you feared that we would abandon your efforts and leave you to fight your battle alone? The brawn without the brains. You haven't changed. In all the years that I've known you, you've always done exactly what you thought was right for everyone else, without taking into consideration any of their thoughts. You disgust me. Now I truly understand the reason why I left you all those years ago. I should have walked out much sooner."

He offered her a coy smile. "Don't delude yourself, you weren't that good," she said, before moving to walk away. Antonio reached out and held her arm.

"Let go," she insisted.

"Listen," he urged.

"Oh yes, I'll listen but will you listen to those creatures which you are about to destroy. Tell me, is it your own inadequacies that you fear or is it because these immortals have something that you can't have? Don't tell me that you are following orders, I won't buy that bullshit. These creatures are different from us, I agree, but they were once human. Something that I can't say about you," she hissed bitterly between her teeth, her words exploding with magnitude within his tortured thoughts.

"I have my orders from the Bureau," he insisted.

"It's alright, I understand; follow your orders. After all that's what the S.S. generals said after the Second World War. The concentration camps were full of soldiers that used that excuse. The only pity is that no one will call you to account for the crimes which you are about to perpetrate. I only hope that the heavens open and strike me dead for helping you. As for the Bureau, after this little escapade, they can take their investigations and stick them where the sun doesn't shine. As of now, I quit," her words were bitter and sharp.

Antonio tried to reason with her but Janet turned and made her way back to the group, which was now some distance behind.

His mind was in turmoil, Janet's words burned deeply into the fabric of his inner consciousness, creating a tempest that raged within. His military training forced him forward, but his human, fragile self, pleaded for him to listen to the reason of his own unregulated mind.

In a daze, he wandered slowly along the pathway in the hope that Janet would catch him up and in some way he could explain his forthcoming actions, for he knew that she could only see things from a black and white perspective. Yet he somehow hoped that she would understand him, this man that followed orders with a loyalty seen in only a few. Self-doubt haunted him. Was he nothing more than a machine, hiding behind excuses? Or was he a freethinking individual? He knew that in some strange perverse way he was both- they were one and the same. One a reflection of the other. As conformity is to rebellion. Rebellion is what is expected of those who will not conform, so therefore, it becomes conformity. It is the following of an expected path. To truly rebel, one must become an individual and swim against the tide of life, not just the tide of humanity.

Four

The mid-afternoon sun hung low in a watery sky, its gentle rays touching the soft grass of the valley's floor. The expeditionary group stood upon the ridge that overlooked this natural splendour as all about the mountains huddled together in a dark confederacy as if to keep its secret and refrain from betraying the trust of its immortal inhabitants who had lived under its protection for centuries. Dark rain clouds passed the sun, provoking fate, calling for destiny to be fulfilled. Antonio stood with a heavy heart, his eyes cast down, unwilling to acknowledge the beauty that presented its self to his senses.

Leon mumbled, "Well, what now? Do we just stand here admiring the view or do we get into some form of action? It's just that its getting dark and I don't want to be around when those things wake up."

"Yes, you're right," Antonio said. "Open the boxes."

From inside each box was drawn several mirrors. Each one a metre across and fitted with a set of connecting pins so that one mirror could be mounted and supported by the other. Fitting them together, Gustave placed the mirror upright and fitted a support to the back, so that it stood without assistance.

"Mirrors! Great. We can do our hair as the vampires pull out our hearts." Leon's sarcastic tone was beginning to unnerve Antonio.

"When everything is set up you'll find out what they are for."

Janet walked past him and glowered. "I think that I've figured that one out already." as she followed the path that led to the valley floor. "I'll make base camp, Gustave. You're with me."

Antonio watched as the pair stepped onto the lush carpet of grass that covered the valley below. Moving slowly they made their way almost up to the caves' entrance before setting down their bags and building a small fire to mark the camp's position. Returning his attentions to the mirror, Antonio lined up the panel so that its reflection would become apparent in less than thirty minutes.

"Alright Leon," he said to his companion. "Let's get ourselves down to the welcoming committee below."

Leon's attentions, however, were somewhat distracted. He was observing the movements that issued from just inside the shadows of the cave's entrance.

"There's something in there, something moving."

"What? Give me the glasses," Antonio instructed.

Antonio took the binoculars and put them to his eyes. Studying for a moment he lowered them and gave them back to Leon.

"Vampire cows. That's a new one on me."

Leon looked through the binoculars; lowering a moment later he smiled more in embarrassment than relief.

"Next you'll be telling me to pull the udder one," Antonio said laughing. "Come on let's join the others."

Several minutes later the group was gathered just outside the cave's entrance and now that they were so close in proximity to this gateway to the underworld they marvelled at its dimensions. From the ridge it looked just like a simple cave's entrance but now, close up, it resembled the portal to another world. A dimension of the unknown. All about the lip of the cave were gentle carvings etching in the harsh stone of the mountain. Carvings that denoted a gentle, harmonious people. A tribe at one with nature.

"Now what?" Gustave enquired.

"Well, we have several more mirrors to put into their positions. One here..," he said pointing to the valley floor at their feet. "...and another two in there." This time he pointed directly into the mouth of the cave.

Leon laughed out loud in a sarcastic way.

"You're expecting one of us to risk our lives and walk into the mouth of the lion. Yeah, man. Sorry! What planet did you say that you were from? You've filled our heads with tales of demons and vampires, killers of the third degree and you expect one of us to calmly pick up a mirror and waltz in there without a care in the world. Fine, when hell freezes over. I'm not a coward but... after you my friend."

"I'll do it," Gustave said in a shallow voice.

"What! Are you all there?" Leon replied.

"I came from the mountains in Germany and moved to Berlin when I was ten. Stories of the un-dead were commonplace. My grandmother would recount tales of the old days to me on winter nights in front of a blazing log fire. My brothers and sisters would be scared out of their wits; they would hide behind the sofa. If we hadn't been so scared we would have seen the funny side of it. And what better way to exorcise those ghosts from your childhood than by confronting them head on? Also, if it's my time to go, then it's my time to go."

"You wouldn't take my camera in and take some photos?" Leon enquired.

Gustave shook his head.

"Thought not. Well, I suppose that there's only one thing left to do. Well, Granddad, I'm coming with you, I do hope that your Grandma was very wrong."

Gustave smiled. "So do I!"

Janet shook her head.

"My, has hell frozen over all ready."

"If you think that I'm losing face to an old man," - he turned to Gustave – "no offence. Then you've got another thing coming. Anyway I want to be the first to get one of those suckers on film. "He..." - Leon pointed to Gustave – "...would have left the lens cap on."

"Before you rush off, I've a present for the both of you." Reaching into one of the boxes Antonio brought out four walkie-talkies and handed one to each member of the group. "Now we can keep tabs on each other. If you encounter anything out of the ordinary let us know."

"Are you kidding? You'll hear my screams all the way back to the village," Leon said, placing the walkie-talkie into his pocket.

Gustave smiled and lifted another of the mirrors from its box.

"Are you going to give me some assistance young man or are we going to spout hot air all day?"

Lifting a set of connected mirrors, Leon and Gustave made their way tentatively towards the cave's entrance. Moving forward, each step seemed harder than the last, as images of horror danced across their imagination. When they reached the gaping entrance they paused, passing concerned glances to one another.

"Age before beauty," Leon said.

"You fail on both accounts, young man," Gustave replied.

Inside the cave, a cool breeze issued from deep below the surface, bringing a comfort to their dark errand. Waiting for a moment for their eyes to become accustomed to the darkness, they traced the direction in which the pathways led, deep into the unholy blackness. Turning to the outside world, Leon shouted.

"Where do you want these things put?" he said, lifting the mirror.

"Use the walkie-talkie," Antonio replied.

From his pocket Gustave pulled out his machine and lifted its aerial. Pushing in the transmit button he spoke quietly into the voice piece.

"Are you receiving me? Over..."

Static filled the cave, soon to be followed by a reply.

"There's a little fluctuation in the signal but that's because it's bouncing of the cave walls...other than that you're loud and clear, over..."

"Where do you want the mirrors, over?"

"One at either end of the passageways...flat against the wall so that whatever is reflected will pass from the cave's entrance and down into the passageway, over..."

Gustave looked to Leon and shrugged.

"Got that?"

Leon nodded his acknowledgement before walking into the shadows, and after several tormenting minutes he returned and Gustave smiled nervously before disappearing into the shadows to complete his own fateful task. Leon's thoughts gathered together in their dark parliament and as the minutes passed he became more and more agitated, imagining abominations beyond comprehension his mind running unnaturally rampant. Retrieving the walkie-talkie from his pocket, he pulled up the aerial and pressed the transmit button.

"Gustave are you there? Over..," he whispered. He was met with a sharp bout of static.

"Gustave are you there? Over..," he repeated. He could feel his pulse begin to race as he stared into the blackness. Then his machine burst into life.

"Of course I'm here, where the bloody hell do you think I'll be?"

Leon gave a visible sigh of relief. Composing himself he answered Gustave in an arrogant tone.

"I didn't know what you were scared of Gustave; it's a walk in the park... easy; we should do this more often... nothing to it..."

From in front of him he could make out the distinctive figure of his companion as he approached. Gustave moved quickly through the shadows of the underworld and he was soon by Leon's side, smiling.

"What's so funny?" Leon enquired.

"We are. Coming all this way into the unknown and neither of us brought a torch. Ironic isn't it? We're so wrapped up in what we've been told that we couldn't remember the most basic of things." Leon laughed and put his arm about Gustave's shoulders as they walked towards the light of the outside world. A bond was growing between the two men.

A dark shadow passed overhead, its bulk foreboding and menacing, neither noticing the towering figure that rose from the shadows behind and unnaturally moved in their direction, gathering momentum. Gustave laughed as he patted his companion's back.

"I would say, a good job well done, wouldn't you my friend?" he enquired.

From behind, an immortal's bony hand reached forward and gripped the soft tissue of Leon's throat, lifting him high off the ground. His eyes began to bulge in fear, his body began to convulse and contort. Terror enveloped him as his fingers, clenching, closed in horror. The flash of his camera fired over and over again, sending artificial light onto their aggressor's face. Gustave fell backwards to the ground in revulsion as the vampire hissed at him, revealing its fangs. Pulling Leon closer the creature held him high as if a prize to his victory, a triumph over the fragility of mortality. Slowly he parted his lips, bearing his sharp hungry teeth, biting deeply into the fleshy neck of his victim, he began to tear and gorge himself upon great mouthfuls of tissue which he irreverently spat onto the floor of the cave before lifting his victim's twitching body high and drinking in the warm fluid that issued from the vast wound.

Falling against the cave's wall, Gustave gagged in terror, the air a prisoner in his throat. Closing his eyes he allowed his head to fall back in an attempt to free his breathing. Opening them, he turned his gaze upwards and found that he was staring into the full face of death. For there, illuminated by the flashlight of Leon's camera, were those members of the tribe that had refused to listen to the warnings of their dream-seer and had elected to stay behind and face their fate. He realised that their eyes had followed his every movement from their vantage point high above the cave's floor and a deep terror-filled scream issued from within, escaping, piercing the air, alerting the world to his dark dilemma.

From his natural ledge above the cave's floor a warrior vampire descended, landing silently only centimetres away. Pausing for a moment, he studied the face of his prey, searching his eye for signs of hate but only finding terror. Reaching out, he gripped Gustave on either side of his head and lifted him harshly upward, his legs kicked violently in the air in the hope of finding a foothold to save him from his torment. The creature lifted Gustave higher into the shadows, holding him firmly, he held him up

LEGACY OF THE VAMPIRE

until their faces were level; blue, immortal eyes looked into those of a mortal, fear-filled and trembling. Seductively, his lips slowly parted revealing his animal instincts, toying with his prey he allowed his tongue to pass over his sharp canines several times. Drawing back his head the vampire hissed and lunged forward, burying his teeth deep into the flesh of his helpless victim.

From the walkie-talkie a voice called.

"Come in Gustave, Leon. Come in. Are you receiving me?"

The airway fell into silence.

Realisation assaulted Antonio's senses. "Quickly!" he screamed at Janet, "Turn the mirror! Turn the mirror!" He rushed urgently to her side "Push it so that it reflects the sunlight into the cave. You have to position it so that it sends a beam off the two mirrors at the back; it's the only way to save them."

Gripping the mirror Janet pushed it slowly until the reflection from its companion upon the ridge touched its own. She could feel the heat of the Sun's searing rays as they raged from reflective surface to reflective surface and eventually into the mouth of the cave. Light danced all about with a brilliance that forced her to cover her eyes, as its presence was almost too strong for her to endure.

"Hold it there! Hold it there!" Antonio screamed as he rushed head long into the mouth of the cave.

Inside, one of the creatures sniffed attentively at the afternoon air, moving slowly towards the caves entrance he observed the mortal that raced to his destiny. High in the mountains behind a shimmer of light gave credence to his down fall, but an understanding of its origins was too distant for his immortal mind to comprehend. It was only as the searing Sun's rays raged ferociously, burning his immortal flesh did the full comprehension of this mortal weapon fill him. He could feel his skin begin to tear and blister as the captured rays of the sun danced and devoured everything onto which it came into contact. It was as if his blood itself were beginning to boil, igniting his soul, touching his very essence. Flames burst from his chest, sending plumes of dense smoke rising to the roof of the cave. Running blindly, the flaming creature stumbled out into the open. Tormented, he fell to the valley floor, his screams of pain filled the valley as he twisted and turned in agony upon the ground, his melting eyes looked to Janet as a saviour as the full impact of the naked Sun ignited him. In an instant only ash existed where the knowledge of centuries had once lay; his existence quenched in the passing of a moment.

Antonio could only watch in horror as the creatures charged past him and out in to the waking world. Quickly he lifted his walkie-talkie and called into it.

"Janet...run for cover..."

Static answered his cries. He could say little else, for all about the stirrings of immortal life drew his attention. Resting hard against the cave wall he allowed himself the look upwards, knowing full well the sight that would greet him. A hundred enraged immortals returned his attentions, their hungry eyes eager to devour his soft, mortal flesh.

Pressing the button on his walkie-talkie Antonio screamed.

"Janet. Turn the mirror again, turn it again."

The light from the mirrors reflected a second time but this time the reflections did not dull its powers. Great ribbons of light raged along the dark passageways, incinerating all immortal flesh which it had the unhappy consequence to come into contact with. Children screamed, their cries rising high above the smoke that drifted to the ceiling. Great trails of black, acrid soot danced in the air as immortal after immortal was reduced to dust. Holding back his horror Antonio observed as adults twisted and turned upon the floor at his feet in their vain attempts to quench the flames which devoured their children. Not caring for the fate that had befallen themselves, they pleaded with the heavens to rescue their infants, forcing them into the shadows in a vain attempt to protect them against the cleansing light. The searing heat rose within the cave as the light danced by, a third time, forcing Antonio to protect his eyes. He was blind within the chaos; all about he could sense those who had fallen close to him. He could almost taste their pain as he stumbled without direction through this underworld; deeper and deeper he wandered, until he reached the bowels of these forgotten chambers.

His walkie-talkie burst into life.

"Antonio can you hear me? Over." her signal was weak and erratic.

"Yes...keep your distance. Over" he warned.

"Do you still want me to hold the mirror? Over" she pleaded.

"Only a minute more. Out..," he said.

As the smoke slowly lifted, Antonio could see the line of the corridor in which he found himself. The carvings on the walls and floor which resembled those found in the ancient mid-European lands seemed to reach out and touch him. The torch-holders that ran periodically along the walls, their light somehow muted and sad, seemed to invite him to follow their pathway. The gentle paintings of those precious to the Tribe were scattered here and there. Their eyes seemed to observe and follow his every movement. Everything had a somewhat primitive dignity about it. Then, all at once the false sunlight ceased, causing his surrounding to be plunged into a painful darkness.

After a long moment, Antonio's eyes slowly became accustomed to the subdued subterranean light that drifted from the candles. Tentatively he made his way deeper into the domain of the Tribe. Turning corner after corner he found himself confronted by small mounds of dust, a chilling reminder to the ancient hearts that once commanded respect from all who would enter their world.

He soon found himself at the culmination of his journey as he stepped into the main chamber of this dark civilisation, its high ceilings filling him with a wonder never before experienced by the superficial souls of mortals. Great pillars, thicker than a tree's trunk, supported this marvel to architecture. Its design could have been presented to him by the gods themselves, for perfection touched him. Great sheets of stone, polished over the centuries now resembled black marble, its sheen glistening as if water. Intricate carvings surrounded the pillars and reached to the heavens, and where pillar and ceiling touched, great issues of black rock hung as if fruit, waiting to be devoured by the gods.

Allowing his eyes to grow accustomed to the sheer darkness he searched the expanse of the hall before him, his eyes sweeping nervously across the dark crevices of the chamber. It was at this moment that a soft moan gripped his senses, filling him with a deep cold fear. Slowly, Antonio turned until he could see the faint outline of a broken discarded figure lying in the shadows several feet from him. Moving tentatively closer, he was horrified to discover that this dying fractured mortal was none other, than his companion on this perilous journey.

"Gustave," he called as he lowered himself and supported his comrade's head.

"Can you hear me?"

Looking closer, Antonio realised that because of the extent of Gustave's injuries, death was only a moment away. His eyes flickered open and a slight colour returned to his cheeks.

"Ah...my friend...did we get them?"

"Yes all of them," he replied.

"Good..." A harsh pain shot through him, causing his body to spasm.

Antonio gripped tightly onto his hand in a vain attempt to comfort Gustave.

"Leon's dead...The bastards killed him. He was only a child..."

Antonio nodded in recognition of Gustave's words. Pulling his walkie-talkie from his pocket he called Janet.

"Come in Janet...are you there? Over."

Almost immediately his answer came.

"Yes, is everything all right? Over."

"Gustave's in a bad way. Over."

"I understand. Out."

Antonio tried to raise a signal but only static met his endeavours.

Several minutes passed before they could hear movement in the passageway. After a moment Janet stepped from the shadows carrying a basic medical kit under her arm and a semi-automatic weapon in her hand.

"Taking no chances?"

Antonio enquired with a slight air or relief as he took the medical kit from her.

"Well, who knows what's down here. After seeing that thing come racing out of the cave I'm preparing myself for anything."

"I taught you well."

Taking a large piece of soft cotton from the kit he placed it upon the largest of the wounds in a pitiful attempt to stem the river of blood that was issuing from this open flesh.

"We need something a little stronger."

Looking down at Gustave he could see that he had briefly lost consciousness. "Well at least he's out of the thick of things. If I can get the morphine from the main medical pack we can ease a little of his suffering," he looked up at Janet. "Do you think that you could stay here and take care of our patient? After all I would be able to get to the camp and back quicker."

"I don't know about that, it depends upon what's chasing me," Janet said, in a vain attempt to lighten the mood.

"Yes you're right. The three of us will stay. Gustave, myself and my friend." This last acknowledgement was directed at the gun, which she held firmly in her left hand.

Taking over the duties performed by Antonio she watched as he disappeared into the darkness, leaving her alone in this inhospitable, immortal world. The natural noises of the world now seemed alien and sinister, filling her with a deep trepidation as the events of nature moved on regardless of the events which it had just witnessed. The sound of water dripping in the distance almost came as a melody to her ears, hypnotising her to its beat, its constant, regular pattern. Time appeared to be lost here, perpetually. Moments could last for hours. Her mind began to wander as the shadows began to culminate.

"Get a grip on yourself...it's all over. It's finished. Our work is done, so we can..."

She broke off in mid-sentence for an unnatural sound came to her attention, a sound associated with man. The almost silent touch of bare flesh upon stone reached her senses, alerting her to this paramount danger. Her eyes searched frantically about the room, piercing the dark shadow and natural alcoves. Her heart began to beat with a gathering pace in her chest, its pulsating presence echoed in her ears. A thin line of sweat broke out across her forehead as a deep fear filled her.

Pulling the Walkie-talkie from her pocket she pushed frantically at the transmit button.

"..Antonio! Antonio! ...Are you there? Now would be a good time to get back here...Antonio!"

Static filled the chamber.

"Damn rocks, stopping the signal...either that or the battery's going flat," Janet cursed, throwing the walkie-talkie to the floor.

Turning her attention to Gustave she pushed the blood-soaked cotton harder onto his wound, this caused him to moan loudly in his unconscious state.

"Hang in there...Antonio's on his way with the morphine. At this rate I'll be fighting you for it," she said, under her breath.

All about her the light from the candles danced as a shadow drifted past. Seeing a reflection across the back wall Janet stood and turned to greet her returning companion.

"Thank God you hurried, I was..."

Her words died in her mouth as she found herself confronted by a vampiric warrior, his blood-stained eyes glaring at her with contempt and hatred. Dropping the gun, her hand went to her mouth to restrain the scream that was building up within. She began to shake uncontrollably as fear filled her every fibre. The creature moved forward until its presence towered over her, blocking out all of the dark light from above. She could almost see the pain exude from his face through the blistered and broken flesh, its raw lines twisted and deep. Savouring his moment the creature lifted his arm and brought it crashing down across her chest, sending her spiralling uncontrollably across the floor of the chamber. The pain of the conflict tore its way through her body, sending waves of pain through every muscle and sinew. Breathless, she lay crippled upon the floor as the vampire advanced, his powerful shadow falling across fragile frame her. Pushing herself up on her elbows, Janet tried to give herself a little leverage so that in some way she could protect herself against this fate that was about to befall her. In her attempts to sit, her whole body screamed in agony, sending intense sharp spasms throughout her whole form, causing her to collapse onto her side and roll over, she found herself face down upon the cold stone floor, blind to her enemy. Closing her eyes she resigned herself to her dark destiny.

His touch surprised her as he lifted her from the floor and guided her to her feet. Opening her eyes she was taken aback as to how human he was, how normal. Her pain began to subside and her strength returned.

"Why didn't you kill me?" she asked.

"Who said that I would not?" his voice was deep and horse.

"Then why have you helped me?" she enquired

"I have not; I would like you to bear witness to that which you have destroyed before it destroys you. I am afraid that I am out of pity, as were you when I came to the reservation of your punishment for our mere existence. Do not delude yourself, you will die."

Janet began to breathe heavier, not in pain but in anger. Anger for being pardoned from the jaws of death only to be returned at the whim of another.

"Yeah? Well not without a fight."

The creature smiled.

"You have spirit. I applaud you. We are evenly matched then, I, with my wounds and you with your valour."

Without taking her eyes from the creature, Janet stepped back closer to the far side of the chamber. Behind her rested the chairs of office that were once held in such reverence by this tribal community, but had now became mere objects of interest, their reason and device lost, antiquities from a forgotten age.

"Trying to hide, little one?" The vampire teased. "My eyes can see into the darkest of corners. There is nowhere to run, nowhere to hide."

Janet stepped back over the broken chairs of office, their polished broken segments difficult to manoeuvre and Janet lost her footing and found herself unbalanced once again and she fell to the floor.

"You make it all too easy," he mocked, as he watched her feeble attempt to regain her composure. "Taste your receipts my dear and savour them well, the score will soon be settled. Prepare to embrace thy maker." With that the creature sprang forward, sending his great bulk through the air and onto her. The instant that their bodies made contact his screams filled the chamber, echoing off the cold walls. Janet could feel the creature's heavy form crushing her as the sound of his laboured breath almost over cast that of her own urgent heart. He tried to rise, his actions stilted, weakened by his immortal exertions. Pulling himself to his feet he looked down upon the injury inflicted by an adversary so fragile. There, from his chest, protruded a long thin sharp piece of wood, a bitter remnant from the broken council chair.

Janet focused her eyes upon her attacker, his wounds bringing to her a self-indulgent, dark delight. "Make it easy do I?" Her words were full of anger.

The vampire fell back onto the floor, pain torturing his soul; a bitter sweetness filled his mouth as thin stream of blood flowing from his lips. He could feel his life essence leaving him, as his immortal soul battled against the inevitable. He could sense himself weakening and prepared himself for his journey into the next realm.

"I salute you," he said, as his life force escaped from its immortal prison. "Underestimation was my only weakness," he whispered.

She watched as a serenity washed across the features of this dying creature as its final breath escaped, leaving only the bitter remains of what once was. The sound of her own life filled the chamber, rising softly to the upper ceiling before gently cascading down to greet her own senses; she began to cry as the reality of her situation filled her urgent soul. She cursed out loud, not for any given reason other than to hear her own voice, alive and well. She closed her eyes and allowed the silence to soothe her dark anguish.

The sound of another living soul drifted high into the air, its presence weak and ailing and her thoughts returned to Gustave, slain and dying. Hurrying to his side she discovered that he was still of this world. Retrieving her gun, she held it firmly in her hand.

"Hurry up Antonio...What's taking you so long?" she implored, standing quickly and turning to look with a lost anticipation down the cold foreboding corridor. However, instead of the anticipated emptiness, which she perceived would confront her, she discovered that space beyond was occupied. An occupation that caused the air to gag in her throat, restricting the scream that was building up from deep within her very soul. Staggering backwards into the comfort of the shadows she lifted the gun and pointed it at the shrouded form.

"What? How? Who are you?"

The question received an immediate answer. The figure slowly lifted the hood that concealed its identity and allowed it to fall backwards. A gentle porcelain face looked back at her, its almost human features soft in the artificial light of the candles.

Smiling, it spoke.

"My name is Elizabetha and your mortal weapon will have no effect upon me," Slowly the creature advanced, moving closer, she kept her respective distance and cautiously circled her intended victim.

"Why did you come here? Why couldn't you leave us alone?" she gently pleaded. "We have not harmed any of your kind, except in self-defence. We are..." she corrected herself. "We're a peaceful race. Now we are nothing. Slain like cattle for the hunger of a paranoid mankind."

"We were following orders," Janet pleaded, in a vain attempt to pull answers from the deep recess of her mind but could not match the magnitude of the question, which had been directed out to her, and so she stood in silence, a pathetic ambassador of this modern world. Her eyes slightly lowered, as if in shame.

"You cause the demise of one of the greatest species which this world has ever witnessed and you do not understand this most simple of questions. Power is truly controlled by the fools. It corrupts the incorruptible and stains the unblemished. How little your kind had advanced, scared of that which you cannot comprehend or understand and afraid of that which you already know. Still you hide from the shadows, and run from the night. You have the greatest weapons of destruction that this world has ever known, advancements in your science far greater than can be imagined. You are the unholy witness, able to see all that you desire and yet you still cower from your childhood nightmares. You destroy us all and do not know why...only mankind could answer with such a statement."

Elizabetha turned and made her way to walk across the chamber but she turned and looked Janet directly in the eyes.

"Do you think that you could ever comprehend the suffering and pain that I am feeling at this very moment? Do you think that you could ever understand the beating of an immortal's heart? How its senses are a thousand times stronger than those of a fragile mortal creature? We immortals feel and sense things in a way that you could not even begin to imagine or comprehend. You follow your mundane lives, struggling to find a path, which will give you guidance. How do you think it feels to have an eternity to explore every avenue? Contemplate every mistake. Ponder every decision," she paused. Gently she continued. "To have that eternity for repentance. Your mistakes grow in magnitude and fester within until your only desire, stronger than that for sustenance, is your own death. Peace. To have eternal rest and to be embraced by the strongest forces in nature. But only when your time is right, not when it is dictated by one such as yourself. An infant in the working of the world, experience has merely brushed itself passed you, lightly inflicting its sorrows upon your brow. If only you could feel the suffering of this immortality, only then could you ever comprehend the magnitude of the events which has passed. Alas, this you will never know or ever comprehend..."

She paused and smiled as a dark thought entered her vengeful mind. "Then again, maybe you could. An eye for an eye. A tooth for a tooth and a life for a life." Moving closer to Janet she reached out her hands and gripped the collar of her shirt and pulled her closer. Her vampiric actions quickly disarmed her captive and sent the weapon across the floor and into the shadows. "The punishment should fit the crime and the actions should match those of the perpetrators. How could you ever feel the passion and pain of an immortal? How could you ever understand the suffering, which you have inflicted upon my kind and myself? And how could your guilt follow you like a murder of black crows, observing your every action? Obsessive and tormenting? You will truly understand how it feels to be immortal, for that is the gift which I will punish you with. The sentence is life; perpetual, sensual, painful, tormented, lonely, immortal life." Elizabetha swooped forward, burying her fangs deep into the soft flesh of Janet's neck. The sweet salt of the blood splashed onto her lips and down her eager throat.

She could feel it raging through her system, giving her that all-important sustenance from which she could create life itself.

Five

Callum's eyes quickly opened; he could sense the sullen evening air as if the world were full of the screams of his departed companions. He could hear their voices, tormented and distorted by pain and suffering. He inhaled a deep, fortifying breath before rising to his feet; he looked about the chamber, all was silent. The destruction that had claimed so many of his kind had mercifully passed. Picking up his humble belongings he followed the undulations of the corridors that interwove their way through this underground labyrinth. As he drew close to the surface his preternatural senses burst into life, calling for him to relish the new night. His pace quickened with ease as deep dark emotions welled up within. His mind turned over and over again those images of friends vanquished, released from their immortal bonds, set free to return from whence they came.

Ahead of him he could see the welcoming sight of the caves exit; the skies were already beginning to darken, sending deep shadows across the mountains and into the valley below. The blazing sunset was already fading into a mild protest against the coming of night. The cool breeze that issued from the valley floor rose up, carrying with it the final scent of winters bloom, a fragrance apparent, yet somehow forgotten. Callum inhaled this gift from nature and waited for the night to claim its domain. A single, isolated tear of pity rolled slowly down his cheek, its salt taste a bitter reminder to the innocent blood shed by the insecurities of mankind. He watched as the clouds fell by revealing the stars that peppered the night's sky, their presence bringing solace and comfort to his shattered soul. He realised that he was alone, not in the mortal sense of solitude but in the immortal sense of eternity: Forever to wander the centuries an outcast of the world, a part of nature and mankind yet never allowed to participate for the fear that manipulates man to perpetuate deeds of good also drive him to follow the darker path of evil. Callum knew that good and evil were only a perception just as heaven and hell, but that feeling of not belonging filled him with a stronger dread almost as powerful as that of the magnitude of death itself.

It was then that her name struck him. Mica, where was she? With all of the torment that had filled him since the genocide of his people he had never given his love a thought. Had she not left the tribe a full day before the carnage, taking with her the hope and dreams of one too weak to proclaim his passion? Where could she be? After all, she had almost twenty-four hours before him, and to a vampire that was almost an eternity. Callum thought deeply, pulling at the very fabric of his mind, recalling information long since forgotten by mortals. One word broke from his lips. "England!"

He knew that she would return to her natural birth place, the only place of true serenity where a vampire could die. Quickly he gathered himself up and stepped into the night, the sun having passed by only moments before leaving its warm presence to greet this traveller.

Six

In a vain attempt to vanquish the bitter wind that swept its merciless way along the street that led to the Ward's home, Ann-Marie pulled her heavy coat about her. Staring through the iron gates that blocked the way onto the driveway of this magnificent house she could almost taste the regal opulence that seemed to exude from every pore of the building.

"Come on! This way!" Susan said.

"Wait a minute! What are we going to tell your mother? We can't just turn up on the doorstep and say, 'By the way, were being chased by a half-crazy vampire that's five hundred years old, now can we?"

Susan thought for a moment.

"I know. I'll tell her that you're doing an in-depth story on me and my life and I've invited you to stay for a few nights so that you can get a better insight into my family and influences. It's all right; she's used to me doing strange things. Like running out of the house late at night and not returning until...Well until now. I suppose she's had a little time to get used to it."

Ann-Marie picked up her bags and followed Susan as she made her way through the gates and up the driveway. She could feel the warm sun touch her naked skin; its gentle rays dancing through the trees that surrounded the garden. Just as they reached the main door to the house Susan turned to her left and followed a gentle pathway that led the way around to the side of the house and took them to the kitchen entrance. The garden was covered in a fresh fall of snow that seemed to cleanse everything onto which it came into contact. Even the frozen pond seemed to fall prey to its tender caress; below the surface the goldfish swam and darted in the water, oblivious to the freezing touch of mother-nature.

Pushing the kitchen door open, Susan urged Ann-Marie to enter, putting her bags down upon the stripped wooden floor, Ann-Marie marvelled at this picturesque Victorian kitchen that stretched out before her. Its old cooking range crowned with copper pots and pans, heather and dried flowers hanging from hooks on the ceiling and walls.

"I think we need a strong cup of tea," Susan said, pointing to the kettle. "...and I'll find Mother and let her know that were here. Don't worry, it'll be all right."

Ann-Marie couldn't help but marvel at the adult way in which Susan seemed to take each situation in her stride, rising to each challenge with little visible effort. Finding the kettle, she filled it with water and placed it upon the lit stove. Sitting close to the range she relished the small amount of heat that came from its gentle flame. It was early morning and the house was not yet alive, the heating system had not kicked into play in readiness for the occupants to roam and ramble at their ease.

Ann-Marie jumped slightly as Susan re-entered the kitchen; her cheeks a little rosier from the warmth leftover from the night before. Unbuttoning her coat she cast it flagrantly over one of the large farmhouse chairs that surrounded the table.

"Mother's getting up, she's in a bit of a mood. I wish I had called her. I've told her that you're here and she's fine. In a way I think that she's looking forward to meeting you."

By the way, if she asks, I told her that I stayed at yours last night and we got talking and fell asleep. I think that she believed me, but if she doesn't ask don't say anything."

"Don't worry, I won't. I can't even explain this to myself let alone try to tell your mother. She'll have both of us carted off to the asylum in a second."

Susan went over to the boiling kettle and lifted it from the range. Turning off the flame she proceeded to pour the water into a teapot and make several cups of tea.

"Milk and sugar?" she enquired.

"Black and strong I think," Ann-Marie replied.

Just at that moment Susan's mother entered the room, her dressing gown pulled tightly around her delicate waist. Urgently she offered Ann-Marie a welcome.

"Hello, it's so nice to meet you," she said, holding out her hand in friendship.

Ann-Marie couldn't help but feel that hospitality was Susan's mother's second nature. Standing, she took her hand and held it tightly.

"Thank you for letting me invade your privacy in such a way. I know that it's a very early time to arrive but after last night I thought that the best thing for me to do would be to get Susan back home as quickly as possible." There was something of the truth in her words.

"Oh, that's all right. I'm happy that you could find it in your time to take such an interest in my daughter's work. Most of the time a journalist would give you ten minutes before they rush off and dig the dirt on some film star or unfaithful politician, camping outside of their homes for weeks-on-end in the vain hope of getting a blurred photograph. No, it is I who must thank you; good publicity is a hard thing to come by these days."

Ann-Marie looked nervously at Susan, her eyes mocking terror.

"Mother, your tea's ready," Susan said holding out a cup, which she took and held for a moment.

"I'm sorry, I forgot my manners. I'm Jennifer, but my friends just call me Jen."

"I'm Ann-Marie and my friends call me... Ann-Marie," she replied, laughing nervously.

"Would you like some breakfast?" Jen enquired. "You both look as though you're frozen to the bone." Walking over to the range she put down her cup and peered out of the window and into the garden. "This British weather is always the same at this time of the year, miserable, miserable or even more miserable. Oh look!" she exclaimed.

"It's snowing, there's a novelty. All we have to do now is wait until summer then we'll get ten different sorts of rain and drizzle. England always looks so washed out at this time of the year. Give me Shakespeare's Somerset any time." Realising that she was rambling, Jen turned to Susan.

"Why don't you take Ann-Marie to her room while I fix something to eat? You'll find fresh linen and towels in the cupboard. I think the room next to yours will be nice, the one overlooking the garden."

Thanking Jen once again for her hospitality Ann-Marie smiled courteously and followed Susan out of the kitchen and up the stairs, speaking in hushed tones as she went.

"That went reasonably well, she doesn't think that we should be locked up and the key thrown away."

Susan smiled as she opened the door to Ann-Marie's room.

"Mum's not bad, as mothers go. She has her moments."

Putting her bags onto the floor Ann-Marie flopped down onto the bed. Exhaling, she closed her eyes.

"And let's hope that she never finds out what we'd been up to over these past twenty-four hours."

"She won't..," Susan said reassuringly. "I'll let you unpack. I'll call you when breakfast is ready" Leaving the room she closed the door behind her.

Lying back onto the bed Ann-Marie allowed the softness of its presence to envelop her, carry her imagination upon its wings into another realm. She lay there dreaming of a more unhurried time. How distant her yesterdays seemed, forever forgotten in the turmoil of the here and now. Yet no matter how much she concentrated she could not eradicate the images that haunted her; images of a creation that should have long-since perished in the hands of time. A creature created by the gods themselves and allowed to hold domain over those less calculating or weaker than themselves. Turning over these thoughts, Ann-Marie contemplated how different these creatures were to man? Was there a difference? And if so, could that difference be measured against those acts of man or was it immeasurable? The mirror to the actions of the world, or the mirror of how things could have been? Opening her eyes, she stood and moved over to the window. Outside the world was waking, the sun rising over the rooftops of London bringing with it the warmth of a new day. Feeling its warm presence upon her skin she smiled a self-indulgent smile and bathed in the light of the morning. A gentle knock on her bedroom door robbed her of these brief selfish moments.

"Yes," she called.

"It's me Susan. Breakfast is ready."

"I'll be down in a moment"

Taking off her coat, Ann-Marie made her way down to the kitchen; there she found Susan and her mother deep in conversation.

"I don't think that I'm too young to stay out all night, after all I am eighteen"

Susan's mother corrected her

"Not yet!"

"My next birthday, which is only three weeks away."

"Three weeks is a long time, and if you keep going on the way that you're going you won't reach eighteen"

Ann-Marie came to Susan's defence.

"I must take some of the blame for Susan's absence last night. It's just that we were deep in conversation and I didn't realise the time. If anyone were to apologise then it should me. I should have made sure that Susan called home, after all I do have your number."

Jen smiled.

"I guess I am being a little over protective. When you have children Susan, you'll be the same. And if you only have the one, as I have, then who knows," she then turned her attentions to her visitor. "Tell me Ann-Marie, do you have any children?"

Ann-Marie quickly answered.

"No! I'm not even married."

Jen was surprised at this statement.

"Why not?"

Ann-Marie thought for a moment before replying.

"Men are like fires, if you don't give them constant attention they grow cold and go out. Anyway, most men think that monogamy is a type of wood," she laughed quietly to herself. "It's strange, I've always had the ideology that my life is my own to live and I found it difficult to do what my partner said just because he was a man, after all this is supposed to be a man's world, why should he get everything his way? I don't know, others have always perceived me as being different. I think that it all stems from my childhood, when other girls were playing mummies and daddies, I was playing career woman, manipulating friends. You know, the things that men do in business and everyone accepts, but if a woman does it she is seen as a bitch. My parents never forced me into being something that I wasn't and I guess I just never got out of the habit. That's probably why I'm on my own now; well, after all, being alone is the easy option." These last words seemed somehow final and cold. Ann-Marie even surprised herself at the finality of her reply.

"Don't you want children?" Jen enquired.

"What we desire and what we achieve are two very distinct and different things, life is never that simple. I understand that I have made a conscious decision not to become interwoven into a solid relationship, as I understand those barriers, which a strong commitment dictates. I guess that it's just not me. I'm more of the deep and meaningful one-night-stand type girl. No fuss, no commitment."

Jen gave her guest a pitiful look as she stood and made her way to the range. "Could you ever perceive yourself settling down, I mean if the right man came along?" she said, pulling out a plate laden with assorted fried foods she proceeded to place in front of Ann-Marie.

Ann-Marie smiled. "Thank you," she replied. Thinking cautiously about her own answer, she paused for a brief moment. "Who's to say that there is a right man? I can remember my mother saying to me when I was a child, that everyone has somebody in this world, it just takes courage to find them. Well, I'm sick of looking; there are times when I think that if I just turn over a rock I would find a more congenial partner than any of those 'Men' on offer on this bleak market place called life. Most of them are past their prime, while the others have just left the comforting arms of their mothers, their

104

ears still ringing with their false flattery while their own mouths are brimming with immature bravado and lies," she looked to Jen, a soft smile reaching across her lips. "I know that I may sound cynical, I don't know, maybe it's the journalist in me, or the love-torn fool. But next time I'm enticed into the dark world of man's comforts, I will think long and hard, for the life that I have built for myself, I will guard with all my heart and soul. No man has a claim upon it; I have forged my own empire and I am ruler of my own kingdom."

Jen sat down and looked into Ann-Marie's soft, brown eyes. "It must be cold up there, alone in your ivory tower, built upon that frigid, barren, inaccessible moral high ground, full of shifting emotional sands."

****

Breakfast over, Susan insisted that Ann-Marie visit her studio at the very top of the old house. Making their way up the winding stairs Ann-Marie recalled their first meeting in the Dane's Art Gallery, she knew that it had been only a few weeks prior, but in her mind an eternity had passed and she had become very fond of her new-found friend.

Just as they reached the attic door Ann-Marie paused. "Wait! When you took those photographs of me in the gallery, did you do anything with them?"

Susan smiled.

"You didn't!" Ann-Marie exclaimed.

"It's not finished, it still needs a little more work."

"Can I see it?" Ann-Marie cried in delight.

Susan opened the studio door and ushered Ann-Marie into the room. Inside, a vast attic window allowed the gentle light of morning to come sensitively pouring, unobstructed, into the room. Its pure light illuminated even the furthest of corners. Moving to the centre of the room, Susan stood before a cloth concealed canvas resting upon its easel. Gripping the side of the cloth she looked at Ann-Marie with hopeful eyes.

"Remember it's not finished, I have to put in a few more highlights. But it's yours, a gift for being a friend and helping me in my hour of need. Oh well, here goes." she lifted the cloth.

Ann-Marie's mouth fell open in delight; she shrieked her approval and hugged Susan.

"My God!" she exclaimed. It's wonderful. It's perfect. Don't change anything."

Susan gave a visible sigh of relief.

"Thank heaven you like it. You can take it now if you want, but leave it outside your bedroom door, the paint's a little wet and it would stink out your room if you kept it inside. There's an old table in the hall at the top of the stairs, put it on that."

Lifting the painting from its easel, Ann-Marie marvelled at its likeness. Falling into her own piercing brown eyes almost reflecting her soul. That long dark hair that cascaded in gentle curls over her shoulders. And those features, as gentle and as delicate as porcelain.

"Oh I can't wait to get this home; I have the perfect place for it."

Susan looked at Ann-Marie with an expression that portrayed bemusement.

"Not this home in London, no I don't mean that place, I mean my real home," Ann-Marie paused. "When this is all over I've decided that I'm going back to Durham. My parents have..." A shadow of sorrow drifted across her life. Correcting herself she continued. "...had, an old farmhouse in the countryside just on the outskirts of the city. It's called Barnstable Farm."

Oh, it's so beautiful there; during the summer the city is so full of life; ancient, yet somehow modern. Years ago I used to love to walk along the river path that went past the old cathedral and music-college. You could really feel that you were part of an ancient culture, something gone yet never forgotten. You were allowed to be alone, to explore your inner emotions. To wander aimlessly, undisturbed along the towpaths and walkways. It was so green, the parks, the fields; you didn't feel that you were in the middle of a city. I had many happy years there. You know, when I was a child at school, a group of us would sneak out during break-times and go into the city centre, we would never get into trouble or anything dubious. No, we would just buy ourselves a cup of coffee at one of the Old World café's, and sit outside and watch the world pass by. Time meant nothing to us then, only something to look forward to with anticipation. Such happy days."

"Why did you leave?" Susan enquired.

Ann-Marie felt sad for a brief moment as memories of her mother drifted back. Funny, it had been some time since she had thought of the pain that her disappearance had brought into her life.

"Time does unfortunately move on. Fate has a way of presenting you with several options in your life and normally they come at some cost. You might not see it then and there, but at some point in your life you will be asked to settle the score. No, Durham has a lot of good memories for me, but it also has a few ghosts and I think that their exorcism is long overdue." Realising that she was falling into a self-induced pity, Ann-Marie looked at Susan and tried to lighten the situation. "Once again, thank you for your gift." A thought of repayment entered her mind. "I tell you what, when were out of this dilemma you must come, with your mother, and see it in its resting place. Be my guest, come to Durham, a returning of the favour."

Susan yelped in delight "I'd love to" Susan said.

****

The day passed at a rather uneventful pace and Ann-Marie found herself being guided around the old house and shown relevant artefacts attaining to the Ward's family history. Everything seemed to drift by her without really connecting. Somehow she could never manage to focus her attentions upon the immediate relevance of her present situation. Her mind kept asking her the same question over again, demanding an answer.

"What would she do when the night came?"

As evening fell the group settled themselves in the main living room of the house; a fire blazing in the hearth brought an almost spiritual warmth to the room, evoking pleasant memories from Ann-Marie's own childhood. Sitting back on the sumptuous sofa she held these memories close to her heart. Daydreaming of a time long since passed.

"Would everyone like coffee?" enquired Jen, "Or should we have something a little stronger?"

"Oh yes!" Susan said.

Her mother gave her a disapproving look.

"I only want one drink," Susan said, a little crestfallen.

Her mother smiled. "I suppose one wouldn't hurt and after all it's nearly Christmas. Would you like a glass of something Ann-Marie?" she enquired.

"Yes, I'd love one," she replied with a smile.

"Good, I think that there's an old bottle or two of red in the kitchen, we can start on them," Jen passed Ann-Marie a mischievous glance as she left the room. Moments later she returned, bottles and glasses in hand. Placing them on the table she began to fill each of the three glasses to the brim with the thick cool red liquid. Picking one up, she offered a toast for the evening.

"Here's to the season that we are about to enjoy. Merry Christmas, everyone."

Taking her glass, Ann-Marie paid her respects to Jen.

"And thank you for having me here," she replied with a warm smile.

"Well we couldn't have you spending Christmas alone could we? Unlike Susan's father. It will be nice to have someone else to fuss over. You see, Phillip is in New York organising Susan's next exhibition, this will be the first time that her work has travelled over the Atlantic; let's hope that it translates well."

"When will he be back?" Ann-Marie enquired.

"New Year's Eve. I really feel for him; do you realise that this will be our first Christmas apart? Even when he worked in the Middle East I would fly over to spend time with him, but we couldn't this year because Susan's London exhibition had just opened and we needed me at this end to keep things going," her words were heavy.

"He'll be back soon," Ann-Marie said, with a reassuring smile.

"Oh, here I am getting all morbid and this is the Christmas season, another drink?" Jen said lifting the bottle and offering it to Ann-Marie.

After several more glasses of wine, her fears, which had haunted her throughout the days had somewhat dissipated, leaving only a warm glow that filled her with a calm presence. Both Susan and her mother seemed to be entering that same frame of mind as the wine began to work its magic, taking from them the inhibitions that seemed to flow between mother and daughter. Jen began to recount the tale of a time before her marriage, when she was only interested in her career, akin to Ann-Marie. A time before Susan's birth, a time when freedom meant the true sense of the word. The wine began to take a stronger hold upon her social and mature rigidity, freeing the inner-self from the restrains of motherhood and allowing the young woman to once again return to the surface, much to the surprise of her daughter.

"I remember my wedding night, that was fun," she began to recount. "We were both innocent, you know what I mean we'd never done, 'It' before. Well, I couldn't believe my eyes and he wanted to put it in the most unexpected places," Jen began to laugh uncontrollably at her daughter's surprised and abhorred expression which appeared to exacerbate her mother's hysteria. "I'm sorry Susan but I don't get a chance like this very often, a time to let my hair down. We should do this more often, a girls' night in," Susan smiled nervously. Ann-Marie reached over and touched Susan's arm.

"Chill out, your Mother was your age once, she wasn't born a mother."

"You can say that again; there was a time when I could laugh and joke with the best of them," Jen said. "Wait a minute, wait a minute," she called "I heard this great joke the other day, one of the friends from the women's net-ball team told it to me. Why do women make worse drivers than men?" Ann-Marie looked hesitantly at Jen before replying.

"Alright I don't know; why do women make worse drivers than men?"

Holding her fingers about two centimetres apart she cried out.

"Because men keep telling them that that's six inches."

Ann-Marie burst into uncontrollable fits of laughter, much to Susan's dismay. Her lack of insight into the joke seemed to add fuel to the fire that was becoming both women's amusement.

"I've got one! I've got one!" Ann-Marie screamed. "Why do women get married?"

Laughing, Jen asked why.

"Because a vibrator can't mow the lawn."

Jen grabbed her sides as a sharp pain of delight shot through her body. She cried for Ann-Marie to stop. The pain of happiness was almost too much for her to take. Tears began to roll down her cheeks. The humorous comments flowed as freely as the wine, each growing in its coarseness at the passing, each distancing the listener from the reality of this real world.

Jen then corrected her stature and asked Ann-Marie a direct question, causing an air of sobriety to fill the room.

"Tell me to keep my nose out of your personal business but you know this morning, when you said that you would never marry, was there something more to it than just losing your freedom? I know that freedom is a big price to pay for such a little reward but it can have its benefits," Ann-Marie took a slight sip of wine from her almost empty glass before answering Jen's question in a very direct and honest way.

"I have this motto. As soon as a relationship becomes hard work I should leave; after all you have to be friends and most relationships don't even have that. It must be terrible having to lie to yourself that everything's going to be alright. You walk around telling yourself that nobody else knows, but they can see the fear in your eyes. It is as if the whole world is in on the lie, a conspiracy that encompasses all of society. It's sad. We've asked men for years to get into contact with their inner selves and express their emotions and when they do, we laugh and tell them to stop acting like children. We want the world. We want perfection. We destroy everything that we touch. We don't realise it but we are the most powerful creatures on this planet. We can live alone. We can raise children single-handed. We can keep a track on the day-to-day events of several people's lives. We can give birth. All this and having to juggle the delicate male ego. Shit! Now, with artificial insemination, we don't even need a man. Black Widow, move over. It's strange we meet this nice quiet chap and fall in love with him. Then we marry him and then we spend a lifetime trying to change him. No wonder the poor buggers are so confused. Have we moved forward in time? Away from that primitive creature that we once were? I think not. We have the trappings of heaven yet we still wallow in pleasures of our primordial hell. Can you answer me a question?" Ann-Marie directed to Jen. "If all women want a quiet life and security then why are so many of us attracted to bastards? We even find ourselves making excuses for them, condoning their actions," Ann-Marie lay back against the sofa; closing her eyes she allowed her head to fall back against the soft cushions. "I don't know, life is too complex; then again if it were just a series of basic choices then we'd all be bored out of our minds by the time we were old enough to make them. Maybe things aren't as bad as we think; maybe that world isn't as dark and foreboding as we first thought. After all many of us survive too old age without as much as a hiccup and yet others seem to court adversity. Fate can be cruel as well as kind. It can take from us that which we thought was immovable. Children have a habit of seeing adults as extensions of themselves; the boundaries between the two are always blurred throughout life. You never think that that bond is ever going to be broken, yet in some cases it is severed. Torn asunder. I don't care how people view it, when you are confronted by such an event in your life it stops you, sometimes permanently, in your tracks. No matter what age you are you still feel the full force of its presence. Be you six or sixty, you're still orphaned. You're left alone on this planet, a mirror to your own mortality. Everyone experiences it, but no two experiences are ever the same. It's as if God were letting you know that he was keeping track of the time that he had given you and those precious sands were slowly falling into the bottomless pit of eternity."

"Funny as the years pass it feels as though those sands were falling at an ever-increasing rate, almost pulled into the darkness of the past by the experiences which we encounter. Maybe that's why I have a greater value than most for myself as an individual, and my own self-worth. I feel that this is my life to live, mine and mine alone. Selfish? Possibly. Why should I bow to another? Live for another's desires, carnal or otherwise? No! I have more respect for myself than that."

Jen smiled respectfully. "Compromise is always a painful thing. Sometimes it feels as though you could burst with anger; scream at the injustice that our partners put us through narrated by their petty whining, but when the times are good it's worth every second. It's life! Nothing is ever cut and dried; it's never black and white. Life is a series of shades of grey, with the occasional colour now and again. Just to brighten up the mundane, something to make it all seem worthwhile."

"That may be so, but it seems to me that the bad times always seem to outweigh the good. Maybe that's because of the times in which we live. Nobody really knows each other, take time to get to know those around them or their place, or even understand their own part in society. Our identity has been stolen by the radicals in this world and replaced with nothing. As people we must conform, become another's perception.

Either that or a distorted character of something hideous. Some creation, far darker than that which was abandoned."

Ann-Marie filled her glass.

"We aren't allowed to be individuals. Men are one thing, women are another; well that's how it's viewed. Stereotyped since time began and those who choose to stand against these rock-impregnated stereotypes, well, they are damned. Cast aside. Instead of being embraced by society they are banished. In this world, too many people hide behind their words, damming others with their hollow accusations and neglecting the very essence of their own being, they turn from that reason why we are all here in this torrid existence and waste that which is precious to us all. We must strive to understand one-another and use this brief period time to make that little difference."

"Maybe our childhood was a different time," Jen said. "The summers were hotter, the colours of spring brighter. I don't know. Everything changes. We need change. You will always find some people who will reject change, those who will fight it, but inevitably they will be conquered by the desire to progress."

Ann-Marie allowed her words to sink into the blackness that was becoming her mind; the wine was working its wonder. She closed her eyes and allowed the distant memories of her past to rush forward and flood her heart.

"You know, for most of my childhood I had perfection in my life. Happiness was something that visited my home every day. It was as constant as the sunshine. Then it all changed. My parents loved me unconditionally. In my eye's they were perfect, never arguing, were always happy and vibrant. Then, it all went horribly wrong and I can remember it as if it were only yesterday. My mother would come up to my room to read me a bedtime story. I was far too old for that sort of thing but I didn't want to tell her, as I knew how much she enjoyed reading to me. In some strange way I think that she enjoyed the stories more than I, and it gave us time alone, together. After she had finished, she would kiss me goodnight and turn out the light. I would watch her as she walked to the door and turn to look back to me. The light from the corridor shining softly onto her face, making her appear almost angelic, as if she wasn't really there. I wanted to grow up to be just like her. To be touched by the same hand that had given her such beauty. I know that all little girls want to be like their mother, but this was different. I thought that if I could hold just a fraction of her grace, a touch of her presence then I would be blessed. She could light up a room with her laughter and dull the brightest of summer days with her tears. Even when she cried you knew that it would pass. It was never inflicted by others only be events. She would mourn the passing of a family pet or a distant friend but it would pass as quickly as it had come and the house would be once again filled with the sounds of her bright laughter. You know the one main thing that I remember the most about her? It's not her tenderness or compassion. It's not even her laughter. No... it's that smile. Her incorrigible smile. She could melt or mend a heart with it. Funny, that was how I remember her on that night. Smiling as she left my room."

Ann-Marie laughed gently to herself.

"That was the last time that I saw her. The next day all of her belongings were gone, her wardrobe was empty, even the pictures in the study that my father had kept on his desk disappeared. He refused to talk about her and in time couldn't even acknowledge that she ever existed. There were rumours going about town that she had run off with another man but I couldn't accept that. Not my mother. She loved me too much to do that. I suppose that's one of the possible reasons why I wasn't any good with men. You see, when my mother left and my father denied her existence, something inside me died and the thought of inflicting that amount of pain upon a child would be too much guilt for me to handle. After all they do say that history had this uncanny way of repeating its self. No! I'm better off being alone, I can't hurt anyone then."

"No....You mean you can't get hurt yourself," Jen whispered.

"I must thank you. For allowing me to spend this time with you" Ann-Marie said in a vain attempt to change the subject away from herself, for in some strange way she always felt vulnerable whenever she talked of her own past. "You received me into your home without a second thought, now you can't tell me that you just did it in the hope of gaining positive press for Susan."

"No, I must admit when you first presented yourself on my step this morning I was a little taken aback, but now that I've grown accustomed to your company I'm looking forward to our time together. It's funny, for a journalist you have an innocent honesty about yourself. And if I'm honest I must confess that I was dreading the thought of Christmas without adult company. One of the best things that I can say about Phillip is that he listens. I don't mean just listens, I mean actively listens. You know that he's taking in everything that you're saying, understanding your situation. He doesn't pass comment, just offers support. When I see the partners who some of my friends ended up with, I sometime count my blessings. Don't get me wrong, Phillip is no angel and thank God! I want something of his personality to get on my nerves, to irritate me. So that I would question myself as to, why did I marry him, in the first place? Why have I spent the past twenty years of my life by his side?"

Ann-Marie heartily filled her glass with a fresh supply of wine.

"Why did you then?"

"I would really love to tell you that I am as besotted with him now as I was all those years ago but I can't, that would be a lie. No, I do love him with my heart and soul but there is something greater than that. He's my friend. I can tell him everything, ask him anything. Ask for anything and if it were not in his power to give it to me he would give me a reason why I couldn't have it. He wouldn't cast my feelings to one side without a second thought. I think that deep down inside, we both feel that people are people and for that simple reason they are different and as a whole we should rejoice in that difference rather than work against it. After all who else should you give your heart and soul to?"

"I would say that you're very lucky, you've got a lovely husband, a talented child and a nice home. Three out of three, most women's dream," Ann-Marie said, with a slight tinge of envy.

"Well, yes. I can take credit for the first two but the latter I don't know. A long time ago when I was young, I used to get involved with a lot of charities and giving to the poor. I don't know if I'm becoming more cynical or just a realist as I get older, the truth is as the years advance some of us become more aware of this beautiful world around us and the problems which it experiences and the other just allow its suffering to pass blindly by. However, because we realise we must find a more practical means to fix these problems, everything stagnates and a solution is seldom found. Blind binding politics is everywhere. It reminds me of when I was a young student all hormonal and full of radical thoughts, I was very revolutionary and would think that all the wealth accumulated by the rich fat cats should be shared, distributed to everyone in a philanthropic, non- egotistical way, but looking back in hindsight I realised that this altruistic act was desired preferably in my direction, but it was only later that the greater realisation occurred to me and that someone has to be proactive enough to create that wealth and that will only ever happen if that individual is creative and motivated enough to do so. Mankind's basic instinct is that of self-preservation and it's alright to want to live in a pure, altruistic world, but altruism lacks motivation and without motivation we would all still be sleeping in caves, throwing rocks at the moon or hiding from the Bogeyman who lives under the bed. I know this world we created is damnable and scary but my biggest fear isn't the Bogeyman; him I can contend with. No, my biggest fear is..." - she purposefully paused and took a breath before looking directly into Ann-Marie's eyes - "Who hides under the Bogeyman's bed?" she whispered.

Susan looked nervously in Ann Marie's direction. She reciprocated with a gentle smile.

Jen smiled, breaking the darkening mood. "You may find that hard to believe looking about you at the opulence all around, but I was not as materialistic so long ago, but children brought out that inner need to feather the nest with pleasantries. No, I'll rephrase that. Having a child was a great excuse to feather the nest. When I discovered that I was pregnant, Phillip and I decided to travel, we spent months in Europe and the Middle East. I bought tapestries in Paris, from the little shop just round the corner from Notre Dame, the one next to the park. Statues from Egypt, we travelled all the way from Luxor to Aswan, visiting all of those beautiful temples along the way." In her mind she began to recall the sights of the years past, the sensation of recall brought back the emotions of inspiration so that her memories felt fresh and experienced anew. "Oh! We saw the temples of Karnack and Luxor. It was as if the years had rolled back, just for us. Then there was The Valley of the Kings, the temples at Edfu, Kom-Ombo and Philae. Egypt was so alive. The past and the present living as one. It was as though you could really step back in time and experience life in the ancient world. I travelled enough for a lifetime in those short months and by the time we came back I was ready to settle down and have a family and I've lived off those memories ever since. No, I wouldn't change a second. I realised a long time ago, that the trouble with people in this modern materialistic world in which we live, is that they spend all of their time trying to give their children all of the things that we, as individuals did not have at their age. Instead of trying to give them all of the things that we do have. The primary of this being …Time. Experience tempers the mind and moulds the character, and experience is free, as is love," Jen poured herself another drink. Sitting back on the sofa she sipped the wine gently."

"I only wish that I could have planned my life in such a way, to see all of those places," Ann-Marie said.

"Planned. Life isn't to be planned; it's to be indulged in. If there's one thing in life that I've learnt it's never plan for tomorrow, for it may never come. Live for the moment, the now. The future does not exist and the past is long forgotten. Too many people hunger for what they once were instead of relishing that which they are or could be; this all goes too quickly," she said, looking about the room. "We make judgements on both ends of the scale, looking up and also looking down," she paused for a brief moments to indulge herself in another sip of the gentle wine. "You know what really gets on my nerves?" she continued. " Phillip and I have worked all of our lives, paid our taxes, tried to help others and just because we live in this big house and have a talented child, everyone thinks that we have very right-wing views and couldn't give a damn about anyone else or the environment in which we all co-exist. Nothing could be further from the truth and yet others will make harsh, snap judgements upon looks, accent, breeding and dress. They perceive that background and upbringing make you a better person. I would say that being able to touch another with kindness would show more of humanity and breeding than the right accent and education, an ability to reach out denotes the true timbre of a person's true wealth."

"Don't forget political stance," Ann-Marie said.

"But politics has always bored me to death. I can only understand that which I observe with my own eyes. I see those politicians in Whitehall cutting back the grants to the school system yet they send their children for private education. Now what sort of system is that?" Her words were becoming slurred as the wine began to take effect. "I've learnt over the years that the best way to be kinder to my fellow man is to help in what little way that I can, as an individual. Power corrupts and those in power couldn't give a damn about you or I. Just as long as they get voted in next time, that's all that they care about. It's funny. The politicians will always try to extract the vote of the poor with lies and false promises and then they will turn to the rich and by using the poor as an example, play upon their insecurities, and so, manipulate the weaker minds of their fellow kin. It has been this way since time immemorial. Politicians. They can all lie, better than the best of us. I suppose there's no wrong or right pathway in life. Why is life always so complex?

Ann-Marie lifted her glass and said, in a rather inebriated tone, "Here ends the party political broadcast on behalf of the up-yours party."

All three women burst into bouts of uncontrollable laughter.

Drinking deeply from her wine glass Jen placed the empty container upon the table and filled it heavily to the brim. Without caution she lifted it to her lips before continuing.

"I know that we have always had a proportion of people in this world who fall below the class system, something which we have labelled in this modern times, the under-class. Those people with low expectation who have lived for generations on benefits. Squeezing the system to breaking point. I mean, c'mon! You can see it on a Friday or Saturday night in any city or town in England, feral children, underage, drinking in parks because they're bored and teenagers getting drunk and losing control in the streets. I know it's happened for centuries but who picks up the mess? Tax payers, people like you or I. It annoys me when you see a child of fifteen or younger pushing a pram with their second or third child rushing behind them, and I bet all from different fathers. I ask you, is that any way to bring a life into this world? It's ridiculous, some of these girls would take more time over choosing the colour of the curtains to hang in their bedroom rather than who is going to be the respective father of their next child."

Susan looked at her mother in dismay and rebuked her sharply "Mother! Don't you think you have drunk a little too much?"

Jennifer moved her head in a slight circular motion before answering.

"Well, I was just saying."

Susan let out a low, dismissive hiss.

"I was just saying," Susan repeated in a slow, sarcastic tone. "...the amount of times that should be put on the gravestone of people bullied at school or in the workplace or children who have ran away from home. Mother, it is said by the ignorant to substantiate their negative actions," she shook her head in dismay. "Oh I give up," she exclaimed.

"Oh, lighten up darling, don't take life too seriously," Jen said, drinking down a substantial mouthful of wine. "It's nice to know that you're a good girl and still chaste."

Susan looked bitterly at her mother before lowering her vocal tones. "Yes mother, but I've been caught a few times... another drink?"

She stepped forward and filled her mother's glass, a look of sarcasm etched upon her face.

Gathering herself together Ann-Marie stood and walked to the far side of the living room, looking out of the window she could see the full expanse of the garden. Its gentle undulations masked by a thick blanket of fresh snow. Looking up she could see dark storm clouds gathering in anticipation of the storm that was sure to follow. A gentle wind began to blow, gathering a few of the already fallen flakes of snow and sending them drifting high into the night sky.

"There are greater things to this life. Creatures that we mortals could never hope to comprehend or conceive," she turned and looked to her companions. "I think that it's going to snow again."

From the hallway the old long-cased clock chimed the hour.

"One o-clock already" Jen said. "I'm off to bed; I want to be up early in the morning having things to do, gifts to buy." This final comment was directed happily at Susan. "I think I'll sleep well tonight, I should, after all the wine that I've drunk." Bending over she kissed her daughter gently on the cheek. "Goodnight. Don't spend too long down stairs; you need the sleep as much as the rest of us. I know you're young but you're not used to drinking wine."

Saying her goodnight to Ann-Marie, Jen left the room and made her way to her bed.

Ann-Marie stared silently out of the window, watching the flakes of snow that were beginning to fall in heavy drifts from the heavens; the storm had come.

"I'm doing it tonight. I'm going to get this over and done with. If I can do all of these things that I've been told then tonight's the time to find out," Ann-Marie spoke without taking her eyes from the garden.

"You can help me if you want but I can do this alone."

Ann-Marie moved back into the centre of the room, sitting next to Susan she took her hand.

"If last night is anything to go by then this is going to be a very bumpy ride. I'm scared, scared as hell, but it's something that I must do. I think all of the wine that I've consumed has addled my brain, in some strange perverse way I'm looking forward to this. I don't know if it's for the adventure or because I want to get it over and done with."

"I'll help you all that I can, what do you want me to do?" Susan enquired.

"Well, I'm going to go to my room to gather my thoughts and get this drunken mind into some sort of order. While I'm doing that could you check on your mother, the last thing that we need is for her to come crashing in on us when we are in the middle of this. I couldn't even begin to explain my actions let alone the situation. As for what you should do? I don't have a clue. I don't even know what I should do myself. Best thing I think is for me to go to my room and practice. Practice what, I'm not too sure. I suppose I should try to remember all of the things that James taught me. Easier said than done."

Her bedroom wasn't exactly cold, but the snow outside the window did very little to conceal the fact that the central heating had switched itself off and the temperature was beginning to plummet at a rather dramatic rate. Lying on the top of the bed, Ann-Marie pulled the bedclothes about her in a vain attempt to preserve what little warmth her body was generating from escaping into the icy air of the room. Her head began to clear as the alcoholic haze drifted passed leaving behind it the shattered semblance of her fragile consciousness. The room began to spin in an anti-clockwise manor, gently at first but gathering speed as she concentrated. She couldn't decide whether this was due to the vast amount of wine, which she had consumed, or if it was the process of travel beginning. Sitting up, she took a deep breath. The spinning stopped.

"It's the wine," she said to herself. "Get a grip, girl. Concentrate!"

Seven

Brushing the soil from his clothes Christian stepped from his provisional earthly resting place. He surmised that his prey had either locked herself into her home or she had left and not yet returned. A noise from the house opposite alerted him to the presence of a stranger, standing in the shadows he observed Ann-Marie's young neighbours leave their home and take a taxi out of the private estate. He watched their departure with mischievous eyes, studying their manner and dress.

Moving to their front door he found little resistance to his effort and gained access almost immediately. The light to the main bedroom was switched on; this he surmised was to give the empty house an occupied look. A deterrent to any would-be mortal invader. Making his way to the bedroom, his vampire hands traced their way along the delicate wood of a Victorian wardrobe, turning the lock, the door swung silently open. Inside he found several designer suits, any number fitting his taste. Choosing one at random he undressed; it was now that he found his predicament. 'In which manner do modern people wear their clothes?' he thought. Searching the room he found several magazines and catalogues, from which he derived an explanation to his quandary.

First bathing then applying several scented perfumes Christian observed a leisurely attitude to his transformation into this modern world. Delicately pulling on the clothes he admired his attempts for several minutes before making his way out of the building.

Standing in the street, strangers passed him by without a second glance. He had truly made the infinite leap into this dark century?

****

The winter night seemed to give Paris a romantic ambience; even the lights from the peep-shows that lined the Boulevard de Clichy seemed to give an air of respect to their undesirable presence. The blues and reds of their neon lights danced across the wet roads, giving them an almost enigmatic feel, these avenues that crossed the city, guiding its lifeblood to their destination. Paris was alive, full of the pulsating desires of life, perpetually turning, as did the sails of the Moulin Rouge. Strangers and friends alike passed one-another, offering Christmas cheer to their kin. The season of goodwill had gathered everyone in its sumptuous arms and offered them hope for the happy season.

It was on this street of the capital that the stranger walked, her long, curly hair hanging heavily down over her bowed head. She had walked blindly for hours, passed the magnificent Romano-Byzantine styles of Sacre Coeur and the simplicity of St Pierre without conversation or human interaction. Wandering, she drifted through the streets, down Rue de la Ponceau and onto the Boulevard Barbes. There she stood watching the world pass before continuing her blind meanderings past the Square of St Pierre and onto Rue Gabrielle. She wandered without direction, absorbing the life of the city, allowing it to carry her upon its tide. Along Rue Durantin and onto Rue Caulaincourt she travelled. Her mind regarded its own presence as an enemy and no longer the friend that she cherished.

Her perfect recollection now haunted her and the desire to remain within these immortal bonds passed, as did the hours of her blind wandering. Never in her immortal existence had she ever felt so truly alone. What would be the point of perpetual existence if companionship were the only thing denied to her? She had lived to serve others; her giving mortal emotions had survived and transcended her journey into this dark perpetuity. Held aloft as a light to guide her through the centuries, a faint reminder of what she once was and what she so desired to be. She derived pure delight from giving. Be it physically, emotionally or spiritually. And now, in her hour of greatest need, she was alone, abandoned by existence itself.

As she passed Cimetiere Montmartre, its reverent majesty seemed to call to her, invite her to partake in its comforts after her arduous journey. Passing silently through the open gates she could almost immediately feel its calming presence as all about her the dead slept in their peaceful slumber. Their worries cast aside in favour of eternal peace. How she envied them, how she longed to join them in their dark infinite dreams. She could sense her human emotions rising to the surface once-again, those emotions that made her what she truly was, the most humane of her kind. Stopping quietly next to a mausoleum, she allowed her thoughts to drift high into the night. Memories of her son, lost forever, cascaded forward, filling her with his spiritual presence. She could see his happy smiling face; hear his laughter in her ears. Falling deeper into the images she began to recall the pain that she had been subjecting herself to, since having the sinister delights of this dark gift of immortality thrust upon her. Its true price was far greater a burden than that of its surmised reward.

Turning to the mausoleum, she placed her hands gently upon the door and spoke, as if in conversation with an invisible companion within.

"How I envy you, I would gladly exchange places with you if I could end this mother's suffering. I am forever to wander this earth, never to find peace or to rest my weary head. Yet you, you have found true perfection. You have not fought against nature but embraced it and allowed the passage of time to take you to your spiritual slumber. I am abandoned by all those that I love. My son. My brother. If you feel their presence, tell them that I love them."

To her surprise, a voice answered her call.

"Is it your own soul that you are praying for or that of your brother?"

Mica turned quickly, her eyes searching the darkness.

"Who's there?"

"I mean you no harm. I have come to help you. I could sense your suffering."

"Who are you? Show yourself," she cried.

"Who am I? I am your friend," came the reply.

"Friends do not hide in shadows they show themselves for what they are," she called.

"Then so shall I."

Slowly, from far off in the distance a figure emerged, his presence was almost inspiring. His appearance and manor could not be distinguished from any mortal even down to his casual stance and demeanour. Almost gliding, he purposefully approached Mica. She marvelled at his soft angelic features and lightly bronzed skin. A colour as soft as the autumn sun.

"Your servant," he said, gently bowing his head and taking her hand.

"My name is Darius and you are Mica, twin to that abomination, Christian."

"How do you know this?" she exclaimed.

"I know a great many things and bad news always has a habit of travelling very fast. Even faster than our kind. In this modern world communications can be as brief as a thought. It's simple; you pick up the telephone and converse with someone on the other side of this cold world. Do you realise that mortals spend their waking hours watching small screens in their homes? Devices that unscramble signals that surround this planet. Images that anaesthetise and dilute the trauma and pain that unfolds before their eyes. And there they congregate before their false gods; self-satisfied in the thought that they are merely a witness to someone else's pain. A 'someone,' to whom they have no allegiance, no equity. An image, pure and simple. Welcome to this long cold winter called life. This modern realm of mortal man."

Darius paused in his introductory conversation for a moment and turned to Mica, offering her a soft mortal smile.

"I knew that you would come to Paris. And so I came to warn you that you are not safe. Others have taken the downfall of the European Tribe as a very bad sign. First your brother incites a revolution and now his gentle sister is one of but a few who survives the destruction of the ancient fabled community. Those vampires that have chosen to follow these modern ways and live within this mortal community now fear your presence and if you were to endeavour to make contact, they would perceive this as a dark omen. Even now, they are out in packs hunting for you, searching for the perceived surviving twin of evil. Your destiny does not lie in Paris. I know that you are seeking answers here, but it is not the culminating resting place for your destiny."

"I don't understand. Why are you endeavouring to help me? How do I even know that you're not part of a plan to help your fellow Parisian immortals in their dark task?" she said.

Darius laughed. "There is a simple reason. A reason that follows each vampire down through the centuries and gives them hope for a true immortality. We are of the same blood. It was I who gave the dark gift to Callum, and Callum who gave it to Christian. And I assume he in turn brought the gift to you. There is a direct line through us all, a line that we must protect. You are still young, an infant to our kind. But there is something else that you should know, something that I asked Callum to keep from his children. Within our blood there is the direct source of the ancient power. We are directly descended from the first immortals, not in a convoluted way as are others, but our line can be traced directly back through only a few of our kind. Those powers that are within you are dormant, sleeping. As they are within a select few. But, if you or any of your kin were to fall into the hand of those who would use that power for their own gain, then an imbalance would occur and chaos would befall our people and eventually humanity. A few chosen mortals also have these powers. Granted, weaker than our own, but powers all the same. Can you imagine the ramifications if one honoured with the dark blood were to drink from such a person? It is beyond contemplation. Others have called this creature to life, darker gods. Not true gods in the human sense of the word, but those creatures that exist within the boundaries of another dimension. Those of the Old World who promote themselves to the adulation of those lesser than themselves. They have awoken from their slumber and are now seeking to reaffirm the power that they once yielded. To stop this you must come into conflict with your own kind. Callum trusted you, which is why he let you leave. I must do the same, I will try to protect you but I can offer little assistance."

Mica looked to the ground as images of her brother came to mind.

"I only wish that my brother and son were here to help me; we are one and the same, bonded by the same blood."

Darius's eyes flashed in anger.

"Your son had passed into the next world and is safe from harm. Your brother however has brought the full anger of the Parisian vampires down upon his shoulders, demonstrating his full nature to mortals, thus risking our eventual detection. He was always the foolhardy one, the rebel. I suppose that was one of the reasons why I chose him above all others."

Mica's eyes opened wide, she stared in horror at Darius.

"What do you mean? I don't understand, Christian is dead. He's been dead for over three hundred years," her voice began to shake.

Darius smirked as mischievous thoughts danced through his mind.

"That is where you are disillusioned my dear, your brother is very much alive and even now he leaves the dark pain of his torment upon everything which he touches, for he is the one who you must set yourself up against."

Mica stared into middle distance as abject disbelief consumed her.

"He can't be alive! I would know. We are one and the same. Our minds would communicate with one-another, we are bonded by immortal blood," she muttered.

"Yes. I know. And that is your downfall. Even as we speak the Parisian vampires are searching for you. If they cannot bring your vagabond brother to council for his actions then they will do it to his kin. They are already asking deep, searching questions. How did you survive the slaughter that has befallen the Tribe? Here you are. Perfection. No scars of battle, or wounds that you suffered to gain your freedom. Nothing! None of our kind will trust you. You are an outcast for no reason of your own. And your brother is not the vagabond rebel that you once loved and followed. He is now a cold-blooded and vengeful killer. A servant to the dark gods. He is the one that you must destroy. I know that these words must be painful, as sure as the pain endured by a mortal at the birth of a new idea, for that is one of the greatest pains to haunt human nature. Yet, you must understand that you are the only soul who could execute this sentence. Your brother's raging desire is to destroy a mortal Communicator whose very existence has now become immeasurably intertwined within the history of immortal man."

"You must help; I cannot kill my own brother. I do not know his crimes. Do not ask me to do this. I've lost him once, do not ask me to do it a second time," she cried.

"Would you rather that his fellow immortals find him and tear his soul asunder? Or would you rather his actions be answered by someone who loves him and can give him eternal rest. Your brother has angered even the most liberal of our kind with his fescennine endeavours; the evidence against his crimes is immutable. He is bent on destroying any bond that could be built between mortal and immortal. We have for too long been outcast in this world, feared and despised. Many are restless and are eager to re-join the life of mortals."

"But they do," Mica insisted.

"No! You don't understand. I don't mean as immortal vampires. I mean at one with man. This Communicator can take from us that which was granted centuries before by the darker powers of the universe. She can rid us of the 'dark gift', and give us back our mortality so that we can end our days in the peace and assurance that death will claim us. You must help us all. You cannot hide from yourself. Look beyond all that you are. Look beyond this distraction that is life, this immortality and experience who you really are."

Mica could feel her heart pounding in her chest.

"Will you help me?" she said softly.

Darius shook his head.

"Then why should I do this alone? This Communicator means nothing to me. She is mortal and will pass into the next realm without a second thought for my suffering. Why should I grant her the protection or assistance of my immortality? After all, it is not I who desires to return to the land of the living. I would gladly join her in her final destination if I could," Mica said, turning in her indifference.

Darius smiled. "Proud words from one so alone. Has fear brought the beast out in the beautiful Mica? Or have you accepted your true nature? I would have expected more from one so exalted, one held in such high esteem by her peers, yet now I find that you make prejudicial judgements before all of the facts are given. If you do not wish to control your own destiny and offer solace to another of your own kind in need, then I will bid you a good evening."

Darius turned to walk way, but Mica's words stopped his departing.

"What do you mean, like me? I thought that you said that this Communicator was mortal."

"Tell me" Darius continued. "Why do you so arrogantly assume that she is like you; why can you not be like her? After all, I did not say that she was a vampire, I said, another of your own kind. Do not try to exheredate yourself. You should not make the mistake of seeing a mortal as only that, a mortal. You were once as they were. A slave to the rigour and pain of their world. It was far from perfection, as is our own. Mortal and immortal are closer in kinship that they would admit. Mortals, for the fear of that which they do not know or understand of our kind and immortals, for they feel that they have transcended that which they once were and have now become that which they so desired. And immortals, a misguided, arrogant race of self-perpetuating lonely souls who are too proud to admit that the only thing that this dark gift had granted them is the insight into their own pain and suffering. After all, instead of a single lifetime to ponder our mistakes and to ask why? We have an eternity to do so, a perpetual life of unrest and torment. We are all multifaceted beings, as diverse as the universe, yet we are all fools. And you my sweet beautiful one are the greatest of us all. You are blind to your own potential. You have powers deeper within your soul that even the oldest of immortals would covet. The line of your ascendants and descendants both mortal and immortal are impressive, something that you should hold dear to your heart. Do not be blinded by your own ignorance, look deeper into your fate and try to understand why an opportunity has presented itself to you at this moment in history.

120

Open not only your eyes, but also your mind and allow the full extent of your pathway of existence to be seen, so that you can follow your destiny with truly open eyes. You have been entwined within your own sorrow for centuries, mourning one who has cast aside any feeling of love that he has ever felt for you. You have been wallowing in your own self-indulgence, a glutton to the pain and suffering of your own heart, ignorant to the aspirations of another."

Mica thought for a moment, his words heavy on her mind.

"Are you trying to tell me that..."

"...that you are a Communicator? Partly, yes. As am I and Callum and so is your brother, but our blood has been contaminated by the dark gift, and therefore, we cannot achieve certain goals and your gift permeates from one darker than most. We have limitations, something that a mortal does not have. Even death has changed for them once they understand the power of the light. They can remain conscious of their mortality, yet exist within their true state of immortality. A true balance between the two. They can live the life of a mortal to return and return over and over again, through birth and eventual death yet they can retain the information that they have accumulated within each of their brief existences."

Looking deep into His eyes, Mica could see the secrets that were hidden deep within.

"There's something else, isn't there? Something else that connects me to this Communicator?"

"When I first heard of her awakening, only weeks ago, I traced back her bloodline and in all cases they led to one point. As do your own. When the news of her coming to the light came to me from the spirits, I prayed to the heavens that she would be strong enough to help us in our goal, but I fear that she will need a powerful ally. Someone truly on her side. For others of our kind will try to destroy her, for they have no desire to return to their mortal bonds and will oppose any who follow that avenue. I also discovered that your brother and this Communicator's history has been inextricably linked for an eternity and he seeks to destroy her through the misapprehension of precluded love. If ever there was a time when you needed to conserve and focus your strength then that time is now. You will need every ounce of both mortal and immortal stamina if we are to succeed on this day. This is a joining of fellowships, a union. Bonds will be broken and connections forged. If we do not use our advantage over those who would oppose us then we are surely doomed from the onset."

"Please! If I am to undertake this task then I will also need your help, how will I discover who this Communicator is? I am frightened and Paris is a dangerous place for me at this moment," Mica pleaded.

"I understand, my kind do not frighten me for I am the oldest of our brethren, with the exception of a select few. My powers are immeasurable in comparison to their own, but I must admit that even I could not slay all those who seek your blood. All that I can offer you is advice. Take it if you will, discard it if you please. It is given freely and without malice. Return from whence you came. Return to that water bound fortress that is your home. Flee to England. Look for the Communicator within yourself. You will not be alone, for one who loves you will find you there. There is also a warning, remember, dear Mica, I know of your pedigree. For it is not only my immortal life blood that courses through your veins but that of an undying malevolent creation whose very soul was untinged by the Original Sin."

Mica closed her eyes as her heart sank into the dark seas of her own insecurities. "One woman cannot change the world, immortal or not."

Grasping onto his fading words, Mica reached into the deep caverns of her perpetual mind and there issued an echo of a stronger incarnation of her true self, illuminating her heart with words of comfort and solace.

"Yes, but this world can change that woman, be she mortal or not."

Part Three

IN THE ARMS OF LOVE.

One

From the living-room window Susan watched as winter's grace appeared to eradicate the world outside leaving behind it the white unadulterated expanse of the garden. She lifted a half-full glass of wine to her lips and indulged herself in the slightest of sips, allowing only the briefest of contacts to moisten her mouth. Looking about the room she recalled the conversations that were held within its strong homely walls in time long forgotten. How the house felt at peace that night, an infinity away from the torments that haunted her at this present time. Looking up to the ceiling she glanced beyond in her mind and imagined her mother sleeping silently in her warm bed, content with her life.

Ann-Marie stepped from the comforting shadows and into the soft light that warmed the centre of the living room. She smiled at Susan and found that her tenderness was reciprocated. Taking this as an invitation she ventured to where Susan sat and looked into her eyes. The only feeling that touched her was that of pity. How one so young could be trapped in such a struggle, she thought. How cruel was destiny?

Susan took hold of her hand. "Is there no way that I can help you if you're in trouble, can't I wake you up?"

Ann-Marie took a deep breath "No. All that will be left of me here will be a husk. The shell without the essence. I'm afraid that I've only got the one ticket and it's got my name on it."

"I'm sorry that you have to do this alone and I don't envy you for the task that you have ahead, but I will create a welcome for your return. I'll build a fire so bright that you'll be able to see it across the centuries and it will guide you back to me," Susan said with a radiant smile.

True to her word, Susan built up the fire until the room was bathed in a warm yellow glow; the shadows that dance and weaved across the ceiling were unhindered by the intrusion of false light and so they seemed to offer a comfort to the world without and within for the only illumination in the room that night was that of the fire that blazed in the heart of this home, offering warmth and comfort to the traveller that lay before it.

Ann-Marie could sense Susan in the distance sitting on the sofa, observing her every motion, but this distraction was soon to pass and in time the world outside of her thoughts faded to an emptiness and a resolute darkness of unnatural sleep filled her consciousness, sending her into the calming realm of dreams, dreams that were somehow base in reality. At first the images that passed her were distant, faded by time, but as the minutes marched forward the screen of her thoughts became clearer and more discernible. She recognised the images but somehow felt as though she were a voyeur into her own past. The thief of her own memories. For the child that danced before her on a summer's day was none other than herself, an infant washed ashore in the turmoil of childhood and into the arms of a mother's love. Ann-Marie knew that she needed to reach further back into her inner self and reclaim the memories long forgotten. She imagined herself standing before the screen, reaching forward, pulling at the very fabric of the images. Just as she felt as though her goal was at hand she fell, tumbling into the darkness of her own imagination. All about her hung the infinity of nothingness, pure blackness. Then slowly there came a realisation, an understanding, a sound. A sound that she recognised. A motion of regular beats and she knew that she was within the womb of her own mother.

Ann-Marie paused. Her mind urged her forward but her heart yearned to be heard. For this was the mother who left her when she was barely eight years old and never returned, taking with her a child's heart and leaving a void in its place. 'She could stay and relive those eight years again, those happy eight years' she thought.

Then she felt herself moving forward and into a deeper darkness, a true world of emptiness, a world of none existence. Destiny had taken this moment from her and it was as if she were suspended in time, no past, no present and no future. A non-being, existing, yet not existing in a vacuous world. She knew that she was there, for she could think, but when she looked down there was no bottom to be seen and when she looked up there was no top, no left, and no right. It was as if she were suspended by the gods, awaiting their next decision. Then once again she felt the caress of a gentle breeze, which was momentarily followed by a great wind which rushed forward bringing with it the images of a past existence. She then began to experience a new sensation, an all too human emotion. The feeling was that of hunger and in a burst of light she was sitting alone being bathed in the evening sun, noise falling all around. She was mortal again but a visitor in a different form, looking down at her hands she saw that they were no longer her own, but those of an infant child. Opening and closing them she marvelled at their structure; noises from all around captured her attention and when she looked up to find their source, she at once recognised the images of a beleaguered and rundown Victorian London street. Women in tight dresses and high hats walked by offering her the slightest of distasteful glances. Looking down once again Ann-Marie realised that she was a street child, an undesirable in these hard times.

From behind her there came a call, a voice rough and hard; she turned to see a washerwoman striding forward with her great hand out-stretched. When it made contact she could feel the harshness of this mother's love and wished to be gone. She could hear the mother scream in her course abrasive tones. "If I've told you once I've told you a million times child, don't come out onto the street."

Ann-Marie struggled to release herself from the woman's grip, turning until she was facing her. The washerwoman stopped and stared at the infant, then raised her arm high above her head hissing as she sent her hand across the child's face.

"I've told you before Victoria, don't defy me!"

The ferocity of the assault sent Ann-Marie falling backwards into herself and once again darkness prevailed. After a brief moment of travelling she realised that her environment had somehow changed. Not in a physical sense, but rather in an emotional sense. She knew that she was weightless, a spirit. But to her senses she could feel an attraction, a drawing of her essence to a focal point. Then there came the sound of air rushing past her ears and a great flash of blinding pure light, then silence. 'Has the nothingness returned?' She thought. She lifted her hand to her mouth, the way that she often did as a child when she was confused or distracted. It was only when the spiritual had made contact with the physical did she realise that she had arrived at her destination.

To Ann-Marie, it felt as if she were being slowly poured into her physical form, she could feel herself tumbling downwards and into the body of her host, she could feel the energies of her spiritual self-rage and torment as they raced to encompass this inhabited husk. She could feel her own spirit interweaving with that of her former self, blending until the divisions between the two were immeasurable and their essence became as if one. Bonded by the blood and torment of immortality perpetuated by mortality, sharing the memories of each-other as they swam into one another's souls.

Immediately realisation gripped her, as all about Ann-Marie could hear the chatter of voices, high and excited. Voices that rose and fell as if carried on the wind. Drifting and growing in volume. It was not until these voices ceased did she realised that all attention was now focused solely upon her. For all of this time she had kept her eyes firmly closed, acclimatising herself to her new surroundings, hoping for the briefest of moments from which she could steal a little more time to become accustomed to her new form. Her fear began to rise within her as she could sense the presence of a stranger sat next to her physical self. Even though she had drifted in the ether of immortality for a brief moment to Ann-Marie it felt as though an eternity had passed and this closeness of another mortal felt as though her very soul were being intruded upon. Slowly she opened her eyes as dark anticipation filled her. For a moment her surrounding resembled a night sky as a thousand lights danced before her unfocused vision. Then, as she mastered her senses, her facilities returned, granting her an uncomplicated view of this world unto which she had fallen. The lights that she first perceived as being stars were in fact the diamonds that were scattered upon the dresses of several women that sat less than a touch away. Allowing her eyes to look down Ann-Marie found that she too was wearing a resplendent dress as beautiful as those of her companions.

A voice spoke gently, offering comfort by its very tone.

"Marie-Anne, are you all right?"

Ann-Marie slowly turned her head and looking in the direction of the welcoming voice. At once she realised that the soft-faced woman that sat comfortingly beside her must have been her mother.

She swallowed hard and spoke.

"Yes mother, I'm all right."

To Ann-Marie's surprise her words were accepted with a smile.

"Is it this talk of witches and ghosts scaring you my child?" her mother enquired.

"No, I'm all right," she quickly interjected, realising the value of this information.

"I know what it is," her mother said, "it's the ball tonight. You're so excited. I remember how excited I was when I went to my first masquerade ball."

Her mother rose from the sofa and walked to the fireplace, carrying herself majestically. There she turned and spoke to her three daughters.

"I know that there has been talk of revolution in France, but we must cast that aside, for tonight is the beginning of Marie-Anne's social life, it's her coming of age," she smiled a comforting smile. "We are going to show off the brightest and youngest jewel of the Beauvoir family and no peasant uprising is going to stop me from showing off my child to the world."

With this her mother opened her fan and fanned her more than ample features. Holding herself, as if a peacock she moved effortlessly to the open door and passed through it without comment. Ann-Marie looked over to the two women who she perceived as being her sisters, she studied their movements and gestures for she knew that a mistake on this night could be fatal. She watched as they sat huddled together, deep in the turmoil of gossip. Their petite frames bulging out of their small, tight dresses. Their faces were painted almost as white as death and their lips as false and as red as blood. Grotesque caricatures of the creature which she had danced across time to confront. Pausing for thought, she wondered about herself or at least this physical form which she had somehow inherited for the briefest of moments.

Looking down, she observed a small pouch that was fastened to her wrist by a delicate ribbon. Upon opening it, she found inside a small mirror and a slim white card. Retrieving the mirror from its resting place she lifted it to her face and was relieved to find that she was relatively free from markings except for a little rouge to brighten her naturally shallow cheeks. Placing the Mirror back into her pouch she lifted out the card and held it just in front of her. To her amazement she had little difficulty in understanding the words printed upon its surface.

The Masquerade Ball

House of the Roussel Family.

Paris

July 4th

1789

Returning her observation to her sisters she listened intensely to their constant chatter, the rise and fall of their shadowed conversation intrigued her, drawing her closer. The elder of the siblings spoke in a hushed, almost inaudible tone; for fear of bringing down the wrath of her overbearing, dominant mother. Urged on by the tentative requests of her sister she recounted the tales passed to her by the maid, who in turn had the tale passed to them by the cook and so on, a tale that grew in voracity and stature as it passed from the misguided lips of fools.

"Go on! Tell us what happened next," urged Rose, the second eldest of the group.

"Gabrielle, you can't leave it there, please."

Knowing the ramifications that her uttering would bring, Gabrielle looked about the room, for she did not want her words to fall upon undesirable ears.

Then she continued.

"I have heard that they were holding black masses in the forest, they were all dancing in the moonlight, naked." A collective gasp issued from her sisters. "After they have danced all night and dawn is about to break-that is the time when they make their sacrifice to the devil."

"What do they sacrifice?" asked Rose, in slow deliberate tones.

Knowing that she had a captive audience Gabrielle played her narrator's part to its extent. "First of all they started with rabbits, chickens and other fowl. Then it progressed to lambs and goats but now they are hunting the country side around Paris, looking for innocent virgins to slaughter."

Rose shrieked in horror as she felt that her sister's words were directed at her.

"Tell me you're lying, tell me you're lying," she said, pleading to Gabrielle.

Gabrielle clasped her open hand over her sister's mouth in the hope of stemming her cries, which would surely bring her mother rushing into the room. Silence fell. She waited; listening intensely for the far off sound of her mother's cobbled shoes on bare wooden floors. But silence returned and her fears were not justified.

"Be quiet you fool, you'll bring Mother running and I've not even come to the best bit. Don't you want to hear about the stranger? The silent one that came from exotic lands beyond? The one who lives in the Château, sleeping by day in the darkness of a locked room. For it is he who presides over these events in the woods, he who dictates the lives of those who follow his god. He who promises life itself."

Ann-Marie stood and stared at Gabrielle. Taking her actions as an objection Gabrielle turned to her sister and spoke in a bitter voice.

"It seems that our studious sister does not condone our chatter, so I will not go further as I don't want to get into trouble." Those latter words were focused directly upon Ann-Marie.

Searching deep within herself for strength Ann-Marie spoke. Her words brought surprise to the group.

"I know who it is that you're talking about" Her journalist talents were now coming to the aid of her quest, for she knew that if she were to offer a gift of information then her sisters tongue would, in time, become loose and the information that she desires would flow as if water from a stream. Gabrielle sat back in her chair, her eyes wide, her lips pursed.

"Pray tell me, little innocent; how do you know of such things? Maybe it is I who should go to Mother and inform her of your actions."

"Feel free, but you will never discover what I know."

Ann-Marie could almost feel the deep sense of desire that burned within Gabrielle's breast.

Realising that the balance between siblings was weighed in her favour Ann-Marie held her ground. She played the coy innocent for all that she was worth.

Sitting back in her chair, Gabrielle smiled. "If you have something worth saying, say it! I'm sure that I've heard it all before, the servants tell me so many things."

Ann-Marie focused her eyes and stared intensely at Gabrielle. Without breaking her concentration she spoke.

"Do you know his name?"

Gabrielle's mouth fell open in surprise. "What! You're not going to tell me that you do?"

Ann-Marie smiled a wry smile. "Well, only if you want me to."

Understanding the game, Gabrielle moved to one side on her chair and offered the space between herself and her sisters to the youngest of the group. Sitting in silence, Ann-Marie smiled to her adoptive kin. It was now, as she sat in close proximity, that she realised and understood the reason for the thick application of powders and paint that concealed each and every feature of her sisters. Being this close up she could see the disease and illness that ravaged their frames, the yellowness of their skin and the dull, decaying light that shone from their eyes. Their appearance made her wince internally and withdraw a little into herself. In a perverse and garish way she was enthralled by their features and the undulations of their tortured flesh. Closing her eyes, she swallowed hard and continued with the recantation of her tale.

"Well, I know more about this stranger than you realise. It's not only you Gabrielle who can talk to the servants but it would seem that you have not been talking to the right ones; those with the most information."

Gabrielle pursed her lips at this rebuff of her contacts.

"I can tell you that he comes from another land far away and he is called Christian."

Rose interjected urgently: "I hear that he's a witch or a sorcerer. He can command the Devil himself to do his bidding."

This seemed to excite the girls, drawing them closer to the conversation. Their questions seemed to be now directed at Ann-Marie.

"Is it true that he can turn into a great, white wolf and hunt the innocent in the night, leaving the château in darkness to search for the lost souls of travellers and beggars?"

Ann-Marie tried to recall the deep dark tales of folklore, which she had heard as a child to give her tale that something malevolent to intrigue her sisters. "I don't know about that, but what I do know is even more frightening." The sisters moved closer. "I know that he is not the only one of his kind" Rose lifted her hand to her mouth in shock, as if to stop a scream from escaping. "Do you mean that there are others like him?" - She looked to the open window. "…out there? How can we sleep safely in our beds?"

From the corridor came the distant sound of footsteps, and Gabrielle knew that her mother was returning. She paused for a moment before leaning over to Ann-Marie and whispering delicately into her ear. "We'll see what a demon your Christian is soon enough, for he is also coming to the masquerade ball tonight."

Gabrielle smiled a self-contented smile as she realised that her words had had their desired effect. This was acknowledged by the shock registered upon her youngest sister's face.

"Be silent now, Mother's coming!"

Their mother entered the room with a great rustle of expensive material as her dress outshone those of her daughters. She looked to her children with delight and smiled.

"The coach is here; are you ready for the night of your life?"

****

It was as if a great bell were ringing in Christian's mind, a bell that informed him that his foe was once again in Dream-time, travelling into the unknown. A deep sense of hate filled him. These emissions from his enemy were growing stronger at the passing of each moment.

Slowly he walked along the city's back streets, a vagabond heart in this cold, cruel modern world. His mind concentrated upon the subject of his deepest, dark desires yet his other senses devoured all else about this immortal creation. Stepping upon the soft snow his preternatural emotions raged with a fire that was almost human. How fragile he felt at this moment in the vastness of time. The pulsating beat that echoed in his thoughts called to him, ridiculed him, brought home to him the fragility of his own immortality.

Without concern for this modern world he walked blindly through the streets, a ghost in this dead city. All about the throng of traffic and humanity raced, blind to the desires of this perpetual creature.   He crossed Westminster Bridge, the Houses of Parliament towering into the skies, their eyes blind to the cries of the world. He began to move forward, closer and closer to his prey, gathering speed as he went until he could not be observed by those with mortal vision. Then, as if in the blinking of an eye, he paused, aware that he was somehow being observed, followed. He stood alone at the T-junction between streets at a place on the outskirts of the city. Observing his surroundings he surmised that the place at which he found himself was now an affluent part of London. The sense of intrusion still haunted him; it was as if he were being watched by the darkness itself.

The pounding of the drum that echoed in his mind grew in volume, almost deafening him, eradicating all other thoughts in his consciousness. He knew now that he had found his quest. Moving several steps along the snow-covered pathway he found himself standing before the gates of the Ward's residence. A deep sense of fulfilment washed over him as he bathed in the metaphorical waters of his own selfish achievement.

****

Susan watched the snowfall in great sheets across the garden and what seemed the whole world beyond. She had been standing at the living room window for some time now, lost in the essence of the night. How calm the world seemed, how at peace with humanity she thought. She closed her eyes and allowed the heavy velvet curtain, which she had pulled back to observe the world, to fall back into its natural place. She breathed deeply and looked about the room; the bright flames from the open fire sent shadows of comforting light dancing across the walls and onto the ceiling. She watched the motionless figure that lay before her, lost in the soft natural light that issued from the fire. To Susan, it seemed as if Ann-Marie was somehow a child again, a baby that needed protecting against the cruel world, and she had been granted that task; as the protector, the giver. She moved over to Ann-Marie's side and looked at her longingly, a deep sense of wonder filled her, Where was she? What was she doing now? Kneeling beside her, Susan took hold of her hand in the hope that this comforting gesture would travel through the centuries and offer support to her new friend.

The waiting was torturing Susan; it had only been a matter of moments since this adventure into time had begun, but since that moment she had never felt so alone. It was as if the world was against her and failure was awaiting their every move. Sleep yearned for her to indulge herself on its banquet; the deep need to rest pulled at her inner self. Burying her head in her hands she rubbed her eyes in the hope of banishing

130

any thought of rest. She stood and yawned loudly, filling her lungs with stale air. Her eyes searched the room aimlessly, passing up and down the walls, across the bookcases and onto the living room door. It was there that they came to an abrupt and horrifying stop. Susan watched in terror as the brass door handle slowly moved. Her heart began to pound as fear gripped her, exploding a thousand dark images in her juvenile mind. There was a gentle click as the locking mechanism, which held the door closed moved and granted those outside entrance into this vulnerable room.

The door slowly opened revealing the pitch darkness of the corridor beyond. Susan could feel pure fear swell up inside of her veins. She began to shake uncontrollably and the darkness seemed to engulf the room, dampening the light from the fire.

"Susan, are you still awake?" A voice enquired from the without.

Susan almost collapsed with relief as she recognised the questioner as her Mother.

"Yes Mother," she said. Backing away, Susan moved to the window in the hope of drawing attention away from the motionless figure that lay before the fire. She watched as the sparrows danced in the garden, searching for food on this cold night. She could sense her mother drawing near and tried to compose herself before confronting her. How simple your life is, she thought, as she took a final glance at the sparrows. Her eyes began to widen as she looked past these natural invaders of nature, past and onto the snow covered stone path beyond. It was the deep, heavy footprints that drew her attention. The snow seemed to have been violated, raped. She could feel the air gag in her throat. She turned and looked at her mother, who in turn looked back at her reflecting the horror upon her child's face.

"What's wrong?" she enquired, with great urgency.

Susan swallowed hard, clearing her throat.

"He's here!"

Jen's expression turned to that of deep puzzlement.

"Who's here?" her words were soft, yet demanding.

But before Susan could reply there came a sound that filled both women with a deep sense of dread. A sound that echoed throughout the empty house. A stranger had entered their home. The sound was that of a child's ball falling from the window ledge and bouncing several times upon the varnished floorboard of the attic bedroom. A sound that neither woman would ever forget.

****

Ann-Marie clutched the small, white card in her hand as she stepped onto the waiting coach: The gentle scent of the night air brought pleasant thoughts to her mind. How she loved the summer and its bright, carefree times. Inside, she sat next to the far window. Beside her sat Rose and opposite were her mother and Gabrielle all looking at one-another, filled with anticipation.

The coach pulled slowly away; turning up the drive it passed into the lanes and off into the splendour of France that was its countryside. Ann-Marie watched the world outside, the country folk tending their fields in the last vested shades of the summer's light. Dusk was falling, bringing with it the comfort of the long shadows that would reach across the world and with its comforting fingers would soothe Mother Nature to sleep. The farming folk waved as the coach passed, a little in respect but also a little in envy. For these honoured few could taste life at its sweetest source. Gathering speed the coach journeyed forward, the late evening was growing darker as the grey clouds of night gathered over-head. Ann-Marie's eyes followed the undulation of the land as it moved effortlessly towards the awaiting horizon; she observed the gloom as it enveloped all about her, gathering everything up in its arms and holding it until the soft light of morning. She now understood the magic that was darkness. The night was an undiscovered time, a time when the immortals could savour their existence and once again step onto the path of man.

It was the urgent looks that were being offered her by Gabrielle that alerted Ann-Marie to the cold dark château that sat silently upon the hillside. No lights burned in the windows, no mortal ventured upon its battlements. It was as if the very life of the building had somehow died, leaving behind this hollow soulless shell. Ann-Marie's mouth became dry and barren. Her speech had forsaken her, taking with it her courage. She could not understand why she was about to place herself into the hands of this immortal demon. Yes, she knew that she had to fulfil her destiny but at what cost, for she knew that if she failed now, in this time, then in the present she would have also lost the battle for her own survival. Gone were the strong words that had echoed in her mind less than a few hours before; gone was the strength that had fuelled her to this very point. If she could turn back time and run away from her destiny, she would without a second thought. Fear is the strongest of emotions and this reality burned itself, deep into her heart.

The château mesmerised her; she could not break its hold upon her emotions. She watched its every movement as the coach slowly passed this great foreboding structure, in the hope of catching a glimpse of the foe that she was to vanquish upon this night. She would fulfil her destiny, or die trying.

****

Christian watched as the small rubber ball bounced several times across the bare floorboards of the attic bedroom. His vampire eyes had neglected to observe the rejected children's toys that littered the window ledge of this vacant room. The window through which he invaded the gentle world of the Ward family was frozen shut by the winter winds, but his talon-like fingernails picked at the ice that had formed at the base of the frame. The window slid open almost silently giving only the slightest of thuds as it rested in the open position. From outside, a strong wind sent drifts of snow into the warm room, that alighted upon the dust covered furniture and floor. As the flakes landed they began to melt staining all that they touched with the pure blood of nature. It was the wind that dislodged the rubber ball and sent it bouncing across the floor, announcing the calling of this immortal intruder.

Inside the room Christian moved silently to the door and turned the handle; to his surprise he found that the door was not locked and he stepped into the darkness of the hallway. His eyes searched for any signs of life but none was forthcoming. He observed the oil paintings that lined the walls, the dried flowers that sat on the table at the end of the corridor and the stairs that invited him to enter the heart of this home. He moved forward but stopped just as he came to the landing, as below him were the stairs, descending into the dark shadows that engulfed this house. Christian sank slowly to his knees and peered at the painting that lay almost discarded against the wall. There sat the image of his foe. The painting of Ann-Marie stared back at him, her beauty filling him with awe. He reached out a finger and gently traced her delicate features; this action ignited a flame that had long since died within his immortal soul. He offered the painting a half smile and sank back into the shadows.

****

Jen held tightly onto Susan's arm as the fear began to rise within her.

"Who's he?" she whispered to Susan.

"You wouldn't believe me if I told you," she replied.

"At this point in time I'd believe anything."

Susan lifted her finger to her lips, a gesture that implied that she required silence from her mother, who complied without question.

"I can only say this once and you must believe me. That thing upstairs is not human and it will kill us if it can," Susan stated.

Jen's expression turned to that of amazement. How could her child express such fantasies? She shook her head in disbelief.

"Don't be foolish. Susan, Ring the police. I'm going upstairs to sort this out," Jen said. This latter action was said in the hope of placating the fears of her child.

"No Mother, I'm not lying. If ever you've believed me in my life, now is the time that I need you to," Susan implored.

"Ring the police," her tone was harsher and less forgiving. "And if it will make you feel better I'll take your Father's fishing knife with me." Opening the bookcase draw Jen took from it a long, sharp knife. "If this doesn't scare him off then nothing will."

She opened the living-room door and tentatively looked into the shadows, her heart began to pound, its fortified resonance echoing in her ears. She turned and gestured for Susan to contact the police; this she did before the shadows surrounded her. Susan lifted the receiver of the telephone; it was silent. She felt truly abandoned. Her eyes began to fill with tears as she stood helpless, a mere observer of her own destiny, a gentle candle battling in the hurricane known as life.

To Jen, her home seemed somehow colder than before, alien, inhospitable, rejecting her attention, it seemed to hide itself in the shadows. She moved towards the soft darkness and allowed it to wash over her as she ascended the house. As she passed the doors that lined the corridors she tried each one in turn and found them all to be secured against the intruder.

Moving to the next landing she stepped onto the stairs and climbed higher and higher into the darker reaches of the house. Never had her family home felt so cold and restless, rejecting her tender touches. Her blood raced through her system as her mind played tricks with the shadows that danced before her. She held the knife firmly in her grip; this comfort was her only sanity in this insane world into which she had stumbled only a few moments before. Looking up to the attic landing she feared this level the most. This part of the house she had never liked, even during the daylight hours, but now in the darkness of night its presence almost touched her skin with its unwanted attentions. Moving silently upwards she somehow felt violated. This intruder had forced her into an action that she would not consider normal and this she resented. She muttered under her breath, cursing the stranger that had disturbed her gentle life. As she climbed the stairs her eyes searched the shadows. She gasped as she made contact with a gentle pair of brown eyes that looked back at her from the darkness. Then, as her senses returned to normality she breathed a sigh of relief as she realised that those eyes belonged to a painting and for the first time in her life she cursed her daughter's talents. She rested against the wall to gather her thoughts before continuing on her journey. Closing her eyes she allowed her defences to wane and the knife to fall to her side.

She was comforted by her own stupidity.

It was from the shadows that the stranger came, his strong features exacerbated by the moonlight, the blue-silver aura seemed to add to his supernatural presence, giving him an almost god-like texture that issued from his skin. His blue eyes radiant in the darkness as he peered at his prey. His mouth opened slightly, revealing his sharp teeth. Slowly, silently he moved forward, smiling a sardonic smile as he drew closer to Jen.

Jen pushed herself away from the wall and turned to continue her journey upward. She recoiled in horror at the apparition that confronted her. Christian smiled a derisive smirk as he mocked her with a paradoxical taunt.

"Boo!" he whispered, in a menacing, yet mocking manner.

Jen's mouth fell open in horror as the demon descended upon her. She tried to protect herself as this abomination loomed over her, blocking out the moonlight. She tried to scream but nothing could escape from her fear-filled frame. She tried to drink in a deep breath, to loosen her throat so that she could warn her child of this abomination that confronted her. Stepping back she realised that she had the knife still in her possession and so swung with all of her might in the direction of the apparition. Christian cried in pain as its blade ripped deep into the flesh of his cheek.

"Bitch!" he screamed, as he fell backwards against the stairs. He was more shocked at his own unprepared action than those of his prey. The time that it took for him to gather his thoughts were brief but they were sufficient enough for Jen to make her escape. Racing down the stairs she called for her daughter to be ready to lock the living-room door.

From below Susan could hear the commotion and the calls of her Mother. Rushing to the strong wooden door she held it almost closed in readiness for her Mother's entrance. Her hand searched the lock for the brass key but to her horror she discovered that the key was missing. She searched her mind for a possible place in which she could find it, the kitchen? The Hall? Her mind drew a blank. She could hear the sound of her Mothers' frantic actions growing closer.

"Hurry, lock the door," Jen cried as she entered the room, her face flushed and sweaty. She slammed the door, sending an echo reverberating through the whole house.

"I can't find the key," Susan pleaded.

"What!" Jen looked at Susan in disbelief. "What do you mean you can't find it? There's a mad man running about the house and you can't find the key? Quick, get the other side of the bookcase and drag it in front of the door."

"Push," Susan pleaded to her mother, for she had no desire to be cut down by this self-perpetuating disease that was Christian. To both women it had felt as though an eternity had passed before the bookcase was in position against the door, but before either could congratulate themselves for their efforts Christian sent the full force of his anger against the obstacle that confronted him. The books from the centre of the case were sent cascading downwards as if a literary waterfall, crashing onto the ocean of wood that was the floor. An almost painful, yielding cry emanated from behind the broken, buckled door. This was followed by a brief silence then a second assault, then another silence. These silences were in no way golden or pure but they were black and hung in the air as if in the form of a great predatory creature, jaws salivating, awaiting its time to strike and take down its prey. The silence grew, expanding, engulfing the house. Jen turned to Susan with a look of horror etched upon her face. "I've just realised that that madman is out there and so is Ann-Marie."

Susan looked over to the form that lay next to the dying fire.

"No she's not, she's over there. Well sort of..."

Jen moved over to Ann-Marie's side and knelt next to her. Observing the almost translucent pallor of her complexion she realised that something was very wrong. She lifted Ann-Marie's wrist and felt for a pulse but could only find the faintest of mortal rhythmic beats.

"I can't feel a strong pulse; something's seriously wrong here, something's very wrong. I think that she could be close to death. We must call somebody. An ambulance, the police. Someone to help her and get rid of that bloody madman from my house."

"No Mother, she'll be alright. We'll be alright, we have to be," Susan pleaded.

Jen swung angrily towards her daughter and gripped her tightly upon each shoulder, looking penetrably into her eyes, she screamed. "Will you explain what the bloody hell is going on? There's some psychotic man running around my house trying to kill me, your friend is, to all intents and purposes, dead, and you're calmly standing there as if this happens to us every bloody day."

****

As the coach entered the thronging streets of Paris, a dark depravity hung in the air itself. From her vantage point, Ann-Marie could see the broken and desolate remnants of this once proud nation stretching out before her. The empty hope that issued pitifully from the eyes of any who had strength enough to raise their gaze to make contact with her own filled her with a deep sense of guilt. Not guilt for herself but for what she once was. How self-important they had become, debauched, they wandered aimlessly, blind to the needs of the common people. Mothers clutched starved infants to their breasts to suckle upon dead flesh just as a nation suckled upon its broken people.

From above, Gabrielle could hear the callings of the coach driver alerting them of a disturbance up ahead. She semi-stood and pushed her head out of the open window and looked up the street. She could hear the sound of rebellion in the air. A sound that was carried upon wave after wave of raw excitement. The coach began to gather speed in the hope of reaching its destination unhindered.

They could see the Roussel residence up ahead; the bright light and silk banners that cascaded down the side of this grand house gave a fairy-tale presence to the whole occasion. As the coach came to a halt a footman stepped forward and opened the door, offering those inside assistance. One by one they stepped into the warm July night. The air seemed to invite them to savour the gentle summer scent of blossom, which it carried upon the soft breeze.

Revellers laughed gregariously, shattering the magic of the night. The party ascended the steps leading to the Roussel residence; inside the splendour could only magnify the poverty to which Ann-Marie had been witness to only a moment before. Great tables were laden with sumptuous food and wine. Vast lakes of Champagne flowed; self-indulgence filled the air, choking the innocent and uninitiated alike.

Gabrielle moved swiftly into the throng of the party, offering a seductive glance to any of the young gentlemen who offered the briefest of glimpse in her direction. Her tiny frame promised a greater seduction to any who would venture close enough to partake of its sensual perfume. Her heavy breasts rose and fell as she overtly indulged in the banquet that was man. These actions seemed to please her mother greatly, almost to the point of encouragement. She would offer slight glances and smile in the direction of her daughter in the hope of ensnaring a suitor to warm her own empty bed. She would open her fan and brush it teasingly passed her lips then close it and hold it gently to her own breast. 'How little courtship had changed', thought Ann-Marie, as she witnessed the rituals of man that had long-since perished in the annals of time.

Realising that her other daughters hung close to her side, their mother ushered them into the main group of revellers. Ann-Marie stayed close to Rose's side for the desire that filled her that night was not that of carnal knowledge but that of success. Her eyes searched the room, eager to find the features that had haunted her nights and plagued her waking hours.

"Where are you Christian?" she muttered under her breath.

Ann-Marie backed away from the main group in the hope of being left alone to continue with her quest. Turning, she walked up the stairs from which she entered the main ballroom; all about her wine flowed and laugher rang in the air. The pain of a nation was ignored on this night and the peripheral indulgences of man were savoured to their excesses. Positioning herself next to one of the large windows, Ann-Marie surmised that she was now far enough away from the main body of the party to be left comparatively alone, however she had not anticipated the unwanted attentions of several eligible bachelors who had already cast their lustful eyes upon her delicate frame.

As the moments passed and the unwanted attentions of her prospective suitors mounted, Ann-Marie could feel the build-up of her fears as she could feel the surmounting odds of her task were stacked against her favour. She smiled externally yet inwardly she pleaded with the heavens to liberate her from this dark task. It was as if she were truly alone in this forgotten realm of history. The memories of her childhood and the pleasures of life were somehow alien to this world that had not yet experienced those transitions that had moulded her nature and viewpoint. The liberation of her wandering soul was the main factor that concerned her now at this point in time. A time that had no beginning, no end. A highway of existence for a perpetual soul that meandered aimlessly, blindly, searching for the only answer that has haunted man since he could comprehend his own being. A question that had been burned upon the lips of poets and philosophers, scientists and preachers. Why? Why, to all the pain and suffering? Why, to all of the joy and delight? Why, to the wars and conflicts? Why, to the prejudice and hate? Why? What was this all for? Closing her eyes a deep chill filled her, casting splinters of dark ice into her very soul and giving her a cold, cold answer. There was no reason. No understanding. No sympathy. Blindness in every order. No sensation. No empathy. No joy. Life for that reason and death because life must have a beginning and an end. At this moment she would gladly return to her modern life, allow another destiny to dictate her end and begin innocently, all over again. She knew that this was impossible, but now, in this hedonistic world, fantasy was her only escape. For this reality and its anticipation's were almost too much for her to bear.

All about, she could hear the attentive chatter of male voices calling and seducing with their hollow flattering words. She opened her eyes and smiled in a vulnerable, coy way. Looking gently at each of the gentleman individually, she offered her apologies and retreated from their attentions. Moving into the main body of the revellers she could feel herself being buffeted and hustled. It was a comforting pleasure to feel mortal once again. The sensation of touch almost thrilled her senses. Looking over to the far wall of the room she could see Rose conversing with a young man; her attention was concentrated and the rest of the world melted into the abyss that was not love. But Ann-Marie desired salvation from this ocean of hungry souls. She pushed passed those blind to her needs. As she moved recollection began to play dark tricks upon her thoughts. Casting shadows of remembrance into her mind. She stopped, her attention now focused in upon herself. She knew that she had been a witness to these events many times before. Could it be her soul reliving the traumas of its transition through the lives of her perpetual existence or was there a deeper meaning to this new sensation that haunted her? She could feel a gentle warmth wash over her. Someone was touching her. Speaking to her. Asking her a question.

"Are you alright?"

"Do you need to sit down?"

"You look a little flushed my dear. I think that this party has taken too much out of you."

Ann-Marie found herself staring at her saviour's chest, not daring to look into his eyes. His voice filled her with a deep feeling of comfort and protection but a deeper fear danced close by. She could feel the soft touch of his fingers upon her flesh as the stranger placed a gentle hand under her chin and lifted her eyes to his own. A blue as deep and as fresh as the ocean smiled back at her. His features were soft and gentle, comforting and considerate. Almost human. He smiled.

"You are beautiful, a vision. No other can match your worth." his voice was comfort itself. Its almost inaudible softness captivated her very soul, carrying her gently into him.

"My name is Christian Pontmercy and I am yours to command," he offered her a deep, respectful bow, and captivated her with his alluring eyes. He offered her his hand. Taking it filled her with an insurmountable pleasure that could not be matched by any experience that she had encountered in this realm or the last. Knowing what he was, became secondary. Fate has cruelly gathered together the essence of her imagination and tentatively mixed it with the fruit of her dark passions and its recipe stood before her.

His touch was almost sensual, light yet strong. She could feel the immense immortal power that flowed through this dark creation. His long nails caressed and teased her flesh, bringing forth the reality of this dimension into which she had cast herself. It was as if she had stepped from the black and white pages of a book and into the vibrant colours of a sensual world.

She followed Christian as he moved majestically, mingling with those present; it was as if he were a vision, a ghost inhabiting this fragile realm. He issued a calmness that touched all those close enough to feel his warmth. Without breaking physical contact they continued up a small set of marble steps that led to a window and out onto the balcony that overlooked the tree-lined gardens at the rear of the Roussel's family home.

Outside, the night mists had descended, bringing with them an almost fantasy appearance to this quiet haven within this pivotal point in the history of Paris, that offered freedom to the masses yet engulfed those blind within that proletariat only chaos and death. The sounds of revolution were distant and forgotten to those who ventured into the paradise on earth. Sitting gently upon a chair, Christian offered Ann-Marie the seat next to his by motion of his open palm. She responded and bowed her head not wishing to allow him to see the pleasure that his presence brought her. Her mind was a blank, she could use her cognitive powers but recollection was lost in the theatre that was once her mind. This creature that she had despised without knowing; feared without understanding, now sat beside her, filling her with a sensual love and understanding that she had never experienced in all of her lifetimes upon the mortal plain. She could hear the sound of her own breath as it gathered pace, deepening as anticipation filled her. The pulsating beat of her yearning heart forced her breast to rapidly expand, giving her the sensation of light-headiness. Looking up into his open, smiling face, she could feel only pleasure. His eyes beckoned for her to respond to his attentions and without thought she found that she was reciprocating his warm and passionate smile.

"You have me at rather a disadvantage madam," he said softly.

Ann-Marie's eye's opened in wonder, which was closely followed by concern.

"After all, I do not know your name. Am I just to call you beautiful for the remainder of the night? Even though, it is a prospect that would delight me immensely," he whispered in a seductive tone.

As she opened her mouth her true identity almost escaped but with a little quick thinking she recovered the situation.

"Marie-Anne, but some of my friends just call me Anne."

"I do hope that in time you will consider me a friend and allow me to call you by that name," he said playfully.

Ann-Marie was captivated by his smile, gentle yet resolute. She knew what he was, what he stood for, what he represented, but this too human creature that sat next to her filled her with a gentle warmth and serenity, far beyond the perimeters of mortal man.

"Forgive me," he said. "I have forgotten my manners. I have not yet offered you a drink. I would deem it to be a great honour if you would allow me to serve you. To be yours and yours alone on such a romantic evening." His blue eyes flashed and Ann-Marie could feel herself falling deeper into him.

"No thank you, not at the moment." she said, her words somewhat hollow in comparison to his own. 'Such a majestic creation.' she thought. 'Could the devil be such a genius?'

"Shall we just sit and watch the moonlight as it caresses the world? For the night is ours to command, our servant. And it will take you anywhere that you desire," Christian gently held Ann-Marie's hand within his own and turned his face to the garden; the light from within the room gave his features an almost angelic texture. Everything about him excited her. His long eyelashes, that bump on his strong Romanesque nose. His thin, uneven lips that parted only briefly to speak. The subtle ocean of his soft, caring eyes. She watched as his great chest rose and fell, almost in perfect time with the beat of nature. It was as if his heart itself were calling to her, asking for her to love him. Calling for her attention.

Looking into the moonlight filled garden, she couldn't help but feel that this reality into which she had stepped had a greater depth than that which she had previously left. Everything seemed vibrant and alive. The colours of the night reached out to her, beckoned her to fall into their arms. For the first time in her life she felt truly at peace with herself, at one with her inner turmoil. Turning to look at her companion she found to her embarrassment that he too was studying her every feature. She blushed and turned slightly away but only enough to ensure his attentions and not enough to offend.

"You are as pure as the morning air, the dew that touches a rose and gives sustenance to the thirsty. Your very presence is to me the blood that gives me life. It is as if our souls were one, joined by the heavens, bound together to savour the delights of the universe as a single creation. I can feel your presence within me deeper than any emotion; it is as if your soul were calling me. Crying in the cold depths of loneliness, and I, I am here to offer you solace, comfort and compassion against this bitter storm called life," Christian held her hand tighter within his own. What would you do if I were to tell you that I could grant you a wish far beyond your imagination's expectations? I could give you the earth and the heavens above; you could have the elements as your muse. The night as your comforter and time as your companion. I could give you a gift far beyond the riches of the Ottoman Empire. The gold of the Pharaohs and the silks of the East. I could show you pleasures that would never end. Experiences which would last for an eternity. Your every desire fulfilled," he smiled.

"But why...why me?" she whispered.

"All that I wish to do is to give you a gift, a sweet dark gift." Closing his eyes he lifted her hand to his lips and kissed her gently.

"Will you walk with me; join with me in this night?" he said.

Ann-Marie spoke without looking at him; her answer was soft yet yielding.

"Yes."

Taking both of her hands, Christian rose and guided her to her feet. Standing silently for a moment he stared lustfully into her soft brown eyes, touching her with his passion.

"I will retrieve my horse from the stables and we will escape into the night, and wander in each other's arms until the dawn finds us."

Closing her eyes she fell into his arms; the sensation of weightlessness filled her as Christian gathered her up and gently lowered her into the darkness of the garden below. Looking up she could see his features awash from the light that cascaded from the room behind him.

From her hideaway, Ann-Marie could see the expanse of the Roussel's garden; never had she been in a place of such beauty, and felt so alone. The night seemed to fall at an ever increasing pace bringing with it the dark shadows of uncertainty that filled her with doubt and pain. Should she fulfil her destiny or stay forever in his arms? She could feel the cyclone of self-doubt within and prayed for it to pass. A sound from beyond the orchard attracted her attention and she lowered herself behind hedge for protection. She could hear the distant sound of horse's hooves upon the damp lawn. From within the mist there emerged the proud figure of a horseback rider. Ann-Marie watched as he moved closer and stopped directly in front of her. He sat motionless for a moment before beckoning for her to join him on the back of his steed. Gripping his hand for support, she mounted the horse. Never before had she been so close to one she had loved so much, putting her arms about his waist she placed her head against the centre of his back and closed her eyes. She could feel the powerful muscles beneath his flesh as he reined the horse to move. In the midst of turmoil she had found serenity.

As they entered the war broken streets, chaos reigned all about, an anarchy that brought a deadly caress to anything that it touched. Yet somehow, this corruption seemed blind to their passion, oblivious to this eternal love as it tore up the Boulevards and cast down the once powerful nobility without mercy. Smoke filled the air from a thousand torches, used to guide a revolution; cries of pain and pleasure rose from all about. These were the starving rats that had turned the tide of history and abandoned the sinking imperial ship that was France.

****

As the trauma of revolution fell into silence behind them Ann-Marie found herself falling into the comfort of the night. History was in the making, evolution and revolution were dancing hand in hand but to this traveller in time the night brought only comfort and consolation to her fragile heart. Even the fierce rage of flames that licked and danced in the air above the Paris skyline only seemed to add a beauty to the soft colours of that July night.

Allowing herself to fall forward onto her lover's back, Ann-Marie could almost feel his strength as his muscles flexed beneath the thin material of his clothing. The sexual attraction almost enveloped her desires, sending them cascading into the deep dark waters of her soul. The gentle movements of the creature seemed to add a rhythmic serenity to her passions, a passion that almost touched the night itself. Placing her head gently against Christian's shoulder she allowed her eyes to wander into the dark comforting shadows of night. The trees that surrounded them seemed to usher them closer, offering their strong arms for protection against discovery, granting them passage into the realms of the lovers unknown.

The density of the forest seemed to gather, collecting its mass as they continued. Above, the sky was now a mere glimpse, as the canopy of this natural ceiling seemed to reject the attention of the heavens. Only the briefest of glances would allow the soft rays of the moon to guide their way on this dark journey. After a moment Ann-Marie realised that these rays were always ahead of them and never upon them, it was as if the moon herself knew that this bastard child of damnation was wandering below her. All about, the darker elements of nature were closing in, colluding, conspiring in readiness for the birth of a dark queen.

Pulling on the reigns, Christian brought the horse to an abrupt halt. Ann-Marie sat back and peered into the darkness that appeared to have enveloped them. All about, the night hung heavy.

"Why have we stopped here?" she asked nervously.

Christian dismounted and reached up to offer Ann-Marie his assistance. Gripping onto his shoulders she allowed herself to fall into his strong heavy chest. Her hands rested submissively against the harsh contours of his breast, alchemising the desires that raged within her.

"We have stopped so that I may once again gaze upon your beauty. So that we may be joined together, forever forged in the tormented parallels of our chaotic destiny. As the sun is to the moon and the darkness to the light, we shall journey forever into the unknown realm of our perpetual tomorrows. As you will be my light, that guiding flame that gives my lost soul direction, I shall be your rock, your steadying force. The purveyor of immortal pleasures, I have only seen a beauty such as yours in one other, a creature of such perfection that I would bow to her presence. She is the personification of all that is good within this world and within my soul. She is the balance between the darkness that is my core and the light that is my hope. Since we began this dark journey a lifetime ago I have always looked to her for the guidance and comfort of her compassion, the gentleness of her soul would invigorate me. Give me life within this life. I honestly thought that she was perfection, an inspired creation, moulded by the gods themselves and sent to entice me, tempt me. But now I find that there is another, a creature of excellence, sent to save me from myself. Save me from my own black memories," Christian gently gripped her hands within his own and lifted them to his lips, kissing them softly he looked into her eyes.

"Who?" Ann-Marie said, in an almost inaudible tone.

Christian closed his eyes and allowed his head to fall gently forward. His face almost human in the soft shadows of the night.

"A one so dear and gentle, so beautiful that all others, save for yourself, pale into comparison. She is the other half of my soul. My identity in life as in death. She is Mica. My sister. When we accepted this gift we pledged our souls to one another, a price higher than either of us could ever have imagined. A debt that we would repay for an eternity or until the heavens themselves would fall from the skies and lie broken at our feet, alone with the dreams of our youth and the aspirations of our infancy. This gift which we embraced brought with it great pleasures and delights but it also carried a great burden and sacrifice. Its darkness would envelop the soul and devour, the very essence that was your mortality, your inner-self, leaving behind a wilderness, a void in the blackness of your heart. We would embrace the dark gift with blind eyes and, ironically, it was the gift that gave us vision, the capacity to look beyond the self and into the inner-self. To touch the perpetual tomorrows and recall the fallen yesterdays. Even though this in itself is a nightmare more than most could endure, it is not this which I fear; no, above everything which my kind may suffer there sits a dark demon. It taunts us, calls to us, brings back the memories of our empty existence and plays them across the proscenium of our thoughts over and over again until it reaches fever pitch and your mind burns as if it were the coals of a blacksmith's furnace. Forging an indestructible chain of memories that hang about your shoulders, weighing you down until the pressure of their presence is unbearable and madness engulfs you. Man has given this tormentor a name and that name is loneliness."

Touching his face, Ann-Marie spoke in soft comforting tones.

"You must have loved your sister dearly; it's as if she were gone, lost from your soul. Has she died?" Ann-Marie asked.

Christian smiled. "What is death but another barrier which we must conquer in time? Let us just say that we are parted and she lives within the confines of another democracy, within which I could not have survived."

"Then why do you not return to her, see her once again?" Ann-Marie said.

"The Tribe has long since become a distant memory for me and I must make my own future, my own pathway in this cold life. I must make you one of my own kind."

"What do you mean, your own kind? Ann-Marie said.

"What would you do if I could offer the world to you tonight? So that you may see with new born eyes, touch with newfound senses? Love with a newfound heart? If I were to offer this gift to you, would you accept it?"

To Ann-Marie's horror she found herself contemplating his words, turning them over in her mind. Blindly she searched for reasons why she should banish this beautiful aberration from her thoughts and cast his love into the dank earth, she could find none.

"Yes!" she heard herself repeating over and over. "Yes! I will be yours until the end of time."

Christian smiled and pulled her close to him, he could feel the pulse of her heart against his chest. Gently he kisses her upon the lips, a warm human kiss.

"We must fulfil the desires of the followers and those who worship Caliban. We must sacrifice an innocent soul and give them a new queen."

Gently Christian took her hand and led her through the undergrowth; all about the night fell into silence in anticipation of what was to follow.

"Christian... where are you taking me?" she enquired.

"All will be revealed in a moment my beloved," he replied.

****

He's moving" Jen said. "He's stalking us, manoeuvring his way about the house. I feel like some caged animal, waiting to be devoured." She moved to the bookcase and lifted the receiver of the telephone, silence greeted her urgency.

"It's dead. The snow must have brought the lines down."

"Either that or our friend has made sure that we're in this alone," Susan said.

Jen placed the receiver gently back onto its rest, listening to the night as she did.

"I can't hear anything. Do you think that he's gone? Maybe he's realised that were more than a match for him. I can't stand this; I want to know what's going on." Gripping the side of the bookcase she pulled at the great bulk. "Help me; I'm not going to give in to him. I'm going to fight with every last breath that I have."

The sound of naked wood colliding filled the room, a sound that soon fell into silence. Jen gently gripped the door handle and turned it. It opened with a slight clicking sound. Peering in the shadows Jen could only make out the reflection of the hall light as it danced across the glass of the long cased clock.

"I think that he's gone" she whispered. Opening the door a little further her eyes searched deeper into the darkness. "I can feel cold air; he must have left the back door open. He's gone. I told you that he wouldn't stay for long if he couldn't get his own way."

Jen did not see the green eyes that watched her from the dark shadows below, eyes full of searching desire, yearning for his hunger to be fulfilled. Without hesitation he pounced. Jen fell backwards as fright gripped her soul. In an instant he was about her, pulling at her, yearning for her attentions. She screamed, filling the room with her fear, sending the creature spiralling away in his terror, his fur standing on end.

"Mother!" Susan cried. "It's alright, it's alright. It's only Merlin, the cat from next door. When Christian exited the house he must have left the kitchen door open and Merlin wandered in with the hope of finding a warm place to sleep and something to eat. The Petersons are at a Christmas party and won't be back until late in the morning, they must have left him out over-night."

Jen stood up, gasping for breath.

"If that little sod does that again he won't see another Christmas."

Susan picked up their new houseguest and placed him upon the sofa. Walking to the open door she listened to the silence that concealed the darkness.

"I think that he's gone," she said.

"What did you say?"

"I think that he's gone"

"No before that. Something like 'When Christian left...,'" she looked at Susan with a distasteful glare. "How do you know the identity of this man? Why do I feel like the fool in all of this evil pantomime? There is something that's going on and nothing seems to be adding up. What's got into you? What is going on?"

Susan looked about the room, embarrassment filling her every emotion; quickly she returned their attentions to the danger of intrusion. "We have to check to see if he's in the house. I'll go Mother, you stay here and guard Ann-Marie."

"No way, there is no way on earth that you're going out alone and no way that your leaving me here alone. It's either we both stay here or we both search the house."

Susan looked to Ann-Marie "I suppose that she'll be alright. I get the feeling that he's long gone."

Huddling together for comfort both women stepped into the cold shadows of the hallway, only to be engulfed by their black waves. Behind them the abominable features of their quest peered through the glass from his vantage point in the outside world. His hungry eyes eagerly devouring the presence of his prey.

Together, the women wandered blindly through the cold, inhospitable house. This building that was once their home was now defiled and polluted. Its tender heart was torn from its essence, leaving behind a black and unholy atmosphere. Suspicion hid around each corner and beneath each eve. The long, dark shadows of night huddled together in their parliament, conspiring against the innocent who wandered into their own forgotten world.

It was in the kitchen where this abhorrent defecation was most apparent. All about, an impression of evil clung to the very walls, its taste hanging in the air. The outside door stood ajar allowing all of cold and the naked elements of nature to invade this once sacred haven, bringing with it the inimical tenderness of its touch. The snow was beginning to pile up against the furniture, leaving small snow dunes that criss-crossed the kitchen floor. Jen closed her eyes and gave a heavy sigh.

"What have you done?" she demanded of Susan, under her breath. "What have you let into my home?" Her words were harsh and abrasive.

Susan stammered, searching her mind for an explanation.

"I want the truth and I want to know it all. I must have been mad to let this incident go as far as it has. For the first time in your life that I've allowed you to be responsible for your own actions and you repay me with this," Jen held her hand to her forehead in dismay. "We must contact the police and get help for your friend," Jen paused. "What is wrong with her, has this Christian done something. Attacked her? Stalked her? Is he somebody who she knows, someone from her past? An ex-lover, boyfriend? What? Tell me!"

Susan's eyes opened wide as fear filled her.

"No!" she cried. "You can't get the police, she doesn't want that. She can sort it all out when she gets back."

"Gets back" Jen said in surprise. "What are you talking about? She hasn't gone anywhere. She's lying on our living-room floor in some sort of..."

Susan was about to explain her words but the sound of breaking glass filled the air, shattering their senses and bringing their attentions to an abrupt and decisive halt.

Susan's hand raced to her mouth in a vain attempt to quell the scream that was rising within.

144

"It's him, Christian. He's returned," she said.

Jen looked along the cold dark corridor that led to the living room; its unwelcoming shadows turned her mind against any thoughts of rescue.

"Yes," she reached down and gripped Susan's hand. "And I think that he's got what he came for," she said, closing her eyes as shame washed over her.

****

As she stepped into the clearing in the forest Ann-Marie was captivated by the magnificence of her surroundings. Great trees reached to the heavens, their branches meeting overhead, framing a prefect moon. Soft clouds reflected the chaos that reigned below as their gentle white complexion were bathed in an aura of red, echoing the turmoil that raged as the revolution fell all about.

"It's beautiful, isn't it?" Christian said, watching the horizon as the flames that engulfed Paris captured his imagination. "How cleansing. It's as if the world needs to be vindicated of its sins and the only way to achieve this is by bathing everything which is perpetrated by the unclean hands of man in an ocean of fire. Flames to soothe and comfort the innocent and dispel the naked desires of the unworthy."

Unnoticed, Ann-Marie had moved from his side and now stood facing a great precipice; a vast pit crudely dug in the forest floor. Reaching over the lip of its far side stood a great mound of earth, prevented from returning to its earthly origins but a man-made barrier of wood. Looking deeper into its dark shadows she could almost taste the presence of decaying flesh below. Her hand came to her mouth in disgust.

"Christian. What is this?" she said pointing to the pit.

Moving to her side, he took her hand and smiled.

"All shall be revealed in time my dear." Guiding her, they moved to the centre of the forest opening. There, they found themselves before a great stone alter, carved with the symbol of a pentagram. Upon this, sat two silver goblets and a sacrificial knife.

"The time is almost upon us. I can sense them moving closer. The followers of the discipline. The worshipers of Caliban," he said.

Ann-Marie strained to hear the lightest of sounds carried upon the night air, but none was forthcoming.

"What do you mean? I can't hear anything."

Christian looked to her.

"After this night, my dear, you shall hear and see everything, your every desire shall be fulfilled and you shall want for nothing." Turning from her he whispered to himself. "And you shall have an eternity to regret it."

From all about, hooded figures entered the opening, their bowed heads held in reverence for the creature that stood before them. Gathering, they stood in two direct lines adjacent to the altar in anticipation of the events to follow. Christian moved from Ann-Marie's side and stepped closer to the altar. Slowly surveying the disciples he smiled, revealing his teeth.

145

"Thank you for coming to me on this night. How fitting it is that the old should be destroyed, as the new is about to be reborn. Look to the horizon and see the demise of all that which you once worshipped. Gone are the soft beds of roses and the lap of luxury. Man has turned against man and been brought down by his own indecision. Your fragile world has come to an end and the dawn of a new era is about to come, a new, stronger civilisation is about to stand tall. You are all followers of the truth; you have turned from the new gods and returned to the old. It is as it was written in the pages of history that man would always return to his first master. For too long has he followed the desires of a shattered religion, blindly complying with the yearnings of a splintered and segregated hope in this faithless world. I am here to offer you choice, a difference. Follow the teaching of my master and become one with infinity. Death need no longer be the end of your existence, this barrier that is held as a threat by other religions, a time of damnation, for you all can be banished for an eternity. Immortality can be yours. Turn the wheel and break the chains of life, do not allow the weeds of your indifference and uncertainty to grow and choke the road to your own personal Eden. You can achieve anything which you so desire, your destiny is your own to command. Forge your own religion. No longer shall you be seen as a disciple to a blind faith. For us immortals shall not be the gods whose light shines apparent and guides their followers, showing them the way to their heaven or offer them salvation for their sinful souls. No! Our light shall shine, it shall light the fuse to confrontation and those who oppose us shall die. Through confrontation comes change and our words shall sweep this world."

Christian turned to Ann-Marie and held out his hand.

"Tonight. There is to be a new queen, a sovereign to this dark realm that will cover us all. We shall start where others have finished. We shall strive to move past the barriers placed upon our minds by others and reach into a realm of thoughts far greater than anything perceived by mortal and immortal alike. We shall not conquer destiny, we shall 'be' destiny. Life, death, infinity and power shall all be ours."

Standing by his side, Ann-Marie could feel the full impact of his words as they burrowed themselves deep into her mind, burning as they touched. History that had not yet been was repeating its self. Echoes of future events were cascading through the annals of time and ringing their truth in her soul. She knew that these events were yet to come, yet had already been. It was as if she were a silent witness to the unfolding pages of history, pages that reached out before her. Briefly touching the tainted soul of man before falling into the black abyss of oblivion.

Feelings, which she could not atone, rose from deep within as a tide of selfishness enveloped her, blinding her to truth. She had cast aside the desires of time and now languished in a bed of pure carnal indulgence. Holding tightly onto Christian's hand she turned away from that destiny, blind to the dark lamentations of history.

"Your Queen!" he cried.

Respectfully, each figure bowed and moved slowly away.

"Let the ceremony begin," Christian demanded.

A deep, rhythmic tone rose from the worshippers as they gathered and moved closer to the altar. From beyond her vision Ann-Marie could hear the cries of an innocent, cries that echoed a fear that lay buried deep within her breast. Her breathing became laboured as anticipation filled her. Anticipation that was soon to be followed by horror, for, from deep within the depths of the dark forest she could see the tortured figure of an abandoned soul. Without care or consideration two of the hooded followers dragged the sacrifice closer to the altar, their urgency bruising and tearing at her soft naked flesh. Her cries haunted the air with their pitiful demands.

"Why are you doing this to me? Please, set me free." The figure twisted and turned. "Somebody help me. What have I done to deserve this?"

Her voice brought a strange recollection to Ann-Marie's thoughts. Yet it was only as the open moon allowed its gentle light to fall upon her features did the identity of this captive reveal itself. Ann-Marie could feel her stomach beginning to turn as fear filled her eyes. Eyes that were witness to this abomination, an abomination that was in her name. Her lips repeated a single name over and over again.

"Gabrielle!"

Gabrielle ceased her struggling and looked directly to Ann-Marie, thinking her a saviour she pleaded for mercy.

"Marie-Anne. You must help me."

The sight of Christian standing majestically behind her sister brought revulsion to Gabrielle's mind.

"What have you done to my sister you animal, you creature of Satan? Marie-Anne, do not listen to him. He is a sorcerer, a demon. He will bewitch you; cast his dark spells upon you. Run if you can, save your soul."

Christian moved closer to the captive figure until their faces were almost touching.

"Such strong words from one who is about to fulfil their destiny. Shall we see such bravery when your own demise is upon you? The reaper shall be your lover and death will be your dowry." With an uncaring wave of his hand Christian motioned for the ceremony too begin.

Ann-Marie moved nervously to his side.

"You see my dear, life must come to an end and these bonds must be broken. For you to truly achieve your destiny you must renounce all that you once were and sever these connections that you have to your mortality," he said.

She watched in horror as Gabrielle was lifted high into the air, as naked as the skies above. Her slender body contorting and twisting in fear, slowly, she was lowered upon the altar and held in readiness for Christian's dark intentions.

"Life is a transient thing," he began. "…and this world is a harsh place. To proclaim your rightful position in this existence you must take from the weak and support the strong. For only by example can we lead, only by courage can we deliver."

"I offer this humble creature for your pleasure Lord Caliban. It is in your name that I shall take from her that which she holds most precious, her life, and give its perpetuation to another, more worthy of your blessing."

Slowly he allowed his cold fingers to trace across the veins of Gabrielle's neck and down onto her chest. She shuddered at his touch as repulsion enveloped her. Fixing his eyes upon those of his victim he stared into her soul, raping her of all that was innocent, devouring the good, leaving nothing but hatred in its place. Gripping tightly to her throat he pulled her close to him, his breath urgent with a darker passion.

"Taste the bitter sweet pleasures of your death my dear, for few can see the face of their deliverer into this next world."

With a speed too fast for mortal eyes to see he fell upon her, his sharp teeth burying their harsh presence into the soft landscape of her flesh. He could taste the bitter sweetness of his triumph upon his tongue as he drank deeper and deeper the delights of his immortality. He could feel the presence of this innocent's elixir as it burned and bathed his soul.

Breaking from his feast he opened his mouth and allowed the cold night air to fill his lungs and calm his passion. He could feel the pulsating rhythms of his heart increase as the echoes of another faded into oblivion.

Regaining his composure he looked to the almost lifeless form of his victim. Smiling he blew her a mocking kiss. A kiss that fell upon cursing lips. Moving closer he allowed his own lips to touch those of his victim.

"Where are your strong words now?"

Kissing her forehead he whispered.

"Sleep, for this darkness shall consume us all one day."

Gabrielle lifted her almost lifeless arms and rested them around Christian's strong neck. In his arrogance, he allowed her attentions to continue unchallenged. This was to be his fatal mistake. With the remaining strength that filled her dying form she pulled him close to her, cradling him in her deadly embrace. Summoning all that was good within herself, she prayed for vindication before burying her teeth deep into her executioner's neck, and there she tore and bit at his harsh perpetual flesh. Immortal blood issued from his open wound and onto her mouth. A great crimson rainbow filled the air with the very essence of damnation. Staggering, he pulled himself from her embrace and fell to the ground next to the altar. His gasping vulnerable form, filling his followers with doubt and fear. Their god had fallen at the hands of one so innocent, slain by a gentle beauty.

Ann-Marie rushed to his side. This once-proud creature that filled her with strength and direction looked back at her with pitiful pleading eyes. Tears of blood ran in rivers down his hollow cheeks and onto his lace shirt, the crimson tide of its presence devouring the innocence of the soft white material, leaving only a bloodied witness to the event which had passed.

"Help me!" he whispered with a tortured voice.

Indecision gripped her, self-doubt haunted her. Reaching down she placed her arms about his neck and lifted him from his graceless demise. Turning to seek assistance she found herself alone in this cold dark night. His once strong followers, strengthened by his immortal boasts had fled into the forest, searching for comfort and understanding at the falling of their dark angel. In that briefest of moments his credibility had flown, like a dove upon the autumn winds.

Staggering in an unholy dance, Ann-Marie guided her love blindly. Her mind tormented by the words of a life that she had long since forgotten. She knew now that she must find the remaining threads of her destiny and achieve her goal. This life was not her own to command and she had deceived herself into thinking that this parallel existence could replace that which she knew was her own. This full, compassionate, vibrant life that filled her with a sensuality and direction has to be set free. The destiny of another depended upon her unselfish deeds. Looking at the broken form of her lover, she pleaded with her inner-self for strength to achieve her task. A strength that was supported by the images of her sister's pleading, bloodied face, searching for her redemption. Here, at her time of death, she could only think of another; as her life-force left her mortal form she pleaded with the powers of darkness to save Marie-Anne's soul. How insignificant she felt. This Communicator who could live within the boundaries of a thousand lives and yet could not see past the desires of the one. Blinded by love and driven by lust. She knew that she had to fulfil that which had been, and so, closed her breaking heart against the events that were to follow, she urged herself to embrace that which had been written in time and was whispered to be her true destiny.

"This is for you, dear Gabrielle," she said, gripping tightly onto his weakening body, his once strong limbs were now cumbersome and restricting, as his strength wept from his mortal wound. Christian was beginning to lose consciousness as Ann-Marie pulled him closer to his final destination. Looking through tear filled eyes, she took a final glimpse of the love that she was soon to lose.

Within, it felt as though her heart would break as he drew her closer in a comforting embrace. She felt as if she were a mother betraying the trust of her child, casting him unloved into a cruel and savage world. Holding him, she looked into his sorrowful, half open eyes. Even now, they evoked deep feeling that betrayed her thoughts.

"Remember my love, that I will love you with all my heart until the end of time. In the years to follow look kindly upon my actions and see them for what they are. The actions of one who loves you and not one who desires to see your downfall. You have brought to me in this brief moment of time, a feeling of true happiness. For the first time in my life I feel truly alive, and for that I bless you." Looking away from Christian Ann-Marie recalled the words of another. "You were right James. Some wounds do get deeper with time."

Closing her eyes, she allowed the weight of Christian's body to pull him backwards and downwards. She watched as he fell silently into the blackness of the pit, engulfed by the dark, hungry shadows, taking with him the very essence of her soul. All about, the night fell into silence as a requiem to their love. The only sound that could be recognised was that of her own sobbing, deep and mournful.

Her delicate hand pulled and pried at the wedge that secured the housing that restrained the earth from returning from whence it came. With urgency, she gripped the softwood and urged it to comply, then, without hesitation it relinquished its hold upon its prize and released its treasure. Slowly the earth began to fall into the pit, gathering speed as its mass moved forward, until eventually his burial mound was complete.

Destiny had righted itself and Ann-Marie had never felt so alone. It was as if her soul, her spirit had been stripped, leaving only the hollow shell that was once her form.

"Farewell my love," she said, as she turned and walked to the altar.

She refused to turn back for she knew that this was truly the end. Her mind now turned to the dark images of her fallen sister and the mortification, which she felt for her own selfish actions and emotions, which she had experienced. These chagrin desires would haunt her for an eternity, for now she knew how cruel destiny and prophecy could be, for they could both be upon you and you could be blinded by your own knowledge to such a degree that the reality of your situation would only become apparent as the final curtain were about to fall.

As she moved closer the soft light of the moon revealed to her that the altar retained little evidence of the events which had passed. There was no blood, no suffering and no body. Ann-Marie searched all about but she could find no signs of her lost sister. A deep sense of dread filled her, bringing with it the desire to leave these sorrowful times, urging her to return to the perceived safety of her own natural world.

A gentle rain fell from the skies; to Ann-Marie it was as if the night were mourning the events which had passed. Lives destroyed and changed beyond recognition. Sitting next to a tree on the edge of the forest opening she could feel the corners of her mind fading to black and realised that her time upon this realm would soon be over. She allowed the images of the events to cascade backwards, through the dimensions of her dark thoughts. These images became twisted and contorted as they merged with those of her own time and the space between. She could feel her soul as it rose from deep within; its urgency almost frightened her. This captive creature of perfection yearned to be free; to wander through the corridors of time and once again be at one with the essence that was nature.

Lying back, Ann-Marie watched the light of the heavens. Above, shooting stars crisscrossed the skies, signalling the demise of a once powerful empire and the birth of a new regime. All about there was the strange presence of death and change, which haunted the land and the people within. She had tasted her fill. Urging her mind to fulfil its task she fell deeper into herself.

Images of past times began to unfold as the powers of her talent began to draw her essence forward. The soft winds of the astral plain carried her upward and into this other realm of existence. How she wished that she could lose herself in this astral world, forever to wander through these avenues of possibility. To become one with the universe and leave the suffering of that which was left behind. Higher and higher her spirit climbed into skies of the forgotten realm, her soul was as weightless as air, free from the torments, which has so recently haunted her conscience.

She could feel her spirit falling in readiness to return to her mortal form, her limbs were becoming heavy as their presence became apparent. As weight enveloped her, drawing her down and into her mortal bonds. The great speed at which she was travelling came to an abrupt halt as she entered her fragile form, thrusting her spirit forward. She could once again feel the cumbersome rigidity of her mortality as she struggled to regain consciousness; opening her eyes she was surprised to see that a great plethora of white, greeting her vision. Her senses danced with danger. The anticipation of warmth and serenity was nowhere to be found. The only emotion and sensation which filled her were those of fear and coldness.

Sitting up, Ann-Marie realised at once that she was outside in the open air. Looking about she recognised the Ward's garden. The world seemed somewhat magical as a gentle fall of snow issued about her.

"How did I get out here?" she said out loud.

A gentle voice spoke from behind her, a voice that brought the dark fears of recognition.

"Remember my love, that I will love you with all my heart until the end of time..."

Ann-Marie turned and looked directly into the eyes of her beloved. Smiling she gasped.

"Christian!"

Lunging forward he gripped her throat.

"Bitch!" he hissed. "How I hate you. You left me for dead. Burying me for an eternity. I would have given you the world, immortality, and how did you repay me? By allowing me to become a banquet for the worms," he pulled her face close to his own, their lips almost touched. "You have fulfilled your destiny and now your presence is no longer required."

Ann-Marie could feel his grip about her throat tighten as his fingers buried themselves deeper into her flesh. For some unknown reason she did not struggle but somehow welcomed his actions. She longed to be released from this mortal restriction. Christian moved his head away and observed her expressionless face. His eyes searched her features for the slightest form of supplication to his actions, as none was forthcoming he gently released his grip.

"Do you wish to die?" he said.

Ann-Marie did not reply.

Slowly, he became angry at her detachment and allowed this to show in his features. Opening his mouth, he revealed his decision.

"Do you want me to break your brittle soul, mortal beloved? Cast you down into the dark seas of eternity? Forever to be lost in the heavenly oceans of contemplation and regret? Life is brief, yet death is for an eternity."

Ann-Marie did not answer.

A rage well up within him. He screamed.

His rage was stemmed by the intrusion of another. From the house there came the distant sound of footsteps. Christian allowed his grip to relax upon his nemesis and Ann-Marie fell silently to the snow. He stood slowly, utilising his senses to search the shadows before him. The footsteps were growing nearer, gathering pace as they progressed. Then, as quickly as they began they ceased. Christian's eyes searched the darkness; he could sense no changes in the atmosphere. Turning, he returned his attention to his victim. To his surprise the figure that stood before him was not that which he anticipated.

"Boo!" Jen said, before bringing down the full weight of discarded lead guttering, which had fallen off the house that previous winter, across Christian's head. This impact sent him spiralling backwards into the snow, great rivers of blood running down his forehead.

"Quick, Susan! Get Ann-Marie and get into the house," she screamed.

Christian stood, reeling from this conflict. A deep hatred filled his eyes. The blood, which flowed down his face, stopped and receded until eventually his features returned to their vampiric perfection.

A witness to this unnatural event, Jen stepped back in horror.

"What are you?" she said.

"Your worst nightmare, come to life," he said smiling, revealing his identity.

"Yes. And I'm yours," a voice said from behind.

Christian turned quickly, before him stood the fragile form of Susan, a blazing torch in her hands.

Almost at once he realised the complexity and ramifications of the danger into which he was now placed. For he knew that his immortal flesh would be consumed within moments by the hungry passions of a naked flame. He stepped deeper into the shadows in an attempt to minimise his contact with this danger. Smiling, he acknowledged his limitations and bowed to his adversaries.

"How the fragile have found their strength. Quite the passionate protector. Defiance brings out the beauty in you my dear, a beauty that I will savour as I devour your soul. Yet, my hungers have been appeased and I would hate to waste a good vintage upon the spoils of sport. So I bid you farewell. Ladies, till we meet again." With these words he vanished, too quick for mortal eyes to see. Melting into the shadows of the night.

"Let's get her inside" Jen said pointing to Ann-Marie. Looking back to Susan, she marvelled at her initiative. "How did you know that he would be afraid of fire?"

Susan glanced back at her with sheepish eyes.

"I didn't. But now it means that we have one more weapon on our side to aid us in our struggle against this dark creature."

Two

The savage winter winds screamed as they darted and danced their way in and out of the broken, tumbledown ruin of the desolate farmhouse. A sole sentinel, watching the world pass by from this remote, forgotten vantage point at what initially appeared to be the very edge of the known world. Life had long since left this once thriving homestead, taking with it the ring of laughter and happiness that would fill the air, rising like a sweet tender kiss of love and filling this home with a mortal warmth and joy. Yet, those rafters that once felt the gentle caress of love, now felt the bitter sting of the merciless wind as it bit deep into its rain soaked timbers. Timbers that lay broken and forgotten, the old to the young, no longer of any visible use, disregarded, allowed to melt back into the earth from whence they came, leaving no trace of their time or their interwoven actions with those whom they once loved or cared for.

For now, the farmhouse that was built so strong, for those who wished to control the forces of nature lay battered and broken by the elements which they sought to tame. It lay, as if savaged by animals, dying in the cold winds of winter, its beams, the ribs to an open chest.

A faint movement came from within; not from one who sought shelter on this abhorrent night, but from one who sought solace. Stepping into the cold night Callum could feel the wind lash and tear at the delicate embroidered material of his clothing. Pulling at them like the gnarled fingers of a beggar tearing at the opulent cloth of the garments rich apparel, sending the fur lined cape that hung about his shoulders outwards as if the wings of a great bat. Pulling it about himself he set forth into the night, not caring in which direction his wandering would take him; blindly he marched on, his mind a carnival of emotions. A subtle light from a sorrowful moon offered him guidance as he walked silently through the trees and down the mountainside.

He recalled the memories of endeavours lost and opportunities missed, and in some perverse way he felt happy within himself. For these were the emotions which haunted him in his mortality. Loneliness was his most fervent of companions, an honest soul mate. She would never leave you, never lie, never abandon your hopes, for there, constantly in the back of his mind she would linger, awaiting his call for her to once again join him on his lonely quest through his existence. The centuries have somehow faded from his thoughts leaving only a distant shade of grey in their place. These were not the harrowing times that tormented his soul, the times which brought dread and uncertainty. No. These times, which he despised the most, was the here and now, the present. The past could be looked upon with the soft light of recollection, its sharp painful corners could be moulded and smoothed by the tools of experience, yet the harsh reality of the present would tear and strip your soul, exacerbated by the cold touch of loneliness.

****

By the time that he had exercised the demons of his past, Calais was almost upon him; the night had fallen by bringing him one step closer to the end of his painful existence. For years he had suffered at the hands of his knowledge, tormented by his intelligence. Within the tribe he was seen as the one to be followed, looked up to. Yet never in his time within the comfort of their walls was he allowed to have self-doubt, anxiety and trepidation. He was the strong, building block of their society that could never fall by the wayside. A mantle, whose weight was almost unbearable at times. How blind others

153

were to his own desires and uncertainties, his needs were dismissed and his concerns abandoned.

This was the past, in a time when his soul could no longer fly into the heavens and touch him with a brief moment of happiness. This would all change; he was now master of his own destiny, the writer of his own history. He would sail through the sea of life, savouring the delights, which he would encounter, blind to the desires of others, and yet he knew that this all would ring hollow without the presence of his one true love.

His mind once again turned to Mica. His Mica, the one who could cast aside the clouds of doubt and fill his heart with light so strong that he could see the future as a road peppered with possibilities and opportunities. His immortality could be an adventure rather than a curse.

Three

She realised that her journey was almost at a conclusion as she saw the soft outline of the English coastline through the light fog that seemed to have enveloped the little ferry since it left its homeport of Calais. The seas had been kind, offering little resistance. Yet now, in anticipation of her confrontation, the black waters of the North Sea began to buffet the little boat. Its valiant metal hull almost paling into insignificance as the great waves that rose and fell against this great canvas of nature that was the sea. White foams splashed across the decks, bring a salt texture to the very air itself. Her immortal eyes did not recognise this ecological invasion, for her mind brought back to her senses images that were surmised forgotten. Images of a time long passed, a time that had fallen into history, almost lost forever.

Standing there, before her beloved England, Mica could almost touch the images that cascaded before her. Centuries before she had left these welcoming shores with the hope and desire of fulfilling a distant dream. Searching for the reason for her existence, a mortal lost upon the sea of life. She had cast aside the trappings of their charmed life and with the blind aspiration of discovering the link that bonded herself to her lovelorn brother, she marched impetuously into the unknown. An action that she would regret for an eternity.

Now, in the culmination of a thousand daydreams she had returned, a stranger to her own shores. Closing her eyes, she allowed the cold winter winds to wash over her. Their bitter sting purging her dark thoughts as Darius' words returned to claim her once again.

Voices began to rise from the far reaches of the ferry and Mica knew that her time upon this craft was coming to an end. The difficulty which she had experienced boarding in Calais almost drained her of her preternatural energies, a conflict which she had little desire to repeat. How complex it was now. In her time, travel was an adventure, a learning process, and a confrontation of cultures. Yet now people were tagged and processed, ushered and escorted, and regarded with suspicion. It had turned from a gentle under efficient pastime to a strong over bearing efficacious machine, which catered for the masses and rejected the individual. If this were the precursor to this modern world, then Hell had truly devoured this Earth.

Lowering her eyes, she looked at the dark waters that invited her to rest in their gentle caress, gripping the brass railing that encompassed the ferry she stepped over it and gently lowered herself onto the outer edge of the boat. There she stood in brief contemplation before falling silently into the dark waters below.

Four

The dark tunnel stretched out before him, a triumph to architecture. This monument to the aspirations of modern man had truly turned back the clock of time and forged a link once again with those nations whom nature had torn asunder. With his perceived divine right, mortal man had defied the verdict of natural balance and re-written his own history. Setting himself above the hand of divinity he manipulated and moulded the element to achieve his desire, a desire that would be fulfilled at any cost. This tunnel that spanned an angry sea would bring salvation to the sanity of one lost in his own immortality.

Callum watched as the magnificent trains sped past him and into the depths of the open earth. He marvelled at the speed at which they travelled, how science had progressed he thought, how different the world had become. For too long he had remained cocooned within the comfort of his own world, safe within the confines of his segregated existence. Watching these triumphs of man he realised how little his mind had grown. He was lost, trapped in the annals of a time past and the transition into this realm of thought may already be too much for him to bear, for the comprehension of these thoughts filled him with a deep anxiety and sorrow. Had he wandered for too long in the serene pastures of conformity, becoming an innocent bystander to his own destiny. And now, when he wished to participate in the action and reactions of life, he realised that he may already be too late.

For centuries he had proclaimed that the only way forward for his people was regression. They should segregate their existence from all others and live without contact with the outside world, yet he knew in his heart that this would eventually lead to an inflexibility of their thoughts and their eventual return to that baser animal that they once were. It was now that he realised that their minds needed the stimulation of progression, the desire to move forward and achieve. These simple human desires had been looked down upon by the elders for what they were. Simple human desires. In their arrogance they had perceived that their immortality had granted them the insight to tame the world and yet they could barely co-exist with the world around them. How wrong they had been. How blind to their human emotions. For deep within their preternatural being resided the remnants of a once mortal heart.

Stepping upon the platform, Callum observed the strange boarding rituals, which each individual undertook. The passing of a book, the checking of their vehicle. It intrigued him, inspired him. These uniformed inspectors moved unquestioned about the platform, their actions respected, honoured. Realising the possibilities, which were now open to him, Callum faded into the human chaos that consumed the station. All about, the organised confusion surrounded him, concealed him, and comforted him. He watched as great screen above his head relayed images and information, he marvelled at the complexities of this world. How inspiring this new life could be.

In the far reaches of the platform stood a small café frequented by such individuals. Moving closer, Callum could see a small group of officers seated around a table, conversing over the day's events. His heart raced, for this would be his first contact with this modern world. But, just as he drew close, the group stood in anticipation of returning to their work. They chatted lightly, laughing, then made their way along the platform. Turning, Callum watched their actions, memorised their walk, stature and body language. He devoured as much information as he could, for this creature that moved before him had evolved in a very complex creation, far beyond that which it once was.

One of the officers paused and bid his companion to continue and made his way to relieve himself of his recent infusion of refreshment. Callum followed him as he passed through several segregated zones of the station and into the realm reserved for those employed by the system. Silently he allowed the stranger to finish his task before rendering him unconscious. The taking of life had always been a necessity for Callum and never a reality. Exchanging garments he was surprised to find that the officer's uniform was a close match and he hurriedly made the transition. Retaining his own clothing in his shoulder bad, he left the security of the restricted zone.

Recalling the movements of modern man he stepped out onto the open platform. Slowly he moved closer to one of the waiting trains, his senses sweeping the minds of those around in anticipation of detection, yet the thoughts that returned were those of normality and confusion. Entering the train he marvelled at the complexity of the structure, its steel walls and open chambers fascinated him, inspired his imagination.

All about he could hear a plethora of voices as the train began to fill with passengers; his heart began to pound as fear gripped his thoughts. Looking about he searched for a place of concealment. At the far reaches of the carriage stood a long vehicle, its smoked windows concealing the identity of its traveller. Quickly he made his way over and opened the back door; Callum was surprised to find it empty, save for a long polished coffin. Smiling at the irony of his situation he stepped inside and closed the door behind himself. Unlocking the catch of the casket he lifted open the lid and peered inside, there rested the remains of a young woman, her pale complexion reflecting that of this intruder to her immortal rest. Pushing the corpse to one side Callum lowered himself inside and closed the lid behind himself. The darkness of the coffin brought a strange comfort to his mind.

Five

Stepping from the cold waters of the sea, Mica could feel the warmth of uncertainty fill her emotions. Above her the cliffs of England towered majestically, their presence striking yet foreboding. She could feel her heart beginning to race as her eyes followed the line dictated by the pathway, which led to the cliff's top. How she hated heights; this mortal trait which haunted her infant years transcended the barriers of death and now plagued her into this immortal existence. Her fears had no standing in fact, no credence in experience, yet they hung about her as strong and as debilitating as they had always been. Gripping the handrails of the lower stairway she urged herself to climb; rigidly, she forced herself upwards. Closing her eyes she concentrated upon the task ahead. Below her the gentle sound of the sea crashing upon the shore gave the night an almost musical rhythm; wave after wave touched the soft sands before receding back into the cold black waters. Nature continued, blind to the concerns of others. Above her head seagulls turned and dived, their cries echoing through the silence of the night, shattering the peace of this timeless scene.

Half way up the wooden steps Mica paused as fear gripped her thoughts; closing her eyes she took several deep breaths before turning to look back at the shore. As she glanced down to the beach her emotions erupted, sending spasms of fear through her soul. Falling back Mica gripped the handrail of the stairway and held on as if her life depended upon this.

"Come on" she physically said to herself, in the hope of appeasing her doubts and offering the comfort of a voice to her inhibitions. "Just keep your eyes closed and stand up," she continued. Gripping tightly to the rail, she lifted herself precariously up, her legs shaking as she stood. 'Now one foot in front of the next and don't look down.' she thought. Lifting her foot slightly off the step, she slammed it hard down upon the one above, this she did in ever increasing exaggeration until eventually she reached her destination. There she collapsed upon the soft grass that covered the cliff's top.

Rolling onto her back she opened her eyes and stared to the heavens. A cloudless sky greeted her. The stars above glistened, their presence as enduring as immortality, bringing to her a deep feeling of serenity for now she knew that she was home, she had returned to her homeland and the heavens welcomed her.

Six

As the shuttle pulled into the station Callum could feel the slowing of the engines and realised that he was coming to the end of his journey. Opening the lid of the coffin he climbed out and sat quietly in the vehicle. His senses searching his surroundings for any sign of detection, passive emanation returned, bringing with them a comfort to his inhibitions. Reaching back into the coffin he placed the body of his companion back into its position of eternal rest before locking the lid. Moving to the window, he watched as the train entered the station and came to a halt. All about, chaos reigned supreme as life erupted onto the platform at the train's arrival. 'How magnificent,' he thought. 'This modern world shall be an adventure rather than a curse.'

As the automatic door opened, Callum summoned from deep within himself all of his dark strength and raced forward as fast as his immortal muscles could propel him. His actions were too quick for human eyes to witness and so he reduced any event of confrontation with those who would suspect that his intentions were anything less than desirable in this new land.

Pausing to take notice of his surroundings, Callum observed the place in which he found himself. A vast man-made road stretched out before him, its direction passing almost into infinity. He could only marvel at this world, as a new-born would cry at the light of a new day. He felt reborn; the slate of his past life was now wiped clean. Turning, he searched for direction, reading sign after sign until his eye fell upon a name which he recognised from his own time. LONDON. This was the direction that he would take; this place would be the starting point for the journey of the rest of his life.

Seven

Watching the heavens, she allowed her mind to wander to times past, happier times. A time when mortality was her prize and the love of another was her only desire. How they would play in their innocence in the meadows of England, twins of sunshine and rain. One soft and caring, the other vibrant and alive. How they complimented each other, reflected one another, lived to be together. They were as if one. Bonded by more than just blood, it was as if their souls were joined and no one could tear them asunder. How innocent he was then, how gentle. The memories of her forgotten brother came flooding back, filling her with a warmth that touched her very soul. She recalled his long, curled hair that fell in ringlets about his shoulders and down until it touched the centre of his back; how alike they looked, how distinctive. She even recalled with a kindness the harshness of his transition as he entered the Tribe and rejected his mortal life, casting aside the trapping of their sibling bonds. She remembered her first reaction when she saw him with his shaven head; how sad she felt inside, yet she refused to show her emotions for fear of bruising his tender soul. To her he would always be her brother, always in need of her protection, her guidance. Had time really twisted his mind and forged a monster beyond her recognition? Closing her eyes, she tried to imagine how, if any, his features had changed in the centuries since they last met, but a blackness filled her thoughts bringing only pain instead of comfort.

They had always been bonded by an invisible force that guided one to the other, yet now she felt so alone. How she craved to feel his gentle arms about her, comforting her. His level thoughts would always bring to rights the desires of her wandering heart, easing the suffering in her hour of need. Could this gentle creation of God really have turned into this abomination foretold by Darius?

Sitting up, she recalled his words as she watched the dark storm move over the horizon, bringing with them the cold snows of winter.

"You are the only soul who could execute this sentence." How unemotional he seemed, how final. Her mind then turned to thoughts of the Communicator. This creature whose powers could change the direction of their destiny, redirect them from the path, which they perceived was their only choice. How desirable it would be to have mortality once again, to have a conclusion to this eternal suffering. Her mind turned to Christian and a hope burned bright that this new mortality would turn him from the dark path, which he had chosen to follow and back to her loving embrace.

"Christian. Where are you?" she said under her breath. Almost immediately the images of his past life raged across the screen of her mind. Her telepathic powers focused and came into action, bringing to her the pictures that she so desired, pictures of each and every event experienced by her brother, since his re-birth into this modern life. People, places, times and actions were all hers to experience. Yet these pictures differed from those that rested in the soft place within her heart; these images portrayed a darker creature, a creature driven by desire and hatred. All at once she could feel a bonding and knew that their minds had been linked. She could see with his eyes, feel his emotions, his desires. Darkness enveloped her, crushing her; images of Ann-Marie, past and present haunted her, plagued her thoughts. Ann-Marie's home and that of the Ward's passed across her mind. As the seconds fell by she realised that this mind into which she had inadvertently entered had somehow changed. Its darker essence almost engulfing her, suppressing her own identity. Drawing herself back, she tried to escape without detection, but even as she forged her retreat she could sense her brother's intentions. It was as if he were absorbing her, connecting himself to her. Draining her of all that was good. Their lives were truly a double-edged sword. For as she had capacity to enter his thoughts, he too, had capacity to enter her own. She knew that this two-way bond could never be permanently severed, but with the passing of the centuries the signal had weakened to an almost silent background noise, lulling Mica into a false sense of security.

Concentrating, she pulled her thoughts back into herself, retreating to the sanctity of her own domain. Opening her eyes she was surprised to be confronted by the serenity of that winters night, above the stars shone with their gentle emissions, peppering the heaven with their magical presence. Allowing the stormy seas of her mind to settle, she concentrated upon the events, which she had recently witnessed, but as she searched the images that assaulted her senses a deep feeling of horror filled her. For she realised, as she had plundered the archives of Christian's thoughts then he too would have reciprocated this intrusion and he would know everything, which she knew. Darius' words, the fall of the Tribe, the powers locked deep within the Communicator. Everything!

Eight

Even though her period in the snow had been brief Ann-Marie felt as though the cold of the night had chilled her soul to its very core. Sitting next to the open fire in the Ward's home, a heavy woollen blanket about her shoulders and a strong warm drink in her hands, she felt somewhat hollow and empty as if her return had taken something 'special' from her. The events of her encounter replayed themselves over and over in her mind, recalling the gentle face of her lost love and the harsh tribulation, which she perpetrated against him. She had damned him to an eternity of immortality in the confines of the cold earth. How bitter her love tasted, how weak her excuses. It was now, as destiny confronted her, that she felt truly lost in this world.

Jen broke her concentration as she entered the living room carrying a tray laden with assorted cakes.

"Are you alright? Getting warmer I hope?" she enquired.

Ann-Marie smiled. "Yes thanks."

Susan closely followed her mother into the room, carrying a large pot of coffee.

"Good, I'm pleased. Now will someone tell me what the bloody hell is going on before I lose my temper and beat it out of you? And don't try to flannel me with some cock-and-bull story, I want the truth. After the events, which I witnessed tonight, I would believe in anything so don't hold back on my account. After all I'm in the frame of mind that if you told me that fairies lived at the bottom of our garden I would believe you, no questions asked."

Susan looked to Ann-Marie for guidance.

"Don't look blindly at each other for help, I want to know and I want to know now," Jen stated, in a raised voice.

"Christian is a vampire and he's been hunting me because I killed him," Ann-Marie said returning her eyes to the flames of the open fire.

"Well if you killed him he looked pretty much alive to me so I guess some one's got their information wrong," Jen replied.

"I didn't kill him in this time," Ann-Marie interjected.

Jen opened her mouth to reply but paused in amazement.

"What! I don't understand, what do you mean? Not in this time."

Susan sat on the sofa. "You have to have an open mind Mother. I can only accept what's been said because I've experienced some of it at first hand."

Jen sat heavily on the sofa next to her daughter.

"I'm still finding this all a little difficult to comprehend. Sorry, but sane people don't rush around chasing dead people or vampires."

Ann-Marie sat forward. "Tell me with an open mind and in all honesty that you did see how that creature healed his own wounds, a wound inflicted by you yourself only a moment before."

162

"I must admit that I cannot give you a plausible explanation that would vindicate that evidence, but I'm sure there must be a reason," Jen answered.

"What happened to your open mind?" Ann-Marie said sarcastically. Jen shrugged her shoulders. "Look, I can see that this is getting us nowhere," Ann-Marie continued. "Maybe it would be better if I just left and you can forget this whole incident. Get your life back to some form of normality."

Susan stood up. "You can't, what happens if he comes back?"

"You're both talking in riddles, it's all complete and utter nonsense," Jen said.

"Oh, shut up," Susan cried. "If Ann-Marie walked out of that door now you would be signing her death warrant. Do you want to have that responsibility upon your shoulders? We're not making this up. Can't you see?"

Ann-Marie stood and made her way to the door.

"It's alright Susan, your mother may be right; it may be for the best. If I go then I may take the danger with me."

"That's the first sensible thing that you've said all night," Jen replied.

"It's alright, I'm going. I'll ring a taxi from the corner. I've enough money. I'll call back tomorrow and pick up the rest of my things," Ann-Marie stepped into the hallway, her eyes filling with tears. Susan hurried behind her.

"Don't leave!" she cried.

Ann-Marie turned and took hold of her hands.

"If anything happens come straight to me. You know where I live," Ann-Marie searched her pocket for an address card, retrieving one, she handed it to Susan. "It's better if I go, I'll see you tomorrow," she gently kissed Susan on the forehead and made her way to the front door. Turning she offered her a brief smile before opening the door and stepping out into the cold winter's night.

Susan stood in silence in the hallway, her eyes filling with tears. "Don't worry, I'll call you," she said under her breath. Opening her hand, she read the address on the small white card, which Ann-Marie had given her.

Masquerade Ball

House of the Roussel Family

Paris

July 4th 1789

****

A gentle drift of snow was beginning to fall as Ann-Marie stepped through the impressive gates that guarded the Ward's home. The night was somewhat calmer; it was as if the danger had passed, taking with it the fears of her recent experience. Walking down the deserted street she allowed her thoughts to wander through the avenues of her mind, replaying the possibilities of the recent events of her past life. Realising the folly of her dreaming she dismissed her meandering recollections and placed them to the back of her subconscious. To her delight, at the junction of streets, there stood a motionless taxi, which she hailed. Inside she gave her directions and sank blissfully into the warm leather of the seat.

****

Jennifer Ward raged blindly about the living room, demanding explanation of her daughter's perceived reckless actions.

"I can't understand you, you're eighteen and yet you're living in some fantasy world. For years you've been demanding responsibility and when I give it to you, you repay me with this. Did you think that I would swallow this fantastic story? Vampires and demons. I've heard it all now. You need treatment. Not as much as your friend, I agree; she's really gone overboard. I've got a mind to ring her editor in the morning and get her struck off or whatever they do to disreputable journalists. Then again if I did that Fleet Street would be a ghost town. Don't you see, this is all make believe? This Christian is probably some jealous boyfriend who she dumped and now he's trying to get even. She invented this vampire rubbish to string you along. When she interviewed you she probably thought you were a nice, impressionable young girl whom she could manipulate and carry alone into her dream world. Everything has an explanation, even what happened tonight. You must admit on a scale of one to ten, and using Ann-Marie as very weird, then her boyfriend would be quite high in comparison; at least an eight. After tonight, compared to her, Jack the Ripper would be a nice house guest."

Susan looked up, her eyes full of tears. "You don't understand. I believe her. We both went through certain things - you could never understand."

"That's what I mean; she's brainwashed you into believing her stories. I think that it would be better if you went to bed, things will look better in the cold light of morning. Tomorrow you'll realise that I am right and you'll feel the same way. Then we'll put this all behind us and get on with our lives."

Susan shook her head in disbelief. "I only wish that you could have been there..," she said before leaving the living room and making her way to her bedroom.

Recalling the events of the day, Jennifer smiled to herself briefly as the absurdity of their contents filled her mind.

"Vampires! Ha! Whatever next?"

Looking about the room, she contemplated leaving the clearing of the remnants of destruction until the next morning, but thought better of that decision and set about clearing away the main bulk of damage. From the kitchen she brought a small dustpan and brush and a large, plastic refuse sack into which she put several of the damaged books which had fallen from the bookcase during her confrontation with Christian.

"What a mess!" She repeated over and over again as she sorted damaged items from those which could be salvaged. The flames from the hearth filled the room with a strange almost serene glow which danced lightly across the living-room walls.

Turning her back to the main wall, Jennifer got down onto her hands and knees and began to sweep up the fragments of the broken glass ornaments. She shook her head in disbelief at the destruction that had visited her home.

"Strange, these things had survived travelling around India, two house moves and an infant child and that woman manages to break them with very little effort. Typical," she said, muttering under her breath. She continued cleaning as the night passed slowly, in the vain hope of returning her home to some form of recognisable normality before the new day was upon her.

Concentrating hard upon her task she did not notice the thin film of dust that was beginning to fill the air, a dust that emanated from the walls of the room. A thin crack appeared in the far wall, expanding as the seconds passed until it almost reached from floor to ceiling. Plaster began to crumble, leaving a thin white powder upon the floor. A powder that increased in volume as the seconds ticked by. The crack had now grown horizontally, expanding from its original few millimetres to several centimetres, ever increasing as time fell by.

Unobserved by Jennifer, the atmosphere in the room began to change. The warm glow of the fire's flames which sent soft shadows across the walls began to contort and twist as if pain were pulsating through their very essence, tearing at them, possessing them. Slowly the temperature began to fall, creating an inner ice upon the windows of the room and leaving a thin film of frost upon the sofa.

The aperture that stretched across the living-room wall was expanding at an alarming rate; it was now big enough for a man to step through, yet silently it grew.

Susan sat in her room, contemplating the words which were so harshly thrown at her by her Mother. How could she convince someone so sceptical of the events which she herself had witnessed? How could she ever hope to rebuild a bridge of trust which she knew was now lost and swept away by a river of perceived lies? Standing, she took a deep breath.

"I'll make her listen. I'll sit her down and tell her the truth and I won't let her leave until she's listened to everything that I have to say," she said to herself, before leaving her bedroom and making her way downstairs.

Most of the far wall was now a portal into another realm, a portal through which things could pass or be passed. Jennifer knelt upon the living-room floor, sweeping the final remnants of glass onto the dustpan. Behind her, a barbaric creature began to force his way into this fragile dimension. A great claw-like hand reached through dimensions and into the room. Gripping the cold air it pulled the bulk of his frame closer to this world. Another powerful limb reached into this realm, followed by a great muscular leg culminating in a cloven foot. An expanse of chest ripped its way through the portal, leaving only the head now to become visible. Two great horns pierced the room, and below them pushed a forehead, then finally a face. A face that personified evil itself. Two great, yellow eyes searched the room in the hope of finding his quest. His red skin was pulsating with the sensation of life.

Susan stepped into the hallway, her mind a turmoil of questions. Blindly she walked into the living room. Looking to her Mother, her actions came to an abrupt halt as she observed the abomination that stood behind her in all his glory. Realising that her daughter had entered the room, Jen paused in her work and looked half-heartedly in her direction.

"If you've come to tell me more tales of horror then save your…" Her words faded to nothing as she realised that the look which was etched upon her daughter's face was that of pure horror. Slowly she rose to her feet and turned until she faced the source of her daughter's dilemma. The creature smiled a sardonic smile as it offered her a mocking bow.

A name raced to the front of Susan's mind, sending spasms of fear deep into her heart.

"Caliban," she said.

The creature looked to her and offered her a smile as he bowed once again.

****

Closing the door behind her, Ann-Marie was strangely relieved to be alone in her own home once again. These familiar surroundings brought a calming, almost comforting serenity to her thoughts. How dramatically her life had changed over these past few days, and yet how little her surroundings had. They reminded her of her innocent former self. Sitting quietly in the living room, the darkness surrounding her, she allowed her thoughts to wander. How drastically destiny had changed her life and re-forged her thinking. Even the most significant of events to touch this modern world's history paled to an inconsequential episode in comparison to that which she had experienced in her brief encounter with the immortals.

She began to fall deeper into the darker side of her emotions, allowing her imagination to control her consciousness and draw conclusions inexperienced and untouched by her encounters. She could see his face over and over again in her mind, calling for her to join him in his immortal adventure. She could almost touch the soft pale undulations of his features as she recalled the innocence of his smile. A single tear of regret slowly ran down her cheek.

"What a fool I've been. Destiny is never written, but made."

Wiping the tear from her cheek she stood and stretched herself in the hope of relaxing her muscles.

"You could do with a nice, long, warm bath," she said to herself. "Clear your head and relax your body. It's all past now, it's time to get on with the rest of your life."

As she climbed the stairs she tried to clear her mind of the images that remained. She found herself casting back her thoughts to those eyes which haunted her, their blue ocean colour washing over her emotions. If they truly were a window to his soul, then she had witnessed a softer side to this nature.

Opening the bedroom door she switched on the light and stepped into the room, its familiar fragrance greeted her and offering her a reassuring comfort. At the far reaches of the room the door to the en-suite bathroom stood slightly ajar and Ann-Marie could see the distinct signs of movement from within. Her heart began to gather its pace as anticipation gripped her. Walking slowly to the door she pushed it gently, allowing it to swing silently open.

The stranger inside stood with her face turned from view, her delicate frame offering a false sense of security to Ann-Marie as her demeanour denoted weakness. Slowly the stranger turned, speaking as she did, until her face was in full view. The stranger's eyes remained closed.

"Please, do not be alarmed, I am here to help you. We are followers of the same destiny you and I, and we must join forces if we are to achieve our purpose," her words were slow and deliberate.

"Who are you? What do you want, and how did you get into my house?" Ann-Marie asked.

Mica opened her eyes. This simple action caused Ann-Marie to gasp. For the eyes which greeted her were those of another. Slowly she moved closer.

"My name is Mica, I have been asked to come to England and guide you. The powers that balance this universe have understood the dangers that are about to confront man and so those who would normally be opposed and segregated must link together for the desire of the one history. Our history. Not the history of mortals or immortals but the history of us all. There is an increasing danger that could destroy this fragile existence within which we all exist. This is the reason I have come to you, for you have encountered a thousand dark delights over these recent brief moments of your life and so would be open to the words which I have to say. You are now less sceptical than others of your kind, less judgmental, open to the old ways." Pausing, she thought for a moment. "There is also another reason for my coming; you see there is a lost soul which I must find in the hope of exercising the demons who have haunted my heart for centuries, demons who are known to us both, for you see I am the sister to your spiritual lover. Christian is my brother."

Ann-Marie stepped back into the bedroom, her mind collapsing about her.

"What do you want from me?" she enquired.

"Your assistance, that is all," Mica replied.

"Are you..?" Ann-Marie began.

Anticipating her question Mica spoke.

"Am I the same as my brother, a Vampire? Yes, we are twins. Not identical, but twins none the less. For centuries I had thought him dead and now that I find him in the land of the living, I must return him to his rightful place," Ann-Marie's eye's opened wide. "Yes my dear," Mica continued "I must return him to his place of rest for his recent actions are beyond redemption. He could bring down the very fabric of all our existence if his deeds were to continue to go unchallenged."

"He has always been a renegade, a vagabond," she said fondly, "...but I feel that his recent actions have been fuelled by the urgencies of another."

Ann-Marie sat on the bed.

"Forgive me for my ignorance but I thought that my part in this passion-play was drawing to an end, that I had fulfilled my part in all of this."

Mica smiled. "Your part within this 'passion play,' as you call it, has only just begun. You see, you are the pivotal pin within this whole situation," Mica sat next to her. "You are a Communicator, as am I. But your powers go far beyond the imaginings of any such as I, or my kind."

Mica paused. "How could I explain myself in an easier way?" she said to herself. "History, your history. If you look into the past you will see that there have been

167

hundreds of semi-Communicators; they pepper your world and reach out through your time. Joan of Arc, Alexander the Great, Michel de Nostradame and Shakespeare are but a few. Great thinkers and philosophers, fighters and peace-makers, they have moulded minds and left ripples that cascade through time and history which even now, centuries after their deaths, hold the imagination of your modern world. Their presence is stronger now than it has ever been, for they have conquered the human imagination and remained an enigma that burns bright in your history; yet the power which each of them possessed would fade into insignificance if put into comparison with your own. They are but a mere candle compared to a raging flame. You see, you possess a talent given to only a few. A talent that could bring comfort or suffering. And with that talent comes responsibility and a price far greater than your imagination could ever comprehend. I personally have only known of one other Communicator who had been granted such a great power and he abused this for the fulfilment of his own desires. As you humans say, 'Nothing in this life is free', and he paid a price, a price which torments him to this very day."

"You see, centuries ago one of your own kind discovered the secret to immortality and after bathing in the flames of perpetual youth he denounced the powers which forged him, and so brought down their anger and as his punishment they made him one of their own. Raging from their judgement he sought recompense for his sentence and so cast down this dark plague upon the earth in a futile attempt to appease the anger which welled up inside him. He created all that you perceive as evil; he is our dark father, and we are to suffer as he has, never again to walk in the gentle touch of a summer's day, cast our wandering eye upon the soft horizon of a winter's morning or savour the touch of another living soul. Never again bare the fruits of a mother's labour or the delights of a mortal's expectations. And this, he cursed us with for an eternity. We are to mirror his suffering, his torment.

"I don't understand," Ann-Marie said.

Mica smiled. "You understand more than you realise. I will try to explain. For every force within this universe there must be an opposing force, its opposite. A balance to right the laws of nature. For every Yin there is a Yang, each a polar opposite to its brother; yet each containing a fragment of the other's soul, so that it will never lose sight of its reason for existing within the confines of the finely-tuned universe."

"No, no. I understand that part, but what I don't understand is, who is he and how could I have had something to do with him when he died - or un-died - centuries ago?" Ann-Marie said in confusion.

"He is Caliban. To all intents and purposes you could call him our god. Not in the same sense as your Christian God or other gods. He has no spirituality. He is as physical as you or I, whereas your gods are worshipped for love he would be worshipped with fear and mistrust. The definition of the word god in his sense would only be as a status rather than something divine," Mica paused, for she knew that her next words would be the hardest to say. "Your connection with Caliban? You are his Yang. He has decimated the lives of a thousand innocent souls by blindly granting them this immortal horror and you have the power to restore to us that which we most desire, our mortality, so that we may once again feel the soft rays of a summer sun and know what it would be like to have a destination for our suffering," she took a deep breath. "To be able to die. To know that this purgatory could end. To have my weary bones placed into the earth and for them to return from whence they came. A dream, which I thought only too painful to contemplate. Yet now, with your intervention, anything could be possible."

"I know that this may come as a bit of a surprise, but why me?" Ann-Marie exclaimed.

"Why not you?" Mica replied.

Ann-Marie thought for a while. "Why not someone else? Why not you, why not Susan?"

Mica stood. "The girl from Christian's thoughts," she said to herself. "Tell me about this 'Susan'."

"There's not much to say," Ann-Marie began. "She's an artist who I met when I was covering a story. I'm a journalist, and I write about people's lives. Well, we met and strangely there was some kind of bond between us. At first I didn't sense it, but as time passed I could feel it grow and in some strange way I felt very protective towards her."

"Your emotions may be unintentional. If I were Caliban I would try to deceive you if I could. You see, he cannot take you into his world; you must enter it of your own volition. Tell me," she continued. "Do you have any immediate family?"

Ann-Marie shook her head.

"I thought not. He is trying to get to you through another."

"Through Susan?" Ann-Marie asked.

"The life of an immortal is different from that of a mortal. Our lives are diverse and erratic, our destiny un-marked. Yet mortals have a path to follow. A path that is dictated long before their re-birth and if those elements of darkness so desired to manipulate that pathway and create a different destiny, then they could, through subtle cunning means."

Ann-Marie's hand slowly moved to her mouth as she contemplated Mica's words.

"Why Susan?"

"This scenario is a little different, as there could be a number of possibilities. First of all, she could be a pawn in his game of power. She could be as you are, a Communicator. A weaker, more convoluted strain of the dark blood but a Communicator none the less. If this is so, then the rules which we are following are re-writing themselves as we speak. For now, better to bait with a bigger fish than with a smaller one; one which you care for, have strong emotions for. If you think about your situation, then it is apparent that Caliban has played his cards very well, for you cannot disinherit yourself from your inner feelings, and abandon the hopes of another whose whole world relies upon your actions and understanding. Your feelings would betray you as sure as a false friend, and you could never leave her to face this onslaught alone."

"I still don't understand the reasons behind his persecution of Susan," Ann-Marie said.

"I, too, have thought of this and I feel that this next possibility, peppered with the essence of that which I have recently mentioned, could be our answer. Mortals can be born and re-born for centuries until their spirits have transcended the physical and ascertained enough information to reach for a higher plain. Your immortal soul hungers for understanding and insight; this is why the re-birthing is so essential, and this is where our solution lies. I feel that Susan is in some way connected to him, from his own past. The extent of which, I do not know, but the bond is very strong. For if it were insignificant then this matter could have a been resolved in an easier way than first comprehended, but, if not, if she were to play a greater part within this game, then I feel that our troubles have only just begun."

"Well, we have him," Ann-Marie said in delight. "If she is a Communicator as am I, then he cannot take her into his domain without her full compliance."

Mica offered her a smile, and yet felt that the solution had been achieved with an ease that could only denote failure.

Ann-Marie turned away from her and thought deeply about Susan and the events that had confronted one so young.

"It's so unfair, life. She doesn't deserve all of this. It's all so unfair," she said.

"When would you like her to experience life? If she were kept away from all forms of confrontation and experience until her consciousness could comprehend that which befell her, then her mind would be a blank canvas for an eternity, unblemished by the traumas of learning and understanding. Is life really that unjust?" Mica said. "Is it really so unbearable to have it this way, or do you desire to have an order to the universe, a greater continuity so that everything is fair, just and balanced? I could not comprehend anything more abhorrent. To know that all the suffering that befalls you, all fear that torments you, all the tragedy that haunts you, everything which you know to be unjust in this life, is that which you truly deserve. To know that each dark shadow that is cast over your life has been forged by your own deeds, this would drive me to destruction. To be confronted by this and more would be beyond my contemplation and endurance. No! I disagree. My desire is for my destiny to mirror the chaos that is my life, this life, which is fair and just. We all must confront the demons of the world and the demons within ourselves so that we may grow and become stronger. Granted, some may fall by the roadside or be consumed by that demon which they pursue, but rather that than no demon at all."

****

Caliban smiled as he stepped from the portal and stood to his full height. His great wings stretched out, touching the walls on both sides of the Ward's living room.

"What do you want? Who are you?" Jen stammered, as pure fear gripped her soul.

Caliban fixed his expression and looked directly to Jen. "Such harsh words from one so beautiful. I have come to invite my companion to dance with me across the dark shadows of my world, a world that would bathe in the light of her beauty and once again be touched by the angels of heaven, as would be my heart," he said, offering her a mocking smile.

"There's no way that I'm going to allow you to take my baby with you. You'll have to kill me if you think that I'll let her go with such a disgusting creation as yourself."

Caliban bellowed, his laughter filled the room and almost shook the foundation of the ancient building.

170

"Don't mock me," Jen screamed, motioning Susan to stay behind her and out of the view of this tormentor.

"Mock you? I do not mock you. I am only surprised at your humility."

A look of puzzlement swept across Jen's face.

"Your perception has deceived you my dear. Your understanding of this situation is clouded by the hatred that befalls you, for it is not the daughter that I have come a calling, but the mother."

Jen swallowed hard as revulsion gripped her.

"What! Me? I don't understand," she said.

Moving hastily forward, Caliban's arm reached out and gripped her Jen's, his great fingers clasping tightly about her.

"Come my dear, melt into my arms and let us depart, there are a thousand dark delights that I wish to share with you."

Jen fought his attentions, but her mortal frame was no match for this creature's muscular bulk. She could feel her feet slowly slipping across the floor, giving way to his stronger force and taking her in the direction of her waking nightmare. Fighting him, she turned to Susan and screamed.

"Run! Run as fast as you can, get Ann-Marie. Hurry."

Caliban smiled, for he now knew that his trap was set and the victim baited. He then turned his attention to his guest, lifting her delicate frame from the floor he drew her into his embrace. Holding her tightly for a moment, he savoured his victory before stepping back into the portal; instantly the room was filled with a blinding unearthly light, which vanished moments later. Susan rushed to the wall, but where there had once had been a vast portal only silence filled the air. Hammering with her fists upon the plaster she discovered to her dismay that the doorway was closed solidly against her. Turning, she rushed out of the house and into the cold night air, not caring if she were to be confronted by any manner of darkness. The only thought that fuelled her now was that of salvation, and she knew that its solution lay in the hands of another.

****

Mica's tone was becoming a little urgent.

"I'm sorry if my words sound calculating or cold, but it is the way of the world. If I were to know all of the answers to life and death then we would not be having this conversation. I know that this life is unjust and uncaring; but that is life, get used to it. Eventually we become that which we most despise. No matter how much we try to turn that path of our soul against the grain of our emotions we will always find that that road upon which we travel will always lead back to ourselves. You can only help others by helping yourself. If you have a goal, which you must achieve, or an aim which you must reach for, then try. Even if you fail you will be transforming your perception of this life. Others will see your endeavours and could possibly be inspired by your trials, thus mirroring your task, your struggle. In the process they open their own minds to their world. Can you not see? We all travel this world alone. Some realise their potential while other never truly find their niche in the structure of this life, but that is what is meant to be, that is life. It is this difference which is the celebration, not conformity."

Mica placed her hands together, as if in prayer, and held them to her lips. "I am sorry if my words are harsh, but all that I am trying to purvey is that life is for each individual to lead alone and each decision which is made is made by the one."

Ann-Marie stood up. "You're right. I'm sorry, it's just that Susan is so helpless, so innocent."

"Please do not apologise for your compassion for it is commendable. I only wish that others in your world could savour a fraction of this beauty and hold it within their hearts as a mirror to their own actions. Maybe it is I who should apologise. Here I am, a creature no longer human but superhuman. Yet, with the experiences of a myriad of lifetimes I cannot understand the actions of my own kind. I confront you with a thousand demands and expectations. Me, a creature of folklore and fantasy, and I expect you to believe in all that I am and all that I say and do. Forgive me, my ignorance betrays me."

Mica turned to the window, her eyes watching the horizon. "I'm sorry but I must leave, dawn is but only a few moments away. Please rest," she said to Ann-Marie. "Rest in the comfort in which I must sleep through the day, light hours, as must all others of my kind."

"One final thing," Ann-Marie said. "Why doesn't Caliban allow you all to become mortal again? Surely this power could be used for good? If he allowed this then would it not show those higher that he has accepted his past indiscretions and that he is responsible for his punishment?"

Mica stood in the doorway, her head resting against the frame. "If only it were that simple. Caliban has been forged by the hands of a greater force and their actions cannot be reversed. I can understand in some simplistic way his suffering. To see all of that which you have devised to appease that suffering disassembled, but that one desire coveted by yourself which could never be attained would become unbearable. To see all of your dark fledglings around you relinquish their chains of suffering which have weighed heavy upon their shoulders for century's running free into this mortal world would drive him to destruction. Even though on the outside he has the form of a demon, inside he is as human as you or I. But his dark fate is to remain physically as he is."

Mica turned to leave.

"Where will you go?" Ann-Marie enquired.

Mica paused for a moment. "I have not thought, but I will find somewhere."

"You could sleep in the attic. There are no windows and only one door which can be bolted from the inside," Ann-Marie said.

Mica smiled. "I bless you for understanding and the trust which you have placed in me."

****

It took Ann-Marie several hours after sunrise to fall into a deep, almost fathomless sleep, a sleep un-hindered by the pressure of a dream world and images of a haunted mind. As the day turned and the evening fell across the skies Ann-Marie began to stir in her slumber but this awakening was not a natural occurrence. From outside of her world there came an urgency, a constant demand for attention. Ann-Marie opened her eyes and sat up in bed, the room was bathed in a gentle orange glow from the world outside. The noise repeated itself over and over again, growing in urgency. Climbing from her bed she put on her dressing gown and went to the window that over looked the open street, below she could see the torment face of her friend. Opening the window she called out.

"Susan! What's wrong?"

Tears ran in rivers down Susan's small cheeks. "It's Mother. He's got Mother."

A cold chilled filled her soul. Taking the house keys from her pocket she threw them to Susan below.

"Ley yourself in, I'll be down as quick as I can," she said before she urgently dressed.

When she entered the living room she found Susan sitting in silence upon the sofa, gently rocking back and forth, her legs pulled tightly to her chest. Rushing to her side, Ann-Marie placed her arms about her shoulders in a vain attempt to offer her comfort.

"What happened?" she enquired.

Susan did not reply.

"Susan what happened? If I'm to help you, you must tell me."

As her friends face turned Ann-Marie could almost feel the pain that was held within her innocent eyes.

"After you left, something came. It took mother. It came through the wall."

"Christian?"

From behind, there came a now familiar voice.

"Caliban!" Mica said, standing in the doorway.

Ann-Marie turned and looked at her.

"How? And why take Jen?"

"How better to entice the fly into the spider's lair? I had deceived myself into thinking that we were safe but I now know that this was a delusion." She entered the room.

Ann-Marie looked back at Susan and found that her once crying eyes were now filled with a dark rage and hatred.

"Who is she?" Susan demanded.

Ann-Marie went to speak, but Mica lifted her hand as a direction to pause.

"Who am I? I am your friend. I am here to help you get your Mother back, for I know the ways of this demon. I know his name, his life, his thoughts, and if you would grant me the pleasure of your presence then I will aid you in your endeavours."

Susan was transfixed by her eyes.

"You look like..," Susan began.

.".My brother. Christian," she closed her eyes briefly and smiled, "You are correct but do not judge us both in the same light for the darkness that surrounds him is his and his alone. He is solely responsible for his own actions."

"But you're..."

Once again Mica anticipated her words. .".A vampire. How astute of you to perceive such a thing, but once again do not allow your prejudice to cloud your thoughts. I offer you assistance with an open and gentle heart; it is your decision if you are to take that which is given with love and understanding, or to reject it and fight this war alone."

Mica offered Susan her outstretched hand of friendship.

"Can you really get my mother back?" Susan said.

"I cannot promise that which I do not know, for the future has not yet been written, but what I can promise is that I will do my best or die trying."

Susan stood and gripped Mica's hand. "That is all that I ask."

Mica smiled.

"Tell us exactly what happened, leave nothing out. We need to know everything in its minute detail."

****

As Susan began to relay the tale of her mother abduction, outside the darker clouds of night reached across the heavens bringing a comfort to the world. A world in which a stranger to this time wandered, his mind ablaze with the images of this modern life. Callum crossed streets and entered courtyards, ambled through alleyways and churchyards, his inquisitive thoughts propelling him deeper into this mechanical age. The neon lights of Trafalgar dazzled him as he moved through the pulse that was this city. Life seemed to exude from its very core, carrying all those who felt it presence upon its tide and into it consumer pleasure. How times had changed, evolved. In his time the coming of the night spelt danger and mothers would hold tight to their breast the young ones for fear of their downfall, yet now, with the coming of night, came the opening of life. Life seemed to erupt and flow onto the streets in abundance, life that savoured the moment and hungered for the pleasures of the here and now. He passed dancers and street entertainers, mime artists and clowns as he wandered blindly through this vast metropolis, this altar to the pleasures of the night.

Slowly, he began to drink in the euphoric hedonism that surrounded him until he felt as though his mind would burst with the pleasures which confronted his senses. A tide of extremity washed over him, warming his soul. A tide that would soon turn into an ocean, deep, cold and foreboding. For just as he had drifted blindly into the hedonistic life an image, brief but unequivocal, assaulted his senses.

Within the turmoil that was this life stood an image, as immortal who was as lost as his own soul. An image, which curtailed the fantasies, which enveloped him and brought recognition to his thoughts. Yet as quickly as recognition had found its place, the stranger had vanished. Callum forced his way through the crowd, in the hope of experiencing the aura of his adversary but as he reached the place upon which his nemesis stood the only sensation to greet him was that of the cool winter's night. Closing his eyes he sent out a signal in the hope of tracing the destination of his foe; he could sense his closeness, his fragrance. But those images that returned were fragmented and broken by the presence of the mortal souls that danced and moved all about.

****

Slowly Mica's expression turned until it was fixed and cold.

"What's wrong?" Susan said, breaking off in mid-conversation

"Callum. He's here. He's in England and he knows the whereabouts of Christian."

"How do you know?" Susan enquired.

"All vampires are connected by a psychic bond, but some are stronger than others. As Callum and I are bonded by the same blood then our signal is stronger than most, which is why I can sense him. Our bond cannot travel great distances, to surmise that it could span continents would be false. It can, if we are lucky, reach several miles. Even then the signal that returns could be erratic and broken; also it is accessible by all who are sensitive to its emissions. Secrets, which are kept from mortal minds, are as open and as accessible as water to the immortals, flowing wherever the tide decides to take them. He feels so close," she took in a deep breath and let out a gasp. "Callum! He's close to Christian."

Callum opened his eyes as recollection filled him, bringing with it a pleasure far deeper than anything, which he had ever experienced in his past. A single word broke from his lips. "Mica."

At the direction of her signal he forged his way through the thickening crowd, as desire burning within his heart. Along the busy city streets and into the heart of this capital he searched, lost in this modern maze. Crossing Westminster Bridge he could see great plumes of tar smoke that drifted into the night air from the barrels that lined the roadside. The flames within that had raged for most of the day were now subdued and offered the passer by comfort on this bitter night.

Mica smiled. "History is forging a path to our door, whether we like it or not," she looked to Ann-Marie, then to Susan. "I think that it is about time that we gave our assistance to your Mother and bring this whole traumatic episode to an abrupt and final conclusion."

****

As they entered the Ward's home Mica could almost touch the anticipation, which seemed to permeate the air; it was as if the house itself were awaiting the outcome of their tribulations. Slowly she made her way into the living-room. The atmosphere was still in turmoil, a witness to the recent events.

"Tell me exactly what happened," she said to Susan.

Susan immediately walked to the far wall.

"It was here, there was a great doorway, and it took up most of this wall; that was how he came in. I was standing there," she said, pointing to the doorway. "And Mother was there," she said pointing to the position where Ann-Marie stood. "He came in through the wall, stood for a moment then took my mother."

"Is there anything that we can do?" Ann-Marie said.

"Yes. But it will take all of the powers that you already have at your disposal and also a few which you do not know about, if we are to turn back the pages of time and re-open this wound."

Ann-Marie looked at her with a deep sense of puzzlement. "I don't understand; how can we reopen the wall?"

"Turning back time," Mica replied.

Ann-Marie's mouth fell open. "What? We can't..." But just as she was about to display her ignorance she quashed her words before they escaped. "And how do you propose that we do that? she continued.

Mica smiled. "One Communicator alone could not achieve such an endeavour, but three together, especially with one so powerful, may be able to achieve such a task."

"What do you mean, three?" Susan said.

Mica took hold of her hand and looked into her eyes. "We do not have time to explain as time is that which we pursue. Just understand that you have a power deep within yourself and when this is all over I will gladly show you how to harness and tame this great beast within. For now I would ask you to follow me blindly, do as I ask and do not question anything which I decide. Then, and only then, we may have a slim chance of returning your Mother to you."

Susan nodded in approval.

Mica held out both her hands and motioned for her companions to do the same. "Please, join hands and form a circle and no matter what happens do not break this circle, for if you do you could create hell on earth. For we are using the most primordial powers that exist within this universe to do our bidding, these powers are unstable and erratic and need the guidance of a strong mind. What you must do is concentrate upon 'turning back time.' Focus your mind; create the image of a giant hourglass filled with sand falling grain by grain, each a lost second passing into infinity. Concentrate upon the sands, focus your energies and purge your mind of dark thoughts. Send your thoughts forward and demand that time do you're bidding. Force back the grains of sand into the upper part of the hourglass, reverse all that is natural and manipulate the very fabric of physics. Then concentrate those energies upon the wall in front of you until the portal created by Caliban's appearance. Then and only then I will give you the signal to cease in your actions. We must all stop simultaneously, otherwise we will return to the here and now and your mother will be lost forever, for we cannot achieve these actions a second time and the doors to this time zone will be barred against us, forever."

Mica looked to her companions. "Let us begin."

Ann-Marie closed her eyes and allowed herself to fall deeper into her thoughts. Almost immediately she could feel the pressure of her present surroundings melt away. In her mind's eye there drifted a far-off light and glowed in the darkness of her consciousness. As her thoughts gathered momentum the object drew closer. She could make out its features, its shape. A giant hourglass, brimming with sand, enough to engulf a desert. Turning and falling the glass sped towards her inner eye; its shining contours blinding her briefly as the light from her inner-mind were reflected upon its surface.

"Slow it down," Mica said. "We are now one mind, we shall see as the other and feel as the other. We shall have no secrets, no place to hide our doubts. Concentrate your energies upon the glass. Slow it."

Almost immediately the glass began to reduce it speed until it eventually hung in the air just in front of their vision. As it turned Ann-Marie could sense the magnitude of its presence, the air was filled with a great turning sound as each traumatic revolution was followed by another.

"Concentrate upon the falling sand, send it back into the upper-body of the glass," Mica instructed them.

Focusing their collective attentions upon the giant grains of sand, they concentrated, hoping for their deliverance. The glass of the great structure began to vibrate, its body rejecting the outward intentions of these invaders to its natural process. It's whole form vibrating in objection for this incursion into its own time-space.

Susan could feel herself weakening as the pressure began to build within her mind. Sensing her plight Mica offered her support.

"Concentrate, it will all be over in a moment, you are strong enough. Then you will be reunited with your Mother."

Ann-Marie concentrated, focusing her weakening energies upon the sand. And, to her surprise, slowly it began to reduce its speed, until it eventually became a slight trickle.

"That's it," Mica said.

This great tormentor that was time was slowly being brought to heal by these flowers of a winter's tale. Those once-salivating jaws that hunger for mortal flesh and dark death-knell heart were silenced by the urgings of a fairer soul. Then, the sand abruptly stopped flowing. Holding the continuity that was life itself at a standstill. The world fell into a void of nothingness, it was neither here nor there, past nor present, lost nor found. It was as if it were hanging by a golden thread suspended in the heavens, an undecided world, lost to the attentions of the immortal gods, spinning in the black void that was its fate.

"Force time back into the top. Will the sand to rise," Mica urged.

Ann-Marie could feel her blood coursing through every vain in her ephemeral form. She felt as if the pressure of her mere existence were building to such a culmination, that her very soul would explode.

Slowly the sand began to rise, drifting upward into the upper-body of the monolithic hourglass, gathering speed in its ascent."

"That's it, that's it," Mica cried.

The hourglass was paused in its revolution but slowly it began again in an anti-clockwise fashion, opposing that which was natural. The gentle vibrations, which they had encountered were now becoming stronger, their presence more dominant.

"Concentrate!" Mica cried.

The glass began to glow as the heat of its unnatural actions conflicted with the very essence of nature itself.

"We must stop!" Ann-Marie cried. But her words were too late, for the glass began to crack and buckle under the pressure excerpted upon its fragile structure. The hourglass shattered, exploding with a voracity stronger than a thousand suns, sending sand outwards into the open universe of her mind.

Ann-Marie screamed as she opened her eyes. Looking about she could see that the room had remained as it had before their endeavours begun. There was no change.

"Where's the portal?" Susan screamed. "Where is it?"

Mica looked about the room, fear filling her eyes. "I don't understand, it should have..."

Just as she spoke a deep rumbling began to fill the air; she looked to her companions. "Do you feel that?" She enquired. Both nodded. "It's happening."

A gentle wind began to fill the room, gathering in strength, as the moments passed, it eventually became a storm. Great bolts of energy danced across the ceiling, illuminating the room.

"What's happening?" Susan cried.

Mica turned and looked to the far wall. "There," she said, pointing to the small crack that blistered and bubbled beneath the paintwork. Slowly it grew in size until eventually it reached upwards, touching the ceiling, where its advancement ceased. Then the crack began to open; stretching outwards until eventually its dimensions consumed the entire wall. The storm ceased and silence once again regained sovereignty over the night.

After looking into the portal's dark and sinister mouth, Mica turned to her companions.

"Ladies, welcome to hell," she said with a jovial smile.

Susan moved closer and peered into the opening, her eyes marvelled at the great stone structures, which towered in the distance. Along each side of the entrance stood a set of powerful walls, majestic and cold in their dark apparel.

"It's just as I imagined it," she said.

Mica smiled. "And that is how it is created."

"What?" Susan said.

"You did not think that this was real did you? It is all taken from our collective imaginations. Everything, which you have seen and will see, has been drawn from the darkest recesses of your most private of places within your mind. Take for instance the hourglass, which we all saw as plainly as you or I. Of course time does not look like that, time has no physical presence, no structure; but for the purpose of our endeavours we needed to derive a positive image upon which we could all concentrate our efforts upon in the hope of fulfilling our task. To each and every one of us, time has always been displayed as sand falling through an hour-glass and so that is the image which we are presented." Turning, Mica looked into the portal. "Here we have another display of our collective minds conjuring an image to which we would all be familiar. These images are born from all aspects of our life, from the present back to our childhood and beyond. Strangely we have derived a prejudice for a place which none of us have ever physically seen, all of the dark patterns of this underworld are as described by the religious and the sycophantic, obsequious in their descriptions of heaven yet damning with their tales of hell. Scenes as painted by Hieronymus Bosch from the fifteenth century pepper this world, tales as described by the priests and common folk haunt our imaginations and colour our view, but please remember that heaven and hell are but perceptions and to some, living within the confines of the Garden of Eden could be perceived as living in purgatory," Mica tentatively looked into the corridor. "We have less than an hour before the portal closes and after that it will remain closed, for an eternity."

Susan moved to her side. "Let's go," she said, stepping into the darkness ahead of Mica; from behind Ann-Marie stepped forward, her eyes following Susan's actions.

"Brave girl," she said.

Mica smiled. "Bravery and stupidity are one and the same thing," she said before following Susan into the portal.

Immediately as they entered they could sense the claustrophobic presence emitted by the stone walls that lined the avenue, its great stone blocks, which made up the body of the wall, were a dark grey and cold to the touch. Above, there bled a wine-red sky, cloudless, its harsh presence mirroring its surrounding.

"Nice place, must come for a picnic some time. " Ann-Marie jested.

"Why do you not like it, after all it was your imagination which created it," Mica said.

"I always wondered what rubbish filled my head and now I know."

Mica smiled. Gathering pace they continued upon their journey, their surroundings perpetual, never changing, as constant as death. As they continued into the far reaches of this dimension a deep sense of its lifelessness filled them, they could almost touch the barren cravings, which issued from the very heart of this creation. Their imagination had given it life yet its soul remained unfound. Stopping at an intersection of stone avenues they gathered their thoughts and questioned their actions.

"What are we going to do? We're here in this lost world and for all we know we are lost as well. Where do we look first to find mother?" Susan said.

Mica pointed back in the direction from which they had come. "We take this road for about eight hundred yards and turn left for another few hundred yards, there you will hopefully find the exit from this world and the opening to your own. As for finding your mother, I would suggest that we look in this direction," she said pointing to a great tower that stood portentously in the far distance, almost too far for mortal eyes to see. Its great turrets reached into the blood red of the sky.

Ann-Marie laughed to herself. "This is like a fairytale. It's like something from my childhood."

"And that is where it is from," Mica said. "As I have said, everything into which we come into contact within this world, one of us will in some fragmented way recognise or understand its meaning. This world is a place of the mind and within the mind, anything is possible. Your darkest nightmares or sweetest dreams could be recognised; it is a place of the soul. And yet this is a place of contradiction for it apparent that it has no soul."

"You know when you said darkest nightmares?" Susan said. "Do you have anything in mind? Such as them?" she said pointing to the skies.

Mica looked up, her eyes searching the heavens. From the direction of the tower there came three flying beasts, vast and expansive of wingspan.

"Dragons!" Ann-Marie said in amazement.

"I think that this fantasy is mine," said Mica. "As a child my nanny would tell me stories of dark knights and Saint George. Of the mythical beasts of Lampton and the dark creations of northern Europe. But it was all Viking folk lore and wives-tales, yet now it is reality."

"Reality which is breathing down our necks," Ann-Marie said. "And I think that we should try and find some cover, I don't want to end up as one of those things main course."

"Prudent," Mica replied. Looking into the distance of the stone avenue she could see a culmination of junctions and a possible place of refuge. "Quickly," she cried, running off alone the Avenue. "Follow me!"

****

Callum was lost in this modern concrete jungle. His senses sent into disarray, searching for the beacon that was Mica. He could feel her presence fading, melting into the euphoria that was this world. Concentrating, he could see the images within her mind, images of places and faces but their pattern was fragmented and erratic, scattered thoughts upon a blind ocean. Unknown to him, their vampiric connection had been severed the instant that she stepped from this world.

****

As they reached the intersection Susan looked back at the skies, above the creatures gathered momentum as they fell through the heaven, descending in their direction.

"They know that we're here, there after us," she said.

"I think that you're right," Ann-Marie cried. "It's as if they knew that we were coming."

"They do," a voice said from behind.

The group turned in unison and looked to the source of the reply, Susan gasped as her eyes fell upon an image, which had haunted her for what seemed an eternity.

"Joshua Cane," she cursed.

"Rebecca," he replied. "Your soul may wear different apparel but I would recognise your presence in any time."

Ann-Marie looked on in amazement. "He's the one from the dream," she muttered.

180

"That I am, my dear, but I can assure you that I am no dream," he said bowing slightly. "And that my presence is now somewhat different to that which it once was." Slowly he opened his mouth to reveal a set of strong fangs. "I am or have become that which you most despise," he said mockingly.

Mica gently walked over to his side and placed a hand upon his shoulder. Looking into his eyes she smiled, her lips closed. "Do you believe in all that you see?" she said.

Joshua's eyebrows knitted. "What do you mean?"

"All I am asking is, do you believe that which you see. This world, us, everything?"

Joshua looked at her with distaste. "Before I was brought here by my master I was blind to the delights of this world. Now I can savour eternity and the pleasures which it could bring."

"Or the damnation," Mica replied. For she knew that his vampiric energies were still in their infancy and his powers were weak. Lifting her hand she gently stroked his face. "There are a thousand pleasures in the next world I can assure you of that and if you help us discover that which we seek then I will promise you that I will show them to you, one by one."

Joshua gripped her hand in an attempt to inflict pain and show his domination. "How could you show me anything? I would desire more than a mortal could give, more..." His words fell short, as did his attempts to rebuke Mica's false attention. His eyes opened in rage which quickly turned to terror as she rounded upon him and pulled him closer. Lifting him from the ground she held him at eye level.

"But how?" he cried.

Mica pushed him against the wall of the avenue, holding him she moved closer, almost until their faces were touching. "Do not try to bargain with me. Your powers are weak and mine are so much stronger, far stronger than anything, which could be conjured by your fragile imagination. Do not try my patience otherwise I shall take from you that which was granted in haste. Do you understand?" Mica hissed.

Joshua could feel her sharp fangs brushing against his flesh. "What do you want?"

"How quickly the tide has turned. I ask of you one thing, the whereabouts of this child's Mother?" she said, pointing to Susan.

A look of fear filled Joshua's eyes. "I cannot tell you for he will kill me."

Mica pulled him closer. "As I see it you have no choice, either you tell me now and he will kill you or you do not tell us and I will kill, both ways you lose."

"Why should I tell you if I'm to die either way?" he said.

"My way you get a head start and a slim chance."

"If we don't hurry neither of us will have any chance," Susan said pointing into the skies. "Those things are getting closer and they'll be able to see us soon. We'll need better cover than this and time is running out."

Mica looked back at Joshua. "The choice is yours."

"Hold on a minute," Ann-Marie said. "Where the hell did he come from?"

Mica smiled and looked at her companion.

"There must be a secret entrance somewhere within one of these walls" Ann-Marie stated, as she placed the palms of her hands upon the cold stones.

"It would seem that your presence is no longer desired" Mica said to Joshua. In an instant she turned her hand and the air was filled with the sound of breaking bone, and his lifeless body fell to the ground.

Susan looked on in horror.

Stepping over the corpse, Mica moved to Ann-Marie's side. "I do believe that your assumption is correct. My vampire senses did not account for his presence until he was almost upon us, hence the wall must act as a screen and the doorway must be close," she turned to her friends. "Look for anything which could be used as a levering system, a button, a brick jutting out of the masonry, something out of the ordinary. It could be our only clues."

Susan looked at her in amazement. "Something out of the ordinary, in this world. Are you kidding?"

Mica smiled and shrugged her shoulders.

Above, the creatures had sensed their presence and began their descent, slowly they circled the heavens as they drifted down aided by the warm thermal which rose from the surface of this damnation alley.

"Hurry," Susan cried. "Caliban's pets are getting closer."

Hearing her words one of the creatures held open its wings and pushed its back legs forward, revealing its razor-like claws. Plunging downwards it screamed in its attack. Susan stood frozen, fear gripping her body and mind. The creature descended, gathering velocity, its cries alerting its companions to its intentions. They too followed their brother and fell from the heavens, claws eager to savour the flesh of mortals.

Blind to the commotion above, Mica's fingers searched the wall, eager to find the key to this dark mystery. Her actions were those of a mortal, driven by fear, for she knew that Caliban and all that he created within this realm would be merciless in their judgements. Perspiration began to drip from her forehead as fear gripped her, frantically she searched but her actions would always return fruitless and barren of hope.

Turning, she looked to Susan, following her attentions she looked to the skies and was filled with a deep dread. She could see the descending demons of her imagination falling upon her and knew that all hope was lost. The raging beasts hissed and snapped as they soared above the avenue, swooping, they fell upon their prey.

Ann-Marie's fingers tentatively touched the undulations of the brickwork, searching, she found a slight indentation and pressed it, releasing a doorway which immediately swung open. Joyous in her endeavours she turned to her companions in delight and found them transfixed by the horror, which approached. Almost immediately she understood the situation and pushed her friends into the secret chamber, throwing herself in after them.

Outside, the beast's claws scrapped across the stone ground, gouging great avenues in its hard surface. Their vehemence filled the skies as they ascended in their ire.

Lying back against the cold surface of the chamber's wall Mica's heart began to rage. Ann-Marie smiled as she looked at her. "My, that's some imagination you have there."

Mica exhaled in relief. "You don't know the half of it."

"Do you think that they'll come back?" Susan said picking herself up from the floor.

"I don't care, if they do we'll be long gone," Mica said. Standing, she looked into the black recess of the chamber, her vampiric eyes reaching into the darkness with ease. "There is a small doorway and intersection about a thirty meters along this passage way. I think that we will find a multitude of answers if we search in that direction."

Susan looked at her watch. "We must hurry, we have less than thirty-five minutes left."

****

Callum stopped outside the Ward's residence; he could sense the disturbance, which the portal had created as if it were electricity dancing upon the ether. His senses could detect the slight residue of her presence. Moving closer he could almost feel the vibrations left by his lost companion which filled him with great anticipation. Entering the house he found it to be in total darkness, save for a lamp that burned in the living room. It was also there that he found source of his concern. The portal had halved in size and was decreasing as he watched. Knowing that his love was lost inside he moved to enter but refrained from doing so. Looking about the room he searched for some means of defence and found it hanging upon the far wall; two crossed Masai spears, tipped with steel. Taking the weapons he marched blindly into the unknown.

****

"What now?" Susan said as they stood at the intersection of avenues. "There are three possibilities, left, right or straight on," she looked to Mica.

"I'm sorry but my senses are all but useless in here, I'm as blind as you are. In the open I could feel something but in here there's nothing, only death."

"Well," Ann-Marie interjected. "I say that we go to the left, that's the way."

"How do you achieve that supposition?" Mica enquired.

Ann-Marie shrugged her shoulders. "I don't know. I was thinking that if this Caliban is sort of a fallen angel or something along those lines then he would sit on the left hand of God. You know, from the Bible. All that is just, sits on the right hand and the rest on the left."

Mica looked at her in amazement. "I suppose that some hope is better than none at all. To the left it is."

Precious minutes fell by as they walked alone the dark avenues and turned blind corners. Image after image mirroring the vast great walls of grey stone towering high above their heads, topped with a great stone lid which greeted them at every turn. Susan could feel her heart sinking as her anticipation was shattered as they reached each blind intersection. She could feel her fear rising in her soul, consuming her mind and bringing dark thoughts to the surface of her consciousness. Images too cold to consider. She watched Mica as she moved slowly ahead, wishing briefly that her mother could have in some way achieved the inner strength shown by this immortal, For she knew that this dark episode would scar her for an eternity. She could sense Ann-Marie's presence as she drew closer.

"Penny for them."

"Sorry," Susan replied.

"Your thoughts, a penny for them."

"I was just thinking about Mother; she was always the strong one, the one who helped me when I was in trouble. Funny how the tables will turn themselves. I know that this will add fuel to the fire of concern, but I felt that I must tell you, when it comes to physical things that we can touch and feel Mother accepts them without question. She's a scientist at heart. She studied physics and environmental science before she went into social work and now finds it easy to say to others that she has an open mind about things such as this but I can tell you that it would be too much for her to comprehend. You see, my Father told me that just after I was born, Mother suffered some sort of break down. The travelling overseas or giving up her career in science or something else triggered this reaction to what was happening to her. Maybe it was the overwhelming responsibility of being a mother which frightened her beyond belief, I don't know, but what I do know is that she has always had black days and I feel that this will sit there as one of her worst."

"Why didn't you tell me?" Ann-Marie said. "If I had of know a fraction of this then I would never have involved her."

"My mother involved herself," her words were cold and surprised Ann-Marie. "A trait which she had a knack of wheeling out when least expected. It's not your fault, if anyone's to blame then it should be me. I held out on her."

"Yes. Because you knew the reaction which she would give you," Ann-Marie assured her.

"No. It's not just that. I wanted something to be mine. Mine alone. Untouched by her interfering hands. She manipulates everything, my career in the art world, my every waking hour and then she says that she's doing it all for my own benefit and I'll thank her in the years to come. It's all backfired on me hasn't it? Now she's the centre of this fiasco and none of it is her fault."

Ann-Marie stopped and held Susan's hands.

"Listen. There's nobody to blame, if we should blame someone then it should be Caliban, after all he's the one who brought us all here. When we get out of this we'll find some reason to it all, you'll see. We'll find her soon and be on our way home."

From the darkness ahead they could hear Mica's quiet voice calling them.

"I think that I've found what we're looking for."

Ann-Marie looked to Susan.

"See. Let's go get your mother back."

184

The chamber that confronted them would have inspired even the most fervent of imaginations, its granite pillars supporting a glass ceiling, granting access to a diffused red light from the world outside, allowing its neutralising glow to illuminate their surroundings. Its soft presence falling upon the black onyx floor, polished to perfection.

"It's like something from ancient Egypt," Susan whispered. Ann-Marie nodded.

Tentatively Mica moved to the centre of the room, her senses dead to her surroundings. At the far reaches, set upon a stage of crystal there sat a great throne, bejewelled and covered in gold.

"Whoever they are, they think highly of themselves," Ann-Marie whispered.

"Thank you." a voice said, echoing from the shadows. Ann-Marie froze, her blood turning to ice as terror rose within. Slowly she turned and looked into the darkness. A set of yellow eyes greeted her attentions.

"Welcome to my domain, please make yourself comfortable, for you will be my guests." Caliban said, stepping into the subdued light of the chamber, his great frame glistening in the subtle red light from above. "Permanently."

Ann-Marie moved slowly back, passing Susan who was unaware of her predicament, her eyes never leaving the aberration that walked before her. Susan turned to discover the source of her companions' torment.

"Bastard!" she cried. Her words echoing about the chamber. Caliban smiled. "How polite of you to remember me, my dear. And after I had invited the two of you to be my guests, for an eternity."

Puzzlement swept across Susan's face. "Two!" She said under her breath. Turning she discovered the place where Mica had once stood was now empty of her presence. Turning she smiled to Caliban. "Two," she nervously reiterated.

Caliban moved to the centre of the room, his actions were contrived and a little stilted. "How can I make you comfortable?" he said sarcastically.

Susan walked forward. "First of all, you can return to me my Mother."

Caliban pouted. "Demands, demands, demands. Such an impetuous young thing, well you always were. Have you never thought of asking yourself as to why I brought you here? Why I have perpetrated such chaos in your insignificant world? Has your immortal spirit truly lost its inquisitive nature, a nature, which I had loved for these past centuries?

He looked deep into her eyes. "How I have longed to feel your presence once again beside me, to know your touch and feel you're hot breath upon my lips. Cast your mind back, recall those lost memories. Can you not remember standing with me before the fountain of eternal youth, watching as I drank my fill of that imperishable liquid? Together we had searched the ancient lands with the burning desire to achieve that which every mortal craves. The days had rolled into years and yet time was immeasurable against our desires. And, at that moment of truth, that moment of commitment, when the empires of the world lay at your feet, you turned your back upon them and against me, spurning that, which was truly yours to have. I have searched an eternity for your spirit, watching, as it was reborn over and over again, I have followed your journey though mortality after mortality, growing colder at each transition. Never being able to touch you or to feel you, never knowing the beauty of your presence, never to understand your reasoning, until now," he smiled. "You do not realise what you have done, you do not know what it is like to see those who you love grow old and wither before your very eyes and to know that immortality will keep you from this comfort so that your pain will grow within your soul, so that in time, that pain will consume you, devouring all that was once good. In my darkest hour I would pray to the immortal gods to release me from this perpetual torment but my cries would go unnoticed and the pain only gathered, bringing suffering and hatred as my solace. How I have longed for this moment and now that you are here with me, once again, I shall place you at my right hand side." Caliban looked from one to the other, a perplexed expression fixed upon his face. "I sense that all is not as it seems."

"He can sense Mica," Ann-Marie whispered. "Take his mind off it."

"So!" Susan shouted. "About you and me: What's the low down?"

Caliban smiled. "You, my dear, have been known by a multitude of mortal names. Miranda, Ophelia, Cleopatra, Diana and there are many others, too many to mention. Your physical attributes may change, grow old and eventually die, but your immortal spirit will always remain the same. I shall always know you as my Nefertiti. That day when you refused to drink with me my heart was torn apart. My life became barren and my immortality a curse rather than the blessing. You do not know how I have hungered to have you here by my side, to see your immortal spirit once again. I shall grant to you that which is savoured by those who pass from their world into the next. Behold, the real you." Caliban waved his hand and in an instant the room was bathed in a soft white light. Susan could feel herself changing. Inwardly she felt as she had always been, but outwardly the sensuality of her flesh began its transformation as the metamorphosis began. Looking down she could see her herself changing, transcending the barriers of time and space. Her skin began to darken until it resembled the soft golden texture of honey, sweet and alluring, a beauty as magnificent as any rose. Her clothing began to change, gone were the harsh materials of this modern life, giving way to the soft manmade woven silks of the ancient world. Pleated and pressed into a perfect garment which caressed and enhanced the undulations of her almost perfect female form. In that instant the transformation was complete and Ann-Marie looked on in both amazement and horror, for before her where her companion once stood, there was now a beautiful Egyptian queen, as perfect as a summer's morning.

Seeing her expression Susan cried out. "What's wrong? What's happened?" she demanded.

"Nothing," Caliban said. "I have only returned to you that which you once were. Observe!" Before her, the floor opened and a giant mirror rose from its depths. As it reached its full height Susan gasped in amazement as her reflection looked back at her.

"Is this me?" she whispered.

"As you will always be," he said.

Susan held out her arms and marvelled at the soft delicate skin, her thin slender fingers topped with long elegant nails. Looking at her reflection in the mirror she took great delight in touching her long black beaded hair that hung in braids down her back.

"Can you not see now why I have sought your companionship, searched for you down the centuries? To me time means nothing, I would reach into infinity to feel your caress. I would search the stars for the merest glimpse of your face," he said.

His words bringing Susan's mind back into focus.

"Time," she whispered. Knowing full well that the element, which she so desires, was now ticking away taking with each stroke all hope for her Mothers' safety. "Where is my mother?" She demanded.

Caliban looked at her sharply, as if her demand had in some way inflicted pain upon him.

"Why should I tell you?" he hissed.

His words took her off guard and for a brief moment she stood in bemused silence. "Well. If you have searched for an eternity for me, transcending the barriers time and space, in the hope of finding some lost love, keeping from me that which I love is not a good beginning. If you grant her, her freedom, then I will stay with you," she turned to Ann-Marie, holding her hand behind her back she crossed her fingers.

"And what would stop you from reneging upon your promise?"

"I will give you my word as a Queen," she said.

Caliban laughed. "Even then you were a liar. I trusted you once and look at the cost which I paid for doing so," he said looking to his appearance. "No my dear, you shall all stay here, your friend and your Mother shall be your hand maidens, after all it was I who perpetrated these events and awoke the sleeping immortal Christian to indirectly pursue you and to bring you me. Your Mother was merely the appetiser, she is of no consequence, I have that which I desire," he snapped his fingers and a doorway in the granite wall opened from which Jen stepped.

"Mother!" Susan cried.

Jen looked at the stranger in amazement, her voice evoking recognition but her appearance was as aliens as the stars. Recognition then filled out her features as she looked to Ann-Marie.

"Where is Susan?" she demanded.

Ann-Marie looked at her with an expression that denoted amazement then she turned and looked to the stranger.

Jen gasped in horror. "What have you done?" she said to Caliban.

He laughed at her impertinence. "I have done that which I desired, for I am lord of this realm and she is my Queen," he said pointing to Susan. "My Nefertiti," looking to Jen he hissed. "You shall obey her desires and see to her needs for we shall be once again joined as one," he looked to Susan. "You will know what it shall be like to finally taste the bitter sweet wine that is this immortality. Forget your life upon this earth, now you are mine."

Jen rushed to Susan's side. "No! You can't do this."

Caliban looked at her in distaste. "Woman! You irritate me. I have listened to your constant whining and complaining, it rings in my ears and offends me as an insect would. You try my patience, a patience which is coming to the end of its tether." Lifting his hand he slowly closed his fingers. Immediately Jen could feel her throat beginning to tighten as she fought to breathe in the stale air. It was as if his fingers were about her throat, squeezing the life from her.

Susan looked on in horror. "Stop it," she cried. Caliban looked to her, a callous indifference upon his face. Susan rushed to her Mother's side in the hope of aiding her plight but she could offer her little assistance and she watched in horror as she fell to the floor, her life force leaving her body.

"Stop it," Ann-Marie cried. "There is no need to do this. Please do not inflict anymore pain upon her." In an instant Caliban released his hold upon Jen and turned his attention to Ann-Marie.

"Very well, but what makes you think that I do not like inflicting pain? Pain and pleasure run in parallels, an analogy which you shall now experience for you shall suffer that fate which was reserved for your companion." Lifting his hand he held open his palm. "Prepare to die."

In that moment Mica was upon him, clawing at his face with her nails, summoning all the dark powers which immortality had granted her in the hope of defeating his intentions. He cried in pain as she bit deep into the soft tissue of his neck, tearing at him, she gouged mouthfuls of his red flesh from this naked, vulnerable place and sent rivers of blood rushing from the wound. He struggled in his torment as shock consumed his body. His yellow eyes flashed, filling with rage. He reached his powerful arm behind himself and swung forwards, gathering velocity as it went. Gripping Mica by the throat he ripped her from his body and held her at arm's length. He hissed at her, as bitter hatred washing across him. She struggled, but his grip tightened, squeezing the immortal life from her. Her eyes turned as the pain became almost too much for her to endure.

"What is this that I find hiding in the shadows?" he screamed. "An insect in the spider's parlour. We all know what we do to insects don't we?" He smiled as he looked into Mica's eyes. He could see her very essence dying within, and derived from this observation an insurmountable amount of immortal pleasure. Slowly her struggling ceased, as her body became weak and all signs of immortal life left her delicate form. He smiled in his indulgence.

A deep pain raged its way through his shoulder, as a dark physical agony devoured him, reeling from this assault he dropped Mica and looked to the infliction. A spear sat deep in his flesh, its point protruding several centimetres from his back. Screaming he pulled at the base of the weapon, pain wracking his body. "No!" In that instant Susan regained her natural composure her eyes searching for the source of her redemption. From the shadows the stranger stepped.

"Get away from her you bastard," Callum screamed as he walked into the centre of the room. He looked to Ann-Marie and smiled, offering her a gentle bow. Holding back the second spear he sent it through the air and into Caliban's side, his rage filling the chamber. The force of the assault sent him falling backwards and onto the floor, away from his intended victim. Callum lifted Mica from the ground and turned to the others.

188

"Quickly, we don't have much time," he said, "Follow me." Gently holding Mica close, he made his way out of the lair of the dark demon.

As they left the chamber they could hear Caliban curse their very souls to damnation.

"Hurry, this way," Callum cried. "It's only a little further in this direction," he said, rushing along one of the corridors. In the distance they could see the faint light of the portals opening; Susan pulled her Mother closer. "Run, I can't lose you a second time." Turning, she looked along the preceding corridor, its emptiness un-nerving her.

Callum stepped from the portal and into the world of mortals, his heart pounding in his chest. Placing Mica upon the sofa he stood at the portal entrance and urged the others to quicken their pace. Ann-Marie was soon to follow but Susan and her mother were still a fair distance behind.

Ann-Marie looked at the portal. "It's closing," she said. "The damn portal's closing," she rushed to the entrance and called inside. "Hurry. You must hurry."

In that moment Susan stepped into this mortal world, closely followed by her mother. At that instant the portal snapped shut, sealing the dimensions. Letting out a deep sigh Ann-Marie fell against the back of the sofa in relief.

Jen began to shake as the reality of her situation touched her; tears of frustration, peppered with relief fell from her eyes. "Thank you, thank you for saving me," she said, burying her head in her hands.

At that moment the portal burst open as Caliban reached through from his dark world; he gripped Jen about the throat and pulled her back into his dimension. Instantly he was gone and the portal was sealed forever.

Susan screamed. "Mother!!!"

****

Mica could feel the pain of her endeavours as consciousness ravaged her thoughts, through the haze that was the world, she could see the familiar face of her friend, caring and compassionate but most of all she could see the face of one who she loved. She lifted her hand to her forehead in a vain attempt to stem the pressure that was building up within. Swallowing, a raw sensation gripped her throat, she let out a delicate moan.

"Rest," Callum said, smiling.

"How did you know that I was here?" she said.

"I followed my heart," he replied.

She smiled, taking his hand in her own she held it close to her heart as the darkness of a dream world enveloped her.

Ann-Marie entered the living room and walked tentatively to Callum's side; she regarded him with a little apprehension as she observed his almost calculated actions.

"Susan's resting, she's lying down in her room, poor thing doesn't seem to realise that her Mother is gone forever, she seems to think that we can re-open the portal and her mother will step out. I haven't had the heart to tell her that it's all over." Seeing that

Callum's attentions were devoted solely to Mica, Ann-Marie expressed her concerns. "Is she all right? She will recover, won't she?"

Callum turned to Ann-Marie. "She will sleep now, not your mortal slumber, but a rejuvenation solace which will aid her in regaining those immortal powers depleted in her conflict with Caliban."

Ann-Marie regarded him with a slight air of suspicion.

"Please, sit," he said. "Ask me anything which you desire, my life to you is an open book. I can understand your situation and how these experiences must have disturbed your mind, I will guide you through all of this if you will allow me."

"Who are you?" she said.

"My name is Callum. I am of the ancient race. I would take it as so that you understand the complexities of Mica's true nature?" Ann-Marie nodded. "I am as she. Immortal. We are from the Tribe, a peaceful race who cast aside the chains of our vengeful immortality in the desire of spiritual growth and enlightenment. For centuries we have lived our forgotten existence away from the prying eyes of man and now we are but a few, for that inquisitive nature which haunts the soul of all mortals has now signed the death warrant for my kind. But before my acceptance of the dark gift I was known as a wise man in the time when I was bonded by mortal restrains. I was born on the place called the Western Islands or the Hebrides, remote and some would say desolate islands off the coast of Scotland around the calendar year 3000, B.C," Ann-Marie gasped at the magnitude of the numbers. "Even from my early childhood I knew that I was different, I seemed to transcend the distractions that consumed the desires of my fellow people and moved into a more, enlightened state of existence. They were happy times, my youth. I had little desire to look beyond the boundaries of my life; to me the world beyond the dark waters that separated my world from the mainland were neither intriguing or enticing, I was happy visiting the other islands, Coll, Jura, Mull, Skye or staying on my own isle, Barra; that was until a stranger visited my village, a stranger who captivated my imagination with his dark appearance and wise eyes. Quickly our friendship grew and he filled my head with tales of the outside world, of great races and monoliths built of stone in lands far off, his stories rang of fantasy, yet I knew that they were always based upon the truth and their purpose was to entice and draw my inquisitive mind into action and force my eventual desire for fulfilment. Darius, for that was the stranger's name, stayed with the village for two seasons before eventually setting off upon his blind journey of discovery, yet this time he had a companion, myself.

Even though our journey lasted for years and only ended at my acceptance of the dark gift, and it was only then that I discover that Darius was an immortal. We would travel at night and sleep during the day, Darius had said that this was to keep our identity from would-be robbers that lined the pathways upon which we were travelling. Oh, the sights which I saw. The birth of Stonehenge, a monolith to which I can proudly say that I had a hand in its construction, from its beginnings as mere rock taken from the great mountains in Prescelly, Dyfed, then onto its eventual triumphant rise over the Salisbury horizon; but its triumph was to end with the march of the Roman Empire. How the Caledonians scared Caesar's valiant Roman soldiers as they raced over the mountains, naked and covered in woad," he said, laughing to himself." Yet, even they could not control the destruction inflicted upon Britain and Stonehenge was desecrated, and it lies now as it had then, broken and decaying against the sands of time, history blind to its sovereign majesty," Callum sighed. "Then there was Christianity and the coming of the Vikings. It was as if modernisation was raging forward and not even history could stop it. I fled from England with the Vikings and found my way to Europe, there I travelled, drinking in the sights and sounds of life, I was immortal then and Darius had left me to grow in my own way; his guidance was always apparent and he would call upon me when I least expected, a father keeping a respectful eye upon his aspiring son. I recall his memory with a fond heart, for he reminded me of my lost mortality; we even meet in these modern times and his manor is as apparent as it has always been. If you were to ask me, of all of the vampires which I know, which one would I say was as close to their original mortal stature, save for Mica, then I would unequivocally call the name Darius," he laughed to himself as fresh thoughts entered his mind. "He even carried with him many of his mortal hoarding traits. He couldn't bear to pass an implement which would cause his interest to burn with curiosity without examining its most trivial of details, and if the opportunity were to present itself then he would claim it as his own. He would carry these objects with him through time itself, correspondence, knifes, Egyptian burial figures, they all went with him, and they all had their use. He was a good teacher and father-figure and eventually through his guidance, I came upon the Tribe and found my vocation as a dream-seer and teacher, I would take those new to the dark gift and show them the potential which could be released from within, and there I settled until tragedy forced me to once again step into the real world," he paused, allowing the silence to come between himself and his words. "Now, there are but a few of us remaining. Darius, myself, Mica and her bastard brother."

"You know Christian," Ann-Marie said in surprise.

"Know him? I created him. He had the potential to tame the world, to aspire to higher things, far greater than anything desired by any of our kind. When I first gave him the dark gift he was as inquisitive as a child, and teaching him was a delight, but I foolishly turned a blind eye to that which drew me to him. His courage, tenacity and all round arrogance. He was everything, which I am not. He is that which I would have desired in my youth and repented in my latter years. I brought him into this life and for that I must pay the price of my foolish pride. We all seek to procreate, and I am no different from most," he turned and looked at Mica as she lay in slumber. "There is one blessing in this desert of curses, he gave me Mica. He created her ten years after I created him, the first of his immortal kin. He was close to death, his immortality leaving him, I can recall it as if it were yesterday, that is one of our failings for we are all blessed with almost perfect recollection, a trait which makes this time upon the is earth unbearable, for we do not have the soft clouds of innocence to mask our memories. Christian had the foolish tenacity to confront one of the old ones, one older than myself, my creator; Darius. Needless to say, Christian almost paid for this arrogance with his life and when Mica found him she paid with his indiscretion with her own. He cursed her for an eternity, damning her soul and exacerbating her suffering so that as the years passed the mere mention of his name would cripple her emotions and send her mind spiralling into a pit of darkness from which she would struggle to return. The only saving grace to enter her life was that of her son, Jess. A delightful inquisitive child who paid for his curiosity with the highest price of all. Now I fear that this darkness will return and I am helpless in my actions."

"But you love her," Ann-Marie said.

"Is it that obvious?" he said smiling.

"I'm afraid so," she replied, laughing slightly. "Does she know?"

Callum looked to the floor as tears filled his eyes. "I am as I have always been, the friend, the companion, the confidant. I am seen as nothing else. It is as if my desires and emotions are second best to those of others, throughout my existence I have been the comforter but never the comforted, never allowed to be weak, never allowed to be, human, I suppose. To a non-immortal, immortality must seem like a great adventure, a great gift but it is not. It is a dark gift, something that pollutes the blood and deceives the mind. It is this reason why I cannot tell her how I truly feel. Our emotions are so heightened that I will die if my feelings are made apparent and are subsequently rejected; it would tear my soul asunder. I cannot live with this need to tell her."

"And yet you cannot live with this feeling of never telling her, you are living in a land of none emotion, none commitment. In some strange perverse way you are playing it safe. Maybe it is your indecisiveness that is pushing her away from you," Ann-Marie smiled and took hold of his hand. "I am sure that you have your reasons for your reluctance to show your true colours and emotions, but believe me the distance between knowing and not knowing is as vast as infinity and if you eventually have your answer, then so be it, but either way, life would be easier to live in."

Callum looked blindly into the air above his head. "I cannot complain, for I am responsible for this. Before Mica came to the Tribe I was happy to carry this mantle of office, in some strange pertinacious way it took delight in the stature and responsibility which it afforded me, but it also gave me segregation. A distancing from that which I desired. At times I craved to be as others, lost in their confusion but the powers granted to me by the dark gift set me aside from others, for my insight and future recollections were seen as divine and so, treated in accordance. I was almost as revered as the holy Qareen."

"Has she never suspected your love?" Ann-Marie enquired.

"If so, then she did not confide in me. In these latter years I have felt her drifting, moving away from the structure of the Tribe and into the solitude and safety of her own world and who could blame her. She had lost the love of a brother who she had surmised for centuries to have perished in the French Revolution and now he too has returned to haunt her, reminding her of that which she has lost and reaffirming that which she cursed him for, her immortality."

Callum thought deeply. "Immortality has a great price. Madness may take the lucky few while the others feel the passing of each second as if it were a weight falling in their heart. It is almost indescribable to portray the suffering, which confronts an immortal to one who has never tasted the perpetual wine of the cursed dark blood. It would be easier for you to tell me of the masquerade of this modern world in a second than it would be for me to have the luxury of infinity to describe to you the suffering which confronts each and every one of our kind throughout their immortal purgatory. The suffering is enhanced, as is the pleasure, along with fear, pride, hatred and every other emotion encountered by mortals and beyond. In essence you become the extremity of that which you are. Some may say that you become the real you, a pure, unpolluted creation. Yet, I would say that this curse runs deeper, it breeds within until, in time, it consumes you, manipulates you and you no longer resemble that which you once were. This symbiotic relationship between nature and super-nature becomes unbalanced and eventually one becomes the victor as surely as the other become the vanquished and an immortal tyrant is born."

"Christian!" Ann-Marie whispered.

Callum nodded.

"You can't blame yourself for the actions of another. It would be the same as expecting every mother to be responsible for the crimes perpetrated by their children or for those descendants born of those who enslaved others centuries before to now requested to stand trial for the dark actions of their forefathers, it couldn't be this way. You must try to separate yourself from your guilt and move forward so that we may achieve a future for us all."

"You are wise," Callum said, looking into Ann-Marie's eyes. "But, there are times when I do feel that this life is a fire in which we must all burn, consumed by all the bitterness which we eventually become. Greed, lust, love and hatred. Our whole existence is centred round our selfish desires; we crave the brief attentions of others and set our aims and expectations high upon the unattainable. Within, we burn until the fire that propels us devours us and only a shell of that which once was, remains; a bitter sweet reminder of those lost opportunities hungered for by our fragile minds. Life is a series of misunderstood communications; no matter how articulate, no mortal or immortal alike, has ever achieved the long-standing desire to put their pure emotional and spiritual feelings into words or conversation. We strive to achieve yet always fall short of our aims. We see the possibility and yet are blind to our destiny, we are lost in the turmoil of our inner battles, a battle which begins at our moment of birth and ends when our mortality ends, yet for some of us this natural state does not occur and a preternatural existence transpires, and within us those desires and inner hopes of others smother and restrict the yearning which we all secretly harbour for, they fester and corrupt until eventually we despise all that we once were and are about to become. We never stand proud and follow our own council, yet freely administer advice as if it were sand, abundant and pure," Callum paused and turned to Ann-Marie, smiling he took his hand and brushed it tenderly along her cheek. "Promise me one thing," he said. "That if you are offered this dark gift, this immortal purgatory that you will reject it for all that it is. For if your pure blood is mixed with that of an immortal your powers will leave you and they will never return and they will take with them the dreams of many of my kind. Your powers, at present, are embryonic but as time progresses you will understand your true destiny and why you have been chosen to follow this dangerous path which you find yourself walking," he looked into her soft eyes. "All mortals wonder at certain times within your brief life-span, whether all of this is worth it and if there is any purpose to all of the suffering? To answer that question I can but propose another question. Could you ever imagine what it would be like to have that question forever in your mind, and to have forever to contemplate its meaning?"

Ann-Marie looked to him with sorrowful eyes for she could feel the suffering, which haunted his soul. "I understand, to you the insignificant cries of a mortal must be as irritating as an insect to a great beast, forever distracting and contemptible within the confines of their insignificant world."

Callum smiled. "A cry in the dark. A lost child. An arrogant illiterate, those are the way in which I would describe mortals. They are searching for the eternal question to life and I'm sorry, but the question has no answer, no meaning. This is it, the moment that is all. Yes the spirit is immortal, but the flesh is not and the pleasures are transient and brief. When the physical dies and the spirit passed on, it forgets the turmoil of its passed life and moves forward to embrace that which it is destined to become. This is the difference between you and I and it is a difference that should be celebrated, as should all differences. Mortality gives you the perimeters within which you can develop and grow, whereas immortality bonds you to that which you once were so that in time you become a parody of the real you, and all that you have to hold onto is the memories of your mortal time in the sun, your halcyon days."

"I think that I understand what you're saying," Ann-Marie said. "But can I ask you a question?"

Callum nodded.

"If we are creatures, spirits who have grown and developed by our constant birth and rebirth then where did we come from? Also, if we advance by these actions, do you remain as you are, for you are locked within this immortal form?"

"To answer your second question first," Callum began. "Yes, we remain stilted within this form, some would say that this is the reason why we have been granted those powers which we have, for if immortality came without this gentle galvanisation then it would simply be that, immortality, a prison for eternity. We would be locked within a shell, the same as man, unable to transcend the barrier of our minds but because this transition which moulds us to such a degree with our acceptance of the dark powers, it changes our perception of everything which is around us," Callum paused, deep in thought. "It can be better explained in this way. It would be like taking one of your modern scientists and proving to them that everything with which they measured their precious theory upon was wrong and the distance between their theologies and perceptions was an infinity from the actual truth. In essence, proving that the world was flat and not round, or that the sun went round the Earth and not the other way, or that death was first and not birth. Can you understand what I am trying to say? While the mind can accept change the spirit can only achieve this through rebirth and if we are to experience the transition granted to man then we must regain that which was once lost. The truth is always seen in the eye of the beholder and yet, the truth is simply the truth. There are no lies within this world, only a perception. That is what gives us the difference, and there is a key as to how the truth is perceived and this gives us lies. We know this, we have encountered it, and immortality has punished us with this bitter truth and yet we have never truly experienced this within our souls for they are as virginal now as they have ever been. Some of our kind are firstborn. New souls, locked forever within the prison of immortality. Yearning for freedom, yet fearing the unknown," Callum laughed gently. "What a paradox. Here we are immortals living in fear of the unknown, of death. Yet, here you are, mortals who must face this dark creation every second of your brief existence and yet you all seem to pass on through your lives without a care for that which will eventually consume."

Ann-Marie thought for a moment. "Maybe your greatest fear is that you understand your immortality, and fear that immortality may not mean forever. There may be a saturation point when the body eventually decays beneath the desires of the soul. After all, who should fear death the most, the hunter or the hunted? The hunted, who briefly feel the presence of their killer before their life is snuffed out forever, or the hunter who lives and breathes death; can smell its stench upon his nostrils and see the blood upon his hands. You will never experience old age, that immanent biological dysfunction."

He smiled at Ann-Marie. "Though in some way our immortality is very sad, for what other reason could there be to living other than passing on your genes, to procreate, and yet, when we create a new life that person becomes immortal and not your genes. Nature is a volatile creature, the world rots and decays, order becomes disorder, it is as if the world is based upon degeneration and malfunction, all focusing upon that immutable concluding event, death."

Callum paused. "You are wise beyond your years, a trait which may serve you well."

Ann-Marie smiled. "And the first part of my question?"

"That is a little difficult. Where did we come from?" he said to himself. "Man has mused over this one for an eternity, and yet the answer is brief and simple. The universe."

Ann-Marie shook her head. "What do you mean? Aliens? Another planet? Another dimension? Genetically altered by some one? What? You can't just say the universe."

"The universe. From whence we came to where we shall return. What once was shall it always be. If you look about this earth you will see that the history of man is merely a distraction; he has placed himself into the heavens in his arrogance, assuming that his history is the one and only and no other should be written. Yet, he negates to understand the true life-span of this ancient world; it has had many races and many false proclaimers to its throne and yet it still stands proud, defiant to the uttering of those who would ravage its resources and rape its lands. We think that we are the personification of genetic and evolutionary matching, the amalgamation of ancient D.N.A. and protozoa, mixed with that magical something, something supernatural. Nothing could be further from the truth. In actuality man is the decaying remnant of a greater race, a once powerful creature which strode this earth with a majestic pride and lived in harmony with everything that was natural. Understanding all and holding compassion above everything. Yet they, too, had their failing and, eventually, through political unrest their downfall was upon them before they could understand or comprehend their innocent actions, for those who deem their endeavours as innocent and righteous yet condemn others for their aspirations are blind to the sensitivity of their fellow creatures and in some strange way deserve to fall before the sword of history. A true history, as witnessed by the stars, blind to prejudice and as incorruptible as a new-born. But they have left their legacy, for we are the sixth sons of this forgotten race and time, we are the penultimate generation of hope, blindly wandering, searching for that which we once were. In his arrogance man has turned a blind eye from the truth and placed all of his faith in science and instead of balancing his knowledge he has mystify it and use it as a tool of power to manipulate others and to coerce them to do his will, this shall be his downfall."

Callum stood and moved to Mica's side. Her eyes were closed as she bathed in a deep slumber. He bent forward and gently brushed her brow. "We have travelled a great distance on this night and there is no turning back. The past is now truly the past and the future is ours to own. For too long I have been silent and now I will stand for that which I believe in and become one with my soul and my emotions, I will strive to understand the desires of myself rather than the yearnings of others. I am weary of this life and the journey which I have travelled has been a long and arduous one made sweeter by the presence of one that I have aspired to be held worthy as to call my own. If my history is to be a cold one then it shall have only a few more pages to turn before the conclusion is written in my own blood."

"Maybe the whole point of this journey is that we should never really reach our destiny. After all, if the whole point of life is to learn then maybe we should accept ourselves for who we are and not for that which we desire to become, for we can never really understand ourselves and if we mask our identity with a false image then we deceive ourselves as well as everyone about us. We constantly underestimate our achievements and the potentiality of ourselves instead of realising our own true inner worth. This knowledge which we all carry within ourselves is infinite in its wisdom, and if we use its power instead of looking to others for direction, when in actuality we ask for their opinion when we desire to ascertain affirmation of that which we already know, we can, in some simplistic way reach for our own potential. If we use this power as a base, then we can truly reach out and touch the stars."

 Realising that their conversation was drawing to a conclusion Ann-Marie stood and made to leave the room, but Callum stopped her by gently grasping her hand. She looked into his sorrowful eyes and smiled before turning to look into the hallway, the dark shadows of night reached across the walls, their presence seemed less intrusive than before, almost comforting. She turned back to Callum. "I know that it's only been a few moment, but I think that I should go and see if Susan's all right, she's been through too much already." Callum released his grip and watched as Ann-Marie walked slowly to the doorway, pausing for a moment she turned to him and smiled. "I only hope that this will soon be over for all of our sakes and for my sanity," she said before stepping into the darkness and allowing the shadows to envelop her.

Callum stood and turned to look at Mica, how his heart was filled with torment and he once again sank slowly to his knees. Holding her hand he prayed silently to the heavens for her deliverance. A prayer from an immortal lost to the blessing of a higher god, a prayer sent from deep within a dark heart. As the images of his love passed across the surface of his mind, Callum could only hope that his aspirations would not fall upon deaf ears. Opening his eyes he stood, looking down at the pitiful, fragile form that was his love, he could feel his heart sinking into an infinite pit of eternal loneliness. Slowly he lowered his head gently onto his open palm as his indecision, which depleted the strength of his convictions, left him once again, lost within his indifference, an indifference which was savagely interrupted as Ann-Marie hurried into the room. "Did you leave the door open? The front door?" she said urgently. Callum shook his head. "Well it's open and Susan's not in her room. If she heard us talking then about her mother and the loss of hope, then there's no saying where she could be now. I dread to think of what may have happened to her."

Callum stood, his eyes ablaze. "Christian would not dare! Quickly, let us search the surrounding area, Mica will be safe here alone. It is forbidden for an immortal to take the life of one of our own and let us only hope that he is beholding to some of our old ways."

As they entered the dark world of night, a gentle fall of snow drifted down from the heavens, leaving a blanket of innocence upon everything, which it touched. Callum stepped into the street, all about the silence of the night was deafening. His senses raced and danced upon the cold air yet returned barren and alone. "I cannot sense her; he must be concealing her mortal signal." Ann-Marie looked up and down the empty street. "If you follow the road up that way," she said, pointing into the darkness. "Then I will go this way into the more populated part of the city," Callum nodded and disappeared into the night, his departure startling Ann-Marie a little, for the realisation and magnitude of his powers became truly apparent to her.

Standing at the intersection of crossroads Ann-Marie felt lost, a stranger in this, her own time. Standing there, beneath the naked light of the street lamp she began to realise the extremity of the suffering experienced by her new found friends torn form their own time and sent unprepared into an unknown, savage, and bitter realm. A realm where innocence was ridiculed and violence applauded. How ashamed she felt at the blatant rape of innocence; a cold shudder filled her.

Crossing the road she could see a soft light emanating from the windows of a local public house. Reaching the other side, she looked in through the windows. How simple life was to those within, this Christmas season has taken hold of all of their souls and how they relished in its self-indulgent debauchery; laughing and making merriment seemed second nature to a normally subdued and grey people. This season seemed to permit the presence of the abstract; a sequester to their natural inhibitions, and a perpetrator to the indulgent. Looking up, Ann-Marie read the sign of the drinking house. 'The Black Sheep' she read. How fitting, returned a thought.

Concentrating, she walking slowly away, slightly envying those inside, blind to the barbarity that was consuming the world as they made merry. It was as she passed the car park behind the public house that her senses came into play, an inner rage consumed her, sending her darker emotions on a roller coaster ride of fear. Her embryonic sixth sense was struggling in its infancy; a struggle that alerted her to the terror that was about to strike.

Looking into the shadows, Ann-Marie recoiled in horror as recognition raped her mind, for there in the darkness lay the discarded remnants of a young girl's shoe, a shoe which Ann-Marie recognised immediately. Slowly she moved towards it, her eyes searching for the imminent danger. Reaching down she lifted the blood stained object and held it close, the deep pain of recognition struck her as tears ran down her cheeks.

"Susan, where are you?" She said turning to look deeper into the darkness of the car park. Her question was imminently answered, for they were lying between two vehicles, resting in the far shadows, a figure instantly recognisable, lifeless and alone. Ann-Marie gasped. Her mind was a blank. Fear filled her. Dropping the blood-stained shoe she hurried over to the body, no longer caring for her own safety. To her horror the wounds inflicted upon her were recent and savage. Ann-Marie let out a gasp as a sickness filled her stomach.

It was the moan that startled her, a moan that represented life. Ann-Marie recoiled in horror for the realisation that Susan was still alive filled her mind with a series of insurmountable questions, question to which she feared the answers. Kneeling down, she supported Susan's head upon her knees and gently stroked her forehead in a vain effort of offering her comfort and solace on this bitter night.

"Help! I must get help," Ann-Marie said over and over again to herself. Looking about she could see that the once thriving streets were now empty and any hope of salvation had gone with them. 'The pub', she thought. 'They'll hear me if I shout.' She could see several strangers moving about inside, their presence enhanced by the false light within.

"Help!" she cried, but the music within seemed to drown her cries. Sitting back she placed her hand gently upon Susan's face. Her eyes flickered open.

"Ann-Marie...you found me...I'm so sorry," Susan said in an almost silent, inaudible voice.

"It's all right," Ann-Marie said offering her a half-hearted smile.

"I heard you talking and when I realised that the portal couldn't be re-opened I was angry and ran into the night, that's where he found me," Susan's eyes looked past Ann-Marie.

Before Ann-Marie could reply a long shadow fell over her, this was followed by the gentle timbre of a soft welcoming voice.

"Do you require any assistance?" he enquired.

Ann-Marie let out a sigh of relief and looked up at the stranger. Her eyes opened wide in horror as his name broke from her lips.

"Christian."

Part Four

THE CONFRONTATION

One

Christian did not see the descending figure until it was almost upon him; it was as if the shadows of the night were rising up against the evil which had poisoned this land. He could feel his immortal flesh tear and rupture from the full force of his assailant's contact, which sent him spiralling blindly into the dark shadows. As he hit the ground, he could see the pure white of the snow turning a deep shade of crimson as his immortal blood wept from his fresh open wounds. A deep rage filled him, urging his black heart to seek vengeance. Quickly, he stood and regained his composure, staring at the hooded figure he sent out an immortal message of warning to this invader to his dark reunion. His warning however fell upon a silent mind, signalling caution to his vengeful hedonistic urges. Christian studied the creature before him, following the strong undulations of his body, his graceful almost liquid movement. Memories ignited the dry tinder of his lost thoughts. Searching, he looked deeper in the hope of discovering a glimpse of his attacker's secret identity, yet his hooded face remained veiled, concealing him from the truth.

Searching, he turned his own mind, Christian recalled the images and faces of companions, both friend and foe, from centuries past, his thoughts raged as urgency compelled him to discover the truth about his assailant. He recalled the followers of the Tribe, his sister, delicate and fragrant, a flower in this bitter wind that is immortal winter, a true beauty of this dark gift. His mind moved on, searching for answers. Cantor, bloated and self-important, cunning of mind but short of imagination. His mind quickly rejected this assumption and drifted forward, recalling faces from deep within the dark recess of his imagination. Clouds of self-doubt thickened and fogged his thoughts casting dark shadows into the furthest of imaginary recesses. Then his mind fell upon his answer; that creature which created him, the only immortal other than his kin who felt any compassion for those of the weaker flesh.

"Callum," he hissed.

The figure stood erect and opened out his arms in a mock gesture of acceptance. He lifted his head slightly but the shadows still concealed his identity, thus mocking Christian in his empty triumph, a triumph of recognition which was short lived as a voice from behind his dark adversary spoke.

"I am here, but it is not I who is your judge upon this night. For I am not the one who confronts you and asks for you to account for your antecedent actions which have brought an insurmountable suffering and disgrace to every dark creation who has experienced the consuming passions of the dark gift. I am not the one who has disgraced the name of our kind and brought a mistrust and hatred from those of our people, which we once called friend and now we fear. For their only desire in this perpetual immortal damnation is to see our persecution and eventual destruction as accountability for those dark deeds, which we were so inadvertently accused."

Christian's eyes flashed in anger. "Have you deserted all that you thought respectful, old man?"

Callum smiled. "Deserted? No, I cannot desert that which has already been destroyed. Sent blindly asunder into the pit of darkness, which is called damnation. To be forever consumed by that black rage which is your master. Our people, who were once warm and compassionate, those who offered you solace in your hour of need, have been brought down by the ignorance of the one. You!"

"Me," Christian hissed. "How am I responsible? I have lain in the earth for centuries, suffering at the hand of this vixen, she has a greater darkness in her soul than any other of our immortal kind could imagine," he said, pointing to Ann-Marie. "She would call me love with one breath and damn me with the next."

"Aye, damned until awoken by your dark master," Callum said accusingly.

"Master! I have no master, I am the lord of my own destiny, why do you imply that I am the puppet of another?"

"You deny that you are in collusion with Caliban?" Callum asked. Christian looked at him in disbelief. "Next you will be telling me that those letters which fell into the hands of modern man, written in your hand, were not perpetrated by your own selfish desires? You arrogantly went against the laws of the Tribe, knowing full well that it is forbidden to write, discuss or communicate anything which could jeopardise a member of the Tribe, let alone the whole Tribe. Yet, give these facts to a mortal and then we find that you have drawn maps, leading the unenlightened oppressors to our very doorstep, bringing with them genocide, which would consume all of our dark children."

Callum's words hit him hard, sending spasms of fear rising from deep within. "I have written no letters...," he paused, as distant memories began to drift into his thoughts. He looked sorrowfully to the ground. "Mica, I wrote to Mica, but gave them to..." His mouth began to quiver as his mind began to torment him with images of death and destruction.

"Mica! What has happened to my Mica?" His hand raced to his mouth as if to restrain himself from screaming.

"Your Mica?" she hissed, stepping from the shadows, a look of repulsion hanging upon her face. "I am not your Mica. Your Mica died that day you gave me over to this purgatory, this immortal death. I, gave my blood to you gladly so that you may have lived, I did not give it to receive this dark blasphemy. You were everything to me; you were my world, my light, I followed you with every beat of my mortal heart. When you left me alone and scared, to seek your destiny you took with you my desires, my hopes and returned years later a changed man, no longer that impetus, tender being that was my brother, the man who lived for the moment and derived great delighted in this gift called life. No. You returned changed. You were a dark deceiver of dreams. One who lied to me, begged for me to help him. I knew that you were close to death and the final gift that I could give to one whom I loved, was my life, the very essence of my soul and you drank deep, deeper than anyone could have imagined." A single tear ran down her cheek. "After the sacrifice that I gave you, you raped my soul and repaid me by condemning me to this darkness, this eternal suffering. Death was my destiny and you even robbed me of that and now I damn you as surely as you had damned me," she paused briefly to compose herself. "I had thought you dead and for centuries, mourned your passing, and now my only hope is for my past misconception to be made into the truth and justice to be written so that my future can be forged, free of your irritating interference."

Christian pursed his lips as her harsh words struck his heart.

"I gave you the gift because I could not live without you. I loved you with all of my heart and soul," he cried.

Mica's eye's flashed. "And I hate you with all of mine."

Her words bit deep. "So be it sister, but remember, you will always be a part of me, I will know what you know, see what you see and think what you think. I will constantly be one step ahead of you. If it is a confrontation that you desire, then that is what you shall receive and this matter shall once and for all be put to rest. I must say this, in defence of these transgressions, which you have brought before me. There is no dark collusion, no alliance; I am alone, as I have always been, now more than ever. Your fallacious whisperings of confederation between myself and the dark one are misguided and as erroneous as your own hatred for those deeds which were perpetrated in my name and are now damning me to this persecution. I admit that I am not innocent, but then again, there is no man who can claim this. You have seen me with blind eyes and judged me on crimes that had transpired centuries ago," he looked sorrowfully to Mica. "This is not why you were granted this immortality. Look beyond your personal desires and into the higher realm of existence that is the pattern of this world. We are greater than man, born into darkness to be his master that is why we were given this perpetually. We are his God!"

"Or his teacher," the stranger said.

Christian looked to the hooded figure and questioned him mockingly. "Pray tell me immortal intruder, what grievance brings you to this makeshift parliament? This court of justice, Are you Judge, Jury, Prosecutor or Hangman? What despicable act have I perpetrated against your gentle soul and caused you to hunt me on this dark winters night?" Christian gave him a wry smile.

The stranger cautiously lifted his hands and gripped the sides of his hood; slowly he lowered it, revealing his identity.

Christian's eye's opened wide in horror as a name spat from his lips. "Darius."

"You are correct in your assumptions," he said as he turned and smiled at Callum. "I have followed this travesty called your life through the pages of time and all that I find is the suffering which you inflict upon all those whom you come into contact with. You are a plague that infects the goodness in others, poisoning their thoughts and turns their minds against that which they know to be right. Your actions are those of a killer, cold, distant and calculating, so that in time your own thoughts are incongruous to your actions. You have disconnected yourself from the real world, absolved yourself from all blame, vindicated your behaviour and given your dark lies a ring of truth. Look deep within yourself, use those all seeing eyes and you will see all that we see. You are guilty as charged."

Christian stepped slowly from the shadows, his heart pounding in his chest.

"So what is to happen now? Three to fight against one. To be executed by those of his own immortal flesh and blood, his closest of kin," he smiled briefly to himself. "Ah! Irony; such a harsh demon."

"The conclusion to your dark existence is not yet upon you. Yet, it looms upon the horizon, the reaper searches for your soul even as we speak," Darius said.

"Why do you not do it now?" Christian cried.

"That would be too simple. After all, we all have our perversions and my own personal one is to see your suffering. In times past you came to me once, an arrogant impetuous youth, full of your own self-importance, and I sent you away to die. It was only the intervention of your sister that brought you back from that brink upon which I had placed you," Darius looked deep into Christian's soulful eyes. "You will see me do this a second time, and this time, there shall be no saving grace."

"I admit that I was arrogant but that is not a crime and my words were as truthful then as they are now, the only thing damaged in our confrontation was your precious pride," Christian said accusingly.

"Do not test me," Darius screamed, causing Christen to step back as fear gripped his emotions.

"What will you do? Strike me dead? Tear out my heart?" he impetuously enquired.

Darius thought for a moment then smiled a satisfying smile. "No! That would be too simple, I will give you a chance, a grace that you neglected to bestow upon your own. Run! Run! Escape into the night and we will hunt you down and destroy you, destroy that beast which you are. We will give you the choice that you denied all of your victims, victims who both directly and indirectly perished at your hand. We will give you the choice to take your own life and save us from fulfilling this dark act. You have one hour from now, if we sense your presence after that time then we will pursue you and destroy you, dispelling your sorrowful ashes to the four winds," he lowered his head and smiled to himself. "Yet, I know the conclusion to this tale, you are weak and cannot execute that final act upon yourself and so we will meet again and next time, I shall be your executioner," Darius turned and looked to Callum. "We shall leave, please bring the remains of his last victim, we shall return to her a little of her dignity, that which has been torn from her tender soul," he then turned back to Christian and smiled. "One hour."

****

Susan's broken and bloodied body lay on the floor in the kitchen of her home, her empty eyes staring into the void above her. Ann-Marie and Mica sat at the table; their hands locked in an embrace of comfort, for fear tormented them both.

"Do you think that this Darius will carry out his threat and go after Christian?" Ann-Marie said in an almost silent tone.

Mica, not taking her eyes from the wall in front of her, answered, in a slow deliberate way.

"The rift between Darius and Christian was forged centuries ago, even before he was immortal, Callum went against his strict wishes and gave Christian the gift and I don't think that Darius has really forgiven him. Time has not healed the wound created by his blatant disregard for his wishes and I feel that my brother is the sacrificial lamb who is being manipulated by those of a greater power in the hope of appeasing the raging fires of mistrust that burn within us all. To answer your question, yes, he will kill him, without a second thought or a glimmer of remorse."

Ann-Marie laughed slightly. "I don't know who the bad guy is any more, Christian, for his dark actions, Callum for creating him, myself for wanting him or you for loving him."

Mica turned and looked to her. "We are all as bad as each other and yet Christian is responsible for himself and I can no longer protect his name."

"You still love him, don't you?" Ann-Marie said.

Mica smiled as tears filled her eyes. "He's my brother, he is all that I have left and soon even that will be taken from me, as has everything which I have loved in this immortal life."

"There is another?" Ann-Marie said.

"What!" Mica replied.

"Another who loves you," Ann-Marie whispered.

"Who?" Mica asked.

"Callum," Ann-Marie said with a smile.

Mica smiled. "I know, I have always known."

"Why didn't you tell him? He's been carrying this love for you for centuries."

"I love him," Mica said. "That is why. I have loved him since that moment when we first met, but I could not tell him for fear is a strong emotion."

"Fear! What do you mean?" Ann-Marie said, turning Mica's face to her own.

"Everything that I have loved, everything which I cherish in this life has been taken away from me and I could not live with the knowledge that I would be damning his soul to eternal torment. If he knew of my love he would pursue it until the end of time and I could not ask him to do this," Mica said gently.

"He would," Ann-Marie said, offering her a reassuring Smile. "It's plain to see, he worships the ground upon which you walk, he is besotted by your presence, he loves you for the gentle creation that you are. In this brief time, which I have known you, all I have seen from you is compassion. You feel the suffering of others."

"That is my downfall so I have been told; when I was given this life I retained my fragile human emotions, holding them close to myself. It was my way of denying reality, defying the events which had happened. I know that I was deluding myself, turning from the truth of that which I really was, but in time my defence became my normality and I could no longer let others close to me, no matter how much I tried. The suffering which I have experienced over these lifetimes had bruised my heart to such an extent that I feel an intense pain every time that I dream, or I allow my aspiration to drift upon the clouds of 'What if'. Now it has become second nature not to dream. My desires are dead along with my life and my aspirations have fallen by the roadside, trampled into the dust of this long journey that is immortality."

"Give it a chance; give him a chance, which is all that he is asking for. Do not deny him, do not deny yourself. This love may just be the gift that you allow yourself that will make this suffering a little more bearable. Some of us do not get a second chance," she said looking at the cold corpse that was Susan.

Mica stood and held out her hand.

"Come, while the need is upon me. Let us go to the others. I will talk to Callum and inform him of my intentions."

Ann-Marie stood. "Oh you sweet talker, romance isn't dead after all," she said sarcastically.

Mica smiled.

As they entered the living room Ann-Marie noticed that Callum and Darius were standing by the open fire, deep in dark discussion. It was only after a moment did they acknowledge the women's presence and cordially bowed as a mark of respect. Their action gave Ann-Marie a deep sense of regard for both men.

"Thank you for giving me a little time with Susan," she said. "It was nice to say goodbye."

Darius smiled. "I understand." Moving to the centre of the room he removed his cloak and leather hip bag and threw them onto the sofa, the hip bag flipping open as it landed. "I will take your friend to her room and arrange it so that her death will be perceived as natural," he said before offering Ann-Marie a second bow before leaving the room. She smiled and looked to Mica, her expressions urging her to purvey her emotions to Callum. Mica's alabaster skin was beginning to flush as embarrassment washed over her.

"Callum," Ann-Marie said.

"Yes," he replied in his natural heavy tone.

"I think that Mica has something that she wishes to tell you."

Mica stood in embarrassment, her heart pounding. "Yes," she muttered. "Follow me, I think that I have something that I must say," she said hurrying from the room closely followed by Callum.

Ann-Marie smiled to herself and sat heavily on the sofa. Pulling her knees to her chest she began to recall the events which had shaped her life over these past few days and a deep sense of regret began to fill her. She recalled her first meeting with Susan in the Gallery and how she had thought her strange, and as time passed, she could see the inhibitions which had haunted her at that age rising in their appearance to the surface of her emotions. How she had changed in that brief time that they had known each other, grown beyond comparison to other mortals, lived beyond a lifetime in a matter of day and yet in some strange way it was as if they knew that they would be struck down before their prime was even recognised. She could feel the tears of her guilt and anxiety rise within her, flooding her eyes and falling down her soft cheeks. The guilt of survival weighed heavy upon her heart, and she felt in some strange way responsible for her own durability and the downfall of her friends. After all was it not her actions, which brought this horror to their door? If she had faced this torment alone then Susan and her mother could have be celebrating life for years to come. Was her weakness responsible? She thought, as her heart sank deeper and deeper into a pit of depression.

Lifting one of the heavy cushions from the sofa, she placed it upon her stomach in a futile attempt to comfort the torment that consumed her. Reaching over she gripped the corner of the second cushion and pulled it towards her, knocking Darius' hip bag accidentally from the sofa. Laboriously she cast the cushions to one side and knelt down in a half-hearted attempt of retrieving the bag's contents, which had spilled out onto the floor. Retrieving several unrecognisable objects, she placed them back into the bag before continuing her search, lifting several papers, which had fallen under the sofa, she was inspired by their vast age, yellowed by time she held them close and dared to read them. The writing upon their time bleached surface mesmerised her, the soft undulation of the letters, almost romantic in their construction, gently gliding and drifting. Then her conscience began to proclaim its distaste at her actions and she made to put them back in their rightful place. It was only as she was about to place them into the bag did her eyes fall upon a word that she instantly recognised. A word that almost burned itself into her mind. MICA. Its strong letters calling for her to read them over and over again, reassuring herself of her perceptions. Slowly, she opened the letter and began to read, as she did so the full ramifications of the true injustice which had befallen her lost love became apparent to her.

July 1789 Paris.

My Dearest Mica,

How I miss you, my deep desires urge for you, how I wish you could come to Paris and reunite with me so that we may walk together in this realm of darkness as a light for all of our kind. The life that I am living here is far from that which I suffered within the confines of the tribe; here, I am accepted as myself and not as others would desire. Oh sister, it is as if a great burden has been lifted from me and I now feel that this immortality is bearable, if only that you could join me instead of following a lost love. Callum loves you yet resents all others connected with you, how he compels, how he contrives.

On the eve of my leaving I did see an ancient soul pass through the mountain close to our home, and later I saw him in Paris, he arrived several days after I had. I feel his presence closing in, it's as if he were following me, stalking me, waiting for my mistakes. His name is Darius, creator of Callum. Please look deeper into his heart for there is more within those so called unselfish desires than first perceived by the innocence of others. I do not trust his all-seeing eyes, for their immortality has given them a cold detachment that compels an even colder heart.

Love Christian.

X

Ann-Marie closed the letter and held it to her chest, the pain within was almost too much for her to bear. "Darius," she whispered under her breath. "He was the one who gave the letters to the church. He was the one who damned Christian."

****

Mica stood tentatively in the kitchen, the soft glow from the artificial light that shone from above gave her skin an almost radiant shine; it was as if she were experiencing the first flushes of youth once again. Her soft eyes looked tenderly onto Callum's face as she studied the soft contours of his subtle features. His solid stature almost angelic in this romantic light.

"Thank you for being my knight in shining armour," she said. "I don't know what would of happened if you hadn't have come to my rescue, Caliban could have killed me. I don't know why I am so surprised. You have always been there whenever I have been challenged by this darkness called life. No matter how harsh this reality confronts my tender soul, I know that I will always have you there to protect me..." - she looked into his eyes. – "...and love me. But one thing intrigues me," she continued. "How did you know where to find me?" she said.

Callum smiled and looked nervously to the floor.

"There's something that you're not telling me isn't there?" she insisted.

Callum lifted his eyes from the floor and looked to Mica's tender face. A feeling of deep guilt filled him. "You may as well know the truth now, for I would have to tell you at some point. Your first meeting with Darius was no accident, he had visited the Tribe only a week before its downfall and informed me that certain letters had fallen into the hands of the church and immediately, I understood the magnitude of the situation. Other letter, written centuries ago, have fallen into the hands of the church over a hundred years ago, but these letters were written by Christian and gave their reader names, places and maps. It would only have been a matter of time before the innocent inquisitive nature of one mortal would urge them forward to quench their desire and eventually they would have stumbled upon our people and everything would have been lost. I can only bless that day when Darius came to me and granted me this information. You see, over these past centuries he had visited the Tribe on a regular basis, unknown to any of our kind, he would tell me of the outside world, bring me the newspapers and communications of the time, keep me abreast of the developments of the world, and it just so happened that his last visit coincided with your departure. I prayed that he would follow your journey closely, in some subtle way guiding you, protecting you."

Mica smiled. "I thank you for your concern but I doubt if I would have been in any danger in Paris, I have been an immortal now for many centuries and even though Darius seemed to think that my life may have been at some great risk there, I am nothing if not precautious when it come to the sanctity of our immortal flesh."

Callum's expression changed to that of deep concern. "Risk, why? From whom?" he enquired.

"The other Parisian vampires," she replied. "Darius told that they had heard of the downfall of the Tribe and they held Christian responsible and those of his blood-line.

Callum thought for a moment before replying. "There are no Parisian vampires. At least none of any importance. Granted there are a few of our kind who choose to live as if mortal, but they have rejected our ways and taken to reclaiming an essence of their mortality through fantasy. They are not in contact with any of the Tribe; I would even go on to say that they shun contact with any of their own kind, other than those to whom they are accustomed. Darius among them."

Mica looked to him with an air of suspicion falling over her. "Please, go on," she said. "Tell me of this mysterious Darius."

" It was the month previous to the last meeting that I saw him and he informed me that Christian's letters had falling into the hands of the church and I knew immediately that our time was running out. He wanted to tell everyone then and there of your brother's betrayal, proclaim that your brother was a devil who would eventually destroy everything which was held sacred by our kind but I asked him to refrain from his actions and he respected my plea, thus allowing me time to consider the course which would best suit the Tribe. On the night which you left he followed you to Paris and eventually to England, keeping his distance, masking his mind, his thoughts and pointing you in the right direction."

"Yes! However, whose direction? You mean I was used as bait, an enticement to bring Christian out from his hiding place. No wonder you found me so quickly in England. Darius followed me from Paris in the hope of finding his goal and you inadvertently caught his signal while you were using your inner mind to find me through my lost thoughts and yet, you have found more than you anticipated," she snapped.

"No, I, we wanted to protect you," Callum said, in his defence.

"From whom?" she returned. "All I can see, everywhere I turn, are lies and half-truths. Deceptions and mysteries. Tell me truthfully, if you can. What are the facts behind this dispute between my brother and Darius?"

Callum sighed. "I cannot tell you the details as I do not know the full extent of the events which have transpired, but I will tell you all that I know. After his undertaking of the dark gift he studied by my side for almost ten years, constantly asking questions and demanding answers until eventually I could no longer fulfil his desire to learn. He then began to ask me of my creator and my teacher and how the similarity between his life and my own had been. He knew of Darius, as he had heard of me speaking of him often in passing, and in the fond way, the way you would comment upon a lapsed friendship. However, he did not know of Darius' strong opposition to his being born into the fellowship. When I first approached Darius to ask his permission to bring Christian into the dark fold he broke into a rage, for I could feel that Darius could see the yearning for knowledge that burned behind his eyes and I think in some strange way it frightened him, that along with the rebellious streak that tore its way through his emotion, it reminded him very much of himself in his younger years, a time to which he did not wish to be reminded. A time when his inner turmoil and battles almost consumed him and in some strange way I feel as though he was trying to protect your brother from the suffering which haunts him even to this day."

"So why did you?" she said.

"I have asked myself that question a thousand times."

"Did you regret your action?" Mica said softly.

"In the beginning Christian was an able student, eager and respectful, but he was always different and when he had learnt from others of Darius' dislike of him he became so enraged that he decided to confront him and demand to know in which way he had offended him, for he knew that at the base of Darius' hatred lay fear, a fear for that which he did not know, but a fear none the same. The day that I gave him his final lesson was the day which he confronted Darius. My teaching was drawing to an end and Christian was searching for a new master to guide him along the path of the dark gift and Christian being Christian arrogantly thought that Darius, being the oldest vampire known to any of our kind, would make an ideal candidate for his desires. Darius however had other thoughts and when they met an almighty battle occurred, needless to say Darius was the victor but his punishment for Christian's insubordination was a cruel one; he drained him of his immortal blood, almost to the point of death and then left him to blindly wander the forest. It was only by a matter of luck or chance that you stumbled upon him and granted him life by offering him your own."

"Why did you not think it reasonable that I may desire to know this hidden information?" she said.

Callum looked up to her and spoke in a harsh yet respectful tone. "You were but a fledgling and the affairs of the ancient immortals were of no concern of yours, even now I am bound by no honour, only that of friendship to tell of these events."

"That may be so, but I am bonded by blood, an emotional tie stronger than any other in the universe. I am sorry, but you're non-committal attitude has damned my brother and for that, I cannot forgive you. Also, if you knew of these events a full week before their occurrence then why did you withhold the information until the night before the downfall of the Tribe? Was it to bathe in the glory of your self-righteous impervious prison which you intellectuals hide within? Your heart may be warm, Callum, but your mind is as cold and as barren as winter, a place where love and tenderness has not yet touched. For centuries you have sat in council over others, strong in your position of self-imposed ambiguity, saying one thing and meaning another, with your slight of phrase you would compel others to follow your actions without objection or confrontation, an impotent blind faith. I would even go to say that you manipulated your position within the Tribe to suit your own fervour. How better to get close to that which you desired, offering comfort and wisdom as your gift, tenderness as your comfort, but at what price? You would watch the world crumble around you; allow the innocent to perish and the just to wallow in the harsh light of suspicion and accusation. You are responsible for the genocide that has befallen us, but most of all you are solely responsible for the damnation of my innocent brother," Mica closed her eyes and turned away, she allowed her harsh words to wash over him.

"I only wish that I could turn back the clock and retrace my actions, then how different this present situation would be. You cannot understand the pain which I am feeling at the moment, I am in purgatory, my soul is torn asunder and my heart is overflowing with dark guilt and could fill an ocean," he said.

Mica turned to him and screamed. "Here you go again. I .I .I, Me. Me. Me. Do you see others beyond your own perceptions or does your world end when reality begins. If only you could look beyond your own selfish desires then I could believe that the suffering which you claim to be experiencing at this moment was real and in some strange perverse way I could offer a fraction of sympathy for the deeds which compelled your action and brought to us these dark times. And yet, all that I see is a self-righteous fool who believes in his own reputation, in his own self-imposed importance. You cannot even imagine this hate which burns my heart at this moment, this hate which drifts upon an ocean of self-doubt for I can feel the lies which issue from your dark immortal mouth," she paused. Breathing deeply, she composed herself. "There is more to this that you are conveying, there are pieces missing within this universal picture, but I shall find the truth," she looked deep into his pitiful eyes. "You do not fully understand that which you have done to me. When I first came to you, and the Tribe, all those centuries past, I was but a child, an innocent, a soul cast upon the rough sea of life searching for refuge, searching for guidance and you protected me. You were my comforter, my friend, my mentor and teacher, the protagonist to my dreams and the preceptor to my dignity; I worshipped your name and relished your presence for I was lost in this world and you showed me kindness, you offered me solace in my darkest hour and always took a great delight in bathing in my joyous reverence, and for that I hate you. As now I find that you were deceiving me, filtering the truth, giving me, giving us all the reality of existence through your own eyes. Keeping us all restrained against the desires which are the very fabric of our beings, damning our urges and restricting our vision, you stunted the development of a great nation for your own ends. Our trite existence has become a mockery of that which it should have been. I can only but assume that the existence which I have lived within these venerable times passed has been nothing if not a lie and my life a parable of its true destiny. I have been made a living mockery and my suffering a dowry to your conspiracy. I damn you for your arrogance as surely as I damn myself for loving you," she said softly.

Mica walked into the darkness of the hallway, her heart pounding in her valiant chest, her senses blind to the surrounding world. She stood in the shadows as tears of freedom washed down her face, for centuries her inner-most thoughts, dark and sinister, had haunted her mind, restricted her almost to the point of destruction and now she could express them, even though her vengeance had ravaged one whom she had held dear she felt exonerated in her actions, for she could feel herself moving closer to the light of her own self-awareness. It was as if the weight of her sexuality was being lifted and a new age was dawning. An age of self-importance. This atrocity to the senses has somehow liberated her, focused her energies and given them a direction, a purpose. The darkness that was once her life was now becoming a distant memory and the reality that was the present made itself apparent to her. She relished its company. Standing there in the shadows, she felt truly alone, it was as if the world were void of life save for herself, a lone traveller, wandering in search of the holy grail that was the sanctity called the soul. She knew that life exited around her as it had always done and yet she savoured this desolate indulgence.

Two

Even now, almost thirty minutes after her death, Susan's extensive wounds still issued cold blood; her gentle frame almost drained of the elixir of life apparent to both species. Darius stood over her body as it lay on the bed; his sad eyes closed in respect for her downfall. Gradually, he began to recite the ancient Egyptian death ritual, calling to the old gods to take her gentle soul and guide it to its rightful place of rest. As the moments passed, a darker sadness began to fill the room as his guilt began to rise within him, guilt for his selfish actions, a guilt that had exiled one and damned many.

Opening his eyes, he knelt on the floor before Susan's body, as if in prayer. Lifting his wrist to his mouth he bit deeply into his immortal flesh, tearing at the wound until a great river of crimson issued out across his hand and onto the corpse below. The instant that this perpetual blood touched her grey flesh the wounds began to heal themselves, closing, the tissue knitted itself together, leaving no trace of a scar or any remnants of her dark confrontation.

Standing, Darius looked at the almost sleeping composure of this once tortured soul and smiled briefly for he now knew that she was truly at rest.

****

Ann-Marie sat transfixed upon the sofa, her mind racing as doubt and mistrust assaulted her thoughts. 'Had this whole adventure been a travesty?' she thought. 'Had every experience, which had befallen her, been a lie? Had she been manipulated by all who she had come into contact?' Her heart began to beat at a rate of urgency as these thoughts filled her mind, turning rationality on its side and replacing it with mistrust and deception. 'Could she have been this foolish?'

Her eye constantly returned to Darius's ancient leather bag as it sat on the sofa next to her. 'What other dark deed rested beneath its decaying surface?' she thought. 'Which other innocents had he damned to a riotous assembly of intemperate fools, fuelled by his dark deceptions?'

Mica entered the room, her urgency startling Ann-Marie.

"What is wrong? I could sense..."

Ann-Marie stood, tears filling her eyes. Her mind urging her to declare the dark knowledge which dwelled within but her heart prayed for her compassion to spare the suffering of anther's fragile soul. She moved to Mica's side and tentatively took hold of her hands, Ann-Marie could almost feel the gentle pulse of life that courses just below this immortal flesh, making her task all that more difficult.

"I don't know how to..," she broke off in mid-sentence for the emotions which rose within her enveloped every moral fibre of her being, sending her into the depths of her darkest dilemma. "I could never put into words the bitter emotions which haunt me at this very moment in time."

"I know," Mica said, her voice warm and soothing. "We have struggled with time and now we are at the conclusion of our efforts. We can all feel the pressure," she embraced Ann-Marie. "You know, as a child I can always remember my mother saying to me that sometimes in life chasing the rainbow can at times bring greater experiences and delight than finding that perceived pot of gold. We were concentrating upon the encompassing events and so we neglected to remember ourselves."

Ann-Marie sharply pulled herself from Mica's comforting embrace.

"No! You don't understand," she began, but a sound from outside the room attracted her attention. Looking past Mica she could see Darius descending the stairs, quickly she hurried to the doorway; turning she whispered.

"Ask me again, sometime."

Without a glance she passed Darius and entered the kitchen, there she found Callum sinking deeper into a dark despair. As she moved closer, she could feel the hatred that almost exuded from his every pore.

"What's wrong?" she gasped.

"I did not follow my own council. I sat arrogantly giving out righteous advice, almost callous in my endeavours. I am pathetic, a fool. Every word of hate that fell from her beautiful lips struck my heart with her truth." Tears filled his eyes. "I could have informed them sooner but I only gave them a few brief days, now I feel each and every one of their passing as sure as if their pain was my own," he looked to Ann-Marie. "I truly feel their suffering."

"I don't understand, who are you talking about? Did you tell her that you loved her?"

"I did not need to. She told me that she loved me, but she also told me that her love for her brother and her love for the truth was stronger. Both of which I have abused and because of that I have lost her forever."

Ann-Marie put her hand to her forehead.

"I don't understand, I'm a bit confused," she said. "Truth? What truth? I wasn't aware that you had lied to her."

"Lies and deception are both the same creature but their meaning is a universe apart. Through my own self-appointed desires I have sealed the fate of over a thousand innocent souls. I have damned her brother as surely as I had damned the Tribe."

"You can't blame yourself for that, it was Christian's letters which brought the downfall of your people, you yourself said that you tried to tell them of the destruction that would befall the Tribe, after all, how could you possibly know the outcome of another's selfish actions..." Realisation enveloped her as Ann-Marie could feel her mouth begin to dry as venom from the pit of her stomach began to rise, bringing with it a deep repulsive feeling. Her thoughts began to connect as those sinister bridges of the mind began to build connections between the splinters of dark evidence that littered her consciousness.

Callum looked at her with pitiful eyes.

Ann-Marie gasped. "You! You were in collusion with Darius."

A single tear of remorse fell from his eye.

****

213

Christian sat in silence within the great walls of Westminster Abbey, at this moment in time he would have sought the solace of any god who would reach out a tender hand and ease the torment that was torturing his fragile mind. All about, the tourists and the faithful listened to the seasonal chorus as the choir sang songs of comfort in their clear, uncommitted tones. Their angelic voices rising high into the rafters of this vast shrine to heavenly immortality.

Christian sat forward on his pew and rested his head in his hands, his dark thoughts haunted his mind, bringing forward the images of the decay and destruction that his perceived arrogance had concluded, tormenting him beyond endurance, he recalled the words thrown at him by Darius. One word in particular; singular in its aim, stuck in his mind. A name that proceeded terror. And, that name was Caliban. He knew that this name stood for the father of lies and the apocalyptic dominator who cursed all of his kind but he could not discover, no matter how much he concentrated and theorised, how his name, other than the obvious, could be connected to such a damned creature. Never, had he sought such an alliance with this condemned creation as he had been so cruelly accused, never, until now.

Closing his eyes, Christian prayed to his dark lord, urging him for his guidance in damning those who would curse and slander his name. In the darkness of a lost realm, his master, a demon of destruction, smiled a wry smile for he had found a proselytiser to his doctrine.

"Will you find my beloved in her next incarnation? Do this, and I will muster an army to fight by your side." Caliban said, his words ringing loud in Christian's thoughts.

Without contemplation he opened his eyes and returned his answer.

"Yes!"

****

A hollow darkness seemed to fall over the Ward's home as the time of Christian's deadline came into sight, the minutes fell forward taking with them any hope of reconciliation for all parties involved in this travesty of fragile emotions. Even the dead lay in silent sympathy to their plight. Darius' blood had finished its duties and Susan lay in her silent, almost regal slumber in the room above. Her flesh, perfection to the art of his immortal powers, unmarked by the traumas, which had damned her and taken her spirit into the next realm.

A gentle wind began to fill the room as dark elementals danced and dived in their mischievous endeavours of Chimerian delights. An uneasy glow began to issue from Susan's resting form as the spirits began to gather and slowly descend into the body, bringing to life a Chimerian nightmare.

****

Ann-Marie stood back in horror, as repulsion filled her senses. Her mind was a kaleidoscope of questions, yearning, demanding answers.

"You...you were in collusion with Darius! Why? Why did you condemn Christian to eternal damnation at the hands of your own kind? I know that he is far from innocent but your actions pale anything which he had perpetrated into insignificance. I don't understand, words fail me; it's as if my understanding of the whole situation had been set in stone and now I find that the stone is riddled with cracks. I don't know who to trust, you're all lying for your own ends. Would any of you understand the truth if it confronted you?"

Her pitiful eyes searched Callum's face, apparent to his suffering, yet her heart grew darker at the passing of each moment, condemning his actions and despising his very presence.

"Why did you do it, what possessed you?" she enquired.

Callum looked up at her, his immortal eyes awash with the bittersweet tears of regret.

"I wanted her to love me. I wanted her to want me. Only me! That's all that I've ever wanted, ever since she came to the Tribe I have wanted to call her mine, but that desire has never been fulfilled. And its pain fills me. My own weakness frightens me. If the whole truth ever came out, Mica would damn my soul for an eternity."

Ann-Marie could feel her inquisitive mind begin to burn as these words ignited the fuse of her suspicion. Rounding upon him she looked directly into his eyes and demanded her answers.

"Why did you desire to bring down Christian? Why this charade?"

Callum looked down at the floor, his eyes full of shame.

"I was jealous; I wanted her all to myself. The thought that Christian may return to the Tribe filled me with a hate so dark that I yearned for his destruction. I realised in time that my own hate was matched by that of another."

"Darius!" Ann-Marie interjected.

Callum nodded.

"He hated Christian, for he was all of the things which he could never be; he also hated him for he was all of the things which he used to be. The years had been hard to Darius and time had mellowed his mind, calming his raging desires and taming his soul. All of those traits which we all blindly admired in Christian. I can recall the day so clearly, Darius and I always met in a secret place, high in the mountains away from the prying inquisitive eyes of others, and it was there that our plan was born. He told me of his deep hatred for Christian and the reasons behind his dark compunction. He had wanted to teach him, guide him, but his deep impetuous temper compelled him to despise all that Christian stood for. The freedom, which he experienced, was envied by all, along with his flagrant disrespect for the society into which he found himself bound. He broke his bonds and became an animal of instinct, a rogue, and a vagabond of the night. And, what does one do to a rogue animal? Clip its wings."

"Or, get another to do it for you," Ann-Marie said harshly. "You've told Mica that she must orchestrate her own brother's downfall, how clinical, how convenient. Your hands remain un-bloodied and she returns a hero to her own kind, the slayer of the darkness that has risen after several hundred years to haunt you all. All parties are satisfied, all demands appeased. Darius is free from the threat of deposition; Mica is a free agent, as accessible to your desires as you are free to fulfil them. How convenient, how disgusting."

"As Pilate once uttered, '…there is blood upon my hands.' Callum said, in a quiet, almost reverent tone.

Ann-Marie's hatred for him evaporated away in an instant.

"I don't understand," she said.

"Can you see, I couldn't share her with anyone? Nobody. I wanted her all to myself," he began to sob heavily.

"What? What have you done?" Ann-Marie said with deep concern.

Callum looked at her, tears streaming from his eyes. "I was the one who compelled her son to walk into the daylight, I told Jess that it was safe and now my lies weigh about my shoulders as sure as if they were a great chain of guilt, a chain that grows in stature at the passing of each immortal second. How I relished my own intelligence as I told him that his mother would adore his innocent actions of damnation, she would see how brave he was and love him all the more," Callum swallowed hard, holding back his tears. "And I watched. I watched from the sanctity of the shadows as her only child was ravaged by the deadly rays of the sun. I watched with a selfish heart as the hungry rays devoured his soft flesh and tortured his soul and in that instant, he was gone, forever. You know what pains me more than this, more than this cold action? The justification which I felt in atoning my darkest desires. For years I was rejected as her attentions fell upon the needs of another and I naively hoped and wished for the removal of this obstacle, and then my path forward could be achieved."

Ann-Marie closed her eyes in horror.

"Please do not tell her," Callum pleaded.

"Where would I begin? How I have misjudged others, how wrong I have been," Ann-Marie said, her harsh words spoken in a subtle tone. "You saw her only child as a mere obstacle to your yearnings, I don't know whether to pity you or to despise you."

Callum stood and walked slowly to the kitchen door. Ann-Marie allowed her eyes to follow him.

"Tell me," she said. "How do I fit into all of this? There is no way in heaven or earth that you could convince me that this was all an accident. That these events which have recently passed, were a random confrontation of circumstance into which we found ourselves drifting. I think not."

Callum, standing in the doorway replied.

"You are right. Everything, which you have experienced since the beginning of this tale, has been a fabrication, even down to the events, which transpired within the hospital. Chance had taken control over several of our endeavours, however that chance has worked within our favour."

"Until now," Ann-Marie said.

Callum bowed. "It would seem so."

"Was James part of your little play?" she enquired.

"Partially. He is a spiritual creature, a gentle and philosophical being; whose only desire is to see the furtherment of man's understanding of his perpetual soul. In the past, his spirit had been the teacher of those previous who could call themselves Communicators. I must surmise that all of that which he told you was true."

"By whose perception?" she said.

Callum lowered his head.

"I can see the conclusion to this scenario even as we speak," she continued. "We destroy Christian, Mica falls in love with you. Darius continues on his blind travels and I use my powers to grant the loving couple mortality so that they can sail off into the sunset and live happily ever after. Think again. Do you still believe that Mica will have anything to do with you? Especially when she discovers to what extent your presence has had within all of this? I won't have to say a word, she is not a fool, and your emotions will eventually betray you as sure as your guilt will burn within you, a fire that propels the pain of your malignant knowledge and consumes your every passion until your suffering becomes insurmountable."

"I'm sorry, but I will not be accountable for your actions; I will not partake in your sordid masquerade. Even if I could freely give to you the gift of mortal life, then I would gladly deny it. After hearing of the judgement and torment, which you have perpetrated against those whom you profess to love and care for, then I would not bargain for my own safety. After all, who am I in all of this? Only a fool whom you have manipulated, a fool who knows a little too much, and once you have achieved your own goal, like others, I may become expendable."

"I have severely wronged another, an innocent. I also have damned his soul. Was it not I who travelled into the past and cursed Christian for an eternity, sent him into a pit from which you expect that he would never again rise? Yet, with the turning of the centuries you find that your plan is falling asunder and the initial price, which you originally perceived, is far higher than even you could comprehend. Christian has followed me through time for one reason and one reason alone, love. The poor fool loved me and I love him, and now with the intervention of your cold touch I am left alone, the focus to his dark intentions, for it is I who he perceives as the betrayer and you once again emerge from the ashes of this blackness without condemnation or blame, your dark admonition has served you well. So! If you don't mind I will play these cards a little closer to my chest than you desire, and if I were to suffer a little accident before this whole adventure were to come to a suitable conclusion, then I would draw upon all of the powers within me, both born of darkness and of light, and use them against your kind. You need me more than I need you. You crave your mortality, where as I desire never to see your pitiful face ever again."

"What will you do?" he enquired.

"More to the point Callum. What will you do?" she replied.

Before he could answer Mica stepped from the shadows of the hallway and moved silently to his side. Immediately she was concerned by his drawn appearance.

"Are you alright?" she said to Callum.

He looked at her with guilty eyes, before lowering his head and hurrying off into the safety of the shadows in the hallway. Mica moved into the light that filled the room and looked directly at Ann-Marie.

"I don't know if it is the pressure of the situation or the climax of a thousand years of waiting but I get the distinct feeling that all is not as it should be," she focused upon Ann-Marie's eyes, the deep blue of her own washing over the soft brown. "Will you answer my questions?" she enquired. "I have searched for centuries for a friend such as you, a light in the darkness of this world. Somebody upon whom I could bear my heart and soul, only to that person could I ask such a question, a question that demands the truth, and if you sanitise that truth at this fragile point within our relationship then I will realise that my perceptions were in fact misconceptions and I will trouble you no further."

Sitting quietly on one of the kitchen chairs Ann-Marie thought, her mind calm in its madness. She looked away from Mica and spoke, her words soft yet commanding.

"Isn't it funny, that we never know when love between two souls begins, yet we know the precise moment when it ends?" She paused. Turning to Mica, as soft tears of bitter knowledge fell from her eyes. "Would you have me tell you the whole truth, everything? Even though it would bring to an end this trust which you, immortals have held in one-another for centuries? Even though it would turn you from your present course and give a new direction from this detestation which drives you? If it were to give a reality to the futile suffering which has haunted you for centuries and give reason to that innocence which has also been betrayed? An innocence, which has been felt by those other than yourself.

No. I would never lie to you, or withhold the truth. I would try, impartially, to give you the facts and allow you to summon your own conclusions. But remember, my words are spoken in protest both to those who demand their presence and to those who perpetrated their being."

"Answer me one thing before we begin," Mica said. "Have I really been that blind?"

Ann-Marie closed her eyes and lowered her head.

"Your innocence has been both a comfort and a virtue."

Mica let out a deep sigh.

"My innocence has made me a fool. Will you tell me the truth?"

"Ask of me what you will," Ann-Marie raised her head and looked to Mica. However her line of vision did not fall upon that which she expected, it reached past Mica and into the hallway, concluding at the aberration that stood in the comfort of the soft shadows. A harsh gagging sound issued from deep within her closed throat. Mica's eyes opened in concern, her mind racing, filling with concerns connected to the ailments, which haunts the fragile existence of mortals.

"Are you alright?" she called, rushing to her side. "Calm yourself, I'll get Callum," Mica said, turning her attentions to the door, opening her mouth to call she froze in horror as the apparition advanced into the bright light of the room, its dead flesh scraping across the harsh surface of the kitchen's polished floorboards.

"Susan!" Ann-Marie screamed.

It was Ann-Marie's scream that brought Callum and Darius rushing into the kitchen, their vampire senses ablaze, the image that confronted them caused both men to maintain a respective distance from the demonic form which stood in the centre of the room.

"What is it?" Darius exclaimed.

"Susan?" Ann-Marie said, in a perplexed tone. "Yet it can't be," she looked to Mica. "Can it, could she have survived? Has Darius' blood made her an immortal?"

Mica concentrated upon the delicate form that stood before her, a suspicious air washing over her. Her eyes narrowed.

"There is more to this than is initially perceived. Do not trust your senses, for there is a deception afoot."

Susan stood before them, her eyes closed tightly.

Ann-Marie moved to step forward.

"Wait!" Mica said, holding out her arm to stop her. Slowly, she turned to Callum and motioned for him to step closer, gradually he edged his way tentatively forward, sliding across the stone tiles of the floor. Eventually, he stood by her side.

"What has happened?" he whispered.

"I don't know," Mica replied. "These powers are far beyond anything which I have encountered. I know of no one who can bring deceased flesh back to life, once the soul has left then the elementals have domain over whatever remains. It has always been that way."

"I know, but the blood of Darius should have protected this fragile form from the attentions of the curious," Callum said.

Mica thought for a moment. "That much is true, but what if the direction were dictated by another, one stronger, a power far greater than either you or I could comprehend. A fallen angel by chance."

Callum's eye's narrowed.

"Caliban," he whispered.

Instantly, the creature opened its eyes, revealing two brilliant white globes where once there were delicate mortal eyes searching through the darkness of life. Ann-Marie gasped as the creatures head moved in an almost mechanical stutter turning from side to side, stopping after each sweep of the room; it began again with its purposeful calculating movements.

Callum rushed at the creature, but a deathly grey arm raced through the air and abruptly made contact with his harsh immortal flesh, sending him spiralling onto the floor. Its touch sent a cold chill to his heart. The creature smiled as it bathed in its shallow victory. Callum righted himself in readiness for his second assault. The creature moved forward, gathering pace until it eventually hit Callum with the full force of its body. This time, however, its expectations were not realised and he gripped the abomination tightly about the soft tissue of its neck. Lifting her, he drew her close to his own eye-level.

"What have we here?" he hissed, as the creature's legs kicked out below her, searching for the comfort of the ground. Gently he began to squeeze Susan's silken flesh until her very life's breath escaped from her throat. Unable to comprehend the situation into which the elemental within had placed this decaying form, it urgently searched for a means of its spiritual hegira.

The creature's hands, which hung by her sides, now rose level with Callum's shoulder; purposefully they arched themselves until they resembled two great claws which she brought hungrily down upon his cold immortal flesh. Tearing, they searched for the soft flesh of his eyes and mouth, in the vain attempt of perpetrating its freedom. Rejecting the pain, Callum concentrated his grip causing Susan's face to bloat and pucker with pain.

"Stop it!" Ann-Marie screamed.

The creature fell limp, as if dead. Callum released his grip slightly, cautious of the way of the elementals. He looked to Darius who returned an apprehensive stare.

"What should we do?" he said.

Darius thought for a moment. "I would suggest that we dispose of this thing as quickly as possible for it is apparent that our enemy has joined forces with our appointed God, and each of them have a grievance against us both."

Ann-Marie pondered the scene that unfolded before her, her mind a kaleidoscope of torment. She turned to Mica.

"I know that this thing is not Susan, but its very presence gives me an uneasy feeling, how can it be..."

Mica interrupted. "It's her body, but once the soul ascends to a higher realm of existence the mortal flesh is susceptible to the attentions of those creatures that were born only of spirit, those creatures who watched mortals with avarice and covernance. Yearning to have that one thing which we all take for granted. Flesh. And when the opportunity arises to savour this delight, even for the briefest of moments, that moment will be seized. However I fear that this moment which we see before us has been manipulated, contrived, by one who would desire to see the downfall of us all."

"Christian," Ann-Marie said.

"Mica nodded."

"How we have all misjudged him," her words were soft and appealing. Ann-Marie said.

Mica's eyes narrowed as a dark cloud of suspicion entered her thoughts.

"What do you mean?" she said.

Ann-Marie smiled and turned her attentions once again to Callum.

The creature's eyes slowly opened, however, instead of hard white spheres there were two soft mortal eyes, glistening as tears of relief flowed down her cheeks.

"Ann-Marie," Susan said, her words were as soft and as gentle as a summer breeze. "Help me," she tentatively implored. Ann-Marie bit her bottom lip and looked to Darius.

220

"Could it be her? Could her soul have returned? Could she have reunited with her flesh?"

Darius shook his head.

"No! Once the soul has gone it had departed in search of greater things."

"But what about when I went back in time? My soul left my body and it was soulless, that was for a greater time than has transpired here. After all, she is a Communicator as I am, could she not have travelled into another realm as danger loomed in the hope of returning when safety had been restored. Think about it. If you damn her now, then you have surely killed her for a second time. And both of your hands are already awash with the blood of innocents."

Darius narrowed his eyes and looked suspiciously at Callum, who in turn looked to Ann-Marie then onto Mica. Realising the weight of her words Mica lifted her hand and placed it gently upon Ann-Marie's shoulder. Ann-Marie looked into her eyes and smiled.

"When the times comes you will tell me?" she said.

Ann-Marie nodded.

Three

Caliban sat in silence, enveloped by the shadows of the chamber, he stared in revulsion at the colour of his own flesh, his ancient thoughts melting into the dark recesses of his tortured mind. Images of his love still haunted him, torturing his senses and bringing a deeper sensation of isolation to his lonely heart. He sighed as the pain of his solitude bit deep.

Something distracted his thoughts, brought his senses back to life and he realised that he was no longer alone in the chamber. Rising, he walked to the centre of the vast room, bathed in the soft light from above his eyes searched the shadows for the identity of his intruder.

"Show yourself," he demanded.

From the far reaches of the chamber the stranger stepped, his eloquent suit and reserved demeanour gave great presence to his stature.

"You asked and I came," he said.

"Christian." Caliban said.

Christian bowed, his eyes never leaving those of his host.

"How you immortals have perfected your dream-time, the projection of the soul. I salute you in your endeavours," Caliban said. "I assume your reasoning for entering the lair of your immortal creator is to gain assistance in your fight against those who have wronged you?"

"Among other things," Christian said.

Caliban laughed. "I can see a dark confederacy forming between you and I and this dark coalition may procure a tentative union as I may require your skills in a time forthcoming, as I can feel the dark emanations of deceit brewing as we speak. I also require your assistance in locating the next emanation of my beloved, who I feel will soon be reborn on your earthy plain." Caliban looked wistfully upwards. He lowered his eyes purposefully and looked directly at Christian. "Name your price."

"How eager you are to negotiate our covenant," Christian said.

"No! I am not eager, but weary. If this treaty were not made with you then it would be forged with another. I am tired and I am not in the mood to play games of negotiation. What is your price?"

"An army, powerful and loyal to me alone. I need an army to destroy those who have slandered my name and reputation," he said.

Caliban thought for a moment. "Agreed, but this army will have its limitations. Were you to fall in the midst of battle then so would your forces, they will evaporate as sure as the mists of a summer's morning for I shall make them from your imagination, creatures born of thought. And, if for the briefest of moments those thoughts were to stop, then your armies would return from whence they came; your imagination. Thus leaving no trace for your enemies to follow, for your enemies shall remain yours and yours alone."

Christian looked at Caliban with suspicious eyes. "Why the limitations?"

222

Caliban laughed loudly. "You do not think that I would grant another immortal a vast army without limitations? How am I not to know that you would turn this great fighting force against the one who created it? No Christian, the odds shall always stay in my favour."

Christian laughed. "You are wise."

"That I am, but I am also tired. I have roamed these dark realms for over ten thousand years and with the longevity of my existence has come the depletion of my once puissant powers."

Christian smiled.

"Do not deceive yourself," Caliban continued. "I do not see my deposition for centuries yet to come and you shall not be the one who is the perpetrator of this act. It has already been written, who my successor shall be, and I am glad to say that it shall not be you."

Christian walked slowly towards him. "And what if I were to fall in battle but rise again, would I still be held to our bargain? After all I do not wish to enter each new century with a tariff upon my soul."

"Agreed, there shall be only one 'tariff' as you put it, but I can guarantee that you shall return begging for my assistance in the years to follow," Caliban said.

"My side of this unholy alliance is for you to bring down my enemies, correct?"

Caliban nodded.

"How do you expect me to fulfil the desires of your side of this barging, by finding the wandering soul that is your soul-mate?"

Caliban sat back in his chair. "I do not expect you to find her."

Christian looked at him with perplexed eyes. "I don't understand."

Caliban let out a gentle, almost human laugh. "Sometimes neither do I. Truthfully I do not expect you to find her but the very hope that you may, gives this empty immortality, a veneer of tolerability. I do not expect you to succeed and yet I yearn for your success. I have followed your path throughout your immortality, from that day which you were born to darkness and on until that day when you were reborn to this modern world. After all, was it not I who awoke your spirit and called you from the cold earth, in the vain hope that you would assist me in my endeavours?"

"Why do you not search for her yourself?" Christian enquired.

"Do not be a fool." Caliban snapped. "I am the firstborn of this generation and the price which I pay for this pitiful honour is my imprisonment. Granted I can leave this dark dungeon for a time but that time is limited and I fear that my search would be for an eternity. Amusing isn't it, I have an eternity to search for my lost love and yet in the very time within which we all exist my moments are limited. Perception is a deviant thing. To others, I would be seen as a God, a creation of the heavens, an immortal whose powers transcend the barriers of man and yet nothing could be further from the truth. If the facts were known I am all of these things yet none of these things. Admittedly, I was transformed by those of a higher realm, granted immortality. And yet if you were to look deeper you would see the similarities, which run through us all. I am no god, I am a creature. To mortals I would be seen as a demon, a devil. However if fate had decided to be kind and I did exist and evolve alongside man, then my presence would have been accepted without question and indifference; yet because I am the product of his nightmares, a creature of his fantasies, I am persecuted and damned," he laughed to himself and turned to Christian. "I had already anticipated your answer and discharged an elemental to cause chaos among the ranks of your enemies. When you desire your forces, use your preternatural powers to summon their presence and I shall dispatch Legion; An army of pure darkness."

****

Callum tightened his grip upon Susan's throat.

"Ann-Marie, help me!" she implored. Her words were weak yet unmistakeable.

"It could be Susan," Ann-Marie cried.

Darius rushed passed Callum and stood before her, his arms outstretched he rested them gently upon her shoulders. "I can guarantee to you that this is not your friend. I would not lie."

"Help me, he is lying, it's me Susan. Stop them, they're killing me," she cried.

Ann-Marie put her hands over her ears and looked at Mica. "Stop them."

Mica shook her head. "They're right, that thing before you is not your friend, she has been sent to torment you," Mica turned to Callum. "Kill it," she said in a cold calculating tone.

"No!" Susan cried.

Callum looked to her in surprise.

"If you do not kill it then I shall," Mica said.

Susan's body fell motionless. Almost immediately, the true nature of the creature jerked into life.

"Bitch!" It hissed, staring at Mica with its cold callous eyes. The creature struggled in Callum's grip. "My master will devour you all, tear at your souls until you plead for his mercy."

Mica looked harshly at Callum. Closing his eyes he flicked his wrist, a loud breaking sound filled the kitchen as Susan's broken body fell to the cold kitchen floor.

Ann-Marie gasped and closed her eyes. "To die once must be unthinkable, but to die twice must be damnable."

Callum stepped over the body and watched as it slowly writhed, its broken figure giving it an almost mechanical presence. A slight vapour began to issue from the form and rise into the air.

"What's the hell is that?" Ann-Marie exclaimed.

Darius looked at the thin mist that hovered over the body. "It's the essence of the elemental which inhabited the shell that was once your mortal friend," he looked to Callum. "I think that it is time that we leave this room," Callum nodded his approval.

"The safest place is the living room. Granted there are many windows there that could grant access to any who wish us harm, but on the reverse of that theory, they can also grant us a variety of exits. Also, there is a fire here to help warm our mortal friend."

In the living room, they all positioned themselves in a place from which each of them could derive the greatest of comforts on this harsh night. Callum and Darius stood on either side of the blazing fire while Mica sat in almost regal splendour upon the wing chair, always observant of her mortal friend who sat in an almost fragile demeanour upon the vast expanse of the sofa. Silence filled the room, bringing with it an air of suspicion and uncertainty.

In the hall the long cased clock chimed four a.m., its perfect chime echoing through the corridors of this vast empty house.

"Where do we go from here?" Ann-Marie said, breaking the silence.

Darius leaned forward, his hand resting upon the marble mantle-shelf of the fire surround.

"Well, if morning comes and we're all still standing, I would suggest that you get away from England at the most immediate opportune moment. There is nothing but danger for you here."

"What about Christian? Do we still pursue him, track him down as though he were some animal?" Ann-Marie enquired.

Darius narrowed his eyes; he could feel the suspicion emanating from Ann-Marie. "Even in the brief moments since our first meeting the elements of this dark allegorical tale have changed beyond recognition; to you, our kind were but fables, legends from a time when people believe in witches and demons. I can understand that the mere comprehension of our existence would place your modern scientific theories upon its head and damn their understanding, which has grown from the practice of your scholastic mentors for centuries. To mortals everything must have its reasoning, its answers, its boundaries, its solutions and its place within the structure of perceived lives. Man cannot comprehend that he is no longer the head of the food chain, imagine if you can the false arrogance that has propelled him from the vast African plains and urged him to wander across the lush and pleasant lands of the earth. Even after the sands of a thousand centuries have fallen by, he cannot place himself in the mind of another living creature. To him all life is a sport, killing come natural, desecration, second-nature," he paused. "You see, when we accept this dark gift we accept the ties that bind us to its devotion, its mantra. No matter who or what we are, we must abide by the laws of the universe, and even this darkness that consumes us is born from the light. If we were to turn our backs against this then we would be denying the very essence of those powers, which had created us. This is why I feel we must pursue Mica's dark brother. He has turned his back against the sacred laws, he has manipulated the minds of the innocent, and it is inevitable that he would grant the dark gift to any who would follow his empty teachings. He would inform the world of our existence, just to bring down the very fabric of both our and their society. I can see him now, as if a child, deriving a great delight from the chaos that would ensue. No! The man that we all knew in the past is not the creature that parades before us now; in his arrogance, he has been consumed by the hatred of his own kind and will stop at nothing to see its final destruction. The magnitude of this evidence stands before you.

Just look with merciful eyes at that once powerful race that lived in harmony with nature and man."

Ann-Marie sat forward. "Should we not show him mercy?"

"Mercy!" Darius screamed. "Why should we show him mercy? He did not show such mercy when he sent the innocent of our kind into eternal damnation, their suffering perpetrated through his arrogance?"

Knowing that the pain of her words would cut Mica to the bone Ann-Marie held back the dark evidence that proclaimed the innocence of her brother. However, she sent Darius a message that chilled him to his very core. "Now who is arrogant?" She said standing. Callum looked to her, his eyes ablaze with fear. "You blindly assume that we will take your words for the value which you proclaim, if there is one thing that I have learnt in this mortal life that is never to take anyone or anything on its face value. Let's say, just in a hypothetical way, mind you, that Christian is innocent, then wouldn't we be damning his soul for an eternity?"

Darius leaned back against the fire surround, his mind in turmoil.

"What is your point?" he snapped.

"My point is," she said. "If Christian were innocent, then who is guilty?" She looked Darius accusingly in the eyes. Callum closed his eyes and sighed. The room fell once again into silence.

****

Caliban sat in silence, his mind in turmoil. The images, which had recently assaulted his senses, were now returning bringing with them the bitter sweetness of their memories. Standing, he slowly moved to the centre of the chamber; there he remained, bathed in the subtle light from above. Stretching out his arms he cast the dark shadow of an inverted cross upon the stone floor of his prison. He closed his eyes and called to the heavens.

"To the lords of a higher realm. To the gods Ra, Ma`at, Thoth, and Anubis, I call upon you to grant me your eternal power, to guide me upon this quest and grant my servant your armies of perpetual darkness. To the kingdom of the lower realms I plead to you for your assistance, bring forth your dark deceivers to blind my servant's enemies and send their minds into that bleak pit of mortal confusion. To all the demons and elementals of this darkness that surrounds us, I call for your service. Send forth your followers to destroy those who would stand before me."

A gentle breeze began to drift through the chamber, gathering pace as it progressed, until it concluded in a vast hurricane of emotions. Dark demons and lost souls drifted all about, sending their cries high into the room.

****

"Let's concentrate upon the task ahead," Mica said. "The relevance of allocating blame has passed beyond the point of indifference. Christian's actions have spoken for themselves. We must confront him on common ground and send him back to his eternal rest."

Ann-Marie interjected. "You don't understand what you are saying; you don't know all of the facts."

Mica looked at her in confusion. "That may be so, but I do know my brother; he is a selfish and arrogant creature. Also, I trust the guidance of my fellow kinsmen; has the evidence that has been placed before you by both Darius and Callum, not turned your thoughts against the demon who has pursued you across the centuries? His only wish is to see the flame of your existence extinguished, for an eternity. Do not deceive yourself, he has love for no other."

"Will you blindly take the evidence of those whom you have always trusted, without question? Just because their council in the past has been succour to your raw emotions, do not deem their every word as truthful, as I have been informed in the past, truth is only but a perception. In my time, we do have things such as blatant lies. No-one is infallible, free from the dark yearnings of deception; you place your trust in the arms of others too freely, look to yourself for your own council and take control of that which is already your own," Ann-Marie said before turning to Darius. "Mark your time well, for your secret is only as safe as I am."

Darius looked to Callum, a bitter expression tormenting his features. Callum looked to the floor in shame.

"There is also another saying in your modern world," Mica said slowly. "That two and two can sometimes make five."

Callum made to speak but Darius held up his hand to prevent him. He looked angrily at Ann-Marie.

"Well. The choice is yours. Do we follow our original plan and bring down this demon? Thus wiping the slate clean and hopefully eradicating the indiscretion of others, casting them back into history from when they came with the hope that they would never re-emerge upon the surface of this tumultuous life. Alternatively, do we wait for your dark destroyer to find you, to strike you down, take you with him into this next realm? Before you make your choice remember that you are the only hope that our kind has to return to its life of mortality, a dream that burns within us all. Every immortal desires that second chance, that brief hope," he paused. "Remember, the choice is yours, and yours alone."

"You bastard!" Ann-Marie said, before turning away from him and leaving the room.

Darius watched her, a wry smile dancing across his lips. He looked to Mica. "Now that we have that one cleared up, shall we make the plans for the assault?" He said.

"Sometimes, you disgust me," she said standing and following Ann-Marie out of the room.

Catching up to Ann-Marie, she gently took hold of her arm.

"Are you alright?" she enquired.

Ann-Marie smiled and nodded her head. "I'm sorry but..."

"There is no need to explain, I'm sure that you have your reasons. All that I can say is that I am not as blind as you perceive. I do not wander through this life with closed eyes. I see more than others would credit me for," she smiled. "Your burden is a heavy one and the sacrifice that you make with your silence is commendable. However, even though I do not know all of the fact that surround the past and present of my brothers jaded history, I can understand that it would be better for us all if his tormented spirit were laid to an eternal rest."

"Even if he were truly innocent?" Ann-Marie said.

Mica closed her eyes and lowered her head. "Nobody is truly innocent," she answered. She opened her eyes and looked at Ann-Marie. "Shall we join the others and make our plans?" She looked at the hall clock. "Time is running out."

Darius looked at Ann-Marie cautiously as she entered the room, his eyes narrow and piercing. He stood arrogantly against the fireplace. "I must apologise if my words were a little too harsh," he said in a sarcastic tone.

Ann-Marie sat on the sofa opposite. "Your apology accepted, your words were strong, purposeful, some could say arrogant. For a brief moment there you almost reminded me of Christian."

Darius reeled at this harsh castigation of his half-hearted apology.

Mica smiled.

"Shall we get on?" he said. The others nodded their approval.

"Let me inform you of a few facts," he said to Ann-Marie. "Vampires are immortal, but they do have their limitations. However, these limitations do decrease with longevity. Sunlight, to a new-born this is a certain killer. The rays of a new sun will devour the flesh of an immortal in an instant, as time progresses our skin can compensate for the searing harshness of its light and several of our kind can bask, briefly, in the splendours of the day."

"Are there many who can do this?" Ann-Marie enquired.

"Other than myself, I only know of a few others. Cantor, the first born of Caliban's dark disease, and Kha`ba and Amasis, his offspring."

"Can you not call upon them, ask them to help us?" Ann-Marie asked.

Darius smiled. "I am sorry but I cannot. Once, many centuries ago, they were as I am, wanderers through the cities of this modern world, but as man progressed and times changed they found the vast vicissitudes between that which once was and that which life had become, insurmountable, unbearable, and so returned to the mountains high above the Bayuda Desert."

Ann-Marie allowed his words to sink in before asking another question "Did they not procreate, have offspring, create more vampires?"

Darius smiled. "Two. Brothers of the higher realm. Sons of the Pharaoh. They offered them the dark gift and they freely accepted it. The first, Djoser, a valiant and noble warrior, quick of mind and strong of heart. He was wise in his understanding and vast in his knowledge. His soul was gentle but his hunger for the hunt was insatiable. I can remember him battling with a great lion in the Nubian Desert, tearing at the beast with his powerful hands. He rose triumphant, unscathed. He was a true god among men. He welcomed the dark gift with open arms. I have not seen one such as him for centuries."

"And the other," Ann-Marie enquired.

"The other..," Darius said. "The other stands before you."

"Can we call upon your brother to help us?"

Darius laughed. "My brother is a wanderer, a lost soul, hungry for the teaching of man. He has turned his back upon the pleasures of the flesh and now studies with those of a higher realm, the Qareen, his hunger is now of the mind. I bless him for his tranquillity. I'm afraid if I knew where he was then I would already know his answer. He would tell me that the troubles of mortals do not concern him and they should be allowed to hold their own parliament without the restriction of those who would deem themselves of a superior understanding."

"Yes, but this does involve immortals."

"That is so," he said. "But the answer would still remain the same."

Ann-Marie sat back on the sofa. Alright, what else? Sunlight can kill him. What other weapons do we have at our disposal?" She looked at Darius, then to Callum. "Don't just stand there in silence. What else?" Her words were harsh and urgent. "Knives, silver bullets, crosses, garlic. What?"

Mica sat forward on her chair. "Fire."

"Fire. That's it!" Ann-Marie exclaimed.

Callum Nodded. "I'm afraid so. The immortal flesh is ancient and so is easily combustible."

"Brilliant! What do we do? Say to Christian, 'Stand there for a moment while I set fire to you.' Yeah, I can just see him agreeing to that one," Ann-Marie said sarcastically.

Darius smiled. "I'm sorry if you cannot comprehend the situation but they are the basic facts. We do not cower from the crucifix or shy away from garlic, neither do we turn ourselves into little bat and flap about the streets in search of nourishment. Metamorphosis is impossible for most of our kind, except for a chosen few, those of the pure blood. Those who can trace their line of descendant back past the knights of Templar and into the realms of history and back to 'she who has no name.' We are creatures of everlasting life and the only thing that can destroy us is fire, be it from the rays of the sun or from a naked flame. Anything else is conjecture or fantasy."

Ann-Marie nodded her acceptance of his words.

"Now we need to find a place of neutrality. Sanctified ground, a bridge, a holy place," he said.

"A bridge?" Ann-Marie enquired.

"A bridge," Darius said. "A symbol of transition."

Ann-Marie thought for a moment. "The closest bridge to our locations is, Westminster Bridge."

Darius smiled. "Then that will be the location of our final battle."

In the skies above the Ward's home, dark clouds of malevolent preternatural energy gathered and collided in their cabalistic urgency. High above, the forces of darkness were congregating, in readiness for their assault.

****

"Don't you think that it would be dangerous to take Ann-Marie with us? After all she is mortal and her flesh is weak," Mica said.

"If we split up then that would mean that one of us would need to remain behind to protect her, thus depleting our forces which would put us all at a tactical disadvantage. No, it's either we all go or we all remain," Callum said.

Mica reluctantly agreed.

"Well, how do we get him onto this Westminster Bridge?" she enquired.

"Darius looked to Ann-Marie. "With a little persuasion," he said, smiling.

She was about to reply when her embryonic communicative powers pulled at her senses, alerting her of the impending danger that was about to ensue them all. Her head jolted sharply back, causing her neck to tighten at her reflexes

"What's wrong?" Mica screamed, rushing to her side.

"I don't know," Ann-Marie cried. Inside her mind the image of the skies above came into focus, its dark and sinister apparel-sending a shiver through her whole form. "They're coming. There's something coming!"

Callum moved swiftly to her side and took gently hold of her hand. "Concentrate, use your powers. Look into the image that you see, tell us who is coming."

Ann-Marie concentrated, her mind was a-rage with images. Her body locked in convulsions, sending spasms of pain throughout her whole being. She lunged forward. Instantly the trauma ceased. She lifted a shaking hand to her lips. "I think they're here."

Callum looked to Darius with open amazement.

Instantly the windows to the room shattered, sending splinters of razor sharp glass in all directions. Mica threw herself over the fragile mortal form of Ann-Marie, protecting her with her immortality. The lights above began to splutter and blink as the cold of the night air invaded the living room.

"Everyone remain calm," Callum whispered.

The lights returned to their normality, bathing the room in an unnatural yellow glow. Mica held tight onto Ann-Marie's hand as they stood.

"Can you sense anything else?" Mica asked her. Ann-Marie shook her head. Mica then turned to Darius. "What now?"

Darius looked about the room. "A hasty exit. The safety of this one is paramount," he said pointing to Ann-Marie.

Leaving the house, they stepped into the bitter unwelcoming night. Darius pointed to the cyclone of dark colours that were turning in the skies above, and for the first time, Ann-Marie could see true fear in his eyes.

"We must hurry," he cried. "I can feel Caliban amassing his forces."

Callum took hold of Ann-Marie's hand, in a vain attempt to offer her comfort. "Which way is it to this Westminster Bridge?" he said.

She turned and looked at him, a deep depressive wave washing over her mind as she lifted her hand and pointed to the epicentre of the storm. "Directly below that," she said.

"He knows!" Mica cried. "The bastard was reading my thoughts."

"I was counting upon that," Darius said. "It will make this journey all the sweeter."

"I know the way," Ann-Marie said. "I've lived here long enough; I know the place better than I know my own home town."

 Leaving the grounds of the Ward's home they hurried off along the deserted streets, Ann-Marie took a backward glance at the house which had welcomed her with open arms and she now left it without a heart. A sadness filled her as she lost sight of its majestic presence, for not only was she saying farewell to a place, she was also saying farewell to her friends, her fallen comrades who had not been strong enough to withstand the rigours of the torment that pursued them. Onward they hurried, through empty avenues and deserted street, onward and forward, blindly marching towards their own oblivion as all about the soft petals of winter fell, leaving a blanket of brilliant white snow upon the ground.

Soon they were into the main throng of the city, passing Knightsbridge and Belgrave Place, Buckingham Palace and Victoria Street. Forward they searched, leaving behind New Scotland Yard and Westminster Abbey, Margaret's Church and The Guildhall, until they eventually found themselves standing in Parliament Square. Behind them ran Great Saint George Street and before them stood Westminster Bridge. Above, the bell of Big Ben residing in Elizabeth tower struck half past the hour, they had reached their destination as the heavens grew darker and black clouds collided, sending ebony rainbows across the night sky.

Darius sniffed the night air. "I can smell burning," he said.

"They're resurfacing the roads with black pitch; you'll be able to smell the tar barrels that they leave overnight, the workmen do it as a kind gesture to the homeless, it gives them somewhere to keep warm. You sometimes get a few of the hooligans running around and causing damage but the police come and move them on."

"Is this the only bridge here?" Callum enquired.

Ann-Marie thought for a moment. "This is Westminster Bridge or Parliament Bridge and that takes you into Lambeth, then there's Lambeth Bridge, Tower Bridge, London Bridge and so on. Does this mean that he could be on any of them?"

Darius turned and pointed to the tower that held the bell of Big Ben. "What is that?"

"That is the Houses of Parliament, the governing capital of the whole of England. All of the country's politicians meet here and hold council," Ann-Marie replied. "Not far is Westminster Abby, the home of the Church of England."

Darius laughed. "Then this is the place. His arrogance would call for him to fight his final battle in such a renowned company."

Ann-Marie looked at him in amazement. "Yeah, right! What do we do now? Wait for him to turn up?"

Darius smiled. "He is already here."

Christian watched as the group approached, his eyes ablaze with rage. From their distant demeanour, he could see that they were unaware of his vast invisible army of darkness, which stood behind him, an army of the dead which was eager for battle. He savoured their arrogant approach as they marched heroically onto the bridge and into their own oblivion.

"What do we do? We don't have any form of plan, or strategy," Mica said.

"We do not need one," Darius said. "After all we are four against one."

Ann-Marie watched the dark figure ahead of her as she slowly stepped onto the bridge, her heart began to pound in her chest as the dark lies that haunted her began to surface and pull at her conscience. She knew that this creature was in no way responsible for the events, which had preceded, and those, which were sure to follow, for he was as innocent as she.

Seeing her anxiety Mica reached out and touched her hand. "It shall all be over in a moment, when it begins keep behind us, use our immortality as your protection."

Ann-Marie could feel her throat becoming dry. "Mica there's something that I should tell you, there's something important that you should know."

Callum threw her a harsh look. "This can wait until another time," he said, his voice trembling.

Mica could feel her suspicions growing once again inside her.

Christian smiled as they drew close and stopped less than ten meters from where he stood. All about the tar barrels let their black smoke drift into the night sky, a fitting testimony to the scenes that presented itself to his mind.

"Welcome," he said. "You have tracked me down through the centuries and now we find each other on this cold, desolate night. A night almost as cold as your jealously," he said to Darius.

Darius hissed.

"Still you hate me. Or is it yourself, or that which you may have become that you hate?"

"Do not play mind games with me, fool," Darius hissed.

Christian smiled.

Darius moved a little closer. "I have hungered for this moment for centuries, I have plotted and connived, I have cheated and lied to bring you to this moment in time, this place in history and nothing and nobody shall take away from me, my victory."

"You already have this battle fought and won in your mind, don't you Darius? Maybe that was your ultimate failing, the misguided insight to understand your enemies. You see, even though, since the first time we met, you have despised my very presence and I have held nothing but respect for you, I have learnt from your actions and understood your mind. Whereas as you were blinded by your hatred, I was lifted and enlightened by your foolish and ignorant actions. I could see you for what you truly were, a child lost in this storm called life. Here you are, a brave and heroic warrior, a dreamer among men, and a visionary. And yet, you cannot see past your own hatred. We are oil and water you and I, and yet we are closer than even twins," he gave Mica a subtle glimpse before giving Darius his full attention. "Love and hate are divided by but a thin line. Brothers of the same emotion, one compelling the other. You hate me for that which you cannot have."

"Relish your insolence, for it shall be short lived," Darius said.

Christian looked to Mica and Ann-Marie. "Ah, my subtle beauties, both as soft as the summer breeze and both as deadly as a viper."

"Ann-Marie bit her lip. "I'm sorry, so sorry," she whispered.

"I do believe you are, sweet one," Christian said. "But your apology is a little late, over two hundred years late to be precise." Momentarily, he closed his eyes. It was as if a dark cloud of regret past over his soul. "How I could have loved you, worshipped you. My queen among these immortal damned. A vision of true beauty and innocence. We could have danced through time, oblivious to the turning of the seasons. What a pair, beloved of immortality. Truly honoured by this dark gift."

He sighed. "How time echoes, and what a parody" He turned his attention to Mica. "Ah sister, blood of my blood and voice of my heart. How it pains me to see you have taken sides against your own kin. Have the years blackened your soul to such a degree? Have all of those years past fallen into none? Those times, both mortal and immortal have been vanquished by the whispered misguidance of another. For these are not the actions of a sister that I once cherished as much as life itself."

"This would not be so if you had not have been so selfish. How callously you condemned the Tribe to the merciless tide of genocide, that swept away all that I knew, tearing asunder the lives and innocence of a thousand immortal souls," she replied the bitterness of her words assaulting his senses.

Christian laughed, as the realisation of the moment became apparent to him. "I see, I see it all now. The dark brother, the rebel, the vagabond and outcast, upon who better to place the blame, who better to stand accountable for the dark actions of another," he looked at Darius with condemning eyes. "I did not think that even you could stoop to such a depth. I applaud you for your inhumanity."

"What? I don't understand," Mica cried.

"Don't you see innocent one?" Christian began. "We are all victims of the avarice of another."

Darius could feel the dark pains of uncertainty rising within; he could feel the harsh reins of power slowly slip away from his hungry grip. "You are more arrogant that I thought. You present yourself in battle, a single immortal against many. I will delight in your downfall."

Christian looked at him and mocked mortal fear. Laughing, he continued. "You surely are a fool. Let me count your army," he said lifting his finger. "One...Two.... Three and my precious mortal make four," he then looked down at himself. "Shall I now count my army?" He said. "One..," he continued, pointing to himself. He raised his head and gave Callum a sideways glance, smiling seductively, he continued. "And too many to mention." Clapping his hands, the veil of darkness that surrounded his army fell, revealing their black and hungry intentions. Great demons stood, their eyes burning, their mouths salivating. Vast, xenomorphic beasts ridden by the dead stood in their magnificence, raging with desire for the ensuing battle. A hundred fallen souls stood as foot soldiers in readiness for their master's orders. His vast army was complete.

"Now Darius, who is unprepared?" Christian said before turning to his un-dead General. Pointing to Darius, he hissed.

"Kill him first!"

An inhuman chaos of screams filled the air as the dark army advanced towards the waiting group. Mica pulled at Ann-Marie and urged her to find sanctuary away from the main throng of the battle but she refused and stood defiant against the horror that tore at her horizon.

"Form a defence, stand in a line," Callum cried." Don't let any of them get behind us. Cover our backs." The group stood, awaiting the onslaught.

Several demons took to the skies and descended quickly upon the enemy, their sharp claws tearing at their immortal flesh. Darius, burning with hatred looked deep into the ranks of the dead in search of his foe. He could see Christian standing arrogantly behind his advancing armies, his face almost human in its pleasure. He turned to Callum. "If we bring down Christian then we will bring down his army; this is Caliban's work. I know. Defeat the General and the other will flee."

"How do you propose we do this?" Callum enquired.

"Bait," Darius said looking past Mica and directly at Ann-Marie. He then sent out a mental message to his companions. 'Step backwards; allow Ann-Marie to be at the forefront of this battle. He will not harm her, she is his love."

Mica turned to him. 'Do not be a fool, his army will kill her.'

'Trust me. We will mark their intellect, if these creatures are as I initially perceived, then I would surmise their minds are not their own and their actions belong to another, they are being controlled by outside elements. Observe, their movements are laboured and weak in comparison to our own; if Ann-Marie were in any danger then we could intercept those who would harm her without undue concern and deal with them accordingly', he answered.

"I'm not going to let her die," Mica cried.

Darius gripped her tightly. "There are always sacrifices in war. Death is a mundane fact."

Mica looked at him in despair. "Go to Hell."

Darius smiled and looked to Ann-Marie. "Ladies first," he could feel his unbridled emotions rage deep within his very core as the restraints of civility became unfettered and his base preternatural being once again reigned supreme over his very soul.

The xenomorphic creatures moved forward, hissing as they advanced. Their riders urging them to destroy all that stood before them. Several foot-soldiers raced forward, their spears held out in front of them. Callum was the first to make contact, he gripped the shaft of the weapon and lifted a soldier from the ground and cast him over the side of the bridge. Another advanced and fell upon Mica. They struggled before she pulled his decaying flesh from her body and held him high above her head, his writhing actions displaying his defeat. She cast him to the ground. The instant that his form made contact with the harsh surface of the road it faded into nothing, leaving no trace of its existence in this dimension. Another advanced and another until the bridge was consumed by their dark turmoil. Fighting broke out all around and Ann-Marie felt weak in amongst this immortal conflict.

Mica hurried to her side, a spear in her hand. "Take this and use it if any approach." Instantly, a demon fell from the skies before her and stood in its full magnificence, his wings outstretched. Lunging forward, he fell upon Mica's delicate frame. She could feel his hot rancid breath upon her face as he pulled her closer. Opening his vast mouth he revealed his fangs and lowered them slowly until they touched her immortal flesh. She could feel the horror rise within, for she knew that his strength was far superior to her own. She struggled but his grip tightened all the more. She closed her eyes and screamed in her mind. Instantly Darius and Callum were alerted to her danger, yet they were impotent to her troubles for they too were amidst the throng of the battle.

The demon looked at her with hungry eyes; he lowered his head in readiness for the meal that would consume his hunger. A hunger that would send him into oblivion. He did not see Ann-Marie as she stepped from the shadows armed with a weapon from the creatures own ranks, there was an unearthly sound as she sent the spear deep into the creatures vast chest, blood and tissue emanated from the growing wound, as she twisted and turned the weapon, savagely ripping his flesh. Dropping Mica to the floor, the demon looked at the mortal who had inflicted this momentous injury, his eyes blinking in blind amazement. Lifting his powerful hand he made to strike down this impudent mortal who had dared stand defiantly before him, however, he could feel his energies leaving his depleting body. He gasped for breath before fading into the night, leaving only a memory where he once stood.

Mica rose to her feet, her hands rubbing her neck. "Thank you," she said, looking tentatively into Ann-Marie's eyes. Her Immortality working to ease the pain and repair the damage inflicted upon her by her conflict. "Please, return to the comfort of the darkness, you are our vulnerability and if Christian were to find you then all of this would be in vain," Mica embraced her. "Thank you once again for my life," she said, before returning to the main throng of the battle.

Standing in the sanctity of the shadows, Ann-Marie watched the battle unfold and in some dark way, she felt that victory might not be theirs. She watched as the demonic hoards fell upon Callum who derived a great delighted in his mastery of the fight, a delight that was short-lived for he strove to defeat his enemies he was brought down by the sword of a demonic warrior. Ann-Marie closed her eyes as the pain of her sight filled her with horror.

"I must help," she said to herself. Opening her eyes she turned to the battle and looked straight into the eyes of Christian. There he stood in all of his magnificence, smiling an almost mortal smile.

"Going so soon, my dear? And after all of the trouble that I have gone to on your behalf," he said. Gripping her, he pulled her close to himself and then he turned to his minions and cried. "Victory is ours."

Ann-Marie screamed and struggled but Christian only tightened his grip. He smiled. "Why do you fight your true destiny? Does the truth fill you with such dark consternation?" He held her, looking deeply into her fearful eyes. "It would seem to me that you are in somewhat of a dichotomy, my dear, and no matter where your choice will fall you will subconsciously follow the darkest of paths." His voice was comforting yet cold. "We are brethren of a darker soul, you and I. We perceive with detached eyes, think with distant thoughts and transcend others with our greater yearnings. Look beyond this mortality and make your choice...But choose well. For goodness reflects the light; and evil, evil bears the seeds of darkness and these are the mirrors of the soul, the reflections of the mind. Your mind."

Ann-Marie struggled; it was as if his words were burning her, their very presence tearing into her soul. "You have a darker side to your yearning, far greater than even I could imagine, become one with your innocence and allow your true potential to express itself."

"No!" Ann-Marie cried. "I can sense the good in you; I can make you good again."

Christian held her close and whispered softly into her ear. "No my dear. I am too far down this pathway, which leads to eternal darkness. I know with a deep conviction that this evil which makes me that which I am would turn you to its will; long before you could to turn me to that path of the righteous and the good which you so blindly follow."

Ann-Marie could sense a darkness drift across her mind as his words bit deep into her soul and consciousness escaped her.

Callum tried to pull himself to his feet, but the pain bit deep into his wounds. Darius rushed to his side. "Let her die and the secrets die with her," he said. Callum looked at him with distaste. "If she dies, then so does the very essence of any goodness which remains within my soul."

The dark army ceased their fighting and returned to the far reaches of the bridge; there it stood in readiness for the second assault. Darius cradled the fallen Callum in his arms as Christian held Ann-Marie high above his head in victory. Her unconscious body limp in its apparel. After a moment he lowered her to the ground and let her lie, broken at his feet.

He looked at Darius. "It is your arrogance that has brought your own downfall. You would blame others for your own deeds and so you shall reap your just rewards. The second time that my army advances there shall be no mercy and your lives shall be forfeit. A fitting end to an eternal battle."

He lifted his hand to signal the second assault, yet his mind called for him to wait. The image that rested before him was incorrect, wrong. There were pieces missing to its overall puzzle.

"Mica!" he whispered. "Where was Mica?"

From behind she appeared, her whole frame compelled by rage, lifting the burning torch in her hands she sent it shattering across his chest. Flames licking and devouring his dead flesh. Screaming, Christian fell back against the parapet of the Bridge. He could feel the heat rising within as the flames ate deeper and deeper into his immortality. His arms flew out in rage, a vain attempt to quench the terror that consumed him. He reached for Mica and gripping her cape pulled her close, looking into her deep cold eyes he whispered.

"Why, sister? Why have you damned me, when you do not know the truth?"

He fell backwards, pulling her closer to the hungry flames.

Realising the danger, Mica struggled with the buckle that held her cloak in place, her fingers moved urgently, compelling her, urging her to free herself from this uncertainty. She could feel the warmth of the flames upon her face as Christian reach out to embrace her. She stood motionless, the apparel of her downfall upon her. In some perverse way she could embrace her demise with open arms and enter the next world with one whom she truly loved and end this bitter torment, forever. In that instant the buckle opened, releasing the cloak. Releasing Christian, she watched with a consuming horror as he fell backwards, his fingers clawing at the material in a vain attempt to save himself from this barbaric end. The inner sensation of his own lost mortality filled him, bringing with it the red river of his own inadequacy and hate, sending shards of a now splintered mind deep into a vast pit of his own madness. The flames raged, sending him backwards against and over the parapet of the bridge and into the sinister dark waters of the Thames below, he could feel his immortality slowly slipping from his body as he sank deeper into the cold cadaverous waters.

Mica held her hands to her ears as her brother's bitter screams echoed through the night. Then there was silence, a vast emptiness that hung heavily in the cold air of winter. She turned and looked to the dark army, and where once a vast fighting force stood, there only hung silence and the mists of a new morning. In a brief instant, her past life was gone.

Lifting Ann-Marie, she rushed to Callum's side. "Are you alright?" she said.

"I've seen better days," he replied, with a rather lack-lustre wit.

"He just needs an infusion of blood. Once he has that, the wounds will heal themselves. How is Ann-Marie?" Darius enquired.

Mica smiled. "Fine, she'll be a little shaken up when she comes round, and this will all be like a dark nightmare," she said looking at the waking city.

Observing Darius' own wounds she enquired of his own health.

"How are you?" she enquired nodding at his inflictions.

"I'll survive," he answered with a smile.

In the Elizabeth Tower the bell of Big Ben struck six o'clock, announcing the coming of the morning, overhead the dark clouds began to disperse, allowing the soft pastel shade of morning to tentatively reach down and caress the city below.

"I think that we should find sanctuary," Darius said. Before the morning rays devour not only the flesh of the fallen but our own.

"Follow me. I know a place that a good friend of mine owns," she said looking at Ann-Marie."

Four

Overhead, the night sky seemed to offer the world a pale blue brilliance as evening fell, clouds that were once dark and foreboding were now soft and comforting, a requiem to the dark events which had recently past. Ann-Marie watched them as they drifted gently across the horizon, the reflective gold and reds of the suns dying rays touching the soft textures of their surface, adding a brilliance to Mother Nature's perfection.

Turning, she walked into the centre of the warm living-room of her modest home. A fire blazed in the hearth as gentle classical music drifted softly into the air, Chopin's Piano Concerto No.1 in E Minor, she thought. How it reminded her of her home, her true home. Out in the wilds of Durham. She sat on the sofa, deep in contemplation.

"You are wondering what will happen next, are you not?" Mica said, entering the room with a small glass of red wine in her hand, she offered it to Ann-Marie.

Taking the glass, Ann-Marie smiled and sank back into her dreams.

"I was only day-dreaming, fantasising about what once was and what can never be again."

Mica sat next to her.

"I would never say, 'never again'. This world in which we all live has a strange habit of making that which we least expect, expected," she said.

Ann-Marie smiled. "You never know, I do feel that I must leave London and return to my family home. Durham is a beautiful place and the countryside is almost perfection itself."

Mica looked at her with cautious eyes.

"What's wrong?" Ann-Marie said.

"I too was born in old Northumberland," Mica answered.

"But your name is French. Pontmercy," Ann-Marie said.

"That is our mother's maiden name, not her married name," Mica said, cautiously. She sat back upon the sofa and gently took Ann-Marie's hand in her own. "I can see our friendship blossoming into something special. When I returned to England, I felt as though my life was almost over and now I feel that it has only just begun. I see now that there is a new chapter to my existence and I would be eternally grateful if you were a major contributor to its writing."

Ann-Marie smiled. "I can't help but feel that this whole escapade is not truly over. I do feel however," she said, looking softly into Mica's ice blue eyes, "...that I should never have loved him, given to him those emotions which either of us, mortal or immortal can ever control."

"No! You were right to have loved him," Mica said, softly. "Life is such a precious thing, to use it to its paramount is a blessing. The mark of a good life is not represented by the elements and memories which we leave behind but the deeds which we do, the lives which we touch and an existence which we have not wasted."

Could love have driven Caliban to such extremes?" Ann-Marie said. "Had the loneliness, which had built up over the centuries, addled his mind, deluded his thoughts?"

Mica thought for a moment. "I don't know, we all search for that special something. Why should he be any different from any other soul? Remember he was once mortal, granted many centuries have elapsed since his baptism to darkness, but those mortal yearnings still stir deep beneath his long dead flesh," she paused for a moment. "It's strange, but within the very fabric of my soul, I cannot help but feel that this passion-play is far from over. It is as if he were searching for something far greater than anything we could ever hope to comprehend. Love is the basis of his desire, but a deeper craving fuels his hunger," she looked to Ann-Marie. "I don't know. Maybe the truth is as simple as we first comprehend; maybe my mind is rambling. After all, I have searched the centuries for the answers to my own innermost questions and now, on this one night, I find my heart to be calm in its own sweet resolution, appeased with its own gentle knowledge. If there is a greater force, a darker agenda to this passion play, then it is better not to be thought about and life is allowed to follow on its own blind course, free from our meddling or intervention."

"Is there such a thing? Is there a darker side to this tale? Something that the most fertile of mind could not comprehend?" Ann-Marie looked away.

"There's something that you're not telling me," Mica said cautiously.

Ann-Marie smiled a nervously.

Mica returned her affection, holding that moment in time close to her bruised heart. Then her soft features contorted, changed, turned to those of solemn harshness. "I know that your soul is troubled but we must cast aside our personal dislikes and distorted emotions. Now, you must answer me a question. Can you remember that secret which you held within your heart for what seemed almost an eternity and tore your soul asunder with its vicious edges and dark lies?"

Ann-Marie nodded and closed her eyes.

"Well, I now for ask you to relinquish that secret and unburden yourself of its truth. Save my blushes, my emotions, I would know it all, I would like to understand the suffering, which you so unselfishly undertook to conserve my tender heart. Please, do not spare my fragile emotions, I am strong and can understand much."

Ann-Marie opened her eyes and looked to Mica. "Even if that information would turn your world upside down, turn those who you once cherished into enemies and those whom you hated with a deep loathing into innocent pawns in a greater misunderstood game? Would you have me rip out your soul and cast it down upon the barren shores of loneliness, so that each and every day after this one there will pass the pain of a lifetime?"

"If our friendship is to mean anything, then this must be so," Mica said. "I will deal with the indiscretions of others in my own way, you are merely the messenger, the vessel which holds these dark answers."

"Very well. In comparison to your immortal aptitudes I am a blundering fool, forgive me for my cumbersome words," Ann-Marie paused and drew a deep breath. Slowly, she looked to Mica, here emotions in turmoil.

"Christian is innocent," she whispered.

Mica laughed. "And how, pray tell, do you come to this assumption?"

Ann-Marie closed her eyes and lowered her head. "Callum told me."

Mica's expression of mirth immediately fell. "What do you mean?"

"It was just after Susan had been killed and Darius set about restoring her body. Before he left the living room he took off his shoulder bag and cast it onto the couch, several articles fell from it," Ann-Marie paused. "There were things from all over the world strewn upon the floor, innocently, I made to retrieve them and there I found a letter, a letter for you from Christian, written in his hand."

"So!" Mica said, innocent in her dark confusion.

"Don't you see? This letter must have been similar to those which were given to the church to incriminate your brother."

Mica almost laughed out loud.

"Letters given to the church by Darius?"

Mica sat forward on the chair, her heart pounding in her chest, her mind a-rage with the truth.

"No! You must be mistaken," tears began to fill her eyes. "I know Darius, I've trusted him for centuries," her thoughts collided in her mind. "It can't be. Oh my God!" she exclaimed. "Darius! Are you trying to tell me that Darius damned them all, he was the one, and Christian was the scapegoat? The perfect criminal," she paused, searching her mind for an explanation.

"But how?"

"Why?"

"How could he do this? He could not do all of this alone, we must tell Callum."

Closing her eyes Ann-Marie held a shaking hand to her mouth. "Callum! Callum helped him," she said softly.

Mica stood in rage.

"NO! Tell me that this is not true. Tell me that you are mistaken."

"There is more, you asked me to tell you of the whole truth and that is what I shall do, you deserve to understand it all."

Mica walked blindly about the room, her hands covering her ears in a vain attempt to mask the words that assaulted her soul.

"Callum had a greater part in this than is first realised," Ann-Marie stood and took hold of Mica's hands. "He is a darker demon than you realise. He would contort the truth for his own ends and when there was no truth, he will invent his own, dark, malevolent and dangerous. For it was he who filled your little boy's head with fantasy and lies, damning his innocence. It was him, he was the murderer, he was the one who urged your son Jess to step into the sunlight, thus removing another obstacle from a mother's love. One less being to contend with for your affections"

Mica screamed as her soul broke. She sank to the floor; tears raging down her cheeks. "Why?" she pleaded.

"He loved you too much. He couldn't bear to share that love with another. He saw Jess as a threat," Ann-Marie said.

"Loved me! Loved me! Is this how he shows his love?" Mica screamed.

Ann-Marie put her arms about her broken friend, in the vain hope of consolidating the suffering, which consumed her. She could almost touch her pain as it ripped and tore viciously through her immortal body.

"What will you do?" she said.

Mica screamed and raged, cursing the names of those whom she had once called friend, her heart, soul and spirit were broken, shredded by the deceit of others, those whom she loved without question and followed without complaint.

Then almost as instantly as the torment consumed her, it ceased. Turning her dark thoughts in on her own mind. She composed herself before answering. "I am not going to do anything, for the moment. If there is a positive aspect to death it is that it ensures that those who are living and are left behind, realise how precious mortal life is. This is how we immortals have lost a precious aspect of our humanity and our immortal soul," she took a deep breath, almost mortal in her composure she smiled. "This chapter to my life shall remain slightly open, I shall feel its festering wounds irritate me as I look upon the faces of those whom I despise. I shall relish the knowledge that I have, and curse them for their dark deeds," she looked to Ann-Marie. "Tell me, do they perceive that you know of their actions?"

She shook her head. "Only Callum," Ann-Marie answered.

Mica smiled. "Please, keep your own council and silence, I shall grieve in my own way, for an eternity if need be and yet I shall derive a great delight from seeing them dig their own grave with their lies and deceptions. Evil is the absence of empathy and sometime a lie reveals more than the truth."

"Will you tell them?" Ann-Marie enquired.

"Eventually. However, first I must do something of greater importance," she said walking to the door. "I need a little time to myself," she said, turning and looked back at her companion, the soft light from the fire's flame washed the room in its gentle glow. "What will I do?" she said to herself.

Ann-Marie's eyebrows knitted in confusion.

"More to the point, my dear," Mica continued. "What will you do?"

"I don't understand," Ann-Marie replied.

Mica looked to the floor, her eyes filling with tears. "There is a way that we may save the souls of those damned by eternity. Those cast forever into the dark pit of confusion that is this plague, this immortality," she slowly lifted her eyes until they met those of her companion. "You could stop this dark torment before its seed has time to eat into the mortal flesh of those who would crave its power, its torturous gift. In time your communicative powers will multiply and strengthen and with this your horizons, and those of time, shall expand until infinity shall be yours to command," she smiled and allowed her eyes to fall once again to the floor. "Destroy the first born before he can savour this tainted death."

Ann-Marie sighed. "I know. But first, I must contend with these other demons, which haunt me. Was I wrong..," she asked, "to love Christian?"

Mica shook her head. "I know, and so did I. No! You were right to love him. In spite of all of his faults, in spite of his wild imaginings and deep desires, he was a special creature. Something that may only bless this earthly realm but once in a mortal's lifetime. If we were to walk blindly through life without the caress of another or, we were to offer a cold solace to the cries of one lost in their own bitter darkness, then that is a crime against your own soul. To be able to give and receive love is a beauty, but to be able to understand another as you have needs a deeper insight and strength into one's self, far greater than others could muster or comprehend in an eternity. It does not matter who we love, or why we love them, it is the aspect that we are capable of loving, unconditionally, that is the true gift. No. Do not doubt yourself; for you have touched that place that most of us can only dream of."

Ann-Marie smile was bittersweet. "And what next?" Mica enquired rhetorically of herself. "What am I to do with my life, with these feelings which bubble below the surface of my soul, sending my every waking hours into a pain that is infinity? In some strange, almost perverted way. It's strange, I wish that I could have joined him, been at one with him in his perpetual rest," Mica looked to Ann-Marie. "Before I stepped into the light of my realisation, I lived in the sanctity of my own small existence. I was sure of who I was and what I would become. Yet now, I do not know anything and understand even less. I'm afraid for the future, for I know that it exists and I am blind to its emotional tempestuous passions. Time itself is a vampires true torment, this incongruous grinding immortality," she took a deep mortal breath. "Do you realise, for years after I was turned to this immortal bitter light that I would pray to God for deliverance from this preternatural torment, but I soon realised that my faith was an absurd euphemism for my own gullibility. You see, faith in its essence positions itself far beyond the realm of requiring proof of some higher deity, and therefore, in its most pure of forms, faith denotes the existence of a God and that in itself is a preposterous solution to the woes of humankind and leaves its haunted purveyor a hollow shell of that which they may have been. There is no God, only blind resonating faith, and that in its essence is the conundrum. For if there is no God, then one must turn to their fellow immortal creators to find solace and comfort for their tormented and battered soul, and in their journey they discover that their own gods reflect and magnify those imperfections recognised within their own tempestuous existence. It is only then that you discover that you are closer to that which you despise rather that than which you desire." Looking blindly to the floor, Mica smiled. "There is no fool like an immortal fool."

Mica searched her soul for bittersweet appeasement, in the hope of contriving assuage against the crimes perpetrated by us all in the name of progress. Progress which is as fabricated as it is unfeeling. "We will always be scared of the unknown, that which we do not understand," she whispered. "For we know ourselves, only too well." She silently walked to Ann-Marie's side, pausing for a brief moment before kissing her gently upon the forehead. Then she turned and left the room, leaving Ann-Marie too bathe alone, in cold silence.

Ann-Marie closed her eyes and allowed the images of her recent emotional revolution wash over her.

"It seems that our dreams do come true," she whispered to herself. "As do our nightmares."

Epilogue

The cold January wind swept along the river, sending tiny ripples across its almost perfect surface. The lights from the surrounding buildings were reflected upon the silver droplets of moonlight that mingled and danced with the black waters of the Thames.

The bridge that spanned the river, a witness to nature's light display, held only one inhabitant of the vast city that reached out in all directions. This was her home for now, the final resting place for her dear departed innocent brother, others had only seen the destruction that issued from his black heart but she had known him before the darkness had enveloped him, she had seen his tenderness, his compassion.

Mica stood in silence, her features softened by the subtle rays of the blue silver moonlight that rained down from above. A hollow happiness filled her, for she could fulfil a dark promise, which she had made to herself almost a lifetime ago. She recalled with a dark satisfaction the images of her lost son, his playful face and bright eyes, his turning nature and soft laughter. How she missed him. A gentle tear ran down her cheek.

She stood for almost an hour upon the bridge, unaware of the world passing her by. In some strange dark way she was contented, this chapter to her life had drawn to its un-natural conclusion and now she could move onto the next, forge new friendships, accept new challenges and right the wrongs perpetrated against her. She would have her justice.

From underneath her cape she drew out a small tan animal skin pouch, putting it to her lips she kissed it gently, then held it close to her heart, but only for a brief moment, before opening it and allowing the bitter wind to carry its contents high into the night sky and eventually down upon the dark surface of the Thames, forever to mingle with the distant light from the heavens above.

Mica watched at the tiny grey particles bobbed up and down, riding gently upon the winter tide. She smiled to herself and pulled her cloak about her shoulders, in her mind she knew that she had reached her destination, yet somehow the conclusion was not as she anticipated. Yes, she had won the war, and yet in some strange malevolent way she had lost the peace.

"Goodnight, sweet Prince," she whispered.

Turning, she took a brief backward glance at the waters below before losing herself in the swell of the capital city.

The grey dust that covered this small section of the river began to break up and sink to the bottom of the black waters, leaving no trace of the child who had once tried to capture the sun and take a gift of light to brighten the heart of a mother whom he loved so much.

Above, the traffic began to screech and roar into life as it slowly made its way across the bridge. Great plumes of thick smoke were sent from the exhausts of the vehicles, drifting, they reached height into the night air, dissipating the pure silver glow that emanated from the moon as it hung in the winter sky. Yet, even the light from the moon could not penetrate the inky blackness of the Thames as it cut its way savagely through the city.

It was from this blackness that the movement began, slowly at first, a turning, a stirring of the dark waters. Thick mud began to rise from the very depths of the rivers bottom, almost contaminating the surface as it gathered in its magnitude, dulling and defusing the pure light that danced across it.

Then, amidst the confusion a hand reached out, pulling at the air it tore at the night sky with its burnt and blistered fingers. Its tortured flesh yearning for the sanctity of life. Moments later the great bulk of the creature broke free from its watery prison and burst out onto the surface. His red eyes filled with rage, a rage that would wreak havoc and destruction upon those had sought to quench the flame of life that burned deep within his innocent heart. The pain without was mild in comparison to the pain that burned within; his mind was ablaze with dark rage. Vengeance compelled him, urged him forward. Demanding compensation, indemnification for those vial acts perpetrated against him.

He allowed himself to float for a while, permitting the cold waters to soothe his blistered and broken flesh. He could feel the strong currents pulling at him from below and so, he kicked his legs out behind him, manoeuvred his body he faced the shore. Then, with a deep clawing action he propelled himself towards the river's bank and the lights that shone from the fires that were lit by the homeless and the outcasts of this society. Those who could find no niche into which they could place themselves, no level upon which they could rest and so they rejected all that they saw and so were, in turn, subsequently rejected by the masses. Those who have turned away from the light to savour the darkness, knowing full-well, that the light desires the darkness within which to shine as sure as the guilty require their excuses of innocence to vindicate their contrition. For these are the true reflectors of society. The true mirror upon which humankind could measure its dark deeds and bring into account, its short fallings, its misdemeanours.

This scattering of unfortunate souls, enveloped in the dark wings of night, were a just barometer to the true temperance of man's compassion to his fellow kin, for these were the veritable vagabonds of this modern world... Christian's kin, his Vagabond Banquet.

THE END.

7671774R00137

Printed in Great Britain
by Amazon.co.uk, Ltd.,
Marston Gate.